# Daughters *of the* Witching Hill

BOOKS BY MARY SHARRATT

*Summit Avenue*

*The Real Minerva*

*The Vanishing Point*

*Bitch Lit*

*Daughters of the Witching Hill*

# Daughters *of the*
 Witching Hill

## Mary Sharratt

MARINER BOOKS
HOUGHTON MIFFLIN HARCOURT
*Boston   New York*

First Mariner Books edition 2011

Copyright © 2010 by Mary Sharratt

ALL RIGHTS RESERVED

For information about permission to reproduce
selections from this book, write to Permissions,
Houghton Mifflin Harcourt Publishing Company,
215 Park Avenue South, New York, New York 10003.

www.hmhbooks.com

*Library of Congress Cataloging-in-Publication Data*
Sharratt, Mary, date.
Daughters of the Witching Hill / Mary Sharratt.
p. cm.
ISBN 978-0-547-06967-8
ISBN 978-0-547-42229-9 (pbk.)
1. Witchcraft—England—Lancashire—Fiction. 2. Trials
(Witchcraft)—England—Lancashire—Fiction. 3. Witchcraft—
England—History—17th century—Fiction.
4. Lancaster (England)—Fiction. I. Title.
PS3569.H3449D38 2010
813'.54—dc22    2009042057

*Book design by Melissa Lotfy*
*Map by Jacques Chazaud*

Printed in the United States of America

DOC 10 9 8 7 6 5 4 3 2 1

FOR MY MOTHER

*Dedicated to the memory of Elizabeth Southerns,*
*alias Mother Demdike.*

*And to Alizon Device, Elizabeth Device,*
*James Device, Anne Whittle, Anne Redfearn,*
*Alice Nutter, Katherine Hewitt, Jane Bulcock,*
*John Bulcock, and Jennet Preston.*

She was a very old woman, about the age of Foure-score yeares, and had been a Witch for fiftie yeares. Shee dwelt in the Forrest of Pendle, a vast place, fitte for her profession: What shee committed in her time, no man knowes. . . . Shee was a generall agent for the Devill in all these partes: no man escaped her, or her Furies.

—THOMAS POTTS, The Wonderfull Discoverie of<br>Witches in the Countie of Lancaster, 1613

## A CHARME

Upon Good-Friday, I will fast while I may
Untill I heare them knell
Our Lords owne Bell,
Lord in his messe
With his twelve Apostles good,
What hath he in his hand
Ligh in leath wand:
What hath he in his other hand?
Heavens doore key,
Open, open Heaven doore keyes,
Steck, steck hell doore.
Let Crizum child
Goe to it Mother mild,
What is yonder that casts a light so farrandly,
Mine owne deare Sonne that's naild to the Tree.
He is naild sore by the heart and hand,
And holy harne Panne,

Well is that man

That Fryday spell can,

His Childe to learne;

A Crosse of Blew, and another of Red,

As good Lord was to the Roode.

*Gabriel* laid him downe to sleepe

Upon the ground of holy weepe:

Good Lord came walking by,

Sleep'st thou, wak'st thou *Gabriel,*

No Lord I am sted with sticke and stake,

That I can neither sleepe nor wake:

Rise up *Gabriel* and goe with me,

The stick nor the stake shall never deere thee.

*A charm to cure one who is bewitched, attributed to*
*Elizabeth Southerns's family and recorded by Thomas Potts*
*during the 1612 witch trials at Lancaster.*

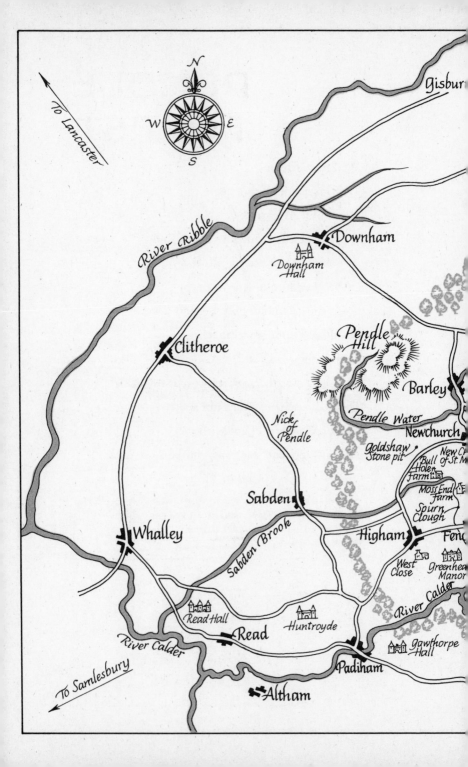

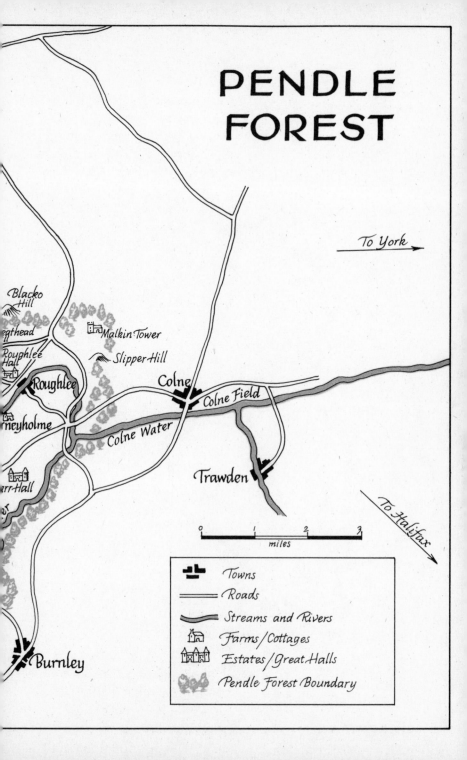

# I

# BY DAYLIGHT GATE

*Bess Southerns*

# I

S EE US GATHERED HERE, three women stood at Richard
Baldwin's gate. I bide with my daughter, Liza of the squint-
eye, and with my granddaughter, Alizon, just fifteen and dazzling as the noontide sun, so bright that she lights up the murk of
my dim sight. Demdike, folk call me, after the dammed stream
near my dwelling place where the farmers wash their sheep before shearing. When I was younger and stronger, I used to help
with the sheepwash. Wasn't afraid of the fiercest rams. I'd always
had a way of gentling creatures by speaking to them low and
soft. Though I'm old now, crabbed and near-blind, my memory
is long as a midsummer's day and with my inner eye, I see clear.

We three wait till Baldwin catches a glimpse of us and out
he storms. Through the clouded caul that age has cast over my
eyes, I catch his form. Thin as a brittle, dead stalk, he is, his face
pinched, and he's clad in the dour black weeds of a Puritan. Fancies himself a godly man, does our Dick Baldwin. A loud crack
strikes the earth—it's a horsewhip he carries. My daughter fair
leaps as he lashes it against the drought-hard dirt.

"Whores and witches," he rails, shrill enough to set the crows
to flight. "Get out of my ground."

Slashes of air hit my face as he brandishes his whip, seeking
to strike fear into us, but it's his terror I taste as I let go of Alizon's guiding hand and step forward, firm and square on my rag-
bundled feet. We've only come to claim what is ours by right.

"Whores and witches," he taunts again, yelling with such bile that his spit sprays me. "I will burn the one of you and hang the other."

He speaks to Liza and me, ignoring young Alizon, for he doesn't trust himself to even look at this girl whose beauty and sore hunger would be enough to make him sink to his knobbly knees.

I take another step forward, forcing him to back away. The man's a-fright that I'll so much as breathe on him. "I care not for you," I tell him. "Hang yourself."

Our Master Baldwin will play the righteous churchman, but what I know of him would besmirch his good name forevermore. He can spout his psalms till he's hoarse, but heaven's gates will never open to him. I know this and he knows I know this, and for my knowing, he fears and hates me. Beneath his black clothes beats an even blacker heart. Hired my Liza to card wool, did Baldwin, and then refused to pay her. What's more, our Liza has done much dearer things for him than carding. Puritan or no, he's taken his pleasure of her and, lost and grieving her poor murdered husband, ten years dead, our Liza was soft enough to let him. Fool girl.

"Enough of this," I say. "Liza carded your wool. Where's her payment? We're poor, hungry folk. Would you let us starve for your meanness?"

I speak in a low, warning tone, not unlike the growl of a dog before it bites. Man like him should know better than to cross the likes of me. Throughout Pendle Forest I'm known as a cunning woman, and she who has the power to bless may also curse.

Our Master Baldwin blames me because his daughter Ellen is too poorly to rise from her bed. The girl was a pale, consumptive thing from the day she was born, never hale in all her nine years. Once he called on me to heal her. Mopped her brow, I did. Brewed her feverfew and lungwort, but still she ailed and shivered. Tried my best with her, but some who are sick cannot be mended. Yet Baldwin thinks I bewitched the lass out of malice. Why would I seek to harm a hair on the poor girl's head when his other daughter, the one he won't name or even look at, is my own youngest granddaughter, seven-year-old Jennet?

"Richard." My Liza makes bold to step toward him. She stretches out a beseeching hand. "Have a heart. For our Jennet's sake. We've nothing more to eat in the house."

But he twists away from her in cold dread and still won't pay her for her honest work, won't grant us so much as a penny. So what can I do but promise that I'll pray for him till he comes to be of a better mind? Soft under my breath, masked from his Puritan ears, I murmur the Latin refrains of the old religion. How my whispered words make him pale and quake — does he believe they will strike him dead? Off to his house he scarpers. Behind his bolted door he'll cower till we're well gone.

"Come, Gran." Alizon takes my arm to lead me home. Can't make my way round without her in this dark ebb of my years. But with my inner eye I see Tibb sat there on the drystone wall. Sun breaks through the clouds to golden-wash his guilesome face. Dick Baldwin would call him a devil, or even *the* Devil, but I know better. Beautiful Tibb, his form invisible to all but me.

"Now I don't generally stand by woe-working," says my Tibb, stretching out his long legs. "But if you forespoke Master Baldwin, who could blame you, after all the ill he's done to you and yours?" He cracks a smile. "Is revenge what you want?"

"No, Tibb. Only justice." I speak with my inner voice that none but Tibb can hear. If Baldwin fell ill and died, what would happen to his lawful daughter, Ellen? Her mother's long dead. Another poor lass to live off the alms of the parish. No, I'll not have that burden on my soul.

"Justice!" Tibb laughs, then shakes his head. "Off the likes of Dick Baldwin? Oh, you do set your sights high."

Tibb's laughter makes the years melt away, drawing me back to the old days, when I could see far with my own two eyes and walk on my own two legs, with none to guide me.

5

# 2

B Y DAYLIGHT GATE I first saw him, the boy climbing out
of the stone pit in Goldshaw. The sinking sun set his fair
hair alight. Slender, he was, and so young and beautiful. Pure,
too. No meanness on him. No spite or evil. I knew straight off
that he wouldn't spit at me for being a barefoot beggar woman.
Wouldn't curse at me or try to shove me into the ditch. There
was something in his eyes—a gentleness, a knowing. When
he looked at me, my hurting knees turned to butter. When he
smiled, I melted to my core, my heart bumping and thumping
till I fair fainted away. What would a lad like that want with a
fifty-year-old widow like me?

The month of May, it was, but cold of an evening. His coat
was half black, half brown. I thought to myself that he must be
poor like me, left to stitch his clothes together from mismatched
rags. He reached out his hand, as though making to greet an old
friend.

"Elizabeth," he said. "My own Bess." The names by which I
was known when I was a girl with a slender waist and strong legs
and rippling chestnut hair. How did he know my true name?
Even then I was known to most as Demdike. The boy smiled
wide with clean, white teeth, none of them missing, and his eyes
had a devilish spark in them, as though I were still that young
woman with skin like new milk.

"Well, well," said I, for I was never one to stay silent for long.
"You know my name, so you do. What's yours then?"

"Tibb," he said.

I nodded to myself, though I knew of no Tibbs living anywhere in Pendle Forest. "But what of your Christian name?" *After all, he knew me by mine, God only knew how.*

He lifted his face to the red-glowing sky and laughed as the last of the sun sank behind Pendle Hill. Then I heard a noise behind me: the startled squawk of a pheasant taking flight. When I turned to face the boy again, he had vanished away. I looked up and down the lane, finding him nowhere. Couldn't even trace his footprints in the muddy track. Did my mind fail me? Had that boy been real at all? This was when I grew afraid and went cold all over, as though frost had settled upon my skin.

First off, I told no one of Tibb. Who would have believed me when I could scarcely believe it myself? I'd no wish to make myself an even bigger laughingstock than I already was.

Ned Southerns, my husband, such as he was, had passed on just after our squint-eyed Liza was born, nineteen years ago. He blamed me for our daughter's deformity because he thought I'd too much contact with beasts whilst I was carrying her. In my married years, I raised fine hens, even kept a nanny goat. There was another child, Christopher, three years older than Liza and not of my husband, but he was far and away from being the only bastard in Pendle Forest. The gentry and the yeomen bred as many ill-begotten babes as us poor folk, only they did a better job of covering it up. Liza, Kit, and I made our home in a crumbling old watchtower near the edge of Pendle Forest. More ancient than Adam, our tower was. Too draughty for storing silage, but it did for us. Malkin Tower, it was called, and, as you'll know, *malkin* can mean either hare or slattern. What better place for me and my brood?

But folk whispered that it seemed a curious thing indeed that one such as I should live in a tower built of stout stone with a firehouse at its foot that boasted a proper hearth when many a poor widow made do with a one-room hovel with no hearth at all but only a fire pit in the bare earthen floor. In truth, my poor dead mother got the tower given her for her natural life — towers named after slatterns hide guilty secrets.

When my mam was young and comely, she'd served the Nowell family at Read Hall. Head ostler's daughter, so she was, and she'd prospects and a modest dowry besides. But what did she do but catch the eye of Master Nowell's son, then a lad of seventeen years? The Nowells were not an old family, as gentry went, nor half as grand as the Shuttleworths of Gawthorpe Hall or the de Lacys of Clitheroe. The Nowells' fortunes had risen along with the sway of the new religion. Back when Old King Henry's troops came to sack Whalley Abbey, the Nowells sent their men to help topple the ancient stone walls. The King rewarded their loyalty by granting the Nowells a goodly portion of the abbey's lands. One of Old Man Nowell's sons went to faraway Cambridgeshire to make his name as a Puritan divine, or so I'd been told. Far and wide, the Nowells let it be known that they were godly folk. But even the pious are prey to youthful folly.

My mam, before her fall from grace, had been an upright girl, so the young Master Roger could hardly discard her as easy as he would some tavern maid. And that was why Mam was given Malkin Tower for the rest of her life on the condition that she never trouble the Nowells of Read Hall. Far enough from Read, it was, for them not to be bothered by the sight of her, but it was close enough for them to keep watch of her, should she seek to blacken their good name. My mam and I were never respectable — respect costs money and we hadn't two pennies to rub together. We'd Malkin Tower to live in but no scrap of land for grazing sheep. Most we could manage was a garden plot in the stony soil. By and by, I think the Nowells had fair forgotten us. When my mam passed on, bless her eternal soul, the tower was in such poor repair they didn't seem to want it back. So I stayed on, for where else had I to go? It seemed they preferred to have no dealings with me and that it shamed them less to allow me to carry on here like a squatter, not paying a farthing's rent.

My natural father died some years back, happy and fat and rich. His eldest son, my own half-brother, also named Roger, had become the new master of Read Hall, part of it built from the very stones his grandfather's servants had carted away from the ruined abbey. Younger than me, was my half-brother, by some twenty years. Rarely did our paths cross, for the Nowells went to church in Whalley with the other fine folk, never in the New Church in Goldshaw with the yeomen and lesser gentry. But once, of a market day in Colne, I clapped eyes on Roger Nowell. Impossible to miss him, the way he was sat like some conquering knight upon his great Shire horse, blue-black and gleaming, with red ribbons twisted in its mane. That was some years ago, when my half-brother's face was yet smooth and unlined. A handsome man, he was, with a firm chin just like mine. I looked straight at him to see if he would recognise his own blood kin. But his sharp blue eyes passed over me as though I were nowt but a heap of dung.

Over the years he'd become a mighty man: Magistrate and Justice of the Peace. We in Pendle Forest were careful not to cross him or give him cause for offence. On account of my being a poor widow, he granted me a begging license. Did it through the Constable without speaking a word to me. And so I was left to wander the tracks of Pendle Forest and wheedle, full humble, for food and honest work.

But gone were the days when Christian folk felt beholden to give alms to the poor. When I was a tiny girl, the monks of Whalley Abbey fed and clothed the needy. So did the rich folk, for their souls would languish a fair long time in purgatory if they were stingy to us. In the old days, the poor were respected—our prayers were dearer to God than those of the wealthy. Many a well-to-do man on his deathbed would give out food and alms to the lowliest of the parish if they would only pray for his immortal soul. At his funeral, the poor were given doles of bread and soulcakes, so my mam had told me.

The reformers said that purgatory was heresy. It was either

heaven for the Elect or hell for everyone else, so what need did the rich have to bribe the poor to pray for them? We humble folk were no longer seen as blessed of the Lord but as a right nuisance. When I went begging for a mere bowl of blue milk or a handful of oats to make water porridge, the Hargreaves and the Bannisters and the Mittons narrowed their eyes and said my hard lot was God's punishment for my sin of bearing a bastard child. Mean as stones, they were. Little did they know. Liza, my lawful-begotten child, was deformed because her father, my husband, gave me no pleasure to speak of, whilst Kit, my bastard, borne of passion and desire, was tall and beautiful and perfect in form as any larch tree. Ah, but the Puritans would only see what they wanted to see. The most so-called charity they doled out was to give me half a loaf of old bread in exchange for a day laundering soiled clouts.

But I'd even forgive them for that if they hadn't robbed my life of its solace and joy. In the old days, we'd a saint for every purpose: Margaret for help in childbirth, Anne for protection in storms, Anthony to ward against fire, George to heal horses and protect them from witchcraft. Old King Henry forbade us to light candles before the saints but at least he let us keep their altars. In the old days, no one forced us to go to church either, even for Easter communion. The chapel nave belonged to us, the ordinary people, and it was the second home we all shared. Dividing the nave from the chancel with the high altar was the carved oak roodscreen that framed the priest as he sang out the mass. We didn't stand solemn and dour during the holy service, either, but wandered about the nave from one saint's altar to the next, gazing at the pictures and statues till the priest rang the bell and held up the Host for all to see, the plain wafer transformed in a glorious miracle into the body and blood of Christ. Just laying eyes upon the Host was enough to ward a person from witchcraft, plague, and sudden death.

When I was twelve, they finished building the New Church of St. Mary's in Goldshaw to replace the old crumbling chapel of ease where I'd been christened. The Bishop of Chester came to consecrate it just in time for All Souls' when we rang the bells the whole night through to give comfort to our dead.

Back then we still had our holidays. Christmas lasted twelve days and nights with mummers and guizers in animal masks dancing by torchlight. The Lord of Misrule, some low-born man, lorded it over the gentry to make poor folk laugh. The Towneleys of Carr Hall used to invite all their neighbours, rich and poor alike, to join their festivities. Upon Palm Sunday everyone in the parish gathered for the processions round the fields to make them fertile. After dark the young folk would go out to bless the land in their own private fashion. Everyone knew what went on, but none stood in our way. If a lass and her young man had to rush to the altar afterward, nobody thought the worse of them for it. I went along with the other girls, arm in arm with my best friend, Anne Whittle, both of us wearing green garlands and singing. Cherry-lipped Anne loved to have her sport with the boys, but mindful of my own mother's fate, I did nowt but kiss and dance and flirt in those days. Only went astray much later in life, when I was a married woman and sore unsatisfied, seeking my pleasures elsewhere.

In my youth, upon May morning, we arose before dawn to gather hawthorn and woodruff. We'd dance round the Maypole and drink elderflower wine till the very sky reeled. At Midsummer's, upon the eve of the feast of John the Baptist, we carried birch boughs into the church till our chapel looked like a woodland grove. Bonfires blazed the whole night through. Some folk burned fires of bone, not wood, so that the stench might drive away evil wights from the growing crops. Most of us gathered round the wake fire of sweet apple wood where we danced all night, collapsing upon the grass at sunrise. On Lammas Day the reapers crowned the Harvest Queen and one year, by Our Lady, it was me, a lass of fifteen, crowned in roses and barley, the lads begging me for a kiss.

Old King Henry was dead by then, and we lived in hope that

the old ways would live again. Crowned in roses, I led the procession of maidens on the Feast of the Assumption, each of us bearing flowers and fruits to lay upon the altar of the Queen of Heaven. Only weeks later Edward the Boy King sent his men to smash every statue in our church, even that of the Blessed Mother herself, whilst we clutched ourselves, full aghast. They tore down the crucifix over the high altar and burned it as though it were some heathen idol. They destroyed our roodscreen, outlawed our processions, and forbade us to deck the church with greenery upon Midsummer or to bring red roses and poppies to the altar on Corpus Christi. They set fire to our Maypole, forbade us to pray for the dead, or celebrate the saints' feast days.

Six years on, weakling Edward wasted away and his sister Mary Tudor promised to bring back the old religion. For the five years of her reign we had our holidays again, our processions, our mass with swirling incense, and the sea of candles lit for the saints. The Towneleys, the Nutters, and the Shuttleworths paid for the new roodscreen, the new statues, altar cloths, and vestments. We had our Maypole and rang the church bells for our ancestors on All Souls' Night. But our joys soured when the news came of the heretics Mary burned alive, near three hundred of them, their only hope to end their agony being the sachets of gunpowder concealed beneath their clothes. Our Catholic queen was nowt but a tyrant. Before long Mary herself died, despised by her own husband, so the story went.

With Queen Elizabeth came the new religion once more to replace the old. The Queen's agents stormed in to hack apart our new roodscreen. But they could not demolish the statues or the crucifix this time round, for the Towneleys, Shuttleworths, and Nutters had divided the holy images between them and taken them into hiding in secret chapels inside their great houses. In those early days, some said Elizabeth's reign couldn't last long. Anne Boleyn's bastard, she was, and it seemed half of England wanted her dead. On top of that, she refused to marry and produce an heir of her own religion. Yet the Queen and her crushing rule had endured.

In truth, the old ways died that day Elizabeth's agents sacked our church. For the past twenty-odd years, there had been no dancing of a Sunday, no Sunday ales like we used to have when we made merry within the very nave of the church. Though the Sabbath was the only day of leisure we had, the Curate refused to let us have any pleasure of it. No football, dice-playing, or card-playing. Magistrate Roger Nowell, my own half-brother, forbade the Robin Hood plays and summer games, for he said they led to drunkenness and wantonness amongst the lower orders. Few weeks back, the piper of Clitheroe was arrested for playing late one Sunday afternoon.

The Curate preached that only the Elect would go to heaven, and I was canny enough to know that didn't include me. So if I were damned anyway, why should I suffer to obey their every command? Mind you, I went to church of a Sunday. It was that, or suffer the Church Warden's whip and fine. But I'd left off trying to hold myself to the straight and narrow. Perhaps I'd have fared no better even if the old church had survived, for hadn't I been an adulteress? But still my heart was rooted, full stubborn, in that lost world of chanting, processions, and revels that had bound us together, rich and poor, saint and sinner. My soul's home was not with this harsh new God, but instead I sought the solace of the Queen of Heaven and whispered the Salve Regina in secret. I swore to cling to the forbidden prayers till my dying day.

I am getting ahead of myself. Back to the story. That evening, after Tibb first appeared to me, I hared off in the long spring twilight, heading home to Malkin Tower. Wasn't safe to be about after dark. Folk talked of boggarts haunting the night, not that I was ignorant enough to believe every outlandish tale, but I was shaken to the bone from seeing the boy who disappeared into nowhere. The moon, nearly full, shone in the violet sky, and the first stars glimmered when, at last, I reached my door.

Our Malkin Tower was an odd place. Tower itself had two rooms, one below and one above, and each room had narrow slits for windows from the days, hundreds of years ago, when guardsmen were sat there with their bows and arrows, on the look-out for raiders and poachers. But, as the tower had no chimney or hearth, we spent most of our time in the firehouse, a ramshackle room built on to the foot of the tower. And it was into the firehouse I stumbled that night. My daughter Liza, sat close by the single rush light, gave a cry when she saw me.

"So late coming home, Mam! Did a devil cross your path?"

In the wavering light, my girl looked more frightful than the devil she spoke of, though she couldn't help it, God bless her. Her left eye stood lower in her face than the other, and whilst her right eye looked up, her left eye looked down. The sight of her was enough to put folk off their food. Couldn't hire herself out as a kitchen maid because the housewives of Pendle feared our Liza would spoil their milk and curdle their butter. Looking the way she did, it would take a miracle for her to get regular work, let alone a husband. Most she could hope for was a day's pittance for carding wool or weeding some housewife's garden.

Ignoring her talk of the devil, I unpacked a clump of old bread, the gleanings of the day's begging, and Liza sliced it into pieces thin as communion wafer.

Liza, myself, Kit, and Kit's wife, also Elizabeth, though we called her Elsie, gathered for our supper. Kit hired himself out as a day labourer, but at this time of year there was little work to be had. Lambing season had just passed. Shearing wouldn't come till high summer. Best he could do was ask for work at the slate pits and hope to earn enough to keep us in oatmeal and barley flour. Elsie was heavy with child. Most work she could get was a day's mending or spinning.

When we were sat together at the table, my Liza went green in the face at the taste of the old bread and could barely get a mouthful of the stuff down before she bolted out the door to be sick. Out of old habit, I crossed myself. I looked to Kit, who looked to his wife, who shook her head in sadness. Elsie would deliver her firstborn within the month and now it appeared that Liza was with child as well. First I wondered who the father could be. Then I asked myself how we would feed two little babes when we were hard-pressed to do for ourselves. We were silent, the lot of us, Elsie doling out the buttermilk she had off the Bulcocks in exchange for a day's spinning. Our Kit gave his wife half of his own share of bread—wasn't she eating for two?

Then I found I couldn't finish my own bread, so I passed it to Kit before hauling myself out the door to look for Liza. By the cold moonlight I found my poor squint-eyed broomstick of a girl bent over the gatepost, crying fit to die. Taking Liza in my arms, I held her and rubbed her hair. I begged her to tell me who the father was, but she refused.

"It will be right," I told her. "Not the first time an unwed girl fell pregnant. We'll make do somehow." What else could I say? I'd no business browbeating her for doing the same as I'd done with Kit's father, twenty-two years ago.

After leading my Liza back inside, we made for our beds. I climbed to the upper tower. Room was so cold and draughty that everyone else preferred sleeping below, but of a crystal-clear evening I loved nothing better than to lie upon my pallet and gaze at the moon and stars through the narrow windows. Cold wind didn't bother me much. I was born with thick skin, would have died ages ago if I'd been a more delicate sort. Yet that night the starry heavens gave me little comfort. I laid myself down and tried to ignore the hammer of worry in my head. The Church Warden and Constable were sure to make a stink about Liza. Another bastard child to live off the charity of the parish. They'd fine her at the very least. She'd be lucky if she escaped the pillory. Sleepless, I huddled there whilst the wind whistled through the thatch.

When I finally closed my eyes, I saw Tibb, his face in its golden glory. Looked like one of the angels I remembered seeing in our church before the Queen's men stripped the place bare. Out of the dark crush of night came his voice, sweet as a lover's, gentle as Kit's father was in the days when he called me his beauty, his heart's joy. Tibb's lips were at my ear.

"If I could," he told me, "if you let me, I'd ease your burdens, my Bess. No use fretting about Liza. She'll lose the child within a fortnight, and none but you and yours will know she fell pregnant in the first place."

My throat was dry and sore. Couldn't even think straight.

"You're afraid of me," he said. "But you shouldn't be. I mean you no harm."

"You're not real," I whispered. "I'm just dreaming you."

"I'm as real as the ache in your heart," he whispered back. "You were meant to be more than a common beggar, our Bess. You could be a blesser. Next time you see a sick cow, bless it. Say three Ave Marias and sprinkle some water on the beast. Folk will pay you for such things. Folk will hold you in regard, and you won't have to grovel for the scraps off their table."

*What nonsense.* The Church Warden would have me whipped and fined for saying the Ave Maria—and that was but mild chastisement. Catholics were still hanged in these parts, their priests drawn and quartered. I told myself that there was no such boy called Tibb—it was just my empty stomach talking. I rolled over, pulling the tattered blanket to my ears.

He wouldn't give over. "It runs in your blood. You've inherited the gift from your mam's father."

I shook my head no. "My grand-dad was an ostler. An honest man."

"He was a horse-charmer, if you remember well."

Tibb's voice summoned the memories. I was sat on Grand-Dad's knee, and he jostled me so that I could pretend I was riding a bouncy pony whilst he chanted the charm to St. George to ward horses from witchcraft. *Enforce we us with all our might to love St. George, Our Lady's knight.* Grand-Dad died when I was seven, but he'd taught my mam all his herbcraft for healing beast and folk alike, which she, in turn, had taught me, though Mam herself had no dealings in charms.

What a marvel. Grand-Dad working his blessings in the stables at Read Hall, beneath the Nowells' very noses. He must have served them well, kept their nags healthy and sound, so that instead of reporting him for sorcery they became his protectors. Perhaps that, indeed, was why the Nowells had given Malkin Tower to Mam—it did no good at all to vex a cunning man by treating his daughter ill.

Still, the knowing made the sweat run cold down my back. To think that I carried this inside me. I could not say a word, only pray that Tibb would vanish again and leave me in peace.

"My own Bess, do I need to give you a sign or two? You'll see what I've said of Liza will come to pass. Now I'll give you more knowledge of the future. Before the moon is new again, Elsie will bear a son."

In spite of myself, I laughed. "Any fool can see she's carrying a boy from the way she's bearing so high and wide. I don't need a slip of a lad like you telling me about wenches bearing babies."

My mocking didn't put Tibb off. He only coaxed me all the more. "They'll name the lad Christopher after his father, and you'll see your Kit's father in the little lad's face, my Bess. You'll feel so tender that the years of bitterness will melt away."

Tears came to my eyes when I remembered my lover who had given me such pleasure before he bolted off, never to show his face again, leaving me to bear my shame and endure an angry husband fit to flay me alive and the gossips wagging their tongues and pointing. My husband refused to give the baby his name, so that was why my Kit was named Christopher Holgate, not Southerns. As punishment for my sin, I was made to stand a full day in the pillory in Colne marketplace.

"That's not all I can tell you of your future," said Tibb, nestling close, his breath warming my face. "In time, your Liza will marry an honest man who will love her in spite of her squint."

"Fortune-telling's a sin," I squeaked. In this the Curate and the priests of the old religion had always been of one mind. A dangerous thing, it was, to push back the veil and look into the future, for unless such knowledge came from a prophecy delivered by God, it came from the other place, the evil place, the Devil. Diviners and those who consulted them would be punished in hell by having their heads twisted backward for their unholy curiosity.

But Tibb carried on in a voice I couldn't block out. "Liza will give you three grandchildren."

How seductive he was. If only I could trust him and believe that my Liza would be blessed by the love of a good man, a happy family.

"Her first-born daughter will be your joy," Tibb told me. "You'll love her till you forget yourself, my Bess. A pretty, impudent lass with skin like cream. A beauty such as you were at her age. She'll be your very likeness, and you'll teach her the things that I'll teach you." His voice sang with his promise.

"What else can you tell me?" I asked, my heart in my mouth.

Opening my eyes, I dared myself to look him in the face, but I only saw the stars shining in the window slits.

Poor beggar women mustn't allow themselves to be led astray by foolish fancies. *Have some sense for once,* I told myself. So I did my best to put Tibb out of my mind. Life carried on, same as it always had. I went begging or took what work was offered to me. Spent an afternoon on my hands and knees, scouring Old Master Mitton's henhouse in exchange for a loaf of bread, a cup of ale, and a bowl of thin gruel. As I scrubbed that stinking henhouse, Tibb and his promises seemed worlds away. How daft to think a woman such as I could ever charm or bless any person or thing.

After my work, I washed myself in the brook before heading home. Our Kit was gone, having found work at the slate pit, but Elsie was sat there in the firehouse with a face stark and clenched as winter. At first I thought her time had come.

"What is it?" I asked, the sweat rolling off me. "Have your waters broken?"

Lips glued together, Elsie pointed to the dark corner where Liza lay upon her pallet. The blankets and linens had been stripped off and were soaking in a bucket of cold water to loosen the red stains. My Liza was wan, her breathing shallow, but I could see no regret in her face. More like relief and silent thanksgiving.

"She took the tansy," Elsie said, speaking cold and hard.

I looked to the rafters where my garden herbs were strung and, indeed, the stalks of tansy with their shrill yellow buttons were gone.

"You've no business growing that evil weed in your garden," Elsie went on, "knowing what sin it's used for."

"Oh, shut it, Elsie," I told her.

Bustling over to Kit and Elsie's bed in the bottom room of the tower, I stripped off the blanket and carried it to Liza, draping it over her. Took my girl's hand and pressed it in my own.

"All will be well," I vowed.

Next I laid hands on Elsie's shoulders.

"You'll not breathe a word of this," I told her.

My hard grip set her trembling. She dipped her eyes and clutched her belly, so big it looked fit to burst.

"You'll not tell a soul," I went on. "Even our Kit. Our Liza never miscarried. She never fell pregnant. You understand my meaning?"

If the Constable and Church Warden were quick to punish girls who carried bastards, there was no telling what they would do to a wench who made herself abort — or, indeed, to the one who had provided her with the herb.

Elsie clutched herself and nodded.

Sore and aching though I was, I dragged the bucket of soaking blankets out to the brook and pounded them against the stones, scrubbing with lye soap till my hands were raw, till the last trace of Liza's blood had vanished out of the wool.

None of this was Tibb's doing. Liza had taken her fate into her own hands, brewed a strong dose of tansy, swallowed it down, and waited till the herb opened up her womb. Just as I might have done those many years ago if I hadn't been so soft and still in love with the man who had given me such happiness, only to abandon me.

Less than a week later Elsie went to her childbed and I delivered her firstborn — a son, as I knew it would be. Our Kit was so happy he wept. Liza, dry-eyed, helped care for the baby whilst Elsie recovered from her confinement. As soon as my daughter-in-law was on her feet again, we took ourselves to the New Church in Goldshaw to have the child christened. The Curate spoke the Gospel over the baby but refused to trace the cross on his forehead with holy water, for he considered such things to be popish sorcery.

Soon shearing season was upon us, and Kit had work every day for a fortnight. Liza, Elsie, and myself went from house to house to comb and card the new wool, Elsie bringing little Christopher along in a rush basket so she could nurse him. Walking homeward by dusk, I twisted my ankle coming down a steep track and had to hobble the rest of the way with one arm round Liza's waist. Come Sunday I let the rest of them go off to church whilst I stayed home to mind the baby. My swollen ankle was propped up on display in case the Church Warden or one of his lackeys barged in to see why I hadn't shown my face.

In truth, I was grateful for these few hours of ease with my new grandson. So sweet and perfect little Christopher was. Couldn't keep myself from taking him out of his swaddling to count his fingers and toes, then I trimmed his tiny nails gently with my teeth, for it was said that infants with long nails grew up to be thieves. I rocked and sang to my darling till he smiled. Couldn't remember when I'd last been so happy. That Sunday was the hottest we'd seen all year. Since the others were gone, I'd taken off my kirtle and was wearing only my thin smock whilst I was sat on the bench beneath the elder tree. My kirtle was hanging from the tree branch so I could slip it back on in a hurry if I heard the Church Warden coming. But for now I delighted in the cool shade and the singing birds and my baby Christopher cuddled in my arms. Elderblossom scented the air. Folk called it a witches' tree, but that was just foolish talk. In my mind, it was a tree of many gifts. I made elder cordial from the foamy white flowers and elderwine from the purple-black berries.

Little Christopher gazed up at me with innocent eyes, his fingers wrapped round my thumb, till he nodded off. Lulled by the sunlight, I leaned back against the tree trunk and, breathing in the elderflowers, slipped off to sleep as well.

His curling golden hair haloed by the sun, he bent over me, and I was young again, beautiful enough to dazzle him. *All I ask is one kiss.* His mouth sought mine. Tilting my face to his, I surrendered, just as I had before, a faithless wife taking her pleasure with a travelling pedlar. How he kissed me.

I awoke with a whimper as a hot tongue bathed the underside of my left arm. In the heat of summer, I'd gone stone cold and couldn't say a word, only clutch the baby tight. By God's grace, the child still slept. I had awakened to see a great brown dog pressed against my knee, slavishly licking my arm.

Though I willed myself to order the dog away, I couldn't speak. My throat was dry as dust. In a panic, I tried to say the Pater Noster, but I couldn't remember the words. Quailing, I awakened Christopher who shrieked. The brown dog trotted away, disappearing through a gap in the hedge.

Though I'd dreamt of Kit's father, it was Tibb's kiss that burned on my lips, Tibb's visitation that made every hair on my body stand up. And then I knew that, unlike Kit's father, Tibb would never leave me, as much as I sought to banish him. It was useless trying to fight it or deny it. He would be with me always.

# 3

TIBB APPEARED TO ME almost daily, most often at day-light gate, though sometimes in the blue quiet of morning or in the black hush of night.

"Why are you here?" I asked him. "Why do you keep coming?"

He smiled and told me, "My lady sent me to look after you." But he wouldn't say who that lady was.

I struggled to make sense of it. Cunning folk I knew, by name and reputation at least: the midwife down in Colne, the herbwife over in Trawden. Did they have spirits such as Tibb? If so, they would scarce admit it for all the world to hear, for dealing with spirits was sorcery and the Bible said suffer not a witch to live. But, then again, you were only a witch if you used your powers for evil. Cunning folk did good. I'd heard that the Trawden herb-wife had once cured a man of palsy. Fact was, people had need of charmers, for who else was there to treat the sick? Even suppos-ing a person was rich enough to hire a physician, such doctors, with their lancets and leeches, were more likely to do harm than good to a body. In the old days, the monks of Whalley Abbey grew medicinal herbs and they'd a prayer and blessing for every illness, even holy relics to heal those with serious ailments, but the brothers were dead or in hiding now, so it was either seek out a blesser or suffer without end.

I made myself remember my own grand-dad, the light in his eyes. When I tossed in the throes of some ague, he'd only to lay his hand upon my brow and chant a rhyme under his breath for the fever to ease. Had he a familiar? Following my memory back far as it would go, I recalled the spotted bitch that seemed to follow him everywhere, yet the animal had never drawn close enough so that Mam or I could touch it.

Mam wasn't a cunning woman, but she had known a thing or two. Long ago I'd heard her tell of the fairy folk. They were not like us mortal beings. Neither were they angels or demons or even ghosts, but a middle race that lived betwixt and between, made of a substance so fine that they could appear and disappear at will. Only the blessed and the mad could see them. My grand-dad had sought out their magics; many a horse he healed on account of their aid. They dwelt in a world apart from ours, yet it was very near. They'd a queen, the Queen of Elfhame, near as beautiful as Our Lady. She dressed all in green and rode a white mare with thirty-nine bells tied in its mane. Fleet as the bride of the wind, she'd ride, the music of those ringing, singing bells echoing through the forest. *My lady sent me to look after you.* Was Tibb, then, one of the elvenfolk, the Queen of Elfhame's host?

With such things churning in my head, I thought I'd gone stark mad. Yet on the outside, nothing much changed. I was still Demdike, the beggar woman of Malkin Tower, mother to one bastard and to one squint-eyed spinster too poor to afford a spinning wheel.

But Kit and his family moved on. It was Elsie's doing. To be honest, she'd never warmed to Liza and after I upbraided her for scolding Liza about the tansy, she'd taken to fearing me, too. I could see it in that fretful flicker in her eyes whenever I took her little son in my arms. She'd try to snatch him away, only Kit would wrap his arms round her and say, "Peace, Elsie. Let my old mother show some affection to her grandson."

Kit's words were of little use. Elsie carried on as though I'd toss little Christopher headfirst into the bubbling soup pot soon as her back was turned. So she badgered and nagged till Kit at last agreed they could move down to Sabden and stay with her brother's people. I was happy, at least, that Kit found steady work in a stone-cutter's yard. Strong as a bull, he was, shouldering those great slabs of slate as if they were no heavier than a lamb's fleece.

Once he and his family moved to Sabden, I only saw them of a Sabbath. Pained me, it did, to see so little of Kit and my grandson, though I confess I didn't miss Elsie much. Why my Kit had to marry such a wet, jumpy thing was beyond my understanding. But he was a dutiful son, sending me what money he could spare. For the rest, Liza and I were left to our own devices. Two masterless women living in a tower.

Liza found what work she could whilst I wandered my lonely way begging. More often than not, I'd be walking along Pendle Water or up over Stang Top Moor when I'd see him out of the corner of my eye. Then my Tibb would take his place at my side. I'd be covered in the dust of the road, swatting at midges and flies, and he'd be fresh and clean as the first morning of spring.

"Go down yonder track," he said one morning. "You'll come across a lamb that's sore lame. Poor thing is bound to die anyway. Wring its neck and hide it in your bundle. None will be the wiser. You and our Liza can have meat this night. Later you can bury the bones in your garden."

"Hold your wicked tongue," I told him. "I might be a beggar but I'm no thief."

He grinned. "That's a sharp temper you have, my Bess."

In truth, I'd grown impatient with his mischief. "If you think you're so clever, why can't you cure my Liza of her squint?"

He sobered and bowed his head. "What God has done, only God can undo."

"What's the use of you, then, if you're only good for tempting me into getting hanged as a sheep thief?"

"I can reveal the things that lie hidden," he was quick to tell me. "What have you lost? I'll tell you where it's gone."

"Kit's father," I said, tart as anything. "Always wondered where he wandered off to."

Long before Tibb first appeared to me, I confess I was once

desperate enough to seek out a tinker woman who claimed she could tell fortunes. Paid her a penny to tell me where my lost love had gone. Took my money, that charlatan had, and told me a pretty tale of my lost Jake being pressed against his will into the Queen's Navy. He had died at sea, so she said, pining for me till his last breath.

Tibb was more forthright. "My Bess, sometimes you're too soft for your own good. He was a rogue, your Jake. Had a girl like you in every town and village on his way. Your Kit has a score of half-brothers and -sisters scattered across two counties. If you'd any sense, you'd have scorned his impudence."

"Does he still live?" I asked.

"Aye, he lives. In Halifax. In his son's house, off Doghouse Fold." Tibb's accuracy in such matters fair took the breath out of me. "Don't ask me to spirit you away to visit him, for you'll not like what you see. Your Jake's a helpless, toothless old wretch by now. His greedy children—"

I scowled.

"His greedy *lawful* children," he corrected himself, "have taken his house, his possessions, and his money, banishing him to a bed in the garret. His wits, his health, his memory, all are gone, Bess. Though he lives, he's a mere shade. His stingy daughter-in-law dishes out one meagre bowl of gruel to him in a day and leaves him to lie in his own piss."

"Enough!" I cried. Such a lot was too cruel for any man, even the one who had used and betrayed me. That night I would pray for Jake.

Tibb wandered over to a birch copse where bluebells grew in a cloudy swath. "I'd never abandon you to such a fate." He sat himself down in the soft grass, then stretched out his arm, beckoning me to rest a spell beside him.

"So you're more faithful than other men?"

"You're a fine one to talk of being faithful," he said. "Letting your husband wear the cuckold's horns. But to answer your question, my Bess: Yes, I am true. You may count on me."

"At least you're useful in that sense."

This made him laugh. "At last, my Bess, we are of one mind."

"If you know so much, tell me this. Where may Liza and I go to find work tomorrow and more in payment than stale bread?"

He smiled, showing off his fine white teeth. "Anthony Holden's, down at Bull Hole Farm. You'll have meat in your belly without risking your neck to steal a sickly lamb."

"Why Anthony Holden's?" Liza demanded when I roused her in the morning. "Last time he had no work for me. Chased me off his land, he did. Hates the sight of me."

"Just this once," I said. "If he sends us packing, we'll never go there again, I promise."

On that brisk morning I led the way. We skirted Blacko Hill, then walked along Pendle Water, passing through Roughlee with its manor house where Richard Nutter lived. Like his father before him, Nutter had remained true to the old faith. Of late, rumours had gone round of him concealing Jesuits, a new breed of priest come over from France as part of a secret English mission. Courting ruin, that was. Both Nutter and the priest, if discovered, would be done for high treason and dragged off to Lancaster where they would first be hanged, then cut down whilst still alive and disembowelled, left to die in slow torment before the spitting mob.

The year before last Nutter had taken a new bride, young enough to be his granddaughter, so I'd heard. Kept themselves to themselves, the Nutters did, so I'd never clapped eyes on the lass. But I fair wondered what kind of girl would choose to bear such a yoke, not only to marry a sixty-year-old man, rich though he might be, but to risk her life sheltering Jesuits. I wouldn't trade places with her for all the money in the world.

Liza and I pressed on by way of Thorneyholme into Goldshaw, past the New Church and the stone pit where I first met Tibb. Felt like an age before we finally reached Bull Hole Farm. As we trudged up to the farmhouse, a brown dog shot out of nowhere and bounded up to meet us. The hairs on my skin stood on end when that beast thrust his muzzle into my palm.

26

"Are you not well?" my daughter asked me. "Told you it was too far to walk on no account."

"Tell me, Liza, did you see this dog when you last came to Bull Hole?"

"I recall seeing a black dog, not a brown one." She shrugged. "But farmers are like to keep more than one dog, as a rule."

She dropped to her knees, took the dog's great head in her hands, and rubbed it behind the ears. Had a soft spot for God's creatures, did our Liza. Her bad temper vanished. For a moment I was worried she would spend the rest of the day fussing over that infernal beast.

"Enough of that," I said. "We've come to find honest work."

The brown dog scampered away, as if to lead us to the farmhouse door, but when we reached the house, there was no sign of the animal. A woman's head appeared in a window, then the door flew open. Sarah Holden was stood on the threshold, hands flapping in alarm.

"Away from here, you squint-eyed devil! We've a sick child in the house and more than enough bad luck. Be off before I have my husband turn you out the gate."

Hiding behind Mistress Holden's skirts, small children sneaked glances at my Liza, who decided to amuse her onlookers. Throwing back her head, she rolled her eyes in contrary directions till the children shrieked with laughter. Ignoring her antics, I strode up to the door and put my foot in before Mistress Holden could slam it shut.

"Is that any way for a Christian to greet her neighbour?" I asked her.

"You're no neighbour of mine," she said.

No neighbour of hers, indeed! Did we not take communion at the same table, I was about to argue when, to my astonishment, a passage from Proverbs came to me, one of the Curate's favourites.

Smooth-tongued as Tibb, I quoted the Bible verse: "He that giveth unto the poor shall not lack; but he that hideth his eyes shall have many a curse."

When I said the word *curse,* she whitened, her lips pressing down, but I knew she could not dispute what was written in the Good Book. At a loss, she was, and what did I do but turn that to my advantage?

"Have a heart, Sarah Holden. I'm old enough to be your own mother. Liza and I have travelled all this way because we've no bread left in our house. Not a single egg. My girl has a squint, it's true, but she won't bring any bad luck in your house, I swear. Have us work outdoors, if you will. We could weed your garden."

The woman shook her head. "Weeding's children's work." She sighed. "If it's honest work you're after, you can scrub out the scullery. There's spinning to be done, too."

"My Liza can spin beautifully," I told her.

The children leapt and clapped their hands, begging Liza to do the trick with her eyes again till their mother shooed them away.

Leaving Liza to do the spinning, I scrubbed out the scullery myself. By noon I was near finished. Meanwhile the smell of lamb stew and baking bread wafted in from the kitchen, and I was hoping and praying Mistress Holden would invite us to her table. We'd keep our mouths shut and sit well below the salt, to be sure.

From the kitchen I heard Anthony Holden and his farmhands tramp in the door, heard Sarah Holden call her servant girl to fetch ale from the cellar. The mere thought of ale made my mouth water, though if Mistress Holden was stingy in her brewing as she was in everything else, it was probably weak, watery stuff. I rinsed out the clouts and was hanging them to dry when, from out of the kitchen, came a roar that stopped my heart.

"That bug-eyed slattern!" Master Holden shouted to his wife. "You let her in the house and she's spoiled the ale!"

"No, sir." Liza's voice came tight and scared. "I never touched your ale, sir. Never even looked at it."

"You cursed it," he said. "You're ruled by the Devil, you ugly thing."

I rushed out of the scullery to see my daughter quaking before him. Master Holden had left the door wide open. Outside the brown dog was stood watching. All my hackles were raised. I pressed my hands together, then stepped between Master Holden and Liza. Mistress Holden, the children, and the servants were stood round, afraid to even speak with the master in such a temper. I lifted my chin and tried to convince myself that I wasn't afraid of him.

"Sir, if your ale's been cursed, it wasn't the work of my Liza. That I'll swear upon your Bible. But if you show me the ale, I can lift the curse."

If anything, my words left Master Holden looking even angrier, his face flushed a deep plum. The one thing that held me riveted was the sight of the brown dog. He was sat down now, one huge paw resting on the threshold.

"You claim to have the power to lift a curse?" Master Holden spoke with contempt, as though I were an idiot not even fit to scrub out his wife's scullery.

"Sir, you just accused my poor Liza of cursing the brew. If you believe she has such powers, merely from her squint, which was given to her by God, why can you not believe that a simple woman such as myself can bless and lift a curse?"

Never in my life had I spoken so bold to my betters. It was as though Tibb were stood beside me, whispering the words in my ear. Master Holden was struck speechless, probably wondering whether to backhand me for my cheek. But I didn't cower.

"Master Holden," I said. "Sure there's no harm in letting me try."

"Ale jug's on the table," he said. Then his mouth clamped up and he looked fair powerless to say anything more.

The brown dog lay down with both front paws resting on the threshold.

Head buzzing, I crossed the slate floor to the scrubbed oaken table and put my hands on either side of the jug. I was silent. Everyone was. If I couldn't do this, they'd call me a liar. Holden would chase me off with a switch. But before I could founder another second, the words came to me, sweet and pure as Tibb's voice.

Three Biters hast thou bitten
The Heart, ill Eye, ill Tongue:
Three bitter shall be thy Boot:
Father, Son, and Holy Ghost,
In God's name.

And then, before Master Holden's unbelieving eyes, I chanted five Pater Nosters, five Ave Marias, and the Creed, all the while remembering how, a lifetime ago, my grand-dad had murmured the Latin words over me whilst I lay fevered.

"That's popish nonsense," he said, but his voice was shaky and uncertain.

Ignoring him, I turned to his wife. "Mistress Holden, if you could please bring me a mug."

Without a word, she handed me a clean pewter tankard, the best she had in the house. Her eyes were lowered like a servant's when she pressed it into my hand. I poured ale into the tankard and drank. Wondrous cool from the cellar, the ale was. As I'd suspected, it was on the weak side, but refreshing just the same. I took a good long swallow before setting the tankard back down.

"You brew good ale, Mistress Holden," I said, though that was stretching the truth a bit.

Her husband poured himself a tankard and drank. "It was spoiled before, I'll swear to it. Sour as bad fruit. But now it's right again." He looked at me with something close to fear in his eyes.

"She's a blesser," his wife said, casting her eyes down to the floor.

"Where did you learn such things?" Master Holden asked me.

"God has given me this gift, sir."

No one could fault me for calling on God, I thought, and

everyone knew that magic could be of the good sort. With my prayers, I'd allied myself with heavenly powers, as any respectable cunning woman would do. Miracles and wonders had always been part of the old religion. Light a candle, pray to a saint, and, with the saint's intercession and God's grace, your wish could be granted. When one of the Towneley wives could not conceive a child, she went on a pilgrimage to St. Mary's of Walsingham and, within the year, she was pregnant. Now that the shrines lay ruined, what could people do but turn to cunning folk?

The Queen herself, I'd heard it said, employed a conjurer in her court—Dr. John Dee. Surely Elizabeth would not do such a thing if she believed him to work evil. Folk said that Dr. Dee could read the mysteries of the stars and turn tin into gold. Different laws, there were, for the rich and the poor. The highborn could hold fast to their astrologers and alchemists even if their laws forbade us simple folk our magics. What if the Holdens accused me of calling upon unholy spirits? My stomach curdling, I looked to the open door. The brown dog was gone.

Mistress Holden, having recovered possession of herself, bade everyone to come eat. Knowing our place, Liza and I sat below the servants at the very foot of the table.

"Some trickster you are," my daughter whispered in my ear. "How did you fool them?"

I told her to hush up and put on a grateful face for the food we were about to receive. After the prayers, the maidservant ladled out lamb stew, the first meat I'd tasted in months. Tibb's promise had come true—I had to give him that. Whilst I ate, I made sure my head was bowed, meek and humble, over my wooden trencher. But I could feel their stares. The Holdens, their children, the servants, and the farmhands were all gawping at me. Word would go round. By Sunday when Liza and I walked to the New Church, everyone from Colne to Whalley would be saying that Demdike of Malkin Tower had charmed the ale at Bull Hole Farm. Could I endure the gossip and the looks that would follow me? Heaven knows, they'd said enough about me already.

The stew and bread were rich and good, filling my stomach.

Proper meal like that was enough to put a glow on Liza's cheeks. If you looked at her from the side, you hardly noticed her squint, and, apart from her wayward eyes and her skinny frame, she wasn't a bad-looking girl. Had her father's glossy brown hair. Her neck and wrists were graceful, her bosom well-shaped—that she had from me. For a moment I allowed myself to fancy that I had the power to bless more than ale. Could I charm one of the farmhands sat at this table so that he would turn his heart to my Liza? But the lads just kept staring at me. Couldn't even read the look in their eyes to tell whether they were nervous, awestruck, or simply curious. Only when the maidservant rose to collect the empty trenchers did I notice young John Device gazing at Liza. Shy lad, he was. Never opened his mouth unless he was spoken to first. When Liza swung her head round and threw him a big grin, he blushed and bolted out the door. So much for that.

"Spinning's done, scullery's clean," Liza said. "Time to be on our way—unless there's anything more they want you to *bless*."

How could she make light of what I'd done? My head still rang and, in spite of the good food, a coldness settled in my belly. I fair trembled at the thought of stepping out that door only to meet the brown dog again. At any rate, it was time to ask the Holdens for our payment.

The housewife and her husband were stood on the far end of the kitchen, their heads together as they spoke in low voices. Then they both looked at me.

"Mother Demdike," Master Holden said.

I was stood to attention, pleased that he hadn't just called me Demdike. "Mother" had a certain ring of admiration about it, the most a woman of my station could hope for. For the first time in my life, I'd an inkling of what it would mean to command respect.

"Could I ask you for one more thing before you go on your way?" So careful and soft-spoken, the master was with me now. Hard to believe this was the same man who had railed at my Liza less than an hour ago. "I'll pay you for it. I'll give you a capon, a dozen eggs, and a dressed hare besides."

Suddenly it seemed my labours were worth more than stale bread. I wet my tongue, searched for words. "If it's something I can do, Master Holden, sir."

My first thought was that he wanted me to bless one of his cows. Tibb had already taught me the charm for ailing cattle: three Ave Marias and a sprinkling of water. But no. Master Holden wasn't even thinking about his herd.

"It's my son," he said. "My little Matthew. He's poorly."

Mistress Holden clasped her hands together, and I saw the red rims round her eyes. Before I could find my voice, Master Holden was leading the way up the narrow, creaking stairs, and Mistress Holden was coming up behind me, so I'd no choice but let them take me to the chamber where the child lay in a trundle bed at the foot of his parents' bedstead. Liza was left behind in the kitchen.

Of course, I'd heard of young Matthew Holden, the sickly child never seen in church, but I'd never laid eyes on him before. He looked to be about four years old. His eyes were sunken, his skin waxen and dull whilst he lay there like a poppet. I wanted to tell his parents no, nothing could be done. One look at the boy was enough to tell me it was hopeless—this child wouldn't make old bones. Mostly I was afraid. My stomach turned and I longed to be far from the room. The Holdens could keep their capon, eggs, and hare. Charming ale was quite a different matter than blessing a sickly child. If I failed, if I spoke the charm and the child's condition worsened, or if, God forbid, he died, then I would be done for. The Holdens would accuse me of bewitching the lad and that would be the end of Mother Demdike. I'd be stoned or drowned or worse.

I was about to flat-out refuse when Master Holden dropped to his knees beside the trundle bed. The sight knocked me sideways. So the loud-mouthed blunderer had a soft spot. I watched him lay a tender hand on the lad's brow.

"His heart and lungs are weak," Master Holden said. "Last winter he fell ill and never recovered his strength."

Mistress Holden knelt on the other side of the trundle bed and whispered fond words to the child before looking up at me. "We called in a doctor," she said. "But he demanded three pounds. We couldn't pay—"

"Sarah!" her husband admonished.

Mistress Holden flushed in her shame of admitting to a person as low as me that she and her husband could not afford a physician. "Can you not help him?" she asked, tears in her eyes.

What a strange thing it was to be stood in their bedchamber with the master and mistress on their knees before me.

"A sick child is a serious matter," I said, so reluctant that I couldn't meet their eyes.

"Please," Mistress Holden said. "At least say you'll try."

One look at her face was enough to remind me what it was like to be the mother of an ailing child. When my Kit was only two, he fell ill with a terrible fever and I'd sworn that his death would be the end of me, only we both were lucky and he pulled through.

My knees ached, my whole body was sore from the long walk to Bull Hole Farm and from the hours spent scrubbing out the scullery. I gazed out the chamber window, wondering what to do, when I saw the brown dog stood below, staring up at me. Sinking to the floor beside Mistress Holden, I took the child's clammy hand. Listless, the little boy stared up. Resigned to his fate, he was. Hadn't any hope left inside him of ever getting better.

"Have you lungwort in the house?" I asked his mother.

She shook her head.

"I'll bring some tomorrow and brew him a tonic." Then I stroked the child's sallow face. "Best if you leave me alone with him for a spell."

After his parents had let themselves out of the room, the first spark of life shone in the boy's eyes. He looked nervous.

"Your parents asked me to bless you," I confided. "What do you say to that, Master Matthew?" I chafed his limp hand between my own. "Wouldn't it be a grand thing to rise out of this bed and go out and play with your brothers and sisters?"

From outside the window came the sound of children's laughter.

"Fancy being out there with them. A fine day, this. You could be sat in the grass with the sun on your face. See the flowers and your father's new calves."

"You stink," the lad told me. "You're dirty."

I laughed. "So your sickness hasn't struck you dumb then. If I'm dirty, my lot is better than yours. Least I do more than lie abed all day like a great lump."

A spot of colour entered the child's cheeks and that made me go soft. Though my back hurt, I lifted Matty from his bed and carried him to the window.

"I'm only a poor beggar woman, but I can wander wherever my fancy takes me. Once I was sat way up there, atop Pendle Hill." I pointed out the window where the hill rose to touch the sky. "I could see all the way to the sea. But you're a prisoner in this room. Have you never prayed to get better?"

The boy watched his brothers and sisters, who squealed and chased each other whilst they should have been weeding the garden.

"Tell me this, Matty," I said, making the child look me in the eye. "Do you want to get better or do you want to lie in this chamber till you waste away?"

The boy's eyes were huge. "I want to get better," he said in a tiny voice.

My skin nettled. My eyes misted. It was as though I could look into two worlds at once. The child's spirit was snared in some dark place indeed, fettered at the bottom of a cold, dry well. A powerful charm it would take to raise him up into the light. The years flowed backward till I was a young woman stood in our church in the days of Mary Tudor. Above the new-built roodscreen was the fresh-painted image of Judgement. Christ the King was sat upon his throne between the glittering gates of heaven and the yawning maw of hell. Beside heaven's gate Saint Peter was stood, holding the keys. At the very same time,

I looked through the Holdens' window to see the brown dog lie down upon the grass.

The blessing seized me. The words flowed from my tongue, whilst the inside of my head buzzed like a swarm of bees.

> What hath he in his hand?
> A golden wand.
> What hath he in his other hand?
> Heaven's door keys.
> Stay shut, hell door.
> Let the little child
> Go to its Mother mild.

I saw a picture, painted on the church wall, of Our Lady, clad in black, weeping at the foot of the cross, but even as she wept, she seemed swept up in a blinding vision.

> What is yonder that casts a light so far-shining?
> Mine own son that's nailed to the Tree.
> He is nailed sore by the heart and hand.

Lastly, I saw the Angel Gabriel, all in white, holding a lily.

> Gabriel laid himself down to sleep
> Upon the ground of holy weep.
> Our good Lord came walking by.
> Sleepest thou, wakest thou, Gabriel?
> No, Lord, I am stayed with stick and stake,
> That I can neither sleep nor wake.
> Rise up, Gabriel, and come with me,
> The stick nor the stake have power to keep thee.

Inside the child was a well of deep cold. My head a-flutter, I held him fast till that ungodly chill drained out of him and into me. Held on to him and chanted till his skin no longer felt clammy, but was warm as bread fresh out of the oven. All my warmth poured into the boy. When I tucked him back into his bed, I was shivery and faint, though sunlight streamed into the close little chamber. Had to hold on to the bedstead to raise myself to my feet. Staggered to the door, then called out to the Holdens, who flew into the room to behold their boy with his new-flushed cheeks and gleaming eyes. The child grasped his mother's hand, told her he would pray to get better and that he wanted to see his father's new calves. I was so weak by then that I had to go down to the kitchen and sit a spell. Liza spoke to me, the Holdens spoke to me, but I hardly knew what they were saying. A bell knelled inside my head. Even when I closed my eyes I saw the brown dog.

When I could finally stand on my feet again and was well enough to wobble home, Liza had to carry the capon, the dressed hare, and the dozen eggs—a basket in each hand.

"How did you do that?" my daughter demanded. First off, she'd thought I was putting on an act like some quack at Colne Market. Now she wouldn't shut her gob about it. "You never did such a thing before."

I was too drained to speak. Took my last strength to drag myself back to Malkin Tower, where I collapsed upon my pallet. Anyone could see that the illness had left young Matthew only to enter me. Never mind the victuals the Holdens had given us —I could barely swallow a cup of broth. Couldn't rise from my pallet for a fortnight, but I sent Liza to bring the Holdens the lungwort.

Whilst she was gone, Tibb appeared and let me hold his warm hand for strength.

"Why didn't you warn me?" I asked him, tears in my eyes. "If I'd known it would be like this—"

"Would you have refused to bless a sick child? I don't believe that for a moment, my Bess."

My sight blurred. The way I shuddered and ached, I feared I would never be right again.

Tibb stroked my hair. "In future, it will be easier on you. You're new to this is all. Lie back and rest, my Bess. You've earned your sleep."

He covered my eyes with his soft palms, and then I tumbled

into a shimmering fever dream. Three paths led off into the blue-bell wood. One led to the right, another to the left, but some tug inside made me set off down the middle path as I called out after Tibb, begging him to show himself. Instead I saw a lady come riding upon a white horse. Rapturous lovely, she was, her red-gold hair shimmering like the sun at daylight gate. The woodland rang with the music of the gold and silver bells twined in her horse's lustrous mane. Lifting her hand in blessing, the rider smiled as though she'd known me since I was a babe. *My lady sent me to look after you.*

The haunting chimes of those bells brought back my memories of the old ways. A girl again, I joined the procession round the fields to encourage the corn to grow high. We chanted blessings over the springs to make them pure. Yet when I looked round, I saw no crosses, no priests, just the young maids and the young men wandering off into the fields of waving green barley. Again the lady appeared, riding a graceful circle round me. Fresh and new as unfurling spring leaves, she was, but older even than the popish faith. She was not the Queen of Heaven, but a queen of earth, Queen of Elfhame.

When the fever broke, Liza was sat beside my pallet with a piece of lamb pie from the Holdens. I fell upon it with a hunger that made her laugh.

"Little Matthew's well better," she told me. "Today he left his sickbed. Ate at the table with the rest of the family. Stuck his head outside before his mother called him back. Then he was sat with me whilst I was winding wool."

I smiled. At least my sufferings weren't for nothing. "You brewed the lungwort for him?"

"Aye." She looked me over, her eyes strange. "Tell me, Mam. Did you have the powers always? Or did they come to you all sudden-like?"

I stared up at the thatch and told her I needed my rest, but she wouldn't stop pestering me.

"You've always sown them herbs," she said. "If we'd nowt else, there were them weeds of yours."

"And a good thing for you," I said, thinking of the tansy.

"But when you blessed Matty Holden, you'd no wort with you. Could you not teach me, Mam?"

"It's not something you want to be meddling with. Look at the state it's left me in."

"Teach me the charms, Mam, please! I've a good memory."

"Child, there's more to it than just words."

"Folk think my squint is enough to curdle butter," Liza said. "If my eyes can curse, sure I could bless if I set my mind to it."

The notion had lodged itself in my daughter's skull, and there was nowt more I could say.


When I was well enough to show my face in the New Church again, I was stood at the back with the other poor folk, whilst the yeomen and gentry sat in their pews. I tried to put on a good face, keep my thoughts on the hymns and scriptures, ignore how the Curate stared at me, how everyone looked my way. Word had certainly gone round.

My old friend Anne Whittle couldn't take her eyes off me. Of all the people in that church, she knew me best, for we'd been best friends during our girlhood, always sharing the other's company back in the days of the processions, our loose-flowing hair crowned with the garlands we'd woven for each other. Such a beauty my Anne had been with her green eyes and her tresses the colour of flax. In secret I used to fancy that she was some high-born lady left by mistake in a labourer's cottage. Full of herself even as a little lass. Burst her spleen if any dared to belittle her. Her temper was fierce enough to make a grown man whimper. Anne forged her own way in life. If one door was locked to her, she'd find another, ever resourceful, never one to give up when she had her mind set on something.

Catching her eye, I smiled. Her hair, like mine, was grey now, yet her eyes were as keen as they'd ever been. Like me, she'd been luckless in marriage, at least in the beginning. Wed her sweet-heart, she had, the best-looking man in Pendle, so she swore, only he'd a wandering eye, and a few years down the line, after her girl Betty was born and the son who didn't live, our Anne found her good man lying in a haystack with Meg Pearson. So what did my friend do but sneak up with a bucket of cold ditchwater and drench them both. In a voice loud enough to be heard from Trawden to Clitheroe, she told her husband that he could have his trollop, for he'd not be welcome in their marriage bed ever again.

When he died not long afterward, Anne shocked everyone by taking another husband, ten years younger than herself. Though folk had surmised she was too old for bearing by then, she birthed her youngest girl, Anne, a golden-haired child pretty as her mother had been in her youth. Now that my friend's second husband was dead, people had taken to calling her Chattox, her maiden name having been Chadwick, in order to tell her apart from little Annie, her daughter.

Anne had stood by me in my hour of deepest humiliation, when, twenty-two years ago, the Constable pilloried me for adultery. Pregnant with Kit, the pedlar's bastard, I shrank inside myself, my head and hands locked into the stocks, my face blackened from the sheep dung the crowd lobbed at me. Not caring what anybody thought, my Anne barged her way through the throng to take her place before me. Though I trembled and sobbed, full sorry for myself, she chatted with me as though we were market wives sat over cups of strong October ale.

"My first husband was an adulterer, as you well know," she'd told me, her face so close to mine that our noses touched, never mind that I was spattered with filth. "Nobody put him in the stocks, but when I threw that cold bucket on him, his member did shrink. God's foot, our Bess! You should have seen it."

Full blasphemous, she teased that she'd pray to Saint Un-cumba, the patroness of women who wished to be rid of their husbands, and with God's grace the saint would help me get shot of Ned Southerns one way or other. So Anne jibed and told bawdy jokes till I roiled with laughter and could no longer pity myself or even feel shame for what I'd done.

If that wasn't true friendship, what was? A sad thing that we only saw each other of a Sunday now that we'd no more holidays or the leisure to do much besides stand for hours in the church on the Sabbath or toil for our bread the other days of the week. Her cottage, over in West Close, lay five miles from Malkin Tower, over an hour's journey by foot.

What I wouldn't give to turn my back on those prodding eyes in the congregation, link arms with her, and set off through the meadows as we used to do. With the strange turn my life had taken, I needed her more than ever. Full of longing, I shot her another glance. Full brazen, she winked.

After the hours of preaching were done, Anne, bless her, was first out the door with her daughters in her wake. I made to follow, hoping to catch up, but as I stumbled blinking into the sunlight, Master and Mistress Holden waylaid me. Little Matthew was stood between them. How proud and pleased the parents looked, how they beamed at me, and how glum was that little lad's face. Wager the mite half-wished he was still ill so he could spare his ears the Curate's dreary sermon. But anybody could see how Matty was thriving since I had blessed him. Whether it was by my charm or by the lungwort, only God could say. After the Holdens had thanked me again and taken their leave, I saw Anne waiting for me at the wicket gate. So I told Liza to go on without me, and Anne sent her two girls home, Betty watching over little Annie.

Mindful of eavesdroppers, my friend and I strayed from the road, finding a narrow track that cut into the green near Pendle Water. The mossy earth cushioned our bare feet as we wove our way between birch trees and felt the dance of sun and shadow upon our faces.

"Tongues are wagging about you, our Bess," Anne said. "Always had a surprise up your sleeve. Now I turn round and you're a charmer."

"I know you don't hold with such things yourself," I was quick to say.

Ever the sceptic was Anne, far too full of common sense to suffer those who claimed to work miracles. *All that chanted drivel,* I'd heard her say before. *Worse gibberish than what we had to hear from the old priests. Give me a good herbwife to lay on a poultice, but spare me the incantation.*

"It's a dangerous path you're treading," she said. "Did you not hear about the conjurer over Burnley way?"

I shook my head. Living at Malkin Tower, I could not keep track of the gossip the way Anne could, living as she did between Burnley and Fence.

"He used the spell of the sieve and shears to discover the whereabouts of stolen goods. The Magistrate had him arrested. He was sentenced to be pilloried not once, but four times, Bess: in Clitheroe, Whalley, Colne, and Lancaster. And he's been warned that should he ever deal in sorcery again, he's to be hanged."

Considering how I'd barely endured the pillory that single instance, I couldn't fathom how anybody could bear to go through it four times. Perhaps hanging would be kinder. Overpowered by everything, I just wanted to hide myself away and never speak about this to anyone again. Yet I could never conceal my true face from Anne.

"Spells and spirits," she said. "It's not what I would have wished for you, love."

I gazed into her eyes, green as the moss beneath our feet.

"By Our Lady, I didn't wish this on myself either."

Struggling over my every word, I tried to describe what had come over me that day at Bull Hole Farm, how the powers I scarce understood had surged through me with a will of their own and I their mere vessel.

Anne's mouth folded upon itself. Her steady eyes blinked. Pale and quiet, she bowed her head. First time I ever saw our

Anne at a loss for words. What if this drove a wedge between us? She might be half-frightened of me now that I'd passed into this murky place where she couldn't follow.

"I can't just walk away from it," I told her, fair helpless. "Can't pretend it never happened."

"No, indeed," she said at long last. "No one will let you. They'll come banging on your door at all hours, calling on you for this and that. Just be careful, love. It's a gift you've been given, but even gifts don't come for nothing. You might have to pay more than you bargained."

With a rush of heat, I remembered how Tibb had appeared to me the Sunday I'd stayed home with my baby grandson. *All I ask is one kiss.* That single kiss had been enough to turn me into a different woman, one who was marked and set apart. Was that the true price and did I rue it? The mere thought of Tibb and his beauty, of how he filled me with awe and set my head brimming with golden light, made me flush like a girl in the thrall of new love.

The strangeness gone out of her face, Anne wrapped her arm round my shoulders. Once more she was my friend, ever practical, quick to think up some joke to make me smile. "Never a dull one, you. Always had to choose the hardest road. Married that shovel-faced Ned when you could have had any lad in Pendle—barring mine, of course!"

Eager to put this talk of magic behind us, I grinned.

"Kindred spirits, we are," she said. "Had to do things our own way, no matter what folk said."

Her arm linked with mine, we headed back. Sermon had lasted an age, the afternoon was wearing on, and our families awaited us. Gone were the days when we could linger together for hours and hours. But before we went on our separate ways, Anne plucked a lacy spray of cow parsley and tucked it behind my ear, which made us both laugh.

"Our Anne, do you think things will ever be so good again as they were back in our day?"

I wasn't talking about the old church, for Anne had never been pious. Far as she was concerned, both Catholic priest and Protestant curate were nowt but long-winded hypocrites. What I meant were the revels and feasts, the delight we'd shared when we were two garlanded girls traipsing into the twilit fields. Our own daughters had never known such a carefree time, only this life of toil and want.

"The old ways are lost," she said, gentle and sad. "Not even them charms of yours can turn back time."

She spoke as any sensible person would do. But after we'd said our farewells and I'd headed off home, I thought to myself that the old ways would never truly die if I kept them alive in my memory. Well important, it was, that someone remained to tell young folk that the world hadn't always been the way it was now.

As Anne had predicted, folk in Pendle Forest would never let me forget what I'd done at Bull Hole Farm. When I went begging, they looked at me differently than before, as though they feared what might happen if they sent me away hungry. Instead of giving me the work of the lowest servant, they invited me to their table, served me what food they could provide, be it porridge or pottage or applecake, with a mug of their best ale to wash it down. Then, after an age of hemming and hawing, they made their request of me. Could I sit a spell with their child or their old mother, with their cow or their lame horse?

The beasts I didn't mind. Adored cows, I did, for their huge eyes and their gentle might. All I needed do was stroke a cow's neck and she'd go soft as lambswool. Drop her ears and stand still and easy whilst I chanted my Ave Marias over her, sprinkled her with blessed water, and let her drink the special tonic I'd brewed. The most skittish horse would nuzzle my neck after I spoke to him and stroked him on the withers and under the mane. Then I'd poultice the nag's legs with elecampane, which my grand-dad had called Horse Heal, for it cured every rash and swelling.

Learned to carry herbs in my bundle: plants to cure cow, sheep, horse, and folk alike. Sick children took the most out of me. Despite Tibb's promises, this never changed. After blessing a child, I was laid up at least seven days. Perhaps it was my fear of something going wrong that left me so weak. Walking on a knife edge, it was. I prayed and prayed that not a single child I blessed would ever die. Grown folk were different. If I blessed an ailing old soul and it was for nowt, no one held it against me. Tried my best to give them some comfort and ease before they departed this world. I liked to see them go with a smile on their lips.

Before long, folk took to asking me for more than simple blessings. Spinsters and widows begged me for love spells, and some folk I'll not name asked me to curse their enemies, but I refused to meddle in any such business. If I wanted to keep my reputation, I could only be seen to work for good and never for evil. So I told people my business was blessing and healing, nowt else, yet despite Tibb's help, there were some whose afflictions were beyond my powers to cure.

Of an August dawn, I walked to Hugh Bradyll's farm, for his wife had asked me to come. The year before Bradyll had broken his leg and the blacksmith had set it for him, but done a poor job, so the bone had mended crooked. Nowadays the sorry man limped about in such constant pain, he could no longer plough his field or herd his cows, and he'd no sons to do the heavy work for him.

Upon reaching the Bradylls' house, I took out my bundle of herbs and blessed the grey-faced yeoman in the name of the Holy Trinity, the five wounds of Our Lord, the Mother of God, and the Twelve Apostles. I spoke every holy verse I knew, chanted the Pater Noster, Ave Maria, and the Creed. But Tibb's voice came low in my ear, telling me what I already knew in my heart: Bradyll's leg would never be right again, that the marrow inside the bone had wasted away.

"This leg can't be fixed," I told his goodwife who was stood

45

there, hands wringing her apron. "I'll brew a tincture of poppy seed to dull his pain, but there's nowt else I can do."

"You said you were a blesser." Mistress Bradyll made like I'd betrayed her out of malice.

"Told you not to bother calling out that lying quack," Bradyll spat before clenching his teeth again in agony.

"In God's name, I've done my best, sir." Had to bite my tongue to hold my peace. "I'm a blesser, to be sure, but no miracle worker. Blacksmith set your leg crooked, sir, and crooked it will remain."

Master turned his head to the wall. "Show that bilker to the door," he told his wife.

My head throbbing, I followed Mistress Bradyll out of the chamber. Her good man was bitter because he was ruined. If he could no longer get about on his two legs, he'd lose his livelihood, lose his leasehold on the farm. Most he could hope for was to learn weaving or somesuch job that could be done sitting down, but even weavers needed their feet to work the loom. He'd have to sit in his bed and card wool like a woman. Couldn't really blame him for his temper or his wife for her tears, but why did they have to lay the blame at my feet?

Meanwhile, I was fit to faint away from hunger. Hadn't had anything to eat or drink that day, and now it seemed that the Bradylls were of the opinion that I hadn't earned any payment at all. Mistress Bradyll opened the door for me.

"Good day to you, Demdike," she said.

But I refused to leave till she had at least paid me in food and drink. Just wasn't hospitable to send a fifty-year-old woman on her way without even a cup of small beer or buttermilk. Holding Mistress Bradyll's eyes with my own, I recited the charm to get drink.

*Crucifixus hoc signum vitam eternam.* Amen.

Hearing the strange words bubble up from my lips, Mistress Bradyll started. She was too young to remember either the old

Latin prayers or the crucifix that had once hung upon our rood-screen. On procession days we had carried it round the fields and pastures to bless the land, the animals, and the crops, for Christ's passion was the promise of life everlasting. Now the cross that hung in our church was stark, bare wood, and those walls, once painted with pictures of the saints and their stories, were white-washed, empty as my stomach was now.

Not waiting for an invitation, I sat myself down at Mistress Bradyll's table and stared at her with unblinking eyes till she shut the door and dragged herself to the pantry to fetch me bread, butter, cheese, and beer. Didn't take my leave till I'd eaten and drunk my fill. I wasn't going to go to bed hungry this night on account of Master Bradyll's bad leg. I kept my eyes level on Mistress Bradyll till she took the hint and packed a bundle of bread and cheese for me to take home to Liza. By the time I walked out her door, she was shaking like a reed, well glad to see me gone.

So back to Malkin Tower I tramped. Didn't know if I'd find Liza home. She might have been spinning at the Holdens' or helping with the threshing at Thorneyholme Farm. Instead I found her sat regal as a duchess upon the bench beneath the elder tree. As the swaying branches, weighted with purple-black berries, cast their shadows over her face, she looked older and wiser, a woman and no mere girl. Two strangers were sat facing her on the good bench she'd dragged out of the firehouse. Ladies, they were, sporting fine gowns of new wool trimmed in velvet and gold thread. Never before had we been graced by such fancy folk.

I was about to barge forward and announce myself when a hare flitted across my path. Tibb's voice whispered in my ear. *Stay back and watch a spell, my Bess. You'll learn something of your daughter.*

The elder of the two strangers spoke to Liza. "We've never be-fore resorted to such measures, you understand, but when needs must." She spoke half in bossiness, half in trepidation. Wanted something done for her, she did. Right plump was our guest, with a lace-trimmed coif to cover her grey hair. I tried to put a name to her face, but she appeared an utter stranger.

"Madam, I can bless as well as my mother," said my Liza.

The cheek of her! She'd sat herself beneath that witchy elder tree to make herself look like a charmer, and she made no show of trying to hide her squint.

"Tell me what I may do for you," said my daughter, speaking smooth as Tibb, who laughed in my ear.

"It's my Alice." The stranger indicated the young woman at her side. "Two years wed and barren as a mule."

"Mother!" Young Alice's voice came sharp as broken crockery. A comely thing she was. Crow-black hair and smooth white skin, cheeks flushing red from her insufferable mother's nagging.

"We made a good marriage for her," the shrew blistered on. "Her sons, should she ever bear any, shall be addressed as Esquire. Her poor father nearly killed himself to raise her dowry."

Young Alice blinked, full miserable, staring down at her small hands. Soft as kid, they'd be. No work for her but sewing and embroidery.

"Yet we've no sign of a babe." The mother went on to explain that Alice's husband had a child by a previous marriage, a daughter, and if Alice had no children, that daughter would inherit the husband's estates. "My Alice," she said, "must have sons. What if her husband has the marriage annulled on account of her being barren?"

Right harridan, the mother was. No wonder her daughter couldn't conceive. What babe would want to be born to such a grand-dam? Judging from her speech, the mother wasn't from the gentry, despite her good clothes, but the wife of some middling merchant hoping to raise herself up through her daughter's marriage.

"Peace, Mistress Whitaker," said our Liza, sounding patient and wise. "What do you want from me?" Liza looked from mother to daughter, her wandering eyes lighting on the girl's downcast face. "Herbs to bless the womb? A charm to help the young lady conceive?"

"There's a curse you must lift," Mistress Whitaker said. "My

Alice is barren because that Chattox over in West Close bewitched her."

"Chattox?" Liza seemed baffled as I was. "You mean Anne Whittle?"

In my hiding place, I could scarce keep myself from sputtering in outrage. Never in all my days had I heard such twaddle. My Anne cursing someone? My Anne, who thought that wizards and their ilk were puffed-up charlatans? She was the last person in Pendle who would meddle in hexes.

"Why would you ever think such a thing?" Liza asked, speaking my very thoughts.

The mother leaned forward on her bench whilst her daughter was sat there, pale and unmoving. "Just after my daughter's wedding, the pair of us saw that Chattox at Colne Market. She passed so close by, not taking care to move out of our way. My daughter trod on her foot."

"It was an accident," the girl spoke up. "I never meant to slight her."

"But slighted she was," said Mistress Whitaker. "I heard her muttering and murmuring under her breath, too low for anybody to make out her words. In God's name, I'll swear it was an incantation."

My skin prickled. Sometimes, it was true, Anne talked to herself—she seemed to value her own counsel and motherwit above all else—but what harm was in that? How dare this woman slander my friend? I was set to burst out of my hiding place to defend Anne's good name when Tibb's hand on my arm held me back.

"Wait a spell yet," he whispered. "There is more you'll learn."

"The Widow Chattox," said Liza, "has no more power to bewitch your daughter than the mice what live in our thatch. But if Mistress Alice has been cursed, I've a charm that will break it, just the same."

At that, my Liza began to recite word for word the blessing I'd spoken over little Matty Holden at Bull Hole Farm. How had she learned it—by eavesdropping? Wench was too canny for her own good. How clear Liza's voice rang out. Both anger and pride tore at my heart.

> Sleepest thou, wakest thou, Gabriel?
> No, Lord, I am stayed with stick and stake,
> That I can neither sleep nor wake.
> Rise up, Gabriel, and come with me,
> The stick nor the stake have power to keep thee.

Then, by Our Lady, I caught my breath to see Alice take something from her velvet purse. Garnet beads, shining dark red as droplets of blood, flashed in her white hands. Her fingers began to work them, one by one, whilst her lips intoned the forbidden prayers. I hadn't seen a rosary since the days of Mary Tudor. Even owning one marked a person out as a traitor. If the Church Warden happened by, he might well report her to the Magistrate who would have her whisked off to Lancaster Gaol. Who was this timid girl, bullied by her mother yet so willing to risk everything for her troth to the old religion? After a moment I put two and two together. She could be none other than the young wife of Richard Nutter of Roughlee Hall, the man who sheltered Jesuit missionaries. At least in their piety, the girl and her husband were well-matched.

When Liza's charm was wound up, young Alice closed her eyes, kissed the beads, and tucked them away, safe and out of sight. The young lady then drew something else from her purse—five shining shillings she pressed into Liza's outstretched palm. More brass than I'd seen in my life. We didn't take money, I wanted to shout. We took capons and eggs and ale and dressed hares, but no coins. Liza had already pocketed them.

My girl declared that she would go through my store of dried herbs and give young Alice the physick she needed to ward off witchcraft and bless the womb. But Liza didn't know much about the plants beyond the quick and timely use of tansy. For all I knew, she'd give young Alice some wort that would poison her, then we'd both be hanged.

Without further ado, I leapt out from behind the blackthorn, as though out of thin air, causing everyone to cry out. Liza's mouth opened wide enough for a hen to nest inside. Never crossed her mind that I could eavesdrop as well as she. As the saying goes, the apple doesn't fall far from the tree.

"Peace," I said, looking our visitors square in the face.

Before the girl's mother could open her flytrap in protest, I took young Alice's arm and swept her into the firehouse, then bolted the door so we would have our privacy.

"So your husband's quite a bit older than yourself, our Alice." Couldn't say what it was, but something in the girl moved me to speak to her in a familiar way, as though she were my own kin. I took her soft white hands in my brown callused ones. "It's God's truth that he's the likely cause of your so-called barrenness. Old seed isn't very quick now, is it?"

Poor thing blushed a deeper red than her garnet rosary beads.

"It's all right, dear. Not a hopeless cause by any means."

Brisk and practical, I reached deep into a clay jar and pulled out pearly heads of garlic. "Have your cook put a clove into his food every noon and evening. You'll not like the smell of it on his breath, I'll wager, but it will help him rise to the occasion, as it were."

She turned her face away from me and seemed so shamed and lost that my heart fair melted away. Not wasting a second, I found some dried woodruff blossom for her, took her cambric handkerchief, filled it with the bloom that smelled sweet and haunting as the first of May, and tied it with a bit of string. Then I closed the girl's hands round that flowery bundle.

"This is for you, to turn your heart to delight. You'll not conceive a child unless you get some pleasure from the act, and I know it's not easy being married to such an old goat, no matter how much land he has."

She lowered her eyes, but I kept on speaking in a low, confiding voice.

"When he comes to you at night, close your eyes and think of the handsomest, most strapping young lad you can imagine. It will work wonders, I promise."

She stared at me, speechless, then her face split into a grin. Her lips parted and she laughed. A shy laugh. I encouraged her, laughing along, till she was roaring, tears in her eyes. How long had it been, I fair wondered, since she'd allowed herself a good long laugh?

"Another thing," I said, wiping tears from my eyes. "You're going to have to learn to show some backbone and talk back to that mother of yours before she eats you alive." I took her kitten-soft hands in mine. "Honest, lass, there's nowt wrong with you. Within the year you'll bear a healthy son." Whilst I spoke, I saw it before me, her loving face bent over the baby who would give her more joy than her elderly husband ever could. "You'll have five children in all. So much for being barren, my girl. One day you'll not be able to remember what it was to be such a slender young thing without any little ones tugging at your skirts."

Young Alice beamed at me with such gratitude, the way I knew she never smiled at her own mother. Then, bless her soul, she kissed my cheek.

In the fullness of time, my predictions came true. Our Alice Nutter of Roughlee Hall had four sons and one daughter. The girl she named Elizabeth, after me.

After Alice and her mother went on their way, I took Liza aside and forbade her to so much as touch my herbs till she had learned their names and uses. Gave her a right scolding, I did. Told her she could recite my charms till she was blue in the face but without the aid of a familiar spirit, the spells were just words and nothing more.

"A familiar?" Her wandering eyes tried to fix on me. "You mean the Devil?"

We were sat in my tower room, the door below bolted lest some neighbour come spying. I watched her back away from me. Her dread filled the air like some awful stink.

"No, Liza. Not the Devil," I said. "I don't have dealings in any such business as that. Familiar's more like an angel."

Then I broke off because that wasn't quite true either. Angels lived in heaven. My Tibb was a creature of earth, of the hollow hills. My poor head throbbed at the confusion of trying to explain this to Liza when I'd scarce grasped what had happened to me.

"An angel?" Liza stepped toward me, her fear turning to hunger.

She saw the power in me, Tibb's power shining inside me like light within a lantern, and she yearned for power of her own. Could any soul blame her? How she longed to be something more than a cock-eyed spinster and the butt of everyone's ridicule. If she was a blesser, folk would think twice before crossing her.

"So how do I come by a familiar then?"

I sighed. "The spirit comes to you, love. You don't go chasing after it."

"Well, how did yours come to you?"

"He just appeared to me one day. I can't explain it."

"He?" All at once her eyes straightened.

I held my breath, wondering if our strange conversation had filled her with such an almighty awe as to cure her squint.

"Tibb," I said. My cheeks went hot as I breathed his name.

Liza sat back on her heels, her eyes never leaving my face. "I'd heard you calling out to Tibb whilst you were poorly after charming Matty Holden. Thought he was some fellow you'd been meeting in private like."

I laughed till I was sore. "Bless you, my girl. Those days are over for me."

But, in a way, my Liza was right. My meetings with Tibb were not unlike lovers' trysts. The rush of joy and fear, the shame and thrill of our forbidden bond, the secret that twined us together.

"He's the power behind my every charm," I told her. "Sometimes he appears to me in the form of a young lad. Sometimes as a brown dog." A shiver gripped my spine. "And just today as a hare."

Liza was speechless, probably wondering if I'd gone mad. Having second thoughts about wanting powers of her own, or so I hoped. Her eyes went on their crooked way again.

"Till you have a familiar, you'll not be able to work a single charm, my girl. I'll teach you of the herbs, but it's best for you to leave the rest of it alone. You don't want to be mixed up in this business." I grasped her hand tight enough to make her look up at me. "You're my only daughter. Wanted to shield you from this, love. Should the tide ever turn and the Magistrate haul me away, I want him leaving you alone."

"Mam, it's no use." Liza spoke up quiet and earnest. "Folk think it runs in our family, that we've the witchblood."

Hearing that word from her lips set me quaking.

"Everywhere I go," she said, "they ask me for blessings and charms. What am I to do?"

I willed myself to be as firm and unmoving as the cold boards beneath my feet. "You're to tell them the truth: You've no powers. If they still want their charms, send them to me. Keep your own name clean."

Late that year, just past Martinmas, I came home from a day's wandering to a dark and empty house. Hearth fire had gone out. Even the ashes were cold. The worst fears chased through my head as I was knelt there, working by moonlight, right frantic, rubbing flint against kindling. Seemed to take an age to spark flame. By the time the peat had caught, my eyes were burning, my hands raw.

Where was Liza, out so late? Had she twisted her foot and fallen into a ditch? Had a mad dog crossed her path, or a pack of lads up to mischief? I prayed to the Mother of God and called out to Tibb to keep her safe.

When the moon had climbed so high as to shine down the smoky chimney, the door opened, its hinges squeaking loud enough to set me gasping. In stepped a wild creature, her skirt smeared with clay and black earth. Her loose, flying hair was full of twigs, dead leaves, and spidersilk. Full a-tremble, my daughter was, stood before the fire, her eyes wandering like mad. When I touched her, she twitched and swayed. Something I'd not seen before shone in her eyes. My girl looked moonstruck, planet-struck, boggart-ridden. Looked like she'd been caught up in a fairy ring and made to dance till she was spent. Her face blazed with wonder, brimmed with shock and bliss.

"This night I've met him, Mam." Her words tumbled out in a hoarse croak. "Met him in the moonlight up Stang Top Moor." She fell against me, clutching me for comfort. "His name is Ball."

My girl didn't need to say another word. I'd no choice now but to train her proper. Teach her everything Tibb had taught me.

So there we were, two women living in a tower, without father, husband, brother, or son to rein us in. Daughters of the witching hill, we turned to magic. Consorted with imps and spirits. We came into our powers, and they grew and grew till folk could not ignore the glimmer in Liza's wayward eyes, the fire that burned inside us both. The magic that ran in our blood.

# 4

SOMETIMES FOLK MADE MUCH of Liza and me for our charms and our blessings. Other times they shunned or even feared us. But most of all, they had need of us.

The corn crop failed in 1587. That winter one in twenty of us in Pendle Forest died of the hunger and clemming, and if it wasn't for the work we did, Liza and I would have likely perished, too. My Liza and I hauled our bone-thin selves from cottage to farm where we did our best to mend ailing cattle and children, and all that labour in exchange for a bit of oatcake or blue milk, maybe an egg or two. Few could afford to pay more.

Sometimes I think the only thing that sustained us were the gifts left in secret outside our door. Mutton pie, barley cake, cellar apples, curds and whey. Liza believed such bounty was the gift of Tibb and Ball, but I suspected Alice Nutter as our saviour. Thanks to my herbs, she was the mother of two healthy sons and, bless her, she'd not forgotten her debt to me.

Ever since Mistress Alice first became pregnant, she and her husband had taken to going to our New Church in Goldshaw, a much shorter ride for her than the grander church in Whalley where Roger Nowell went. Though Richard and Alice Nutter were landed gentry who kept the old faith, they were as bound as I was to show their faces in church of a Sunday and at least pretend to accept the new religion.

When Mistress Alice and I saw each other on the Sabbath, we'd trade our secret smiles, even in that famine year, and she'd invite me to come ruffle the hair of her little boys, pretty as girls in their gowns, for they were too young to be breeched. Her husband looked on, as though puzzled that his young wife should be drawn to someone lowly as myself, but he seemed well proud of her benevolence toward the poor.

Of a Sunday I was always on the look-out for Anne, to see how she fared. Thin as the rest of us, my friend was. Though she greeted me hearty as ever before, I could tell something more than plain hunger troubled her. When I cornered her for a private natter, she told me she was worried about Betty, her eldest daughter.

"She can't find steady work." Anne ducked her head out of the stinging wind as we huddled in the churchyard. "She's a strapping girl of twenty-five and she has no prospects."

Times were so dire that folk in the forest began to steal from one another—the needy robbing the desperate. Broke my heart, it did, to hear of some widow coming home to find her peck of oats gone, the only food she had. Before long, people were at our door begging Liza and me to cast spells to reveal the names of the thieves.

I'd known Kate Hewitt since before Liza and Kit were born. She was married to a cloth dealer down in Colne. We called her Mouldheels on account of all the spinning she did—the wooden pattens she wore were black and greasy from working the treadle. One day she and her good man returned home from visiting relations to find they'd been robbed: her spinning wheel, a pile of woven cloth, and their one pewter plate missing. The Hewitts promised me and Liza enough wool for new cloaks if we could uncover the culprit.

Upon the dark of the moon, Liza and I trundled down to Colne with our wire sieve. Jack Hewitt provided a big pair of wool-cutting shears. Our Kate Mouldheels lit a single tallow candle and bolted the shutters. What Liza and I were about to do was unlawful in the eyes of the Constable, diabolical in the eyes of the Curate—conjuring spirits to learn the name of the thief.

The rite of the sieve and shears had been one of Grand-Dad's charms, so Tibb had revealed to me, unveiling long-buried memories. Grand-Dad, in turn, had learned it from a very old man who had learned it from his grandmother. Ancient, this spell was, maybe even older than the old religion. Heathen magic it might have been, but how could I let honest folk suffer at the hands of the wicked if I'd the means to set it right?

Liza and I were stood facing each other, middle fingers of our left hands upon the handles of the shears to press the blades against the rim of the sieve, which hung suspended. Driving rain hissed down the chimney into the hearthfire, filling the cottage with blue smoke. I heard yelping dogs and knew, with a shiver, that they were Tibb and Ball. My eyes closed, I recited the charm, calling on Saint Peter and Saint Paul, on Christ and Mary to free the innocent and reveal the guilty. Then I bade the Hewitts to name, one by one, the people they suspected of robbing them.

"Alice Gray," Mouldheels offered, but the sieve did not stir. "Jane Bulcock."

Pained me, it did, to hear her naming her own friends and neighbours like that. Did she trust them so little?

"They're innocent," I told her.

"Meg Pearson," she said.

My lip curled at the thought of Meg, that hussy who had lured my Anne's husband away, sporting with him in the haystack those many years ago. If Meg were the thief, I wouldn't feel the least bit sorry to bring down justice on her. But the sieve hung steady.

"Tom Redfearn," Jack Hewitt said.

The sieve didn't budge, but a sweat spread over my upper lip. Young Tom Redfearn was besotted with Anne's younger daughter, fifteen-year-old Annie. They were not yet betrothed—she was too young and times were too hard—but I'd heard that she'd set her heart on him. *Please don't let it be him.*

"Mam," Liza whispered. "Look at the sieve."

My knees knocked to see it tremble. Full expectant, my daughter stared at me. When I did not speak, she took charge.

"Not Tom Redfearn," she said, smooth and business-like. "But someone close to him."

"What about his sweetheart," Jack suggested. "Annie Whittle."

When the sieve remained still, I offered a silent prayer of thanks.

"No, she's only young," said Mouldheels. "More like her mother, that Chattox."

As I struggled not to shudder, the sieve twisted, but did not fall.

Mouldheels frowned. "No. It's the older daughter. Betty."

The sieve writhed between the shears' blades before it tumbled down and struck the slate floor with an awful bang, leaving me so weak that I crumpled to my knees. Outside some thing scratched and scraped at the bolted door. Closing my eyes, I saw the brown dog's great paws. I saw the pain on Anne's face as she had confessed to me how worried she was about Betty, her first born whom she'd named after me. Now my spell had revealed her daughter's crime.

"There you have it," Liza said. "Betty Whittle is your thief."

"Came calling last week, did Betty Whittle." Mouldheel's voice was grim. "Asked if I'd any spinning for her. Didn't trust her within an inch of my spinning wheel, but of charity I offered her a cup of milk."

I fought tears. Why had Mouldheels been so stingy? If she'd welcomed Betty with a generous heart, given her a proper meal and some old bread to take home to her family, it might not have come to this.

"We'll have the Constable on her," said Mouldheels. "And the Magistrate."

"No," I said, lumbering to my feet. Mouldheels had no clue what it was like to be truly poor, as Betty was, had no inkling what it was to gnaw on dandelion root to still hunger pangs.

"What do you mean *no*?" Liza asked, vexed and not hiding it.

Ignoring her, I turned to Mouldheels, taking her hand. "If she's stolen from you, it's not out of wickedness but dire need,

I'll swear to that. Let me talk to her. I'll see to it that she returns what she's taken."

"You're a soft one, our Bess." Mouldheels sounded none too pleased.

"If we don't get our gear back within the week, I'm going to the Constable," her husband told me. "You've seven days."

Next morning I set off early and alone, telling Liza it was best if I spoke to Betty in private.

"Why are you sticking out your neck for her?" my daughter asked me. "I know her mam's your old friend, but Betty's a thief, plain as the nose on your face. Let the Constable sort her out."

"And see her strung from the gallows? What a heartless wretch you are. She only did it on account of being hungry." *Such a fate that could have befallen me if Tibb had not shown me my powers.*

"Do you think Betty was going to eat Mouldheels's spinning wheel then? Betty's too full of herself, that's her problem. If she wanted for food, all she needed do was ask for it like any meek soul would do."

"You'd have me do nothing — just stand aside and see her condemned?"

How was Liza to understand what I owed to Betty's mother? Though Anne believed the old ways were lost, she was nonetheless the keeper of my most deep-reaching memories, the cherry-lipped girl who had seen me crowned Lammas Queen when I was younger than Liza was now. She was the tough, loyal friend who had stood by me at the pillory. I'd march to Lancaster barefoot before I saw her daughter hanged.

Shutting my ears to Liza's protests, I packed my bundle with oatbread and some plumcake Mistress Alice had given us.

Stark winter morning, it was, the grass glittering with frost. The road, frozen hard beneath my feet, forked off in two directions. Stood upon the place where the three ways met, Tibb awaited me. He rested his golden hands on my shoulders, warming me with his touch, comforting as coddled ale.

"Have a care," he told me, "which path you tread."

"Tell me which way I should go then. Would the track to West Close be any good?" So cheered to see him after my spat with Liza, I was light-of-heart, teasing him.

"You and you alone," he said, "choose the road you walk."

I sobered to hear him so sombre. He was talking about so much more than my journey to Anne's this day.

"Can you speak plain?" I begged him.

"Some paths are steep and stony whilst others seem broad and easy, though they lead to misfortune."

"So I should pick the steep path over the gentle one?" I asked, well maddled by his words.

"Once you asked me if I would be true to you," he said. "Have I not been true?"

"Truer than any."

"But you, Bess, are you true?" He spoke as though my entire fate hung upon the answer I gave him.

Even as my eyes clouded with tears that he should doubt me in this, my answer came stout and sure. "True to my family. True to my loved ones. True to the old ways. True to *you*."

"True to some," he said with a wistful smile. "But not to others."

For a moment I was too gobsmacked to say a word. Then my skin burned poker-hot. "That was over twenty years ago!" But the memory of my adultery and my husband's fury came back to me. The hell of the pillory, relieved only by Anne, her fellowship, and the jokes she whispered in my ear.

"Betrayal," said Tibb, "was your undoing those many years ago. Beware betraying again, my Bess, or you shall suffer for it threefold."

I fair wondered what he meant. Who was left for me to betray? I'd sooner cut my own throat than double-cross Tibb or my family or friends. I'd no husband or lover left to cheat. Speaking in riddles, Tibb was. Enough to do my head in.

"Don't weep," he said, kissing my brow. "Just remember my words. Now go on your way, my Bess. Anne has need of you."

61

Be of use, I told myself. With Tibb's blessing, I headed down the track to West Close. I'd show Tibb how faithful I was to Anne and her family. Not one to forget old loyalties, me.

Anne's cottage was tucked between a ditch and a brimming stream with banks of red clay. When I knocked, there was no answer, so I opened the door and stepped inside. Folk poor as Anne possessed neither lock nor key. *Where had she and her daughters gone?*

Cloudy light spilled through two small windows covered in oiled rabbitskin and revealed puddles on the beaten-earth floor — rain had come through the patchy thatch. In the firepit weak flames sputtered and sent thin plumes of smoke curling up into the rafters. Right careless, my Anne had been, to leave a fire burning when she'd gone out. I squatted down to bank the fire when a moan made me leap out of my skin. On the murky far end of the cottage, a white arm reached out from behind a tattered curtain.

"Mam?" a voice called.

*Betty?* Swallowing, I stepped toward that arm that drew back the curtain. Lying upon a pallet tucked into a recess in the wall lay the vision of my childhood friend: Anne Whittle with her hair like spun gold, the loveliest creature I'd ever seen, only she was pale and ill. And it wasn't my old friend, but fifteen-year-old Annie. I'd only ever seen Annie in her coif, which hid her splendid hair. Gazing at her now, I felt a bittersweet twinge, for her beauty brought back my recollections of the happiness I'd shared with her mother, those days that were so far away that they might have happened in another country.

"Our Annie, what ails you?" I stroked the girl's clammy brow.

"Some ague. I hope I'll soon mend." A sweet thing was Annie. Humble, but not sorry for herself. Even in the weak light her green eyes sparked and flashed. She'd the most perfect skin I'd ever seen. Not a pockmark on her. Little wonder Tom Redfearn was smitten. I hoped that after a year or two he'd find enough steady work so that they could marry. Let her have her bliss before hardship stole her youth away.

"Did Mam send for you?" she asked.

"No, but I wanted to have a word with her and your sister."

"They're off looking for work," Annie said. "Mam promised they'd come home with bread and fuel for the fire."

I reached into my herb pouch for my bundles of feverfew, willow bark, lungwort, and coltsfoot. "Let me brew you some physick."

I found the kettle on a shelf and went outside to fill it with clear water from the fast-flowing stream. Back inside, I hung it on the hob over the poor little fire. They'd no more peat in the house, so I blew on the fire, fed it with stray bits of the straw that lined the floor instead of rushes. I even tried to charm the flames, but still it took an age for the water to boil. Since I could find no cup, I poured the herbal brew into a wooden bowl. Raising Annie by the shoulders, I held the bowl so she could drink.

"When have you last eaten?" I unpacked my bundle and dipped the hard bread into the herbal brew to soften it before giving it to her.

"Yesterday my sister had some drippings and oatcake off the Duckworths."

*Had the Duckworths given Betty the bread and drippings, or had she just taken them? What would I have done if I'd a younger sister who lay ill as Annie did?* Too jittery to sit idle, I found a comb made of oxbone and, before I could stop myself, I was gently working through Annie's tangles and snarls. Stepping through the gate of memory, I became a girl myself again, combing Anne Whittle's hair.

"Soon as I'm well again, I'll earn some brass," Annie said, sounding steely and determined. "I'm not afraid of honest work. Betty traded some of her hens for an old spinning wheel. If we took in spinning, we could earn a fair penny. The Asshetons," she said, speaking of her landlord's family, "have plenty of wool."

"A spinning wheel," I said, coming back to the present with an almighty jolt. "Those don't come cheap, our Annie. That would have cost your sister more than a few chickens."

The girl flushed. "What are you saying, Mother Demdike?"

Dropping the comb, I plaited her hair. Though I'd never touched silk, I couldn't imagine it could be any softer than Annie's locks. "Kate Mouldheels's spinning wheel was stolen and she suspects your sister to be the thief. If she doesn't get it back before the week is over, she'll go to the Constable. She says Betty stole some cloth and a pewter plate off her, too."

Took Annie a fair while to find her tongue. I kept my silence, my head bowed down to the floor. To think Betty had been reduced to this. For want of a spinning wheel, she'd thought her family would starve.

"Betty went out today with something tucked beneath her apron," the girl said at last. "She wouldn't show me what it was, but she promised to come home with something to eat."

"It couldn't have been the spinning wheel," I said, thinking aloud. "Too big to hide under an apron."

*Had Betty kept her thieving a secret from her mother, or had Anne known but been helpless to stop her?*

"A pewter plate's not too big." Annie fell back against the pallet. "Will the Constable come round for her?" Her voice broke. "Mother Demdike, she could hang."

"Hush, child. We won't let it come to that. If you show me where the spinning wheel is, I'll return it to Mouldheels before the Constable hears a word of this."

"Up that ladder there." Annie pointed to a wide shelf high in the smoky rafters. There I found Mouldheels's spinning wheel wrapped in the stolen cloth, its warp greasy with sheep lard to make it fuller and warmer. As Annie had predicted, the plate was nowhere to be found.

Before I left I broke out the plumcake for the girl. Being so soft, it was easier for her to eat. But she didn't finish it—she wanted to save some for her mother and sister. Sitting on the edge of her pallet, I chanted my blessings over her till I saw that stricken look vanish from her face. Annie took my hand and kissed it.

"God go with you, Mother Demdike. I'll thank you till my dying day for not going to the Constable."

"All will be well, love. Look after yourself."

The spinning wheel in my arms, the heavy wool draped over my shoulders, I stepped out the door and trudged six long miles to Colne. *See, Tibb,* I whispered to the wind. *See me now. I am true.*

When I finally reached Mouldheels's door, the winter sun had set and I was chilled as the frost-tipped grass.

"Here's your spinning wheel and here's your cloth," I told Mouldheels and her husband. "If your cloth is dirty, I'll come tomorrow and wash it for you so it's good as new. Your plate's long gone, I fear. Now it's between you and God if you'd let a poor woman hang on account of a missing plate."

Mouldheels was careful to inspect her spinning wheel for damage before she agreed to forgive Betty the stolen plate. Just as I was about to faint away in hunger, she invited me to her table for a bowl of steaming pottage and mulled ale. Her good man gave me two lengths of woollen cloth and two brass clasps to make cloaks for Liza and me. I wore them both home, one over the other, and they kept me warm, but, in God's name, it was a ghost-ridden night. Wind blasted though the hedges to send me skittering and crossing myself and crying out to Saint Anne, the Virgin's own mother. The sheep in the fields took the shapes of spectres. I remembered the tales I'd heard from my mam of the Wild Hunter who swept through the sky with his furious horde, the souls of the unchristened dead.

When I finally reached my door, it was barred against me and before I could even knock and shout for Liza, I heard such noises from within, such savage cries and squeals, that I thought the hosts of hell had taken over Malkin Tower. From within my firehouse, the floorboards thumped as though a ring of demons were reeling round. Had the Devil himself come to punish me for dallying in magic?

*Help me, Tibb.* I breathed his name and attempted to pray, but no words would come, so great was the terror that seized me. Off in the distance a cat yowled—or was it something other than a cat? I swore I would die of cold and fright outside my own door. My skin juddered so hard, it felt as though somebody had poured a bucket of eels down my smock. Unearthly laughter shook the door and shutters, and then singing, and such singing it was. With a start I recognised Liza's voice.

"Get up and bar the door," she sang, her words slurring together. She was either hag-ridden or stone drunk.

Up spoke a young man. "Our Liza, you fair take my breath away. None of the other girls ever let me."

My daughter giggled like a mad thing. "Well, I'm not like other girls, am I?"

At that I pounded on the door hard enough to bruise my fist. "Unbar this door, Liza, or you'll have hell to pay."

Inside there was much shouting and banging about. When at last my girl let me in from the cold, I saw that her coif was askew and her kirtle was laced crooked, as if she'd done it up in a hurry. She smelled like a tavern. In the shadows near the smoking hearth cowered young John Device, that shy hired boy from Bull Hole Farm.

Liza straightened herself and put on a smile. "Right worried, we were, Mam, with you out so late! Did you find Mouldheels's spinning wheel?"

I did not grace that with a reply, but stalked past her, sat myself down on the stool by the fire, and rubbed my hands over the flames till I stopped shivering. An empty cider flask lay upon the floor. So thin those two were from our winter of hunger, the single bottle had gone straight to their foolish heads.

"Not a drop left over for me?" I asked just the same.

Liza hung her head.

I turned to the boy. "Come step up so I can see your face. If you're courting my girl, I'd like to have a good look at you."

The lad trembled like a sapling in a gale.

"When's the wedding to be?" I demanded. Couldn't put him at his ease till I had his intentions sorted out.

"C-c-c-c-come spring," the lad stammered. "M-my ap-p-p-

66

prenticeship will be done." Taken a right fright of me, had John Device, which only made his stutter worse.

"And was that your master's cider you filched?" I asked, full severe.

"G-g-got it given," he said, his face bright pink, and I knew at once he was too bashful to lie. This lad didn't have a deceitful bone in his long, skinny body.

"What will you do when your apprenticeship's over?" I looked from him to my daughter. "After what the two of you have been up to this night, it won't be long before the babies start coming."

"Mam!" Liza tried to cut me off, but I silenced her with a glare.

"A family has to live on something." I held the boy with my eyes.

"M-m-master Holden's sons are too young to care for his herd. I'm a good cowman. Best he's ever had, so he says." Talking about cows took his stutter away. "Master will pay proper wages."

Like a fortune-teller, I scryed deep into that boy's startled eyes. "Do you love and cherish my only daughter, John Device?"

"Aye, Mother Demdike, I do." He spoke with such a rush of feeling that I knew right then he was no rogue like the other one whose name I didn't even know—the one who had left Liza pregnant and weeping, with no choice except to swallow the tansy or endure a life of shame. But young John Device was aglow to the tips of his jug-handle ears with new love. My girl, the only one who had ever *let* him, had swept him off his feet. He'd be hers forever. This tow-headed cowherd adored her, squint and all.

Still I didn't leave off looking him over till I was well satisfied. A gangling thing, he was, but straight and strong. If he was timid, he was true-hearted. He'd be good to my girl, gentle to their children.

"Well, I'd best t-t-t-take my leave," the boy said, backing away to the door.

"Don't be daft, our John," I told him. "It's a terrible cold night. You're welcome to bide here. Best leave just before dawn, so you're back at the farm in time to feed the cattle."

Liza flashed me a trembling smile. When she turned to John, her face went so soft I had to look away. So I hoisted myself off my stool and made my way up to my cold, draughty tower room, leaving the lovers to their privacy.

Liza and John tried to be quiet, but echoes of their endearments reached me as I huddled in my pallet and breathed in my hands to warm myself. Tibb had spoken true: My daughter had found the love of a decent, honest man. Soon she would become a wife and then a mother. Off in the future was the granddaughter Tibb had promised me, the one he said I would love like no other. Liza, bless her, had found true joy.

Though my heart was full of thanksgiving, I hardly slept that night. It wasn't the tempest or the cold that kept me awake. Anne filled my thoughts. She must be despairing. Betty was a grown woman, beyond Anne's control. Though she loved her daughter dearly, Anne couldn't save Betty from herself. That girl's lot had been unlucky from the beginning. Unlike Annie, Betty was plain and graceless, dour of face. If Annie had inherited her mam's beauty, Betty was heir to her temper and unquenchable spirit. Ever wilful, Betty would not be one to know her place and obey the law just because it was expected of her. She'd blaze her own trail, even if it destroyed her, and her mam could only look on in grief.

*What would Anne think of me if she knew that my magic had revealed Betty's crime?*

At church the next Sunday, we poor folk were thin on the ground. The hunger had killed off more than a few of us, mostly children and old folk. Two families had stopped coming to church altogether on account of having no decent clothes left to wear; they'd traded every last garment save their undersmocks for food. Even those of us who still had clothes on our backs were a pitiful lot. How thin we were, skeletons with a bit of skin attached. Nowt but crow feed. A tremor gripped me as the knowledge came, unbidden, that this coming year would be better. A year of plenty with a good harvest. A year of fat and new babies. But too late for some.

At the very last moment Anne trudged in, her daughters behind her. Always the last to arrive and the first to leave was Anne. Didn't like to linger in the church a second longer than she had to. Sick with nerves, I couldn't keep myself from gawping at her. She gazed back at me, her eyes full of a sad knowing that tore at my heart.

Betty was looking bitter as bile, keeping her distance and not deigning to look my way. But her mother, much to Liza's consternation, sidled up to me. Anne was well gaunt—probably gave what little food she had to her daughters and took nothing for herself. At least young Annie appeared much improved since I saw her last. Over on the men's side of the church, Tom Redfearn stared at her, his face blazing with devotion, whilst she lowered her eyes and blushed. Liza, meanwhile, winked at John Device.

Anne and I traded smiles to witness our daughters in the grip of new love, the only light in this time of hardship. I ached to take Anne's hand, tell her I'd only interfered out of sore concern for her. Whilst the sermon dragged on, Anne began to murmur beneath her breath, the way she sometimes did, but this time, she had her eyes locked with mine. Beside me, Liza bristled. Others looked our way, too, their faces pale and strained. My spine prickled at the memory of how Alice Nutter's noisy cow of a mother had suspected my Anne of muttering incantations. But soon enough my memory unlocked the mystery behind Anne's words. An old song, she was singing, so soft that only I could hear it—the song I used to sing to her when I teased her.

> Will you go to the rolling of the stone,
> The tossing of the ball?
> Or will you go and see pretty Annie
> And dance amongst them all?

Once upon a time the song was about her, when she and the boys round her had first awakened to her youthful beauty. Now she sang it in honour of her daughter's awakening. Even if our future seemed bleak as bone-dust, the threads of our past bound Anne and me as one.

When the service had ended, Anne didn't tear out the door as though her bum were on fire as was her habit, but stayed close by my side.

Upon the shelf in the back of the church, our Alice Nutter had left out bread for the poor. Betty grabbed a loaf on her way out as did my Liza, whilst Anne and I followed in their wake, walking side by side.

In my anxiousness I couldn't wait till we were alone, but blurted out my words. "Please don't think less of me, our Anne. I never meant to trouble you."

"Bess," she said, her voice breaking. "You're my dearest friend in all the world. But don't go behind my back again."

"Mam?" Liza swung round. "Is she worrying you?" She glared at Anne.

Stood behind her, John looked full bewildered and not a little frightened of Anne, who laughed under her breath even now.

"This is a private matter," I told Liza.

Anne and I strode off together, neither of us uttering a word till we'd left the crowd behind.

"I'm not your foe," I told her when we'd reached the birch wood near Pendle Water. "I acted out of friendship."

No doubt needing to rest her bones after the hours of standing in church, my friend sank to the cold, mossy ground.

"Betty's not a bad girl." Anne looked so thin and frail that I almost feared the stinging wind could blow her away. "We were down to eating acorns and grass, and Annie too fevered to leave her bed. I begged Betty to stay out of mischief, but there's no stopping that girl when she has her mind set. In truth, she did about the only thing she could do. And Mouldheels is fretting about her plate?" Anne let out a ragged laugh. "Dear me! Remember them Robin Hood plays they used to put on before the

Magistrate outlawed them? Stealing from the rich and giving to the poor?"

"Why didn't you come to *me*?" I sat down beside her. "I would have given you anything."

"I did, love. I called by Malkin Tower. You were out and your Liza was entertaining that young man of hers. They didn't see me, but I got a good look at them, at how the two of them are half-starved as it is, so how could I ask any food off you and yours?"

It didn't used to be like this, I wanted to cry out, having to steal just to stay alive. But Anne knew as much, her memories reaching back as far as mine.

"Our Anne," I said, my heart breaking. "How did we get to be so old?"

"I'm so worried about that girl. She could hang." My friend touched my face. "As could you, love, for the spell you performed for Mouldheels."

In the eyes of the Constable and the Magistrate, I knew I was damned as Betty. If thieving was a hanging crime, then so was sorcery. But, like Betty, I'd put my need to feed my family and do for my friends above the law.

"I never meant to betray," I swore to her. "I'd no clue it was Betty. Never even suspected."

For a long while we were sat there, too shattered to say anything, our heads bowed under the weight of our burdens, our hands knit together.

"Anne," I said when I could bear the silence no longer. "Promise you'll come to me next time you're in any sort of fix."

Heading home, I reached a bend in the road to find Liza and John sat upon a stone. John's face was white as chalk. His boot, polished for Sunday, was flung upon the ground whilst his bare foot rested in Liza's lap. I caught my breath at the sight of his ankle, swollen to the size of a cabbage.

"Dear God, lad," I said. "That looks a nasty sprain."

He flinched as I touched his puffy skin.

"Twisted it coming down the track," he said between grit teeth, but I could tell straight off that something graver than the pain was eating him.

Liza, being her practical self, ripped strips of cloth from the hem of her smock. "I'll bind it tight for you, love. You'll soon be right again."

"Aye, if I can stay away from those who mutter bewitchments within the very walls of our church," he said, his voice full of cold anger.

"Bewitchments?" Unable to understand his meaning, I looked to my daughter.

Liza cupped her hands round her beloved's ankle as though to charm away the soreness. "Our John is of the mind that this is Anne Whittle's handiwork."

An icy gust blasting down Stang Top Moor robbed my body of its last warmth. So my friend had stood beside me during the service and sung a song just for my ears—to think that her goodwill could be so misunderstood. Bewitchments, indeed.

I laid what I hoped was a motherly but firm hand on the young man's shoulder. "Anne Whittle is my dearest friend, and I'll not hear any speak ill of her, even you, our John. She's no witch."

"I'm not daft," he said. "Anybody can see how her lips move. But no sound comes out. You never know what she could be saying."

"Perhaps it's none of your concern," I told him.

"You should have a care round her, Mother Demdike." John's solemn eyes met mine. "She was right vexed with you. God forbid you should come to harm."

I struggled to keep my patience with the lad. "Why would Anne want to harm me? She and I have been friends longer than you've been alive."

He answered without a moment's hesitation. "Because you gave her cause for offence. You begged her pardon, didn't you?"

"It was well daft of you, making such a scene in the churchyard for the whole parish to hear," Liza pointed out. "There will be all kinds of talk now."

"I should have held my tongue till I was alone with her," I said, giving her and John their due. "But there's no bad blood between Anne and me, so put that out of your head, both of you. And she's nowt to do with your twisted ankle, our John."

"Anne Whittle has no powers to speak of," Liza said, easing John's boot over his foot and ankle, now bound with the linen torn from her smock. "But *I* have them. And everyone in these parts knows that my mam is the mightiest charmer in Pendle. You're not afraid of *us*, love, are you?"

"Cunning craft is well different from witchcraft," he said. "Every fool knows that."

The year had turned. April, it was, the eve before Liza and John's wedding. Out of Malkin Tower I stole. Our luck was changing, so I prayed, from woe to weal. Everything I passed on my way seemed to promise a good season ahead. Twilight washed the blooming blackthorn, broom flowered brilliant gold, and primroses sprang from the moist earth. Ducking through a gap in the hedge, I headed out across the green meadows. Mare's tail clouds whipped across the fading sky where the new crescent moon sailed high. As I neared the beck, the sun sank behind Blacko Hill.

Daylight gate was that space betwixt and between, neither day nor yet night, when I could see the invisible. As the music of the running beck filled my ears, I called out to Tibb and then he was stood before me, his one foot in the beck and the other upon the clay shore. In the gloaming his eyes shone like two stars.

"I've a boon to ask of you," I told him when he took my hand. "Let there be no strife at Liza's wedding."

John Device, despite my every attempt to reason with him, harboured an unholy dread of Anne, and Liza would rather keep the peace than see him ill at ease. If it had been up to the two of them, Anne and her daughters would have been banished from the celebration. But what a stir that would have caused—shunning an old family friend on such an occasion! If you want good luck on your wedding day, I'd told Liza and John, you must show hospitality to everybody and let none be turned away. So at last they'd agreed that there was no neighbourly way to exclude her, but Liza had taken me aside and begged me to at least keep Anne away from John tomorrow. Her request had left me feeling like Judas.

There was no need to explain this to Tibb, who gazed at me steady, already divining my thoughts.

"Sometimes there's no easy way," he said. "Torn between the one thing and the other. You must know in your own heart where truth and justice lie."

Though I'd warned Anne that some were surmising the worst when they saw her talking to herself, I'd never dredged up the nerve to tell her that my daughter's own bridegroom thought she might be a witch.

"Can you not turn John's mind to others things?" I asked Tibb. "Just for a while at least. Once he's married, he'll have more important concerns, so I hope."

"John's a good man," said Tibb. "I can't make him a different man from the one he is."

White moths flitted round my head. The beck flowed, a fox barked, and nightbirds sang a lullaby to creation. Such a lovely night, brimming with good omens. I allowed my heart to fill with hope. My daughter would wed a loving husband. My friendship with Anne would endure. In time, even John could make his peace with that.

"Give us your blessing then," I asked Tibb. "Your blessing on us all: Liza and John, Anne and me."

"Your wish is my gift," he promised.

At the next day's dawning, Liza donned her best kirtle and the new lace-trimmed coif and collar Alice Nutter had given her. Singing, we made our way over the flowering fields to the New

Church where our guests gathered. Kit was there with his Elsie, her waist already thickening with her second child. Mistress Alice, also pregnant, wore a fine new ruff. The Holdens of Bull Hole Farm had turned out with young Matty, now a robust boy of ten years, and with John's fellow farmhands, who took the place of brothers since our John was an orphan. Mouldheels and her good man were taking great pains to hold themselves aloof from Betty Whittle, who was flirting with everything in breeches whilst her mam and sister looked on and laughed. Kit's boyhood friend, Henry Bulcock, had come with his new bride, Jane, whilst Liza's old friend Jennet Preston had walked over the hills from Gisburn.

When Liza and John recited their vows, I sensed Tibb's blessing inside the very walls of the New Church. Nothing could mar my daughter's happiness. Crowned in white dog-tooth violets, her smile was so wide that it fair masked her squint. Anybody could see how her love for John had transformed her. As for the bridegroom, he looked right pleased with himself, grinning and proud.

After the ceremony, when the couple stepped out of the church, Anne shot forward before I could stop her and planted a noisy kiss on our John's mouth, then pinched Liza's cheek.

"If you're your mother's daughter," she told the bride, "you'll make such sport on your wedding night, you'll keep half of Pendle awake!"

Liza recoiled as though from a snake and threw me such a look, whilst John was stood there, his face drawn in horror, his hand raised to his mouth as though to wipe away the stain of Anne's kiss.

My friend seemed flummoxed. "I was only wishing you well," she told John. "I mean no harm."

Taking her arm, I drew her away. "Peace, the lad's a bit shy," I said.

Happily, my son-in-law's mood soon appeared to lift when the other Bull Hole farmhands pounded his back and teased him that Liza's kirtle was already beginning to swell with their first-born.

Our merry procession wound its way to Malkin Tower. Anthony Holden made room in his ivy-bedecked wagon for the bridal pair and me whilst our friends on foot raced in the wagon's wake, shouting out jibes to make the couple laugh. But Liza twisted round in her seat and put her mouth to my ear, begging me to keep Anne from coming near John again.

"She'll not pester him, I promise," I whispered back. "Now think of happy things. Your wedding day is no time to pick quarrels."

As the breeze stirred the circlet of violets upon my Liza's head, she leaned over to kiss John as though to banish darkness from her mind.

So much joy after those bleak months. At Malkin Tower we gathered for such a feast as we poor souls had not imagined after our winter of hunger. The Holdens had slaughtered a lame calf, which we roasted upon a spit. Alice Nutter brought spiced cakes, a cask of good ale, and another of wine. We toasted the newly-weds and stuffed ourselves till our stomachs were near to bursting. We ate and drank till our laughter made the very stones of the tower tremble.

"Just like old times this," Anne said as she filled my cup.

"You said the old ways were lost," I teased her.

We raised our cups to John and Liza as they danced to the music of Kit's fiddle.

"The next wedding will be Annie's," I said, smiling to see the girl twirling in Tom Redfearn's arms.

"It will be a while yet before Tom earns enough to take a wife," Anne said. "As for Betty, she has no takers, bless her. Think she scares the lads off, she's so eager. In truth, she might stay a spinster."

"Peace, Anne. There are worse fates." I thought of my own unhappy marriage.

Betty danced with one farmhand after another. For her mother's sake, I was pleased to see that she seemed to have lived down the shame of nearly being called out as a thief. She still acted stiff round me though, as if she couldn't quite trust me to mind my own business.

"Listen to that music!" I cried. "Some would say we're too old to dance." I grinned at Anne, daring her.

"Well, *you* may be a grandmother, but I'm not." With a flourish, Anne drained her cup and leapt to her feet. "Let's see what these old legs can do."

Shameless as she'd been forty years ago, my Anne hitched up her skirts to show off her ankles, neat and slender as a girl's. Before I knew it, I'd joined her. Round and round we jigged, pounding our bare feet into the new grass. Two fifty-six-year-old women dancing as though we'd never stop.

When the heavens darkened and the crescent moon rode the sky, the bride and groom retired to their bed strewn in sweet violets. By then many of our guests had wandered home, but Anne and I kept dancing round the bonfire. Laughing and dizzy, we spun, free as the girls we once were. We danced to banish want and unkindness, gossip and ill fortune. We danced to kindle hope. It was April and the world was new. The night swam with stars, and off in the fields lambs bleated to their mothers. Throwing back our heads in glee, we danced till sunrise filled the sky, and then we fell gasping upon the dewy earth.

After the wedding Liza and John did not move away to Bull Hole Farm as I'd feared, but stayed on with me. Since the fields near his farm were overgrazed, Anthony Holden decided to rent the meadows near Malkin Tower. Switch in hand, our John Device drove the cattle to their new home, rich with grass. Each morning at dawn he rose for the first milking. With Liza helping him, he set up a dairy in the shippon over in the next field. The Holdens didn't pay John much in the way of brass, but they let us keep a goodly portion of the milk, cream, curds, butter, and cheese. Every month Anthony Holden sent our John a peck of oats besides. If we would not get rich, we might at least grow stout off this plenty.

The weeks of May and June passed in happiness: John and I watching our Liza bloom as the child inside her ripened. Her hair shone with a rare lustre and her skin glowed healthy and fresh from the good milk and cream. Of a Sunday the newly-weds strolled back from church arm in arm, cooing to each other, whilst I pressed on ahead to give them their privacy. Sometimes I helped in the dairy, and if ever a cow or calf sickened, John called for me at once. The Holdens were well pleased that I was so close on hand to see to their animals. When I wasn't needed in the shippon or dairy, I set off on my rounds through Pendle Forest, same as before, working what charms and blessings as I could.

Our John was a kindly soul. If he'd a fault to his name, it was only his conviction that Anne Whittle possessed some secret sway over me and that if ever I chanced to get on her bad side, she would wreak her revenge by cursing the lot of us. The kiss Anne had given him upon his wedding day never ceased to haunt him.

It wasn't magic itself that he feared. On the contrary, he believed that lawful folk had need of blessers such as Liza and me to shield them from baleful forces. Though he was no cunning man himself, he wasted no time in drawing upon his own charms of protection, clambering upon a ladder to hang a horseshoe and a rowan cross over our door at Malkin Tower. To safeguard his master's cattle, he nailed three horseshoes over the shippon door, and behind that door he hung a sickle and a rowan switch, and behind each beam a bit of cold iron. When he drove the cattle out to graze, he tied holed stones round their necks to guard them from black magic and lightning besides. Fearful for Liza's condition, he had her wear a twisted iron nail on a string hidden down her smock to keep her and the baby safe. Of an evening he threw salt in the fire to banish the evil eye.

It was witchcraft John feared: the teeming and foul powers ever threatening to undo our hard-won good fortune. He knew better than anyone how quick and merciless woe could strike. When he was only seven, he'd lost both parents, neither of them older than twenty-five. When the young and healthy died so sudden, the first thing folk suspected was witchcraft. My son-in-law never spoke of such things in the open, but sometimes I wondered if his unfortunate parents had ever quarrelled with Anne and whether John laid this burden of grief on her head. Then there was the matter of Anne's two buried husbands, especially the first one, that cheating scoundrel, who had died of a wasting disease within the year after Anne had uncovered his infidelity. Of course, I could never believe such things of my friend, but this was how suspicions took root, how they grew and grew with a force of their own.

Despite the pains I'd taken to shield Anne from all this, it soon became plain enough that my son-in-law thought nothing good of her. Our friendship carried on, same as before, only now the shadow of John's silent shunning hung over us both.

# 5

I N THAT BOUNTIFUL SUMMER of 1588, three months after Liza and John's wedding, I was walking past Alice Nutter's fields of corn and barley at Roughlee. Her tenants' little
boys pranced round, armed with slingshots to drive the crows
from the grain. Seeing them at their work, I murmured my own
spells to banish the birds—anything for Mistress Alice who had
been so generous to us at Malkin Tower.

As my eyes followed the path of fleeing crows, I saw the beacon blazing away atop Pendle Hill. Near turned to stone at the
sight. Such fires were lit only in times of dire need. Whilst the
little lads pointed and charged about yelling in their excitement,
I offered up a silent prayer that we in Pendle Forest would be
spared from this evil, whatever it was.

The boys whooped and swarmed toward a rider trotting up
the track and when that rider drew near, I found myself staring
at the stern-set face of my half-brother, Roger Nowell.

"Magistrate!" the boys shouted, some of them remembering
to bow and bob.

"Back away, you lot," he ordered. "You'll spook the horse."

But I clucked my tongue at the stallion. Ignoring the rider,
I stroked the horse's sweat-lathered neck to calm him, then finally screwed up the courage to face my half-brother who towered over me like some avenging archangel, the tip of his polished boot level with my forehead. He was handsome as he was
arrogant: a man in his thirties, heading toward his prime. His
chin seemed to jut out even stronger than when I'd seen him last,

and his hair was the same chestnut brown mine had been before it turned grey. Did he, too, see the likeness between us? Did he even remember he'd an unlawful half-sister, seed of his dead father's folly?

"The beacon, sir," I said. "What news have you?"

"The Spaniards mean to invade." Full impatient, he was. No doubt eager to be gone and to spread the word to more important souls than the likes of me. "Their ships attacked the Queen's Navy off the south coast."

"Christ's wounds," I muttered.

Hunger I'd known and the press of want and going without. When I was five, Old King Henry sent his troops to sack Whalley Abbey and butcher the monks. But a foreign invasion was something beyond my most fearful imaginings.

"The King of Spain," I said aloud, looking up into my half-brother's cold eyes. "That would be Philip. Dead Mary Tudor's husband."

"Indeed," he said. "And should he succeed, our days shall be just as dark as they were under Mary, with decent Christians burning at the stake."

The Spanish would bring back the old religion: the mass and the feast days. The priests could come out of hiding. But it would mean the end of the new church in this country. Families like the Nowells who had hitched their fate and fortune to the Queen's religion would be left high and dry. And what would it be like to be ruled by foreigners, I fair wondered. Did any of us want this, even those of us who had longed for the old ways to return?

My half-brother leaned down from his saddle to scrutinise my face as though trying to decide where my loyalties lay.

"Aren't you that Demdike? That herbwife?"

I could not speak but only nod like some simpleton. What did he know of me, my half-brother? What rumours had he heard? Would he trouble me for my work in charms and spells, or would he try to drive me from Malkin Tower, which, by rights, belonged to him?

"You'd best go see to Alice Nutter," he said, nodding back

toward Roughlee Hall. "When I spoke to her just now, she was looking poorly."

"Yes, sir. I'll go to her straightaway, sir."

Digging his spurs into the stallion's flanks, my half-brother cantered away, leaving me to choke on his dust.

"What did he mean?" one of the boys asked, tugging my sleeve. "What are Spaniards?"

"Folk from foreign parts." With my apron I wiped my smarting, dust-stung eyes. "There's to be war."

My mouth went dry at the thought of our John Device being pressed into the navy and wrenched away from Liza just as she was about to birth their firstborn. If our men were sent away, the crops would rot in the fields. Tibb had not prepared me for this.

But the little lads darted about as though this were some grand adventure. Rubbed me the wrong way, their merriment did, the way they laughed as they pelted each other with their slingshots, playing at war as though it were nowt but a game. I confess I fair lost my temper, shouting at them till they leapt, wild-eyed, showing me a sight more awe than they had the Magistrate.

"Mistress Alice is paying you to shoot the crows, not each other, you dunderheads. Now do as you're told. Spaniards or no, we'll still have to eat this winter."

God willing, we could save the harvest yet, if the women banded together to cut the grain. Leaving the boys to worry the crows, I rushed along to Roughlee Hall to see what I could do for Mistress Alice.

Roughlee Hall was the grandest manor house in Pendle Forest. Richard Nutter's father had built it in the year of my birth. With its walls of golden stone and graceful arched windows of mullioned glass, it looked as though it could endure a thousand years. Rose and lavender bushes lined the path up to the door and offered their perfume to the sultry air. Beds of daisies and chamomile, there were besides. The lawn was so close-clipped that it resembled green velvet. All this I saw by peeking my head round the gate, left open by Nowell after his speedy leave-taking, so it appeared. But it wasn't for me to go knocking on the front door.

Instead I ducked behind the hedge and followed the path well-worn by servants' feet to the back of the house and its warren of outbuildings: the stables and shippon, the dairy and henhouse, the laundry house and storage sheds, all built upon the slope that rose behind the great house. Butterflies and bees danced over the kitchen garden and flitted through the orchard. I was about to head to the back door that was propped open in the heat when I caught sight of the lady, heavy with child, staggering beneath the apple trees. She stumbled and clung to one of the branches to hold herself upright.

"Mistress Alice?"

I took off at a run, my bare feet slapping the dusty cobbles of the yard and then the dry, tickling orchard grass. She started, her head jerking.

"Don't take a fright," I called out. "It's only me."

Seeing her face, I stopped dead in my tracks. Pale as an invalid, she looked, her face damp with tears. I could well understand why she wept, for war was woeful business and such a shock was never good for a woman in her condition. Little wonder Nowell had sent me to look after her. Maybe that half-brother of mine had a heart in that proud chest of his after all.

At first Mistress Alice seemed too distraught to say anything. No doubt she'd come out to the orchard for fresh air and some privacy, only to have me come charging in. Perhaps it shamed her that I'd caught her like this, weeping and undone. But I could scarce bring myself to leave her alone in this state.

"Mistress Alice, if you're feeling faint, it's best to sit a spell."

On this steamy day she had on a gown of thinnest silk, flimsy as a petal, but she was sensible enough to put her own health and that of the child over vanity, and allowed me to help her sit down upon the grass.

"Shall I fetch your husband?"

"This morning he rode for Samlesbury," she said, her voice bleak.

So she had been alone when Nowell stopped by to deliver his dreadful tidings. I watched her brush her forehead, setting her coif askew. One lock of jet black hair came loose to fan across her bloodless cheek. How much she had changed in the six years since I had first met her, that summer day under my elder tree, when she was still a timid young wife who feared herself barren. Pregnant with her third child, there wasn't a trace of girlishness left. The woman I saw before me was a matron. Yet she seemed troubled as she had been those six years ago. Something weighed heavy on her heart.

"Terrible news, this war," I said, wondering if she'd brothers who would be sent away to fight. Her husband himself was far too old for battle.

"God preserve every one of us. I never thought it would come to this." She spoke as though she'd known that there was some great evil on the way, but that it had turned out even worse than she suspected.

"I daresay you know much more of this business than I, Mistress Alice." I thought that her husband might have dealings with the mighty and powerful who knew just what the Spanish had in store for us. "But we might still prevail."

"It's a trap," she said. "One way or another, Nowell means to flush us out."

Her words made no sense to me, and I began to fear that the heat had gone to her head.

"You're dreadful pale, Mistress Alice. Shall I fetch you something to drink? A wet cloth for your forehead?"

"No, thank you. Just sit with me for a while." With her clear grey eyes, she gazed into mine. "You can predict the future, Mother Demdike. You said I'd have five children. Can you tell me anything more of my fate to come?"

"The far-seeing only comes to me in flashes. But," I added, anxious to comfort her, "I'd never had any inkling of bad fortune in store for you. Why should you fear the Magistrate?"

"I think you're canny enough to answer that question your-self," she said.

I could, I thought. Though she and her husband let themselves be seen at the New Church every Sunday without fail, everyone knew that they were Papists and that they sheltered travelling priests.

"Nowell thinks that we want this invasion," she said in a voice like ice. "He thinks we're set to welcome the Spanish, that we're part of some conspiracy to overthrow the Queen."

"But you would never." I stopped short, searching for words. "I don't always fancy the way things are, but better the devil you know than some foreign army."

Above the canopy of apple branches, smoke from the burning beacon blackened the sky.

"I love my country every bit as much as Roger Nowell does." She shook in her anger. "Little does he believe me. He keeps his eyes on us, Mother Demdike."

Her words left me numb. At first I thought she meant that my half-brother was watching the pair of us, and I remembered that look he had given me, staring down from his horse. But as she went on talking, I understood it was the Catholic gentry that she meant.

"My husband and I, the Towneleys, the Shuttleworths, the Southworths." She counted the names off on her fingers. "He means to gain the Queen's favour by uncovering traitors in his midst. He's lying in wait for one or the other of us to slip up and then he'll make his move."

"Hush now," I said, thinking that no good could come from allowing her to carry on like this. "You could harm the baby if you let yourself get so overwrought."

In truth, I doubted that even Nowell would presume to take on the richest and most powerful families, forcing his way into their homes and sticking his nose into every nook and cranny in search of Jesuits—it could backfire on him. Besides, if the Spanish did indeed land upon this shore, both Nowell and Mistress Alice would have plenty more to fret about.

"I'm no fortune-teller," I said. "But I saw you with five children, which means that you and your good man will both be alive and well for a while yet."

She reached for my hand. "Can you say a blessing for my family, to keep us safe?"

"Course I can." I squeezed her fingers.

She laughed soft. "My husband would think it wicked of me to even ask you. But what does he know?" She smiled for the first time since we'd been talking. "God has graced you with this gift and you've used it for much good."

Under the apple trees I murmured my charm over her whilst she listened, her head bowed as if in prayer.

On my way home I witnessed all manner of unrest. Beacons burned atop Blacko Hill and Slipper Hill. Looking east over Yorkshire way, I saw bonfires lighting up the Pennines. Roads and tracks were full of folk running and shouting like lunatics.

"It's a prophecy!" Old Man Sellar yelled out to me as I trudged past his farm, not a mile from Malkin Tower. "The bastard Queen will fall and the holy mass will return."

"Don't let the Magistrate hear you go on like that," I warned him.

Nowell would make much of what the gentry were up to, and yet I wondered if he'd ever spared a thought of what we common folk made of this new faith that had robbed us of our pleasures and joys. To be honest, I didn't give a toss about the Pope in Rome or any plots in faraway lands, but I yearned for the sense of sanctity and protection that hung over us then, the talk of miracles and wonders, a prayer and a saint to ward us from every ill and the solace of the Blessed Mother. Now we'd been left to stand stark and unshielded, to bear whatever cruel lot Providence cast our way.

I sought shelter in a copse of birch trees, resting my brow upon my knees, striving to still my ragged breath and racing heart. And then Tibb appeared, spotless as I was dusty.

"You might have warned me," I told him.

"Of the Spanish?" He knelt beside me, brown breeches on the dry earth. "Calm yourself, Bess. Folk will talk nonsense, but never believe a word of it." He took my clammy hands in his steady grip. "It's not the foreigner from across the sea you must fear, but the devil you *know*."

Sweat trickled down my brow and caught in my lashes, blurring my view of his face. The devil I knew? I grew queasy at the memory of Nowell's eyes boring into mine, and when the vision of Nowell faded, I saw Tibb again, grave as Mistress Alice herself.

"What do you mean?"

"Have a care. Watch your step. Keep yourself out of his sight and mind as much as you can."

Tibb murmured his blessing over me, as I had just done for Alice Nutter.

After he had gone, I struggled to gather my wits. Tibb seemed to be saying that my fortune was somehow entwined with Mistress Alice's, and her a gentlewoman. At least Nowell stood to gain something by going after her and her husband: their fine house and their lands. But how would he profit from going after one as lowly as me?

I dragged myself back to Malkin Tower where Liza and John were sat clasping each other and whispering in their agitation.

"If they send you away, I won't be able to bear it," Liza told her husband.

Landlords could do that—send their tenants off to war. Though we paid no rent, Malkin Tower belonged by law to Nowell. Would he summon our John? My head hurt too much to think anymore. Sick at heart, I trundled off to bed.

The Spanish invasion was the only thing folk could talk about, but before any of our men could be called to fight, the news came that it was all over. Our Queen's Navy had trounced the Armada, so Nowell proclaimed, and had given those Spaniards a right basting, driving them from our shores. Took to flight, they did, and then their warships were battered in summer gales and sank, one after another, to the bottom of the sea.

The Curate said that God's own hand had raised the storms to vanquish the enemy and preserve our Queen. Each of us, whether we were loyal to the new church or the old, offered up our thanks. Alice Nutter and Roger Nowell engraved the same inscription on their manor houses: HE BLEW HIS WINDS AND THEY WERE SCATTERED.

We'd much to celebrate that August: peace, victory, and a rich harvest. Every hand was needed to bring in the wheat, oats, and barley. Our John helped the Holdens at Bull Hole with the scything whilst Liza and I bound the sheaves. When the last sheaf was brought in, decorated like a bride upon her wedding day, folk gathered round each farm for the big harvest supper. Crops were so good that we tried to forget there had ever been famine. Soon we were helping pick apples at Bull Hole Farm and pressing the cider. Sarah Holden gave us a cask to take back to Malkin Tower — it would be ready for drinking come Yuletide. I thanked God and Tibb and all the saints, for this was the most abundant time my family had ever known.

Though I was ever mindful of Tibb's warning regarding Nowell, it was easy enough to stay out of his sight and he'd little enough reason to linger anywhere near Malkin Tower. So I tried not to dwell upon peril and misfortune, but instead prayed to look with clear eyes at what lay ahead.

Elsie's time came in early October. With the Sabden midwife to help her, she bore a girl she named Margaret after her own mother. After the christening, our Liza cradled her newborn niece and stared, full enchanted, at her small, pink face.

"What a lovely little lass. God willing, mine will be bonny, too. Won't be long now." My daughter's belly swelled huge and high. "But mine will be a man-child." This she knew because Ball had told her so.

It was plain to my eyes that Liza was carrying a boy and a big one at that. Her husband, after all, was a tall, long-boned thing. Secretly I worried for her, since she was so small in the hips — the first birth was always the hardest. Liza was so huge, I expected her time to come by the end of October at the latest, but still her belly grew and grew till she could only waddle along, splay-legged as any duck.

"Why's my babe so late?" she asked me, her hands gripping her belly.

I told her not to worry, that I'd seen many a baby born later than expected and come healthy and sound.

At Hallowtide Liza insisted on walking up Blacko Hill, as we'd always done, for our midnight vigil on the Eve of All Saints. Under cover of darkness we crept forth with me carrying the lantern to light our way and John following with a pitchfork crowned in a great bundle of straw. Her cloak drawn to hide her face, Liza brought up the rear.

Once we reached the hilltop, after a furtive look round to make sure no one else was about, John lit the straw with the lantern flame so that the straw atop the pitchfork blazed like a torch. With him to hold the fork upright and keep an eye out for intruders, Liza and I knelt to pray for our dead. In the old days we'd held this vigil in the church, the whole parish praying together, the darkened chapel bright as day with the many candles glowing on the saints' altars. Now we were left to do this in secret, stealing away like criminals in the night, as though it were something shameful to hail our deceased. I prayed for my mam and grand-dad, calling out to their souls till I felt them both step through the veil to bring me comfort.

In my heart of hearts I did not believe my loved ones were in purgatory waiting, by and by, to be let into heaven. There was no air of suffering or torment about them, only the joy of reunion. My mam, young and pretty, worked in her herb garden. She hummed a lilting tune whilst her earth-stained fingers pointed out to me the plants I must use to ease Liza's birth pangs. At the sound of hoof beats, I looked over the garden gate to see Grand-Dad riding up on some old nag the Nowells had lent him. Come all the long way from Read Hall to Malkin Tower to visit us, he had, his smile near splitting his face as he jumped down from the saddle to sweep me up in his arms. He whispered his old charms to bless me and Liza and John.

A long spell I knelt there, held in the embrace of my beloved dead, till the straw on the pitchfork burned itself out, falling in embers and ash to the ground. Our John helped my pregnant daughter rise to her feet, then we made our way home through the night that no longer seemed so dark.

All Souls' Day was no longer a holiday, but just the same Liza and I baked soulcakes of oat, apple, and honey, the way I learned from my own mam, to give to any poor folk who came knocking on our door, but our only visitors were Anthony Holden of Bull Hole and some of his hired men. He'd come to tell our John it was time to cull the herd.

Like Judgement Day, it was. Young John sorted out the good milk cows and heifers and the bull calves from the rest. Some of the young bulls he castrated. Others went with the weak and crooked into the slaughter pen. When the first bullock was led to the killing ground, his bellowing was enough to send the rest crashing round the pen till I feared the fence would break. Our John and four other men fettered the bullock before Anthony Holden himself slit the beast's throat, quick and merciful. Though the animal was well dead, it still heaved in its death throes. So that none of the blood would be wasted, our Liza came with a firkin to collect it. Blood pudding, she said she'd make, and black pudding, sausage and tripe, and she'd pickle each hoof and head.

But the sight of so much blood made her go pale as whey. Dropped the firkin, did my girl, splashing blood over herself. As the cattle in the slaughter pen bawled and charged, so the babe in her womb thrashed with such force that I could see the movement through her bloodstained apron. She swayed on her feet.

I caught Liza under the arms. "Her time has come."

John helped me bring her to the house. Whilst John ran to fetch fresh straw to spread on the floor, I took off her red-spattered apron and kirtle, and found her a clean shift to wear. After setting the kettle to boil, I brewed raspberry leaf and motherwort for my daughter who crouched on the birth straw.

"Lad wants to come out," she said, trying to hold her baby through her own wall of flesh. Again I saw the child kicking and pummelling, making the thin fabric of her smock leap and shake. "Come to me, my little boy."

Liza panted, too weak to stand, whilst I mopped the cold sweat off her brow and waited for her waters to break. Generally a babe stopped kicking before it travelled down the mouth of the womb and the birth pangs began. But this child kept on flailing inside her whilst outside the cattle lowed and wailed. Hours dragged on till we both knew her time hadn't yet come after all. With a heavy heart, I moved her to her pallet, swept the birth straw off the floor, and unbolted the door so the men could come in. Past sunset it was and they were awaiting their supper. They roasted fresh meat on a spit, but my Liza could only stomach thin broth. Next day I rose at dawn to get on with the pickling, salting, and sausage-making. But I collared John and told him that Liza was not to do any work besides stitching till the baby came.

Late at night I crept out the door. Cold air slapped my face and frost-spiked grass pricked at my bare feet. As I squeezed through a gap in the hedge, a great long hare crossed my path. Caught my breath, I did, as it sailed clear over the stone wall in one mighty leap. I'd barely walked another ten paces when a second hare hopped to the middle of the track, its ears and nose a-twitch.

"Tibb?" I whispered. "Ball?"

No glint of recognition flickered in the creature's eyes. It just bounded away.

When I reached the far meadow that bordered the beck, I spied more hares cavorting in the moonlight than I could count. This wasn't right. Spring and summer were the seasons for sighting hares in plenty—not this dead end of the year. What portent was this? Onward I pressed, ploughing a track through the crowd of them till I reached the beck and its rushing waters. Cried out to Tibb, I did. Cried loud, over and over, till my throat ached. When he showed himself, he seemed distant, his face washed silver in the cold moonlight.

"I need your help," I said, fair throttling him for taking his sweet time on a night such as this. "It's Liza."

"Aye, Bess. I know it well." He spoke up solemn as any curate. "In time the babe will come. Everything that is to be will be in the fullness of time."

"Now you speak in riddles. Why are there so many hares and what have they to do with Liza's baby?"

Tibb lifted his face to the moon. "As for the baby, you must love him. Above all, that."

"What are you saying, you daft thing? You think I need you to tell me to love my own grandson?" So sharp was my temper that Tibb faded away. As loudly as I implored him, he did not appear again that night. Homeward I plodded, kicking at the hares as I crossed the meadow.

When I opened the door, I found my Liza slumped before the hearth, tears a-glitter on her cheeks. "Wondered where you were off to," she whispered. "Couldn't sleep for my nightmares, Mam. Kept dreaming that hares were chasing my baby."

*Tibb, how could you abandon me to this?* Trying to hide my fears from her, I filled the kettle and brewed hops to send her back to sleep.

But I lay awake, aching with cold. Edging my way to the window slit of the upper tower room, I looked out to see hares sporting far as I could see, bleached ghost-white under the moon. How they chased each other round and round, having a merry old time, as if this were their world, not ours.

Liza's travails began upon Martinmas morning. First the gush of water, then the twinging that signalled the start of her labour, her womb clenching like a great fist. Again John brought in fresh, clean straw and I brewed raspberry leaf and motherwort. The sun climbed a sky full of lacy mare's tails. Between the pains, our Liza clung to the window frame and declared that the omens were good. We both gazed out that open window till the cold air stung our faces, and we saw not a single hare.

Hands pressed to the small of her back, Liza paced in circles, round and round, ever sun-wise for luck, till the force of her travails forced her down upon the straw. I rubbed her private parts with new butter so she wouldn't tear. Holding her upright whilst she squatted, I chanted and prayed to the Mother of God and to St. Margaret, patroness of childbirth, and begged Liza to hold on and keep pushing. At last a great purple head crowned between her thighs. Then, despite the butter I'd used, my poor girl tore and bled.

Liza's head lolled back, her eyes twisting in their sockets. In her torment she cursed and swore she'd never let John in her bed again. My ears rang from her wailing till the biggest newborn I'd seen in all my days slipped out of her and into my arms. Huge as a full-grown hare, he was. I prayed that this harrowing birth wouldn't be the end of my girl. *Help us, Tibb.*

She collapsed on the straw. First I thought she'd fainted away. Then her eyes opened, and I cut the cord and held up her baby. Eyes filling with tears, Liza begged me to hurry up and clean him off so she could hold him. In trembling arms I cradled him. He was whole and perfect, except for his head which seemed a sight too large for the rest of him. I cleaned out his nose and mouth, and then the lusty little thing punched the air and bawled. Whilst I washed him, a sliver of dread needled me, though I didn't understand why. There was nowt wrong with the boy, nowt I could see. He already showed us his nature, brawny and full-spirited. I wrapped him in his swaddling and tucked him in his mother's arms.

"Isn't he beautiful? My darling boy." Liza was smiling like I'd never seen her smile.

Then, with her last strength, she pushed out the afterbirth, which I cast straightaway into the fire so that the flames consumed every part of it. An evil soul could use the afterbirth for blackest magic.

Next I washed her, stitched her back together again, and laid on a witch hazel compress to still her bleeding. After that was done, I covered her in blankets and called out to our John who had been wandering like a lost soul between the house and the shippon, waiting till I invited him in.

Liza was wan and weak, but grinning like a mad thing as John bent to kiss her.

"Feel how strong our little man is." She opened the swaddling and wrapped her husband's fingers around one tiny, powerful foot, laughing as their son kicked out as he'd been kicking away in her womb for months. "He'll grow to be taller than even you!"

"We'll call him James," said John. "After my father." Such wonder shone upon my son-in-law's face. In his baby boy, I knew he hoped to see his cherished and long-dead father live again.

My own misgivings about the baby weighed heavy, a yoke upon my shoulders. Leaving Liza and John to their happiness, I swept the soiled birth straw off the floor and burned it in the hearth till the flames leapt high as hares. Tibb's voice echoed in my memory. *You must love him. Above all, that.* Then I understood that young James's birth was the turning point of our fortune and fate.

# 6

LIZA WAS WELL BESOTTED with her baby, as was our John, who swanned about with the little lad in his arms, eager to show him off to anybody who came within five miles of Malkin Tower. Little Jamie seemed to thrive. His colour was ruddy and strong, and he'd an appetite like none I'd ever seen. Near drained his mam each time she took him to her breast. He latched on and fed till her teats were bloody and raw.

"Best wean him right fast," I said, but she wouldn't hear of it.

So Jamie grew and grew till folk teased John that Liza had cuckolded him and that the child was the seed of some ungodly giant. Such jests meant nothing to John, who doted on the boy and told all who cared to listen that his son was the picture of unblemished health. I tried to coax smiles from my grandson's lips whilst I cooed and sang, but the boy only drooled, lost in his own world. Our John whittled a bit of wood into the shape of a bird and tied it to a string to wave in front of Jamie's face, thinking to amuse him. But the babe's eyes wouldn't follow the swinging bird. He only stared straight ahead—dull, no spark in him.

"Can't the lad see right?" John fretted.

"He's not blind," Liza was quick to say. Strong sunlight made him blink, so she said, and the sight of a cat made him shriek.

By Jamie's first birthday even Liza had to admit that the lad just wasn't right. He couldn't crawl, only drag himself across the slate floor on his elbows, wriggling like a salamander. When we called his name, he was slow in turning his head, and he could not speak a single word, even to say *mam*. Whilst most little children raise an awful fuss if their mother leaves their sight, it was all the same to Jamie if his mam was sat beside him or some travelling pedlar stinking of donkey dung. If the lad showed no fear of strangers, he was plagued by night terrors.

By the time he was five, our Liza still had to dress him and he was yet in clouts, having no clue what he was supposed to do when his mother sat him on the pot. He could hardly hold a spoon to eat proper but ate with his hands as though he'd been reared by wild creatures. At least by then he was finally walking and talking, though his words made little enough sense. Once I caught him kicking over a piggin of milk he was meant to carry back to the house. When I scolded him, he said he'd done it because a hare was spitting fire at him and boxing his ears. Our Jamie wasn't wicked, nor was he a liar. He was too simple to tell truth from lie, or what was real from his own foolish fancy. Liza and I did our best to set him straight. We spoke blessings over him, drew on our charms and physick herbs, but in vain.

Not an easy future in store for our Jamie. Cruel folk took to calling him Liza's Idiot, whilst kinder souls murmured that he was touched by God. Such talk tore at my daughter's heart. She began to believe that she, a cock-eyed freak of nature herself, had passed down the stain to her son. And hadn't she gazed at the full moon whilst she was pregnant—what if her child had been moonstruck within her very womb? The thought of bearing another stricken child, passing on the curse to yet another innocent life, was enough to make Liza wish herself dead. Every new moon she brewed herself tansy and pennyroyal till her courses came.

At least our John was steadfast and loyal. He stood by Liza and flew into a rage if any dared speak ill of his son. "He might not be a clever one, but he's a good one, which is more than can be said for many round here." John laid the blame for his son's affliction on Anne and her witchery.

"It's nowt to do with Anne Whittle," I kept telling him. "Some children are born that way. Maybe God has some special purpose for him." Best we could do, as Tibb had said, was love Jamie as we would any other child and try our best to keep him out of harm's way.

"Not what I expected, any of this," I told Tibb. At daylight gate in cold February, I was sat atop Blacko Hill, not caring if the temper I was in frightened him off for good. "You promised me three grandchildren by Liza, but I'm left with one who will never be right. Liza's a broken, weeping thing; she's downed enough tansy to make herself barren; and her good man lives in terror of my oldest friend. Can you do no better for us?"

Tibb lifted his eyes to me. "Don't give up hope too soon, my Bess. It might be winter now." He waved a long arm at the naked trees, fallow fields, and the dark clouds smothering Pendle Hill. "Yet spring won't be long in coming. I promise you that."

Stepping close, he stroked my hair till I leaned against him, let him support my tired bones. Spring couldn't come soon enough for me.

A fortnight later I walked home from the Bulcocks at Moss End where I'd blessed a lame horse. At daylight gate, as I made my way along Pendle Water, I felt a flimmer in my belly. Something big was to come.

"Tibb?"

I heard his voice inside my head. *Hurry home, Bess. Your daughter has need of you.* Out of nowhere the brown dog flew out to harry me, nipping at my ankles if I lagged. He wouldn't leave my side till I was ten paces from my door.

I found Liza sobbing over my store of dried herbs. At this ragged end of winter, we were clean out of tansy, pennyroyal, and rue. She crossed her hands over her womb and near doubled over in her desperation. It was the dark of the moon and she'd no bloody clouts to wash. That meant she was bearing. Again I felt the tingling inside me. Sinking down on my knees, I took her hands.

"Welcome her," I said.

"Her?" My daughter was thirty now, still skinny to the bone, but the trouble and care over Jamie had left its mark on her. Wrinkles etched the skin round her mouth and crooked eyes. Her hair had gone thin and lost its sheen.

"Welcome your daughter." My right hand cupped her belly and sensed the life within, stirring and quickening beneath my palm. I closed my eyes to see a golden shimmer, sun spilling through shifting green leaves. I saw a lantern in a dark night, a beacon in a tower. A light far-shining. The beautiful girl Tibb had promised me those many years ago.

Liza shoved my hand away. "I'll have it out. Midwife down in Colne must have some remedy for me."

"Not this one," I begged her.

"What if it's another—" She choked on the word she could not say. "Maybe our John was right all along."

Over the years John's talk of curses and sorcery had worn down Liza to the point where she was too frightened to call upon her own powers. She herself couldn't say the last time Ball had appeared to her.

"My womb's forespoken," she said. "But not by Anne Whittle. I'll not grant her that much talent. Devil himself did this."

"Stop talking foolishness."

"Kit's Elsie—she has five children, each of them healthy and perfect." Liza rubbed her swollen eyes. "That's because she never meddled in the magic. Soon as you became a blesser, she dragged Kit off to Sabden. If I'd known the price I'd have to pay—"

"Hush."

I held her tight, seeking to give comfort, though her words gutted me. Was she saying that she wished she, too, had forsaken me when I'd come into my powers? Did she wish she could be just like her sister-in-law, an ordinary wife and mother and nothing more? I *had* tried to warn her away from this path. Pushing away my own hurt feelings, I rubbed her hair.

"This child you're bearing now will be beautiful, our Liza. She'll be as canny as our Jamie is slow."

"How do you know that?"

"How do you think I know?"

My own daughter gawped at me, loose-jawed to hear me fore-tell the unborn child's future.

"She'll be your pride. Your John will melt at the sight of her. She'll be fierce and loyal and true."

Liza wept and shook her head. "Can't you see, Mam? I've fair lost hope. I daren't trust this."

"You must bear her for Jamie's sake. The lad will never be able to earn his own living. What will happen to him when we're all dead? He needs a sister, a canny sister, to look after him. If you rid yourself of this girl, he'll be alone in the world. Elsie won't allow Kit to take him. Stupid goose thinks he's the Devil's seed."

Liza's tears fell, drenching our clasped hands.

"It will be an easy birth this time," I promised her.

I brewed Liza a tonic to strengthen her womb. I blessed her in the names of St. Mary and St. Margaret. With John saving the richest milk and cream for her, the haggard, haunted look left her and she began to smile again. And so I dared hope that our luck would turn.

# 7

By tibb's enchantment, I found myself transported to a narrow cart track. A flowery tunnel, it was, hedges rising high on both sides, hawthorn buds swelling, soon to burst into lacy-white bloom. The ground underfoot was slick from good spring rain. Blackbirds trilled till a woman's scream rent their song. A man's curses I heard. Frantic feet dashing through the mud. From round the bend, young Annie Redfearn careened, tearing along like a runaway horse, her golden hair flying loose. Somebody had ripped the coif off her head and slashed open the front of her kirtle. She slid to a stop before me, her eyes huge and beseeching. The left side of her face was red and swelling with a mark that would soon darken to a bruise. Cowered behind me, did Annie, as though I had the might to defend her from the terror that chased her. Seconds later I saw him hurtling toward us. More boy than man, he was, but his face purpled in fury.

"Leave her be." I planted myself between him and my best friend's daughter.

One glance was enough to tell me that this lad was born to wealth and property. His mud-spattered boots were made of finest pigskin, his jerkin trimmed in velvet braid. But try as I might, I couldn't put a name on him.

"You're still a young one," I told him. "Go home before you bring shame upon your family, chasing down a defenceless woman. Did your people teach you no better?"

I shuddered as the young man passed right through me as though I were vapour, not flesh and blood. As though I were dead and gone, a ghost and nothing more. Then came Annie's shrieks, unstoppable as blood, till I collapsed on the muddy track that turned before my eyes into rich red clay. Scooping up a fistful of the stuff, I swung round and crammed it into the lad's hateful face till he finally loosened his grip on Annie.

Gagging upon my own spittle, I awoke. My heart rattled loose inside me. My skin had gone cold as the grave.

"Tibb, what is this?" I whispered into the dark silence. "Why would you send me such a nightmare?"

Maundy Thursday, it was. I tried to put the dream out of my head as I set off for the New Church with my family. On that April morning dew gleamed upon the hedges. The meadows were golden with buttercups and the beckside was pungent with bear's garlic and wild onion. I smiled to watch John, mindful of his wife's condition, help Liza over every stile, whilst Jamie skipped along, glad to be traipsing through the fields instead of stuck in the shippon shovelling manure. Out of the hedge leapt a hare, darting across our path. Let out a whoop, did Jamie then, and clutched my arm.

"Calm yourself. It's only a dumb animal," I lied.

The hare cocked its head and gazed at me with soft eyes. I fair expected it to disappear into the green, but it hopped in our wake a quarter mile whilst Jamie babbled fearful about the thing.

"The creature means you no harm," I said, this time speaking the truth. Tibb, taking the form of a hare, was trailing me to church upon Maundy Thursday, though I'd no clue why. Just wasn't regular, this. If he was going to appear to me, why hadn't he done so last night, after the horrible dream, when I'd cried out for him?

Of a sudden, Jamie took off like a sprite, leaping a stone wall and prancing after a yearling horse whose sleek grace struck his fancy. "Dandy!" he kept shouting, trying to grab the cantering colt by the mane. "That's my Dandy." Lucky the poor animal didn't kick his head in.

Trying to do what was best, I made up my mind to deal with

the boy myself and sent his parents on without us so at least they wouldn't be late for church. The Church Warden would be less likely to whip an old woman and a simple boy. Took me a fair while to catch Jamie, who made a game of letting me chase him. When the two of us, red-faced and spattered in field dirt, finally straggled into church, the Curate was well into his sermon. Putting on a contrite face for the Church Warden, I stayed in back near the door, holding tight to Jamie's arm lest he bolt again.

Whilst Jamie wriggled his arms and jabbered to himself, Anne glanced my way with swollen eyes, as though she'd wept the whole night through. Even her daughter Betty seemed downcast and wan. Something cold crawled up my legs as I gazed over at Annie Redfearn. Though her coif was pulled well forward, anybody could see the black bruise upon her cheek. On the men's side of the church, Tom Redfearn looked as though he were watching his own funeral. How unbearable for him to be stood there, bearing the stares and the shame of everybody thinking that he had done this to his own wife. But I did not believe for a moment that he was the culprit. My dream returned, clutching and clawing at me — that strange young man tormenting Annie till I rammed cold clay in his face.

As if reading my thoughts, our Jamie juddered and twitched. Standing still and quiet for three hours was too much for the restless lad. I couldn't keep him from hopping from one foot to the other. The Curate, observing his antics, left off preaching about the Last Supper, the blessed event we were meant to celebrate this day, to speak instead of the Devil, of the Devil's long arm reaching into our lives with wicked temptation. Jamie burst out laughing and slapped both his thighs. Before the Church Warden could charge over with his switch, I hauled the boy out the door. With a whoop, our Jamie broke free of my grasp. He skittered round the churchyard, playing tag with the silent gravestones. I could only shake my head at him.

"You'll be the ruin of us, you daft boy."

A crooked grin split his face. Right pleased with himself, he was, to be out of the church.

"You'll have to go back in again for communion," I told him, for if the two of us did not step up to the communion table, rumours would fly. Folk would say we were afraid of the Host, or unworthy of it, which was ridiculous, in my mind. Hadn't the Curate told us that the Host was not the Body of Christ, as the Papists would have us believe, but only plain, honest bread that we ate in remembrance of our Lord? According to the Curate, the old priests were nowt but sorcerers preying on the ignorant, and when they chanted *hoc est corpus meum* whilst holding the Host aloft, they were really saying *hocus pocus*.

Giggling, my grandson flung himself down upon the Towneleys' grave plot. "The hare what we saw on the way to church had a message for you, Gran."

I folded my arms in front of myself. "And what would that be?"

The boy's eyes fair twinkled, as though he were cannier than any of us had guessed. "Clay pictures," he said, all hushed and secretive.

Again the nightmare reared inside me. I felt the damp weight of the clay in my hand, remembered how I had packed it into the mouth and nose of Annie's attacker so that he could never again draw breath. The thought made me so dizzy that I didn't dare look up for fear of seeing a hare or a brown dog. Then, remembering the Church Warden, I dragged Jamie to the church porch. Looking through the open doorway, I pretended to listen to the sermon whilst Jamie rocked on his heels and counted magpies.

"One for sorrow, two for mirth," he chanted. "Seven for a witch." He spun on his toes. "Let me take the colt home, Gran, please? I'll name him Dandy."

"Hush."

When at last the Curate drew his sermon to a close, too hoarse to drone on any longer, it was time to lead Jamie up the aisle for communion. How my grandson delighted in playing the jester before the long-faced churchmen. Mouth gaping like a trout's, the lad dropped to his knees before the Curate and stuck out his long red tongue. Had to bite the inside of my cheek to keep from laughing. Though they said he was a dullard, our Jamie had a way of twisting every occasion to his own amusement.

"You'd best flog that boy when you get home," the Church Warden told me as I led Jamie out the door.

Pretending humility and obedience, I rushed my grandson away before he could pull a face or do some other fool thing to provoke the man. Bells rang and everybody hastened out of church with the eagerness of cattle let out of the barn for the first time after a long winter. Jamie spirited me away to a shadowy corner of the churchyard.

"What is it now?" I asked him.

"Gift for you." His words slurred. Beneath the shadow of the great yew tree, he opened his mouth and stuck out his tongue, revealing the communion bread.

"And what would I want with that, you silly boy?"

His eyes widened. "For your spells."

"Enough of your nonsense." I clapped my hand over his mouth, then softened my voice. "Swallow the Lord's bread, love. There's a good boy. Look, here comes your mam."

Lad swung round to Liza and stared at her belly, still flat under her kirtle. "Little sister," he said.

"Come along home, our Jamie," said his father.

My family headed out of the churchyard, but I dawdled behind, waiting for Anne. I'd never seen her looking so ill-done-to, her hands clutched to her middle as though someone had stabbed her there. She didn't need to speak a word. I took her hand and out the lych-gate we went.

"Go on without me," I told Liza and John who started at the sight of Anne and me walking arm in arm like sisters. "I'll meet you back home."

John wrapped a shielding arm round my daughter's shoulders and hustled her and Jamie along, out of Anne's sight. Betty had already gone. Annie and Tom were nowhere to be seen amongst the departing throng. If it had been me with a face like Annie's,

I'd have hared home right fast so not to have to endure the prying eyes. My friend wouldn't tell me a thing till we were sat upon the clay banks of Pendle Water.

"Once you made me promise I'd come to you if I was in any sort of fix," Anne said, fighting tears. "Well, now is the time."

"What happened to Annie?"

"It wasn't our Tom's doing," she told me straight off. "He'd never hurt her."

"I know, love. He's a good man. Who did it then?" I dared not speak of the nameless lad in my dream.

"Landlord's brat. Young Robert of Greenhead."

Robert Assheton—I knew him by name and reputation if not by sight. It was common knowledge that he served Sir Shuttleworth of Gawthorpe Hall, Chief Justice of Chester, and that he spent much time travelling with his master. But when he was home at Greenhead, only two miles from Anne's cottage, young Annie would have no respite.

"Look at me!" My friend broke down, helpless and inconsolable. "I'm her mother and I can't protect her. Her husband can't protect her. He's a labourer for the Asshetons. One word from that Devil's son and Tom will lose his livelihood. That bastardly gullion said that if she didn't let him have his way, he'd turn us out of our cottage."

"Have you spoken to the lad's father?" I asked. "Think of the shame, our Anne. His son serving the Chief Justice, then turning round and molesting Annie, and her a married woman."

"Old Master Assheton's off in York, not to return till the end of the month. As for the lad's mother"—Anne made a rude gesture—"she told me to my face that the boy's only young, full of high spirits, and he means no harm. She'd sooner have my Annie whipped in the stocks as a temptress and whore before she'd lay the blame on her precious son. To listen to her, you'd think he shits golden sovereigns out his hole."

"If his parents will do nothing, you must go to the Constable. That would humiliate them even more."

Anne began to cry again. "We've no witness. It's Annie's word against his. Who do you think the Constable will believe?"

My friend's desperation struck me like an iron fist. Though young Robert served Justice Shuttleworth, it seemed there was no justice in sight for Annie. Robert Assheton had acted as he had because he knew he could get away with it. The law of the land protected only the rich. Rocking my friend in my arms, I sought to give her what solace I could. We were just two lowly old women—how could we hope to stand up to the gentry?

"I wish I knew what to do," I told her.

Anne's eyes shone green as the churning water. "We both know the measure of what you can *do,* our Bess."

Her words left me too gobsmacked to speak. Ever since we were girls, Anne had been the doubter, the sceptic, who held all would-be enchanters apart from me, her friend, in deepest contempt. Yet now she was asking me to work magic on her daughter's behalf.

"There must be something, some charm of yours," she said, clasping me tight. "You cured Matty Holden, after all."

Once more the dream wrapped itself round me, how young Annie had sought out my protection, how I'd finally thwarted the lad by slamming clay in his face. I remembered what Jamie had said to me in the churchyard whilst he lay atop the Towneleys' grave plot. *Clay pictures.* I imagined taking a scoop of the river clay I was sat on, imagined shaping it in my hands till it took the form of Robert Assheton. I imagined dropping that clay doll into the fire. Sticking it through with blackthorns. Crumbling it, bit by bit, till nothing remained. Such thoughts left me wanting to spew in the bushes.

Throughout Pendle Forest I was known as a cunning woman. Folk called on me to heal the sick, mend their ailing cows and horses, reveal the names of thieves, bless ale and wombs. On occasion a sorry few had asked me to work curses for their own selfish designs, but I'd always refused.

Some bind I was in now: my dearest friend begging me to use

my powers to curse Robert Assheton. If it had been anybody but her, I'd have run off home right then. Meddling in revenge magic would soil my good name forever. Such spells weren't the business of a cunning woman but the work of a witch. *Witch*—the very word set me trembling.

"You're asking me to work woe," I said.

"Bess, you're our only hope."

If I did this, my immortal soul would be damned to hell. *Have a care,* Tibb had admonished me all those years ago, *which path you tread. Some paths are steep and stony whilst others seem broad and easy, though they lead to misfortune.* If I took a single step on the false path, I feared it would be too late to return to the road of righteousness.

Meanwhile, my dream smothered me. Annie's flailing arms, her beaten face. What if she were my daughter? What wouldn't I do to save Liza, my immortal soul be damned? If young Robert laid a finger on my girl, I wouldn't waver a second before unleashing the darkest magics I could conjure.

"Bess?" Anne gave my arm a shake. "You've gone blue round the lips. Look fit to faint, you do."

"Our Anne, let me think on this."

"Think all you like," she said, resigned. "Meanwhile, my daughter has no refuge." Anne pressed her fists into her eye sockets.

"I'll come tomorrow," I promised her. "I'll bring salve for her bruises."

Anne stared off into the rustling green. "It will take more than salve to mend her if no one stops young Assheton."

That night gave me neither rest nor peace. The straw in my pallet kept poking and pricking me, sharp as a thousand bodkins. When at last I slept, I only dreamt of Annie. Of her bruises, dark as shame. Of her eyes, pleading and forlorn. Wherever I turned, there she was, floating before me like a spectre.

At dawn I staggered, shivering and shaking, to the tower

window. Tibb's voice seemed to hang in the pearly-grey light. *You and you alone choose the road you walk.* Wasn't I already beyond the pale? Though I had cleaved to the ways of healing and blessing, that didn't redeem me in the eyes of the Curate, for I'd consorted with spirits. As far as the men of the church and the law were concerned, sorcery was sorcery, whether it was used for good or ill. I was damned to hell as it stood. If the Constable chose to arrest me, he could hang me, same as a thief or a common murderer.

A voice inside that was not Tibb's but my own spoke up, insistent and defiant. If there was one kind of justice for the high and mighty, could there not be another justice for the poor? What was the use of having these powers if I didn't use them to help my best friend's daughter? Indeed, such magic was the only power a lowborn woman such as I could wield, the only way retribution could be brought down upon Robert Assheton. How could I live with myself or ever look Anne and her daughters in the eye again if I failed them now?

Whilst the rest of my family slept, I hurried off for West Close, cutting through dew-drenched meadows. Clambering over a stile, I looked up to see seven magpies stitching the sky with beaks and wings. *Seven for a witch.* John suspected my Anne of witchcraft, but I was the real witch and all for the sake of my devotion to her.

Onward I strode till I reached a lane enclosed by hedges and high-arching trees, their branches knit overhead. Rooks I heard, loud and greedy, drowning out the blackbirds and larks. With each step my heart pounded harder. No turning back. Then I was stood before Greenhead Manor, smaller than Roughlee Hall, but grand, nonetheless, with ivy climbing its proud stone walls and framing its mullioned windows that mirrored the blue and green morning. So this was young Robert's home. I froze, no more strength left inside me to move.

Then an invisible thread tugged me onward. My soles burned

and I was off down the track that led from the manor house to Anne's cottage. Walking between hedges of budding thorn, I saw not a single magpie, only heard the lambs behind the hedges calling out to their mothers. A clean, fresh scent rose from the earth as the sun climbed higher. Beautiful and pure as a dream, this morning was, and just as fragile and easily torn.

A bridge took me over Spurn Clough where the rushing water in the beck below drowned out the hoof beats coming from behind. Once over the bridge, I was passing round a narrow bend when the rider came galloping, full reckless. He would have knocked me right down had not the brown dog leapt out, snarling and snapping. Eyes a-roll, the stallion screamed, leapt sideways, then reared, his hooves beating the air. The rider, savage as anything, yanked the reins, tearing at the horse's mouth till blood flecked the flying foam. He dug his spurs into the creature's lathered flanks, sending the horse on. The brown dog hurtled after them. Though the entire scene unfolded before me in a flash, I knew beyond a doubt who that young horseman was.

So what could I do but carry on down the track, following the marks left by the horse's hooves and the dog's great paws? Before long the dog prints vanished away, as I knew they would. I came upon a slippery patch where the lad, now unhorsed, sprawled and groaned, his backside well blackened with muck.

"Taken a spill, have you, sir?" I hid my smile. So Tibb had sorted this for me and I'd not have to reach for the clay. "Anything broken? Now, a snapped tailbone is a painful thing. Takes a long time mending, that does. If you don't mind my saying, sir, it's not very canny to ride a green stallion you can scarce master."

My sides ached from the struggle not to laugh as I reached out my arm, making a great show of offering to help him to his feet, but the lad slapped my hand away.

"Keep your paws off me, old bitch. If I see that dog of yours again, I'll take my musket to it." Nowt injured but his sullen pride.

"Dog, sir?" Eyes innocent, I looked round. "There's no dog about. You'd best rest a spell and wait for your head to clear."

Red-faced and swearing, he made to stand up, only to slip in the mud and fall back upon his bum.

"Good day to you, sir." Singing loud enough to drown out his curses, I carried on my way. For a sixty-three-year-old woman, I could move right fast and soon left him behind.

A while later I came to a gap in the fence with the top board hanging loose. Looking into the field, I saw the stallion with his nose down in the long grass, munching away and fair content to be shot of his rider. Bending down, I found the stirrup and stirrup leather the horse had succeeded in scraping off his saddle before leaping through the broken fence. Clever beast. I flung the stirrup over the hedge and out of sight, then scurried off, cackling like a mad thing. Not such a bad morning after all.

When I reached Anne's cottage, it looked abandoned, its door and shutters closed, as though Robert had been true to his threat and banished my friends from their home. I tried the door handle only to find it barred from the inside.

"Our Anne!" I called through a chink in the wood. "It's me."

Her eye appeared in a crack, then the door opened. She drew me inside before barring it again.

In the weak light trickling through the holes in the thatch, Annie Redfearn was sat spinning her landlord's wool with a drop spindle. She hardly lifted her head when I came in. Betty was hunched over her mending, her needle dipping in and out of the mud-coloured stuff. So it had come to this—three grown women hiding behind closed shutters and a bolted door, working in near darkness on a fine spring morning, hiding themselves from the world in case young Robert happened by.

"Our Annie," I said, "I've brought salve for you."

The young woman murmured her thanks but her smile was more like a grimace. She flinched beneath my touch as I rubbed the ointment into her tender skin.

"I'll help you, so I swear," I told Annie, "by any means I can."

Her mother came to me from behind, wrapping her arms round my waist.

"I knew you wouldn't let us down!" Anne cried.

"Hush!" young Annie said in a harsh whisper, shocking us with her temper. "My Tom pried those nails loose from Assheton's fence posts so he could make that door bolt, but fat good it will do with the racket you two are making. Anybody could hear you a mile off."

Before her mother or I could say another word, a furious barking outside the door made my nape go cold as clay.

Anne peeked through the chink, then leaned her full weight against the door as if to block it forevermore. "It's him."

Silent but swift, young Annie seized a knife with a long, glinting blade. Betty grabbed an iron fire poker. Putting my eye to a crack in the door, I watched the mud-spattered boy stalk toward the cottage. Being thrown from his horse hadn't made him give over, not in the least. Angry, he looked, and itching to make Annie pay. Soon enough his fists battered the door. From far away, I heard a howling dog.

"Open up!" young Robert yelled. "I know you're in there."

My friend gripped the bolt and held fast.

"The lot of you are nothing but beggars and squatters," the boy taunted. "Don't pay a penny's worth of rent. And *you*, Betty Whittle, are a thief! I'll turn the lot of you out."

He beat against the door till the purloined nails holding the bolt in place began to give. But before he could force his way into the cottage, I shoved Anne aside, lifted the bolt, and yanked the door open so suddenly that the young man tumbled into me.

"Our Robert, we meet again. Was falling off your horse not humiliation enough?"

"It's *you*," he said, although he didn't seem to know me from a dead fly. He lifted his arm to wrest me out of his way, but I, quicker and stronger than any old woman has any right to be, jumped on both his feet, forcing him backward.

"If I were you, young master, I'd watch my step. Leave these folk in peace, never to trouble them again, or you'll rue it."

He laughed and made to push me aside, but I blocked his path, stepping close enough to breathe into his nostrils. "Now, now, my boy, don't make me go whistle for my dog."

Soon as I spoke, the brown dog appeared, taking his place beside me. The beast growled low, the fur on his scruff raised, his haunches tensed to spring for the boy's throat at my command. First time I ever saw a man's face go green with fear.

Still the whelp had to make a show of his might. He craned his neck to see past me and shouted at Annie. "You can't hide from me. One day this land will be mine, and I'll tear down this cursed cottage."

My fists took hold of young Robert's jerkin. "This land will *never* come to you," I sang out, a cold river streaming through me.

The far-seeing held me in its grip, and I knew that I spoke the truth. So bold was I then that I turned my backside to the brat and farted.

"Nothing like pea pottage for getting rid of bad wind," I said, winking at Anne.

A snarl ripped the silence that followed. I heard teeth tearing cloth, heard the young man yelp in his terror, the dog bark and snap, heard the lad scrambling away. When I finally turned round again, all I saw of young Robert was his filthy arse as he scuttled off home, the dog furious at his heels.

My Anne embraced me. "Thank you, thank you, till the end of my days. If only I could protect her the way you did."

"It's all right," I told her. "It's all over now."

"All over till he returns, twice as vexed as before, with you not here," young Annie said. None of her fear or pain had lessened. "Mother Demdike, I beg you, how did you do that? How did you call that dog from out of nowhere? You don't even keep a dog."

Sheepish, I turned to Anne. "Will you let me speak to your girl in private?"

I touched her shoulder, and then my old friend pressed my

hand and nodded. Her daughter followed me out the door. Nervous, Annie was, looking round to make sure young Robert wasn't lurking about. I led her to the beck behind the cottage, its banks red with clay.

"What I'm about to tell you is secret," I said. "And forbidden. If you care for your mam and your sister, you'll conceal it even from them, for this kind of knowledge can get a woman hanged. Do you understand my meaning, our Annie?"

"I can keep a secret if I must."

Hunkering right down, I scooped up a handful of clay and placed the stuff in her palm. Right maffled was the look she gave me.

"Some women in your place, if they were troubled by one such as Robert Assheton and they'd no other way to help themselves, would resort to desperate means." Here I stopped to draw breath. "Annie, that's clay in your hand. If you'd a mind to, you might model it in the shape of him that torments you, as close a likeness as you can manage. Then you might have a mind to stick a thorn in the clay where his private parts would be, to stay him and bind him. Or you might crumble a bit of his legs to lame him; or his backside to give him an awful case of piles; or his eyes, to dim his sight; or his head to befuddle his thoughts. A truly wicked sort might stick the clay doll in the fire and let him roast like the souls in hell. Of course, such things are sinful and no God-fearing Christian would ever consider doing them."

Annie blinked at me. "Are you saying that anyone who moulds clay might work witchcraft, Mother Demdike? Then there'd hardly be a landlord left alive."

Bright girl was Annie. There was no talking down to her, no hiding the facts.

"No, Annie. The spirits . . . or *a* spirit must be there for the spell to work."

"How am I to get one?" she asked, her face white as birch bark.

"Peace. I'll lend you my Tibb. He'll see to it that it works."

I kept my eyes upon Annie whilst she gazed steadfast at the clay in her hand.

As I cut across a field on my way homeward, Tibb appeared at my side.

"Have I done wrong?" I asked him. After telling Annie of the clay, I was beginning to have second thoughts. A bundle of rattling bones, I was, half-fearing the hounds of hell would chase me down and tear me to pieces for my wicked deed, passing on such unholy knowledge to one as innocent as Annie. But I found no reproach in Tibb's eyes.

"You've kept your word," he said. "You're true to your loved ones."

Yet I quaked to think of Annie stabbing the clay picture with thorns, then crumbling it, bit by bit, as it pleased her. Grim stuff, this was. But Robert had left her little enough choice.

"Tibb, what have I unleashed?"

"Rough justice."

Next Sunday in church, Annie Redfearn seemed a new woman. The marks on her face had faded some, and she held up her head instead of shrinking inside her kirtle. According to the gossip going round, young Robert had left early for Chester, riding his sister's fat old gelding since his own stallion kicked and reared whenever he came near the animal. Hearing that the lad wouldn't show his face in these parts again before December, I was well pleased.

After the service, as I headed out the door, who hailed me but Tom Redfearn. How I blushed to see that tall young man bowing to me.

"I am much obliged." He didn't need to say what for.

Liza and John cast uneasy looks as I said my farewells to Tom and the rest of Anne's family, but on our walk home we spoke not a word of it. Easier to keep our silence than break into a quarrel, for they knew I'd not suffer their speaking ill of my friend.

If John mentioned Anne at all, he called her Chattox, her hated nickname that made her sound like a poisonous toad.

Liza, loath to leave her husband to his brooding, nattered on about cheese-making till our John came back to himself, mild-faced and content. Marching along in their wake, I only half-listened. So many thoughts chased through my head. I asked myself if I felt any different now that I'd done what I thought I could never do: harness dark magic. When I weighed my soul, it felt no heavier than before. After seeing Annie's head held high in church today, her peace restored, I could not summon a sliver of regret for what I'd done. No divine hand swept down from heaven to smite me. I imagined Tibb hidden just behind the hedge, a smile upon his lips, his hand raised in blessing.

That summer our cattle grew fat and sleek, giving us so much cream that even our John began to look a little less scrawny. Jamie grew strong and tall, if no cannier than before, and my Liza flowered. Her skin had a glow about it, her hair a rare sheen as her belly ripened and swelled. Our John said he'd never seen her looking finer, even in the bloom of her youth when he first courted her. As she grew heavier with child, I caught her stroking the babe through the wall of her own flesh and singing cradle songs to her yet unborn daughter. She was in love with her already.

In October our John and his Master Holden drove the fat of the herd to Colne Market and turned a profit. God smiled upon us, so Anthony Holden said, well pleased at the end of such a good year. Sarah Holden then prepared such a Harvest Home feast as never seen before. She welcomed folk from near and far, inviting them to spend the night if the celebration carried on too late. Though I was invited, someone had to stay behind at Malkin Tower to mind the remaining cattle. So I let my family go without me and waved to them as they took to the road. Once I'd lost sight of them, I went to sit under the old elder tree. We'd already stripped the tree of its violet berries. The vat of elderberry wine was steeping and bubbling in a dark corner of the firehouse. With only a few limp leaves still clinging to its gnarled branches, the tree looked tired and used up. Likewise, I was beginning to feel the burden of my sixty-three years.

A strange humour I was in, both restless and melancholy at once. I'd sent my family off to the feast because I craved solitude. Yet my loneliness gnawed at me. If my body wasn't getting any younger, my mind was sharper than it had ever been, my powers rising and stirring, all the mightier after I had risked everything to help Annie Redfearn, and I scarce knew what to do with them. Liza, my one-time apprentice, had forsaken her own gift. I'd no one to confide in, no one who would understand what was brewing within me.

Circling round the foot of Malkin Tower, I listened to the faraway piping and singing. Bonfires crowned every hill, for it was not just the Holdens having a merry Harvest Home. Though the new religion had banished most other festivals, even the Curate agreed that it would be an insult to Providence if we didn't offer thanks for a bountiful harvest. This one night it almost seemed as though the old ways had returned. Children bore their flickering rush lights up Blacko Hill. A game, it was, to see if a person could reach the hilltop without the wind blowing out the light. Every soul in Pendle Forest was off revelling, apart from me. What was I but a lonely old woman in my tower? Everything I had learned, every secret Tibb had whispered in my ear, would die with me. As the cold wind blustered, I imagined my flesh and bones wasting away till I became a boggart floating off in the night to scare decent folk. *Seven for a witch.*

About to go inside, I was, and retire to my pallet when out of the darkness a figure appeared to block my path. Her eyes shone in the moonlight, and she held a pie in her outstretched arms.

"Happy Harvest Home, our Bess," said Anne.

The sweet scent of apple pie reminded me that I'd eaten next to nowt that day, my appetite having failed me till this moment.

"You walked all the way from West Close to bring me a pie?"

Wondered how she even baked it, having no oven. I grinned to think of Betty snatching it from the Greenhead kitchen.

"My feet are well sore," my friend complained. "Are you going to let me stand out here till the moon goes down?"

So I invited her inside and built a hearthfire as grand as any of the bonfires on the high hills. Later our John would scold me for wasting so much peat, but it was Harvest Home and I was finally in the mood to make merry. I cut the pie to share and filled two cups to the brim with last year's elderberry wine, potent enough to make the stars spin in the sky.

"How are your girls?" I asked her.

"Off dancing the harvest in, them two." Anne raised her cup to me.

"Wouldn't it be something to be young again?"

In truth, the heady wine almost made it seem within my grasp to travel back through time.

"You were such a shameless one," Anne teased. "Even when you were married. Your husband didn't stand a chance. You were pretty enough to make the Curate forget half of what he was meant to be preaching."

I laughed myself legless at the memory. "And you! With your golden hair. They all said there was no greater beauty in Pendle Forest."

We fell silent then, mourning what was gone and would never return. Seemed unjust, the way the years had slipped away, robbing us of our pleasures, the love and the lust that had seared us.

"God's foot," I said, "doesn't the world grow drearier each year? Times were never so good as when we were young. Remember when the Lord of Misrule bared his bottom to the Church Warden?"

Anne roared, her hand grasping mine. When her laughter died down, she cast her eyes to the ashes in the hearth.

"What's left for us now?" she asked.

"Our children and grandchildren," I said, then regretted my slip of tongue, for Anne was not yet blessed with grandchildren.

"Even our children grow older," she said after a spell. "Least you have your powers. Must be a comfort, knowing you're not just a useless old woman like me."

"Hardly useless! What would Annie do without you?"

"What would she do without *you,* more like." Anne turned to me. "You taught her about them clay pictures—that's the only thing that saved her."

A draught stole in beneath the door, raising my flesh. "She told you?"

"Did you think she'd keep it secret from her own mam? Does your Liza keep secrets from you?"

I sighed, wondering. My own daughter had washed her hands clean of all I'd tried to teach her.

"At least young Assheton is gone to Chester," I said. "God willing, he'll trouble her no more."

"There's the rub, our Bess." The defeat in Anne's voice undid me. "He'll return for Christmas. Only a matter of weeks. Hangs over us, this does. Already Annie's gone off her food. Tom said he'd murder him if he comes round again—what good would that do if Tom gets himself hanged? I'd give anything to be able to protect her the way you did."

The wind carried the sound of a dog baying to the moon.

"What are you saying?" I asked her.

She leaned close. "You taught my girl. Could you not teach me?"

"Anne." My head swam with wine and my own bewilderment. "You never believed in such things." Looking into the depths of her green eyes, I prayed to see her old doubts arise. But she gazed back at me with the zeal of a convert.

"It's true that I don't believe in saints or miracles or any of that gobbledygook. Don't even know if I believe in God. But you were stood right in my cottage when you summoned that dog. It's not a matter of believing—I saw it happen."

"It's no easy path. Remember, you warned me yourself of the dangers, the price to be paid." Anxious, I was, to talk her out of this, for I'd no desire for my best friend to hang for what she was begging me to teach her. What a fuss Liza would raise if Anne became my new apprentice. John would declare that he'd been right all along about Anne having the power to twist me to her will, that she was a witch, that our doom was sealed.

"You know I'd never ask you for anything trifling," Anne said. "I swear I'd pay any price to keep my family safe from young Assheton."

"Our Anne, I'd roast in the worst fires of hell before I'd let that wretch meddle with you and yours."

With a shaking hand, I filled our cups again.

"Even if I were to teach you everything I know, you'll still not be a cunning woman till a spirit comes to you and that can't be hurried or forced, our Anne. It's the spirits who choose, not us. But please let's speak no more of this tonight."

Setting sombre thoughts aside, we emptied the wine flask, finished the apple pie, and reminisced about our youth till our flanks ached from laughter. Anne sang one old song after another, and what did we do then but rush outside to dance in the moonlight like two silly girls. Jig after jig we danced, spinning and swirling till we were dizzy, and then we threw ourselves upon the grass to gaze up at the wheeling stars. Her loosened hair touched mine and our fingers twined together.

With the harvest moon pouring down upon our faces, I gave Anne my word. I promised to teach her of cunning craft and familiars, of blessing and binding. By and by, a spirit might well come to her. My friend and I had shared so many things in our long lives. Why shouldn't we share this?

# 8

E VEN GIVEN EVERYTHING that came afterward, Anne and I would both treasure that night for the rest of our days. At the ragged end of her life, my Anne would cling to our secret feast like a silk handkerchief, and she would embroider it something fierce to make it even more fantastic. She'd say that we'd shared a magnificent feast at Malkin Tower with sweet butter, cheese and bread, roasted meats, and plentiful wine and beer, all served to us by our familiars, my Tibb and her Fancy, though he had yet to appear to her that night. She would first encounter her spirit toward the end of November when he came in the guise of a black-haired young man.

Speaking of our banquet, she'd say that we'd no fire or even a single candle for light, but that the imps themselves lent us their magical glow, not only Tibb and Fancy, but a host of she-spirits besides. She'd say that some creature that took the shape of a spotted bitch told me, within her own hearing, that she would be granted silver, gold, and great wealth. This was the tale she would live to tell whilst I lay dead. But I am leaping ahead.

During that waning year of 1595, I was careful to keep my meetings with Anne privy, for I'd no wish to upset Liza with her time being so near or to give our John any excuse to fret and moan. Anne and I took to meeting in a copse of trees on Slipper Hill, not far from Malkin Tower, or else I walked to West Close.

In early December I came by Anne's cottage and, finding it empty, walked in the direction of the voices I heard behind the willows and rushes. Anne and Annie were sat on either side of the beck, both of them making clay pictures, for young Assheton was expected back from Chester any day. Mother and daughter jerked their heads in alarm as my shadow fell across them, but then they smiled in their relief to see that it was only me.

Young Annie seemed well jittery as she shaped the clay, but her mam's hands were steady. I thought to myself that it was a good thing Annie didn't have to wrestle with this on her own—she could lose her courage, after all, then it might be too late to save herself.

As the winter sun glinted on the angel-bright hair spilling from her coif, her beauty was enough to dazzle, even whilst she was sat at her grisly task. A married woman of twenty-four, she could pass as a maid of sixteen, she was still so lithe and grace-ful. I could well understand why Annie was her mother's joy, the shining star of her old age—she was like a mirror in which my Anne could see her own lost youth reflected. Such a fond and fierce look Anne gave her daughter when she reached across the beck to take the half-finished clay manikin from Annie's falter-ing hands. My friend's brow furrowed, full-determined, as she put on the finishing touches.

For the life of me, I hadn't the nerve to ask them why they were making two clay figures instead of one.

Returning to Malkin Tower, I found John busy lining Jamie's old cradle with sweet-smelling new straw. Our Liza's baby was due this month. Banishing all thought of clay pictures, I gath-ered clean rags to sew a poppet, no instrument of magic, but a child's blameless toy, with combed flax for hair.

Soon enough Yuletide was upon us and gossip spread like the pox. Robert Assheton had returned to Greenhead feeling miser-able and unwell, swearing that Annie Redfearn had bewitched him.

"You swore that Chattox has no powers," our John told me. "Is her daughter now a witch?"

"You promised you wouldn't go on about that anymore," Liza said to him, her hands clutching her pregnant belly. "Please, love, just throw some salt over your shoulder and be done with it."

"This is well serious," John insisted. "That young Assheton told his father to have Chattox and Annie laid in Lancaster Gaol. He wanted them locked up in a place where they'd be glad to bite lice in two with their teeth."

Listening to those words, I could almost see Robert's hate-twisted face. We were in real danger, Anne, Annie, and me. No telling what could happen to us now that young Assheton was spouting on about witchcraft. I seized my wits, picking each word with care.

"Master Robert's nowt but a moonstruck fool," I told John. "The boy should be ashamed of himself, slandering poor folk and all because he tried to have his way with a married woman who can't stand the sight of him."

John shook his head in disbelief. "You still say Chattox is harmless? I saw young Master Assheton's face and if ever there was a hag-ridden soul, it was him. Where would Annie learn witchcraft if not from her mother?"

My skin began to burn with the many secrets I'd kept hidden from my own family. If my son-in-law knew that I had taught both Anne and Annie, would he run to the Constable? Would Liza herself shun me? A tightness closed round my throat as though a collar of cold iron were choking me.

In my silence, Liza spoke. "Our John's right that Chattox and her lot are never up to any good. If she's not a witch, her oldest girl's a thief. It's only folk's goodwill and charity that kept Betty from being dragged off to Lancaster ages ago."

"Enough," I pleaded. "I'll go to West Close and talk to them myself. Find out what this is about."

I rushed past fallow barley fields haunted by crows. St. Stephen's, it was, the day after Christmas, yet bleak as death. When

I reached the cottage, I found Tom Redfearn digging out the clogged ditch that ran alongside the road.

"You'll find the women inside," he told me, his face etched with worry.

Anne and her two daughters were knelt round the fire. Eyes streaming, Betty cut onions whilst my friend stirred a pot of thin broth into which the onions would go. Young Annie was slapping down wet clapbread dough on the steaming-hot stones that girded the fire.

"Happy Christmas, Bess." Anne rose to kiss me. "You're just in time to eat with us. When the soup's ready, we'll call Tom inside."

Doting and tender, she turned to smile at Annie who looked anxious as her husband, her skin drained and bloodless. Betty swiped at her onion tears and pulled a face. In a foul mood, she seemed, as though resentful her mother was making it so clear that Annie was the favoured daughter.

"Don't just sit there like a clod, our Betty," came her mother's voice. "Go out and fetch another turve for the fire."

Soon as Betty had tramped out the door, Anne sidled close and spoke low and fast. "Ill talk going round about us, Bess."

"Ill talk indeed," I said, a catch in my throat. "The clay pictures—did anyone see you making them? Just the other day I stumbled by and saw you. Oh, be careful, our Anne."

"He says he won't stop till his father has us arrested." Young Annie spoke in a cold, tight voice. Her hands slammed the sizzling clapbread on the stone till the steam rose, obscuring her face.

"That boy is running round like a madman," said her mother. "We haven't had a moment's peace."

Betty trundled in with the peat, which she dumped in the fire, sending sparks flying over her sister. She looked from Annie to her mother to me, the three of us guilty-faced and silent, gagging on our terror of what lay ahead.

"You were talking about young Assheton." Betty sounded

well weary of the things that had been kept from her. She turned to her sister. "Wouldn't it be easier to just give him what he wants so he'll leave the rest of us alone?"

My Anne went dark red as if spoiling to give Betty a right good clouting, when Annie staggered to her feet and threw herself between them. Her young face sagged.

"Speak of the Devil," Annie said.

The four of us listened to the noise of hooves splattering through the mud.

Anne took hold of the fire poker. "You stay inside," she told young Annie. "Never fear. This time we have Tom on hand."

Annie clutched herself. "What if he picks a fight with Tom and Tom gets hauled off for decking him?"

Her mother, Betty, and I rushed out the door, leaving Annie to bolt it behind us.

Astride a fat grey gelding, young Robert was sat, dressed in a cloak of new wool with gold and silver braid. His sword hung from his belt and he'd a tall plumed hat. Not the bedraggled boy I remembered. A sparse beard grew at his chin and his eyes glinted with lunacy. Gaunt, he looked, and haunted, too, as though he'd known no sleep or rest since I'd seen him last. Couldn't sit still in his saddle but rocked back and forth like Jamie at his worst. Even his placid gelding danced sideways, full skittish. I could imagine Annie with the clay doll in her hands. Her hidden away in the cottage this very moment and crumbling away at the head.

"Bring out Annie Redfearn," he commanded as bold as though he were the Chief Justice himself. "I must speak to her at once."

"If you have anything to say, you'll be talking to me, Master Robert," Tom Redfearn said.

Tom stood nearly six feet tall. In spite of the cold, he'd rolled up his sleeves so that the young master could see his muscles flexing as he wielded the shovel. The boy trembled in his rage at being told off by a poor tenant. Yet lowborn as Tom might be, armed with only a shovel instead of a sword, he was twice the man in size and strength. If Tom chose, he could fell Robert with one blow.

Thrashing in the saddle, the boy jerked at the reins, forcing the gelding to pace a tight circle. He pointed his riding crop at Tom. "I'll have my father put you out of this house."

"And if he doesn't?" Well angry, Tom was, his every muscle tensed. Reminded me of a bull set to charge.

"Then I'll pull the cottage down myself."

Tom's reply came stern and strong. "When you come back again, you'll be in a better mind."

Young Robert brandished the whip at Tom, intent on striking his face, when a sooty crow swooping overhead sent the horse spinning, then the beast shied at the whip. Without another word, the landlord's son dug in his spurs, sending the old gelding into a swift, jerky trot.

"One day I swear I'll murder that milksop," said Tom.

"Peace," Anne said in a voice that made every part of me shrink. "You won't have to."

Her eyes hardened as they followed the crow winging away in the direction Robert had fled. The bird could only be Fancy, I thought: Anne's familiar rushing off to do her grisly bidding. A storm was rising inside my friend, the power, raw and new, potent enough to knock me sideways. Anne was so much more than my apprentice. She had it in her to outshine me, to charge ahead where I would never dare go. Like a knife in the gut came the unwelcome knowing that I was afraid of her, afraid of my oldest friend. It was not enough for her to protect her daughter from young Assheton, I realised. She wanted to be even with him. Wanted to destroy him. My own Anne Whittle, who had nothing left to lose.

"Have a care, our Anne," I begged her before I left. "Go too far and you'll get us hanged."

We'd best keep our heads down, I warned her. Make like the

meekest souls in Pendle Forest. Pray that Robert would leave for Chester soon and not show his face again for a good long while.

Anne shook her head at me, her patience worn thin. Assheton was the menace looming over her every waking hour. It was her daughter and her home under threat, not mine. She didn't have the luxury of walking away from this.

"We've the powers," she said. "Why should we not use them? We're damned if we don't."

An awful pall clung to me when I walked home that foggy evening. Anne had been chosen by her spirit, that was true, her desperation drawing a familiar altogether different from Tibb. If Tibb was a creature of earth, sun, and starry skies, Anne's Fancy seemed a son of coldest Saturn, of shadowy places and slithery creatures who hid down dank holes. His was the might concealed in the tiny purple flowers of nightshade. Under Fancy's thrall, my Anne was becoming another woman, one I didn't know if I could trust.

She was her own mistress. She alone chose the path she walked, and there was no pulling her back, for her actions were borne of dire need.

Right late, it was, by the time I reached Malkin Tower. A rush light still burned behind the window. Stepping in the door, I girded myself, thinking that Liza and John would welter me with questions concerning Anne and her deeds. What would I tell them now when they spoke of the rumours of vile witchcraft?

My son-in-law only cried out in his relief that I had returned. He pointed to the pile of fresh straw where Liza huddled, clad in her shift with a blanket wrapped round her. Her time had come, at least a fortnight earlier than I'd reckoned.

"She's been having the pains for hours already," John said before leaving me to my business.

"I thought you'd never come," Liza panted. "You were with *her.* She kept you out so late on purpose."

My daughter's white lips clamped in dread. It appeared that her old fears of bearing another afflicted child had arisen, along with her memories of Jamie's brutal, tearing birth, and the talk of black magic had done her no good at all. Trying to put her mind at ease, I brewed her motherwort and raspberry leaf. I prayed aloud to St. Margaret and St. Anne, but my daughter flinched even to hear that name.

"What if she's cursed me again?" Liza asked as I mopped the cold sweat from her face.

"Anne Whittle never cursed you, love." Once I would have said that she was blameless and had never cursed anybody, but thanks to my own meddling, that was no longer true. "She never wished the least ill on you. Now take a deep breath and stop clenching up."

Her pains were coming fast. If she could bring herself to breathe in time with them, she would spare herself some agony.

"She kissed John at our wedding and things were never right after that. She cursed Jamie in the womb and he was born an idiot."

Raving, my girl was. Women swept away in the dolour of childbirth would yell out the most outrageous things. Some of it was purest nonsense, and some of it was the hostility and regrets they'd bottled up inside and never given voice to before the pain wrenched it out of them. The midwife who helped me when I birthed Liza told me how I'd cursed the whole night through, wishing every possible calamity to befall my husband. The next morning I hadn't been able to remember a word of it. God willing, it would be just the same for my daughter. Between her pangs, I sang bawdy songs to make her laugh, but she would not allow herself to be comforted.

"Only thing stronger than witchcraft is cunning craft. Keep my baby safe from her. Promise me you won't let that woman near us again."

"Hush, love. You're doing the baby no good, carrying on like that."

But she clung to me and pleaded, gripping my hand hard enough to crack the bones. Her eyes gleamed with real horror. Her legs knifed, her whole frame cramping up. As the pain wracked her, she began to sob. To think I had promised her an easy birth. John's worst imaginings had infected her, and now these travails had pushed her to the brink of hysteria. She was convinced that Anne meant to damage her child. Worse still, her dread awakened my own. What I had witnessed that very day in Anne Whittle's face left me floored—the raging powers inside her rising like floodwater. She was in over her head and there was nowt I could do about it.

"She's not your friend, Mam, she can't be. She's using you. Promise me you'll not keep her company."

If Liza kept on flailing, neither she nor the baby would survive. And if I did nothing to ease her panic, I'd lose them both.

Tibb had admonished me to be careful which road I walked, but in truth no road was simple, straightforward, or, indeed, what it appeared to be at first glimpse. Every path was tricksy, full of turns and twists and blind corners with God-only-knew-what dangers lurking round the bend. If Anne had made herself into the witch that folk had long feared her to be, she'd done it to defend Annie. To save my own daughter, I had to make this vow.

"I promise you, love. Now push when I tell you."

Murmuring too low for Liza to hear, I called out to Tibb to preserve my daughter. A rare light began to flicker and pulse in our dim chamber. Though it seemed that only my eyes saw the glow, it touched us both and in that moment the terror drained from Liza's face. Gasping, she bore down.

At daybreak, when the first rays of sun pierced the mist, the baby came, whole and hale, slipping out easy for me to catch.

"Just look at her," I said to Liza, holding up her daughter before I'd even cut the cord. "Look at your girlchild. She's perfect."

Liza cradled and kissed her, her face lit up in wonder.

After I'd washed my granddaughter and wrapped her in swaddling, I sat a spell with Liza, my arms round her, drinking in her joy.

"In God's name, she's a beauty," my daughter said, stroking the chestnut curls already sprouting from the infant's head. Our child of promise.

"Girl's not like her brother," I told her. "You can see that straight off."

Liza nodded. "A canny one, she'll be. You called on Tibb last night, didn't you?" My daughter took my hand. "Your magic's much stronger than hers."

So she'd not forgotten her ranting about Anne or the promise she had begged me to make. Now she'd hold me to that vow. She would expect me to see Anne as our enemy. Could I really go through with such an awful bargain?

"Let me fetch John," I said, turning away so she wouldn't see my sadness.

But when I saw how our John, full tender, wept over his daughter, just as his wife did, my dark thoughts faded. A voice inside me that was mine, not Tibb's, said *family first*. What was stronger than blood?

"The blessed child," said John.

"Let's call her Alizon." Liza smiled to him. "Can't think of a prettier name."

Even Jamie went soft when he first laid eyes on his little sister. Gentler than I'd ever seen him be, he reached out a timid finger to stroke her tiny hand.

Having come so close to touching death, Liza took weeks to heal. I insisted that she rest in bed with no work but to nurse and cuddle her baby whilst I did the rest. I even used the excuse of tending Liza to stay home from church for an entire month, sending John and Jamie on without me. Wasn't it midwinter, after all, when a newborn was most vulnerable? Liza and Alizon needed all the care I could give them.

Kept snug at home, the baby grew plump and rosy. She was quick to prove her cleverness, so eager to latch on to her mother's breast. Afterward the little one raised her huge blue eyes, still unfocused, to the sound of her mam's cooing and she soon learned to smile.

I was so in love with her, so caught up in our circle of happiness, my bliss was near perfect—unless my thoughts strayed to Anne, whom I'd not seen since St. Stephen's Day. I prayed for her and her girls, yet at the same time I longed to shield my own family from the web of dark magic Anne was caught up in. Was I a fickle friend? Would Anne think that I'd abandoned her when she needed me most?

Round about the old feast of Candlemas, the weather turned mild, the roads dried out, and Liza was on her feet again. It was high time we finally had our little Alizon christened, so off to church we went. My thoughts were on Anne. I fair wondered if I could look her in the eye without my face igniting in shame. At least I could take comfort in the fact that young Assheton had left for Chester. Anne and I would have nothing to fear till he returned.

The instant my family set foot in the churchyard, who waved to us but Anne. For the first time in her sixty-four years she'd come early to church, for she'd heard my little granddaughter was to be christened that day. She'd been missing me, so she had. My heart flooded with memories of everything we'd shared, sticking together in good times and bad. How I yearned to go off somewhere private with her and pour out everything I'd been through since we'd parted on St. Stephen's Day. But before I could get out a word, her eyes rested upon the baby in Liza's arms. My Anne bustled over, no doubt intent on fussing over the pretty little thing.

Liza looked to me in alarm whilst John threw himself in Anne's path. He'd a face like thunder.

"You," he said to my dearest friend, speaking loud to be heard by all the gawping folk in the churchyard. "Stay away from my family."

At the sound of his raised voice, the baby began to cry. Liza turned her back on Anne and hurried into church, leaving Jamie to stumble along after her. John took up the rear, glaring at Anne to keep her distance. The others standing round crowded into church as well, as though they'd no desire to be caught out with the old woman my son-in-law held in such revulsion. In a matter of heartbeats, my friend and I were the only two left amidst the gravestones and glowering yews.

The look on Anne's face said more than any of my fumbling apologies could have done. Nobody's fool was my Anne. She knew that things between us could never be the same again.

"Bess," she said. "Your John Device never cared for me, that much I knew, and your Liza's heart hardened against me ages ago. But never did I dream that you would prove such a turncoat."

My eyes filled with tears as I uttered the words it half-killed me to say: that I'd seen a change in her that left me stark terrified.

"It was *two* clay pictures I saw you and Annie make," I whispered so that none could overhear. "Why two, our Anne? I taught you the craft so that you could protect yourselves, but it's gone beyond that — it's gone well beyond my understanding."

Even as I spoke, I saw Fancy's bruising might clinging to her like a dusky cloud. Mute and trembling, the pair of us were stood there till finally Anne broke the deadlock.

"Think you're too good for me now, our Bess? Think I might taint you? By God, I was there the day they near stoned you for adultery."

Holding her thin frame tall and proud, she swung round and strode into church. That day I was the last one in the door. Bowed and defeated, I joined my family. Empty, I felt, and hollow, as though my heart had fallen out of my ribcage.

After my granddaughter's christening, Anne, who was no

longer my Anne, hurried on her way without another word or glance in my direction.

It was Eastertide before I learned that Robert Assheton was dead. He'd fallen ill in Chester, his body wasting, his mind ravaged. As he languished far from home, the lad declared a hundred times over that Annie Redfearn had cursed him. His cousin, the Dean of Chester, buried him in that city, some said to keep Annie from dancing upon his grave or digging up his bones to use in her unspeakable magics. Though he perished round about Candlemas, the news took months to reach me because folk only dared whisper about it. With the young man dead, it was proof that witches lived amongst us. Our John could not even bring himself to look at Annie when she was stood in church with her hands folded in prayer. So awful was the fear that few had the stomach to speak of it, much less make public accusations. Everybody knew that crying witch could backfire. The Magistrate might come to look upon the accuser with suspicion, or the accused witch herself might be declared innocent and live to hurl even more misery upon any who presumed to denounce her.

Yet even this dread might have eased with time had not Christopher Assheton, the dead lad's father, begun to ail at Maudlintide, just before the beginning of the wheat harvest. He didn't point the finger at Anne or her family—he didn't dare. He suffered and he pined, confiding to his daughter Margaret that he, too, had been bewitched, only he didn't have the nerve to name the ones he suspected. By Michaelmas he was dead. All I could think of was the second clay picture I'd seen Annie shaping that last December, how she'd passed it across the beck for her mother to finish. For the life of me, I couldn't begrudge them for what they'd done to Robert, but why his father? Then I asked myself if Christopher Assheton had died of witchcraft or of grieving his son who had died so young and so disturbed. A parent's love is a powerful thing, and at the root of Anne's terrible magic was a mother's fierce devotion to her daughter.

I kept my own part in this business silent. If I'd been bold enough to ask Anne's opinion, no doubt she'd have told me I was a bald-faced hypocrite who did my all to preserve my own reputation as a cunning woman for the sake of my family and our livelihood whilst allowing her and Annie to carry the full weight of blame as the rumours descended. After Robert and Christopher Assheton's deaths, the gulf between Anne and I only widened with more pain, more hurt, till a hell-deep abyss plunged between us. A wrenching thing, it was, when my dearest friend became my rival and foe. Anne had loved me, perhaps more than any other living soul ever had. As my cuckolded husband would have told me, the quickest thing to turn to hate is love betrayed.

Anne's powers rose like a column of smoke in a clear summer sky whilst mine began to ebb. I still chanted my blessings and walked my rounds with my pouch of herbs, but my days as sole cunning woman of Pendle Forest were over. Now we'd Anne to reckon with, Anne who had grown fair unstoppable.

# II

# THE BLACK DOG

*Alizon Device*

# 9

FROM EARLIEST CHILDHOOD, I learned to safe-keep secrets in the chamber of my heart. I knew how to keep silence. Life or death could hang in the balance.

My earliest memory was walking hand in hand with my gran into a manse with arched windows and ivied walls. Five years old, I was, my bare feet padding upon rushes scented with lavender and rosemary, my eyes huge to take in the silver candlesticks, the tables and chairs of massive carved oak, dark with age. A lady came to greet us, her face lighting up at the sight of Gran. Her hair was half black, half silver, reminding me of a magpie's wing.

After whispered words with Gran, Alice Nutter, mistress of Roughlee Hall, led us into a chamber where the shutters and thick draperies were drawn against the July sun. Upon a massive four-poster lay the oldest man I'd ever seen, the lady's husband. So shrivelled and shrunken in on himself, he was, it seemed a marvel that he still breathed. His parchment skin was stretched taut in pain.

"My children are away with kin," I heard Mistress Alice tell Gran. "I've called them home, but I don't know whether they can return in time."

Whilst I stood by, eyeing her every move, Gran set to work with her herbs, brewing them over a fire that blazed in that very room though it was high summer. Poppy seed, said Gran, would ease his suffering. After she tipped the draught into his mouth,

Old Master Nutter smiled, the tightness in his face unfurling some. Gran and Mistress Alice prayed over him with strange words that I knew from their sound and music, for I'd heard Gran chant them many a time, though I did not yet understand their meaning. But I lisped along all the same as I watched Mistress Alice threading dark red beads through her fingers.

Old Master Nutter reached for his wife's hand. "Bring her to me one last time before I go."

I'd no clue what he was on about, but Mistress Alice understood straightaway. She and Gran traded a look, then Gran took my hand as if to lead me from the room.

"You can stay," Mistress Alice told her.

"The child, too?" Gran asked.

"Why should she not see it at least once in her life?" Mistress Alice smiled in sadness. "She might not have another chance."

By now I was well curious, gawping with huge eyes as Mistress Alice went to tap upon a panel of plain wood behind the chimney breast. The answering knock that came from within made me jump. Did goblins and boggarts live inside her walls? Gran put her hands over my eyes, but I peeked between her fingers to see the panel open like a door. Then Mistress Alice invited us both to pass with her into that secret place.

A narrow stair led upward to a hidden chamber beneath the eaves, a place of windowless darkness lit only by pricks of candle flame. A sweet fragrance I couldn't name tinged the stale air. When my eyes grew accustomed to the murk, I gave a cry to see a ghost-white young man staring at us. But Mistress Alice curtseyed and spoke to him, proving that he was a creature of flesh and blood.

Only then did I dare look round the chamber to see the wonders hidden there. A candle in a lamp of red glass hung from the shadowy beams. There was a great table covered in embroidered cloth and above it a cross with a man's tortured body nailed to it. The sight made me twist my head in fear. Then Gran turned me round to face the most beautiful thing I'd ever seen: a statue of a lady with flowing hair and tender eyes, her arms outstretched as if to embrace me.

"That's Our Lady," Gran whispered. "The Queen of Heaven."

Stood upon a crescent moon, the lady was, her lovely head crowned in a circle of stars. Rays of sun adorned her blue-painted gown.

"Once she'd her own altar in the New Church," Gran told me. "Then Master Nutter had to hide her to keep her safe."

I fair wondered what was harder to believe: that this lady's statue had once dwelt within our stark whitewashed church or that the old, old man in the room below had ever been strong enough to rescue anything.

The young man had donned a robe and placed a stole round his neck. Full reverent, he lifted the lady from her niche and bore her down the narrow stairs and into Master Nutter's chamber whilst the rest of us followed behind as if in procession. When the young man set her upon the bedside table, the old man's eyes softened. He'd a look of purest bliss and comfort.

Mistress Alice checked the bolts on the doors and shutters. Meanwhile, the young man fetched all manner of things from his hiding place and arranged them upon a table in the room. A silver chalice and plate, they were, and a silver box, the sight of which made Gran cross herself. In a voice rich as his face was wan, the young man sang the secret words, all the more powerful because I didn't understand them. Gran knelt, tears streaming down her face, and I trembled at the mystery of it, gazing at the star-crowned lady who shimmered in the candle glow. Then the young man raised up a round white wafer, and though I was only five, I knew I beheld something holy and rare.

The young man gave the wafer to Old Master Nutter and anointed him with oils, chanting over him just like Gran would do when she was blessing someone, and I asked myself if he, too, was one of the cunning folk. Before I could catch another glimpse, Gran drew me to the other end of the chamber to give the two men their privacy as murmured words passed between them.

"He's preparing Master Nutter's soul for the next world," Gran told me.

Closing my eyes, I tried to picture the world beyond this one and what it might look like. I'd always thought of heaven as a place made of clouds, but when I tried to conjure up paradise, I saw a deep green wood, thick and lush, with bluebells growing everywhere.

When it was all done and Master Nutter was dozing peaceful with his wife holding his hand, the young man gathered his things to return them to their hiding place. Gran and I needed to wait till the room was clear before we could unbolt the chamber door and go on our way.

Just when I thought the young man would vanish inside the walls like a phantom, he approached Gran, his face full sombre, and asked if she'd anything to confess. Though he was but a scrawny thing, it was a long look he was giving her and one that I knew well even at that age—the look that folk gave Gran when they didn't quite approve of her reputation.

Only a short while ago, Gran had gone down on her knees and wept to hear him sing. But now she stood her ground, stolid as a badger. This man might have hidden power and authority, but so did my gran, and he knew it.

"Peace, Father," she said, and I thought it was well odd she should call him that since she was old enough to be *his* gran. "My sins are between me and God."

"You must not breathe a word to anyone about what you saw today," Gran told me on the walk home. "He has to hide or else he'll be chopped to pieces. Butchered like a pig."

"That's why he never smiled," I said, thinking of how the young man lived in the dark, the sunlight never touching his face.

"Bless him, but he was dour as any Puritan." Gran's eyes were miles away. "Didn't used to be like that, love. Even your mam's too young to remember, but back in my day there was more to religion than all this hush and doom."

As we walked along Pendle Water, hand in hand amongst the birch trees, she told me how she once led the procession on the Feast of the Assumption, a crown of roses upon her hair, how they used to dance within the very nave of the church. Gran was so wise because she remembered the lost things that other people had never known, even that pale young priest.

I knew two things for certain. Most important was that Gran was the most powerful cunning woman in Pendle. When all else failed, she'd the gift to mend what was broken. Mistress Alice's priest had reason to both fear and respect her, and I wondered if the Magistrate himself ever reaped such awe—when had he ever healed a person? In truth, Gran was mightier than any soul I'd ever met. My mother's anger and my father's fears crumbled before her. Before I came into this world, Mam was a charmer, too, yet never anything like Gran, whose match was nowhere to be found. Second thing I knew, sure as my own brother's face, was that Anne Chattox's curse hung over my family in defiance of Gran's powers.

The first sign was delivered not a fortnight after I'd seen the forbidden priest and the statue of Our Lady. On a sunlit afternoon I was helping Gran weed her herb garden. She gave me a catmint leaf to taste but told me to stay well away from the monkshood, for it was potent poison even though its blue flowers were dazzling as the Virgin's mantle.

Gone to Colne Market, my parents were, and my brother was mucking out the byre. So it was just the two of us in Gran's garden, her telling me stories of the Queen of Elfhame riding through the greenwood upon her white mare, when we both looked up to see a woman stood at the garden gate. Leaving me in the mint patch, Gran went out to speak to her. First I thought nothing of it, for folk were always calling on my gran, asking her for a blessing or potion.

But the woman started railing at Gran. "You think you can just wash your hands of us? You made my mam what she is."

Whilst our visitor carried on like a drunken fishwife, her mouth twisted ugly-wide, Gran was stood quiet, saying, "Peace, Betty, peace."

My own parents had told me that Betty Whittle was a fiendish one. So off I bolted to fetch Jamie. Though unkind folk claimed there were sheep with sharper wits than my brother, our Jamie was fearsome-protective of Gran and me. Brandishing the manure fork, he came charging as if fixing to stab Betty through the heart with those dung-caked prongs. Seeing what she was up against, Betty shut her wicked gob and scarpered. Jamie made to chase her, but Gran laid a hand on his arm.

"Let her be, love."

"I'm fair clemmed," our Jamie replied. He always said he was clemmed. I never saw a body eat so much as my brother.

So Gran promised us bread, butter, and soft new cheese from the dairy. Skipping with each step, I led the way to the house but froze at the sight of our open door swinging in the breeze. So that slattern had barged her way into Malkin Tower. There, before our hearth, she'd dumped a filthy old sack.

"Alizon, no!" Gran cried out, but I was a wilful thing, too quick for her to stop.

Pouncing on the sack, I opened it and what tumbled out but a human skull. Empty eyeholes stared back at me, mocking me as I shrieked. Four teeth still stuck to the jaw, fixed in a ghastly grimace. Scarier than the skull itself was the look on Gran's face as she crumpled to the floor. The way she cupped her hand to her mouth, I thought she was going to be sick.

Anxious to give comfort, I patted her arm. "Don't be sad. We can hide it."

"Aye," she said, wiping away tears. "We'd better do just that before your parents come home. Not a word to your father, you two. Thing like this could frighten the life out of the man."

Of the three of us, Jamie showed the least fear. Sometimes it was a blessing to be simple of mind. My brother scooped up the skull as if it were no eerier than a cabbage and tossed it back into the sack.

Whilst I clambered upon the gate to watch for my parents, who were due back from market any moment, Gran gave orders to Jamie, who dug fast and furious behind the manure heap. After he'd buried the skull, Gran had my brother rake fresh manure over the filled-in hole so that Father would never notice it, or so we hoped.

In spite of the pains we'd taken, my father returned home ashen-faced, for he and Mam had passed Betty on the road. My parents could tell just from her smirk that she'd been by Malkin Tower.

"What does Chattox's daughter want from us?" Father asked Gran.

Before Gran could get a word in, Mam spoke up, saying it was bad blood. Though Chattox sought to earn her bread as a cunning woman, folk favoured Gran over her and why wouldn't they, seeing how Gran had kept her name clean whilst there were rumours about Chattox that were too dark to even name. That was why Chattox's family struggled whilst ours prospered.

When Mam reached the end of her tirade, Gran's face clouded as though something needled her, and she said we should pray for Chattox and her daughters. A hard time they were having with Tom Redfearn dead and Annie's new baby to feed. Our gran was a soft one, always making excuses for folk.

Father was soft, too, but he knew danger when he saw it. To ward us from evil, he stirred up the embers in the hearth and cast in salt till the flames leapt and hissed.

This I'll confess: Of my two parents, I loved Father best. I loved him more than the sun and moon, almost more than I loved Gran. Such a gentle soul he was, ever mild with Jamie and me, even when Mam's temper flared. Once, whilst we were out walking along the beck, he showed me a nesting mother duck. Together we watched how she spread her wings to shield her little duck-lings. So it was with Father. If he bridled each time he crossed paths with Chattox or her kin, it was only because he wanted to protect us. I prayed that his love and Gran's magic would be strong enough to keep harm at bay. Yet after Betty's unwelcome visit, I saw that skull whenever I closed my eyes. Though we'd buried it, that thing haunted me and filled my nightmares.

In church I only dared peek at Chattox sideways whilst hidden behind my mother's skirts. Every inch the witch she looked. As old as Gran was Chattox, but with none of Gran's warmth. Her wrinkled skin, thin and speckled with age, barely masked the skull beneath, and when she drew back her lips in what passed for a smile, yellow wolf teeth winked from her gums. Sometimes she was bold enough to grin at Gran, fixing her with her green serpent's eyes, and then I'd see my Gran blink back tears. Even as a little girl I sensed that Gran was sore tormented by secrets from her past and that they'd everything to do with Chattox, her former friend who had turned against her.

A few weeks on, we came home from church to find that the rusty old lock on our door had been forced. Gran's herbs, torn down from the beam where they had hung, lay scattered and trampled. In the place where Betty had left the skull last time were our emptied barrels of oats and meal. My mam began cursing like a bailiff, never mind that it was Sabbath Day. She pointed to the gaping box that had held our linen clothes: our spare smocks and the good collar bands and coifs we wore only at Christmas, Eas-ter, and weddings. Our precious finery earned by my father's hard work, our only possessions that set us apart from ordinary poor folk — all of it was gone. The oats, meal, and linen together were worth a good twenty shillings, so my parents reckoned, more than my father could earn in five years.

"I'll see her hang for this," said my mam. "She'll feed the crows."

"And what would her mother do to us then?" Father asked. If

Mam's face was red as slaughter day, his was white as wax. "Chattox would strike back even harder."

"He's right," Gran said, heaving herself off her stool where she'd sat, silent and brooding through the storm of my mam's rage. "I'll sort this."

Without another word, she trudged out the door, no doubt on her way to Chattox's cottage, leaving us to gawp after her.

Not till daylight gate did she return, limping and footsore, but she shouldered our bag of meal and our good linen clothes. Mam went over the collars and coifs, piece by piece, inspecting them for tears and stains.

"I told them to keep the oats," Gran said. "They're down to skin and bone. Old Anne lies ill and Annie's baby has the colic. Our John," she said to my father, "I gave my word that we'd give them a dole of oats every year and Betty promised not to trouble us again."

Mam was having none of it. "How could you be so witless? Betty robs us and you want to reward them!"

"We won't go hungry," said Gran. "Anthony Holden's a good master. He won't let us starve."

Father remained uncertain. "Oats or no oats, Chattox won't rest till she sees us rot."

In 1601, the year I turned six, summer never came. We'd cold, overcast days, the heavens pelting down rain that flooded the fields and caused black mould to blight the wheat. Pastures turned to quagmires. Our cattle began to suffer afflictions. One cow died, another sickened, a third fell lame, a fourth stopped giving milk. Of the young stock born that year, one was born with the mule foot and another had the waterhead. A third was a weaver calf, pacing ever back and forth till at last it dropped dead.

Worse were the August hailstorms, casting down stones big as robins' eggs. Two of our laying hens we lost to the hail, and

Anthony Holden of Bull Hole Farm lost a foal. Crops of barley, oats, and wheat lay wasted in the fields. God was trying us, so the Curate said, punishing us for our sins.

As we could barely feed everyone at Malkin Tower, our payment of oats to Chattox came to an end. Weren't we living on nettle soup ourselves? That winter Death's hand closed round our throats. Though Father himself admitted we could not sacrifice the dole of oats to Chattox, he could not stop looking over his shoulder, near crazed for fear of her wrath. If she so much as glanced his way in church with that look of bitterness, full of wounding power, my poor father staggered. Before Christmas he took to his pallet with a fearsome ague. Already wasted with hunger, he'd no strength left in him to fight it off. Gran brewed her herbs, laid poultices on him to draw out the fever, blessed him, and prayed over him till she fair lost her voice. But no ordinary physick could mend him. Father fell into strange fits, his limbs lashing out, his eyes rolling. What ailed him could only be witchcraft. Most wrenching was his horror as he swore that this was Chattox's revenge on him for denying her the oats.

Gran worked her counterspells. She threw what salt we could spare into the fire, blessed horseshoes, rowan crosses, and crooked nails, and hung them over every door and window. She stoned a magpie and strung it up on the elder tree out back, yet still the fever and fits would not loosen their grip on my father. Meanwhile, my mother grew frantic.

"You're stronger than she is," Mam pleaded to Gran. "I can't lose him. Please, there must be something more you can do."

Gran took our last living hen, pure black and full mettlesome, stuck her full of pins, then burned her alive whilst chanting her countermagic against Chattox. The bird seemed to shriek out in agony just as an old woman would do. An almighty stink filled the air as first the feathers burned, then the quills, and finally the flesh, bearing the aroma of a good supper till stink erupted from the unclean bowels. The flames raged like hellfire, charring the fowl's bones black. Next Gran took a handful of our precious store of oats, mixed it with my father's piss, made a cake of it, and, having named the cake Chattox, burned that, too.

Wind brewed up in a tempest, battering the shutters and bolted door. It howled down the chimney like the Gabriel Hounds baying for blood. Sparks of fire flew in a whirlwind and skittered across the floor, setting fire to the rushes. Jamie and I lunged round, stamping them out.

When the storm was at its wildest, there came such a bang upon the door, loud enough to rouse Father from his stupor. I ran headlong to Mam, burying my face in her apron, whilst she cradled my head with trembling hands. *This* was my gran's terrible magic. Every part of me froze and I thought I would crack apart. *Who* was stood outside our door? Another knock sounded, causing my father to moan and thrash. Even Jamie spooked. Loud and fast came the pounding. Mam edged to Father's pallet and reached for his hand. I wrapped my arms round his neck and put my ear to his chest to listen to his wild-thudding heart. All the while Gran was stood before the door, holding the bolt firm in place. Each one of us thought it was Chattox on the other side, trying to claw her way in. The spell had summoned the witch to show herself at the house of her victim. But if Gran were soft and showed Chattox mercy, allowing her to step in out of the storm, the spell would be broken and with it any hope of releasing my father from that witch's grip. Up to Chattox, it was, to end this thing. Tears streaming down her face, Gran braced herself against the door as the pounding dragged on and on. A shambling old woman locked out in such weather was certain to die, leaving Father to live.

Malkin Tower seemed to twist round and round, and I fell into a swoon, my arms still clinging to my father's neck.

In dawn's grey light, I awoke to unearthly stillness. In the night Mam had carried me to my pallet. Gran had collapsed in a heap, her head against the bolted door. I watched Mam help her to her stool.

"Is Father better?" I asked.

Neither Mam nor Gran said a word.

The storm had died. Full determined, Mam unbolted the door. The terror of what lay outside made me fly straight into Gran's lap. She caught me in her arms as though I were her last comfort.

What did Mam expect to find when she opened that door— Chattox's rain-sodden corpse? She found nothing. Not a single footprint.

"It can't be," she said. "We heard that knocking."

I just sobbed whilst Gran kept her silence.

"Could it have been the tapping of a branch, do you think? Could she have sent her imp to plague us?" Mam crumbled to her knees beside Gran. "You said it would work."

Wrenching her head away, Gran pushed me out of her arms and into my mam's. Then she hoisted herself off her stool and headed for my father's pallet. Struggling loose from my mother's embrace, I flew past Gran to be the first one to see how he fared.

Father's face was grey as gravedust. His eyes bulged wide, fixed on some almighty terror, his mouth frozen open in a mute cry. His skin was cold as the chill creeping up my back. With a scream, I tore out of the tower as though an army of demons were chasing me. Racing to the top of Blacko Hill, I howled till I was hoarse.

When hunger finally drove me down, I found Gran crouched near her herb garden. Weeping bitter, she hacked the frost-hard earth with her spade, digging dandelion root to boil in a broth that would be our only food now that she'd burned our last chicken. Even after raising the most horrendous magic she could muster, Gran hadn't been able to defeat Chattox but was left to grub in the dirt like the lowliest of creatures.

Seeing me through her tears, she reached for my hand. "Our Alizon, sometimes God is cruel. I'd have given my own life gladly if only he would have let your poor father live."

. . .

A part of me died the day that Uncle Kit and Matthew Holden lowered my father's coffin into the black earth. I fair longed to pitch myself down that dank hole and let myself be buried with him. I shook in my desolation and fury. Chattox had murdered my father and not even Gran had been able to save him. The final insult was that the witch was going to get away with it. Gran had forbidden Mam to breathe a word of it to anyone. *If we go round crying witch, what do you think folk will say about us?* On this Gran was well stubborn. The Constable would take one look at Chattox and one look at Gran and see two old women who meddled in spellcraft and sorcery. Our hands were tied. No justice for my father, only this bottomless loss. A lucky thing for Chattox that she was ill in bed that day, or claimed to be, for if she had dared to show her face at Father's funeral, I would have sprung at her like a wildcat and raked her flesh raw with my fingernails.

I sobbed like an abandoned child, not allowing Gran or Mam to give me any comfort. I wouldn't let anyone so much as lay a finger on me till Alice Nutter, graceful in her dark widow's gown, took my chin in her gloved hand. With her lace-trimmed handkerchief, she wiped my eyes and snotty nose as though I were her own little girl.

Putting her lips to my ear, she whispered words I would never forget. "Your father's bound for heaven, sweetheart. When you miss him, you can pray for him. God will listen and your father will know that you keep his memory alive in your heart."

After kissing my forehead, Mistress Nutter went to Mam and Gran, not saying a word, but clasping their hands and standing with them in silence a spell, her head bowed with theirs.

I turned to my father's grave, now piled high with holly, pine boughs, and ivy. It being the dead of winter, there were no flowers to be had. Mistress Nutter's words rang inside me like a promise: I could pray for Father and he would look down from heaven and know how much I loved him.

A small, thin hand reached out to offer me a bough of sweet-smelling juniper. I found myself staring into the wide brown eyes of Nancy, the Holdens' youngest daughter, one year older than I was. She gave me a shy hug, patting my back till I hugged her in return.

Folk were kind in showing us their sympathy. Anthony Holden paid for the funeral and delivered a sack of meal to Malkin Tower so we wouldn't go hungry. Mistress Nutter rode by to bring us winter apples and a flask of dark-red wine. But nothing could take away the anguish of losing both Father and our livelihood in one blow.

The omens were too powerful for Master Holden to ignore. Not only had his best cowman died, but he'd lost a quarter of his herd, and what could have caused that but blackest witchcraft. Though he made no accusations against Chattox, he'd the good sense to move his remaining cattle from the fields near Malkin Tower back to the pastures near his own home. His son Matthew, the boy Gran had once cured, was now old enough to take Father's place as cowman.

After burying my father, we came back to an empty shippon. No more work for Mam in the dairy, no more fresh milk or cream, butter or cheese. With Jamie too simple to find good, steady work and me too young, Mam wandered from farm to farm, doing whatever was asked of her in exchange for bread.

Though Gran carried on with her cunning craft, she was never the same after my father's death. A filmy grey caul began to creep over her eyes, clouding her sight, till after a year or so, she needed me to lead her round by the hand. Jamie held Chattox responsible for Gran's blindness, but Gran herself said that it was the price she'd paid for living so long when most folk died much younger. There was a price to be paid for everything, so Gran believed.

With Gran losing her sight, we'd every reason to believe that God had forsaken us. If the hardship didn't finish my family off, the grieving would. Our Jamie was inconsolable. Once I found him battering the gateposts with his fists. I had to beg him to stop and I took his hands in mine before he reduced his own to bloody stumps. My brother just couldn't get it through his head that our father had left us to slumber in the sod. Gran staggered round like a ghost as though she blamed our tragedy on her misbegotten spell. As for Mam, it was as though her life had come to an end. By night she wept till the flesh round her eyes was raw and bruised.

For the life of me, I tried to forgive my mam for what happened next. Before I was even born, she'd forsaken her own powers. What she did after Father's demise seemed like madness. If she heard Gran whispering the most harmless blessing, she'd leg it out the door as though she thought that even the most goodwilled healing charm was the Devil's work. If Mam so much as heard me murmur the Ave Maria, she'd order me to leave off with the popish wickedness.

Found religion had Mam, and not the comfort of Gran's old faith with the saints and the Mother of Mercy, either, but the new religion in all its harsh austerity. If I didn't know better I'd say she was bewitched, that she'd come under the spell of the new Church Warden, Richard Baldwin of Wheathead, who singled out Mam for his special attention. His wife being ill, he had hired my mam to help in his household and there she became wise to his ways, learning his Psalms by memory since she couldn't read. Mam spent more time at his home than ours, and when she did show her face at Malkin Tower, she near did our heads in with her talk of sin and brimstone, the chosen few and the damned multitudes. Maybe she believed that if she bore this splintery cross, she could redeem herself, wash her soul clean of shame. In truth, she embraced more than religion during her first year of widowhood.

Goodwife Baldwin was bedridden and ailing, never to recover, and full senseless most of the time. Though a Puritan, Dick Baldwin was still a man with needs he could no longer ignore, and Mam was so lonely, so willing to make any sacrifice to win a man's love again. And so it came to pass. She offered herself to that horse-faced man with a smile like vinegar. Where Father had been gentle and yielding, Dick Baldwin was stern and severe. Perhaps Mam hoped his staunchness would lend her the strength she needed to endure her loss. No doubt, in her heart of hearts, she nursed the hope that he would marry her when his wife passed on, as the woman was sure to do any day or week. Mam was already doting on Baldwin's small daughter to prove her worth as a stepmother.

Meanwhile, she neglected Jamie and me, her own half-orphans who needed her as never before. So what did my brother and I do but learn to place our trust in Gran instead of our inconstant mother. In our loneliness, Jamie and I stuck together like two burrs. If anybody was fool enough to call my brother an idiot in my earshot, I'd lob the offender's head with a rain of earth clods and manure. By and by, folk learned not to mock Jamie when I was at hand. God knew Jamie needed every bit of succour I could give him, for his lot was never an easy one. After Master Holden moved his herd from Malkin Tower, my brother was left to wander from village to farm, begging for work and food.

As for Chattox, she got her comeuppance in a manner of speaking, or at least her daughter Betty did. Though my family had never breathed a word to the Constable of the theft at Malkin Tower, Betty Whittle just couldn't keep herself out of harm's way. Being a witch's daughter, maybe she thought she was too crafty to be caught, or that Gran's reluctance to condemn Betty had proven to the whole parish that she could do as she pleased and get away with it. Then Betty made the mistake of robbing her landlady. On laundry day at Greenhead, Betty was brazen — or gormless — enough to snatch a linen sheet hung up to dry. Wasn't like stealing from poor, simple folk, this. The servants raised the alarm, and the gardener caught Betty round the waist. Margaret Crook, sister to dead Robert Assheton whom folk said Chattox and Annie Redfearn had bewitched, sent for the Magistrate, who examined Betty at Read Hall. Then off to Lancaster she was marched. On account of her poverty, the Judge took pity, sentencing her not to the gallows but to a living death in prison. When Betty did meet her end, it wasn't in a public spectacle, dangling on the end of the hangman's rope. Instead, a month after her trial, she perished of gaol fever, louse-ridden and half-starved.

After that Chattox seemed well gutted, dragging herself round like some sick and beaten dog. No one denounced her now because she had grown too pitiful. Least she seemed to know enough by then to leave my family alone.

Our spot of good luck during those years of mourning arose from a dispute over property boundaries. It came to be known that Malkin Tower and the tiny plot of land upon which it was stood belonged not to the Nowells of Read Hall as folk had believed, but to Alice Nutter, who was the most gracious landlady we could have wished for. A great almsgiver was our Mistress Alice. She would never let her tenants suffer hunger or turn them out of their cottages. Assured that our home at least was secure, Gran, Jamie, and I rubbed along well, just the three of us, resigned to Mam's desertion.

But soon enough my mam returned to the fold. She reaped nothing but bitter disgrace from her dealings with the pious Master Baldwin, who trusted himself to be one of the Elect to inherit the heavenly and everlasting kingdom of his narrow-hearted God. Instead of marrying her, he cast her out as a wanton as soon as she confessed she was carrying his child. Left her to bear his bastard alone did Baldwin, without surrendering a penny to feed mother or babe. Gran brought out the tansy, offering to brew a dose for Mam. She told my mother that she'd be a fool to have this child, but Mam was so heartbroken, so ill-done-to, and she saw this baby as her one consolation, a blameless new life she could cherish. The baby would love her, so Mam hoped, even if Baldwin despised her. Only Gran's fearsome repute as a cunning woman and her vow to reveal Baldwin's shame stayed the Curate and the Constable from pillorying my mother for her out-of-wedlock pregnancy.

Often I asked myself how differently our fates would have spun out had Mam heeded Gran's counsel and never allowed Baldwin's bastard to see the light of day. As it stood, our lives were forever changed. In 1603, the year our Queen died and her Scottish cousin rose to the throne, Mam gave birth to my half-sister, Jennet — borne of Baldwin's unholy lust and my mother's unending grief.

# 10

OF ALL MY FAMILY, I alone could pass as a girl like any other. I wasn't simple like my brother, nor cock-eyed like my mam, nor a bastard like my sister, nor a cunning woman like Gran. Though I loved my family more than anything, I cherished the fact that I wasn't marked out as the rest of them were.

I felt right sorry for little Jennet. Though Mam had named her after Jennet Preston, her dear childhood friend, and though she had insisted on giving her the surname Device so that my sister would at least bear the name of a good and kindly man, Jennet was the cuckoo in our nest, Baldwin's seed growing up at Malkin Tower. With her mousy hair, her pinched face, her cold blue eyes, she was the very picture of him. Like Baldwin himself, little Jennet seemed to spurn Mam's love. Kept herself to herself, that child. If I tried to cuddle her close, she shoved me away.

"In God's name, I wish Mam wasn't so *ugly*," our Jennet told me one morning, lying beside me upon the pallet we shared.

She was seven years old and had wrenched me awake from a dream of Gran trying to fit a wreath of roses round my head. *Time for the procession. You'll lead them all on Assumption Day.*

"And I wish Gran wasn't such a frightful old thing," my sister rattled on in her singsong.

Sitting up, my head still ringing from that dream, I looked to the door leading into the next room where Mam and Gran were fixing breakfast, and I prayed that neither of them had heard the little traitor. God forgive me, but there were times when I fair wished I could pack the brat off and send her back to Baldwin. Let him try raising her.

"Suit yourself," I told Jennet. "Go find yourself another family."

Leaving my sister to chew on that, I dressed and tied my hair up with the rose-coloured satin ribbon Nancy Holden had given me for Christmas. That summer I was fifteen and Nancy was my dearest friend in all the world.

"I'm off to work at the Holdens," I told Mam on my way out the door. So eager was I to be with my friend, I hadn't the patience to wait till the porridge was ready.

"Work?" Mam looked up from the pot she was stirring. "You're more like to while away the hours gabbing with that girl."

"Leave her be," said Gran, winking at me as though she knew just what I had dreamt.

In truth, our gran did look a frightful thing. Her coif was askew and her grey hair, thick and unruly, sprang out every which way, but most unnerving were her eyes, milky and clouded. When she aimed those eyes at you, you'd quail, for she truly *saw* folk with those cauled eyes of hers — saw what they hid inside and was never fooled by their masks or their lies.

"A true friend is the most precious gift," Gran said, smiling wistful, and I thought with sadness how she had once been friends with Chattox before it turned bad.

"I'll bring back bread," I said, kissing Gran's cheek. "And buttercake!"

At Bull Hole Farm, they'd wool to card and spin, cream to churn into butter — more chores than hands in their household. Whenever I was in need of honest work or just wanted to call in, they welcomed me. Even when I was doing some lowly task, it was never drudgery if I could pass some time with my friend.

Soon as I neared the house, Nancy darted out, apron flapping, eyes sparking in her gladness to see me. Taking my hands, she pulled me into the kitchen where her mam made much of me.

"Our Alizon!" Sarah Holden said. "I'll wager you've eaten nothing this day."

Arms a-flutter, she sat me down at her scrubbed table and brought me a bowl of steaming beef broth with barley and onion. Nancy poured me a mug of small beer.

"No use working on an empty stomach." Clucking and fussing, Mistress Holden filled my bowl again soon as I'd emptied it. I think she loved to stuff me because her own daughter was so thin, without much in the way of appetite, and she wanted to set an example for Nancy as to how much a healthy girl could eat.

Nancy's mam wasn't a bit like mine. Sarah Holden had no deformity, no blot on her reputation, but was her husband's stout-hearted wife, her children's proud mother: a broad-faced country woman with strong cheekbones and clear brown eyes.

Though I knew it disloyal of me, and I feared it made me no better than cold little Jennet, I envied Nancy her mother and her happy home. The only daughter left in the house now that her sisters had married, Nancy was her mam's pet and she, in turn, loved to cosset her small nieces and nephews, half-orphaned after her brother Matthew's wife had died having the last baby. Whilst I was sat at the table, the children crowded round to watch me eat, all of them laughing and joking and jibing. Well I remembered the story of how Gran blessed and mended Matthew when he was no bigger than the tousle-headed tot cuddled up by my side. That was why I, Mother Demdike's granddaughter, was ever welcome here. Yet I allowed myself to fancy I was no kin to Gran, but one of the Holdens' own; that Nancy, not Jennet, was my blood-sister; that Anthony Holden, respected by everyone, was my father; and Matthew, strong and kind, the older brother who looked after me.

Children of the sun, the Bull Hole Holdens were, whilst I was a child of the moon. They lived with the warm light a-glow on their faces whilst I dwelled in the shadows. When they left the haven of their home to walk abroad through Pendle Forest, nobody whispered rumours about them. They were spotless.

But envy was a sin, so I tried to put such thoughts out of my mind. Truly it was enough for me to bask in Nancy's friendship and her mother's hospitality. If I spent enough hours at Bull Hole Farm, I could almost believe I was as blessed as Nancy.

Late in the afternoon Nancy kissed me goodbye, and Mistress Holden sent me home with a basket stuffed with bread, cheese, and cake. Even Jennet would smile to see me bringing home such bounty. I was walking past Moss End Farm with nary an evil thought in my mind when a stone whizzed past my face. Spun round, I did then, to see eleven-year-old Isobel Bulcock sat upon the gate and grinning like one of Chattox's imps.

"Witchblood! You've the witchblood! Your granny's nowt but a blind old witch!" The pudding-faced brat swung her grubby bare feet back and forth. "Devil stole her eyes away."

"Shut it, you," I said, turning square to face her.

"Your mam's a whore!" Issy said, growing ever bolder.

Behind the gate a few other children ducked and giggled, daring Issy on.

"Your brother's an idiot. He eats dirt, he's so dim."

God forgive me, but I'd inherited my mam's quick temper. Setting my basket down, I stalked toward Issy. The nearer I drew, the paler Issy became. Her cruel smile vanished and the other children's jeering died. When I was close enough for my breath to hit her face, Issy's mouth hung in a frightened O as though she longed to scream but had lost her voice.

"Mind your tongue, you devil's spawn," I told her, quiet and chill. "If ever I hear you gabbing on about my family like that again, I'll give you something to cry about, our Issy."

Then I turned, picked up my basket, and strode off homeward, my head held high as though I were leading the procession Gran had spoken of in my dream.

Though I did my best to appear calm on the outside, I was seething. *Whores and witches.* That was what Baldwin called us. To think I'd hear those words from young Issy. Her father, Henry

Bulcock, was Uncle Kit's old friend, and Jane Bulcock, her mother, had always been good to my family. If our friends' children could spew such awful rubbish, I fair wondered what our enemies were saying about us.

When I reached the gate of Malkin Tower, my heart lightened to see our Jamie stood there, beaming and proud, holding up a dead hare by its hind legs. God's teeth, my brother had been poaching again. Though I'd no business encouraging him in such lawlessness, I couldn't help but smile to see him so happy. When times were hard, our Jamie always found a way to put meat on our table. Even if he was simple, he did his best for us.

Two days passed in peace. Of an early morning I went to Bull Hole Farm, passing by Moss End, but Issy didn't show herself. On the third day, when I reached home of an overcast evening, tired but cheerful from my hours with Nancy, Gran seized me by my wrists soon as I stepped in.

"Henry Bulcock came by today. He says you bewitched his Issy."

First I could only laugh, but Gran was dead earnest, her face as long as my arm.

"By Our Lady, I never cursed that spoilt chit!" My face burned at the unfairness of the accusation. "What a little liar, that Issy. Gave her the devil, I did, on account of her goading me first, but nowt more. Now I wish I *had* bewitched her. Might at least shut her up."

"Never say such a thing, even in jest," Gran begged me.

Then I saw how truly frightened she was. Had it come down to this, that an eleven-year-old could condemn a person for witchcraft after trading a few heated words?

"Course I didn't bewitch her," I said to Gran. "I haven't the powers."

"Only Gran and me can curse and bless," our Jamie broke in. "We've familiars but you haven't."

So my brother now claimed to be a cunning man with a familiar spirit like Gran's Tibb? A right mess he would get us in if he went round announcing that to folk.

"Don't butt in where you've no business," Gran said to Jamie. "Go on outside. Alizon and I must talk in private."

"Talk in private with Jennet around?" I pointed at my sister who gawped from her perch in the corner as though she wanted to commit our every word to memory so she could blab it about Colne Market.

"Alizon will get the powers by and by," Jamie declared in a voice loud enough to be heard in Yorkshire. "She'll meet her black dog."

"What black dog, you daft thing?" In the whirl of confusion, I couldn't help but raise my voice. "Have you all gone mad?"

"Enough!" Gran's fist slammed down upon the table. A rare thing, it was, for her to lose her temper with us, but when it happened, we quietened down right quick.

Mam grabbed Jamie and Jennet and dragged them out the door, leaving me and Gran alone.

"Now tell me, what did you say to Isobel Bulcock?" Gran fixed me with her sightless eyes as though she could peer into the very depths of my soul.

Full contrite, I took her hand. "In truth, she spoke ill of you and Mam. Said you were a witch and Mam a whore. I told her to shut her wicked gob or she'd be sorry for it."

Gran winced as though a spasm were passing through her.

"Alizon." She drew me close. "Bless you, you're true to your own. But you must learn to mind your tongue. Tomorrow we'll both go to Moss End. You'll apologise to Isobel, and I'll do my all to bring that child back to good health."

## 11

I NEVER WISHED to curse or harm anybody, much less a child, even one so irksome as Issy Bulcock. When I saw her, lying upon her bed, her cheeks pale as mushrooms, I longed to cut out my tongue for fear of speaking so harsh to a soul ever again. Such a state she was in, her skin covered in a cold sweat that made her smock stick to her bony chest, that I near believed I *had* bewitched her. But that could never be. Such powers were Gran's, not mine.

Full calm, Gran stroked Issy's brow, and when she proclaimed that the child would soon mend, we knew it to be God's truth. Issy's parents, and John, her brother, fair wept in relief, as did I. But Gran was not one to allow me to kneel there snivelling like a wet thing when I could be useful. So she bade me fill the kettle, hang it upon the hob, and take the herbs from her bundle. Alehoof, I brewed for Issy, along with dittany, black horehound, and archangel wort. Whilst they steeped, Gran chanted over the child and I prayed to the Mother of God, for hadn't Gran taught me the forbidden prayers, word for word. Five Pater Nosters, five Aves, and the Creed, recited whilst picturing deep inside my heart the Five Wounds of Christ—this could heal a child. This and Gran's physick.

I heard a dog howl from far away as if it were baying at the moon, though it was midday. Always made me tremble and cross myself, that dog's yowling did, for what could it be but Gran's familiar, the font of her magic. Even Jane Bulcock heard it and went a shade whiter as if she were close to fainting, so I took her arm and led her to a stool.

"Peace," I whispered. "Gran's mending your lass."

What would any of us do, I wondered, when Gran died, as she surely must, being nearly four-score years. For all Jamie's boasting the evening before, it was plain to see he'd no grand future as a cunning man. As for our Jennet, she seemed to turn up her nose at any dealings with the cunning craft. True Puritan's daughter, she was.

I remembered the dream I'd had of Gran fitting the garland upon my head. Her hopes of carrying on the family business fell upon me, but I could only disappoint, for I was unworthy of such a calling. I'd not felt so much as a flimmer of magic stirring inside me, no promise of the wondrous force Gran wielded. Most I could do was guide her on her errands now that she was blind and defend her good name with my fists if need be, should any dare speak ill of her. As for my own prospects, I'd be content enough to find regular work to keep us fed, and one day I'd love to marry and have little ones of my own, but ones less bothersome than Jennet, God willing. To be honest, none of the lads round these parts ever turned my head. Still the world was a big enough place, or so I'd been told, and one day I hoped to meet my true love, the one who would set my heart a-light. When I passed the time with Nancy, the two of us bent over our carding or mending, we'd put our heads close and whisper of the sweethearts we'd yet to meet.

Right then, as if harking to my own privy thoughts, Gran hooked me with her filmy eyes and cracked a grin as if to tell me she'd something well different in store for me. "Come, Alizon, love, bring that brew."

My hands were steadier than hers, so it was I who stirred the cup till it was lukewarm, then tipped it gentle into Issy's mouth. God knew I was no wisewoman like Gran, but this at least I could do.

• • •

162

Hours later Gran and I made our cumbersome way homeward, clambering up the breast of a hill. Her breath was ragged and raw. Every sixth step, we stopped and bided a spell, and I did my best to bear up her weight. Any other woman of her years would have stayed home, but folk had need of Gran so to them she would go for as long as she still had strength to set one foot in front of the other. At least our bellies were bursting-full, for Jane Bulcock had the mind to feed us on fricassee chicken, oatbread, and apple fritters. My head was fair floating from her strong beer, which left me light on my feet and made me wish I'd the powers to spirit Gran through the air so that her toes never touched the earth. The thoughts running through my head sounded mad as Jamie's talk. How he loved to go on about foals that sailed through the sky and carried folk on their backs.

Whilst I helped Gran up the rough track, she leaned close. "Alizon, love, when you're next on your own—say you're cutting across the hills to Nancy's tomorrow. Well, it may happen that an animal crosses your path."

My skin went fevered hot when she turned to me with those milky eyes. I wanted to clap my hands over my ears.

"A cat," she said, "or a spotted bitch, or a hare might appear. Even a young man might show himself to you."

Those last words of hers made me hoot in spite of myself. "A young man showing himself to me! Gran, listen to yourself." I'd make any silly jest to turn our talk to other things.

But Gran's eyes still pinned me so I could scarce look away.

"He might take the form of a lad," she went on, ever patient, "but be no lad of flesh and blood. Or he might first appear as a lad, then change into a dog or a cat." She squeezed my hand. "Don't fear it, love. Let it come to you. Never dread such things, for there's power to be found there."

"Familiar spirits aren't for the likes of me," I told her.

How I wished I was Anthony Holden's daughter—just a girl, of whom only ordinary things could be expected. Not one who carried the witchblood inside her. But even my inmost thoughts weren't secret as far as Gran was concerned.

"You'll never be ordinary, our Alizon." The love and the pride blazing on her face were enough to undo me. "I saw you praying for that Bulcock child and a rare light was shining all about you."

Anybody could pray, I wanted to tell her. Didn't mean I was anything special. But then she cradled my cheek with one roughened hand, silencing my protest.

"You've the powers inside you. They lie still for the time being, but one day they'll awaken." She smiled.

I walked on, my arm entwined with hers, only now I felt like the feeble one, her firmness supporting me. We'd reached the crest of the hill when she came to a halt and raised one palm as if to feel which way the wind was blowing.

"Listen," she murmured.

What I'd taken for the pounding of my own heart proved to be hoofbeats striking the earth, raising a cloud of dust. Coming back to my senses, I drew Gran off the track. Who would come riding this lonely way so late?

Up the hill swept four horsemen, but my eyes lighted upon the lead rider astride his blood bay stallion. Well younger than Gran, that gentleman was, but older than my mam I reckoned. Nevertheless, he was a spectacle to behold, his face still handsome with a neat beard coming to a point over his strong chin, which was the sign of an unwavering character. He'd high leather boots with flashing spurs, lace at his cuffs and collar, and a fine tall hat. A marvel that the hat had stuck fast to his head with the galloping over uneven ground. When he saw me and Gran, he reined in his stallion, slowing to a walk. Even then, his horse lifted each hoof high and proud.

There we were, Gran and I, stood before this gentleman. Right civil, he nodded his head and looked me full in the face.

Gran grasped my elbow. "Who is it?"

With her powers, how could she not know? "The Magistrate,"

I whispered. Course I'd seen him before at Colne Market, but never up close like this.

"Where are the pair of you heading?" he asked. Sat there upon his great stallion, it was as though he spoke from the top of Pendle Hill. "Rather late for two females to be out and about."

Gran's hand on my arm went slick and cold, leaving me to wonder why she should be so nervous. He was the Magistrate, not some ruffian come to worry us. What's more, he was now High Sheriff of all the county, or so I'd heard.

"We were visiting our friends, sir. The Bulcocks of Moss End." I shaped each word careful as I could so that he might understand my speech, coarse as gravel compared to his. Our own Curate didn't speak with such grace as this man. "We live only a mile from here, sir." At the last second I remembered to curtsey to show him the proper respect.

"Where do you live then? Slipper Hill?" It became plain that he'd no clue who we were. I'd have thought he'd recognise Gran, for her fame stretched wide, but she was stood behind me, her face fair hidden from him.

She pinched me but it was too late.

"Malkin Tower," I blurted.

"Malkin Tower, you say? You must be John Device's daughter."

"I am, sir." I stood tall at the sound of my father's name.

"What happened to that good man was a sorry affair indeed."

"It was, sir."

"Nigh on nine years ago."

I was well surprised that a man like him had such sharp memory of my father's passing. It wasn't as though the Magistrate had been present at the funeral.

"A pity," he said, "that nobody came to me then, when I might have been able to do something to seek justice for the man."

So Master Nowell knew the rumours that Chattox was the cause of my poor father's death. I drew a deep breath, prepared to condemn her to Roger Nowell, Magistrate and High Sheriff, only Gran near wrenched my arm from its socket. But she didn't straighten herself to face him. She said not a word, only made like a bent and witless crone. That made my mouth go dry, for I'd never once seen her cower.

"A pity," he said again, looking so deep into my eyes that I near forgot I was just a grubby girl on the wayside. "Unless people come to me with their complaints, I am powerless to act on their behalf."

Whilst I stared up at him, dumbstruck by the might of his words, he seemed to glance behind me to make out Gran, who was unmoving as any tree stump.

"Best get the old beldame home before dark," he said.

With a flash of his spurs, he and the other men rode on. Soon all that remained of Roger Nowell and his retinue were the hoof prints their horses left behind.

Gran gripped my arm till it ached. "You *fool*. Never let yourself be dazzled by the likes of Nowell. And don't you dare speak a word to him about Anne Whittle."

I shook at the force of her fury, then asked myself, for the very first time, if she were not misguided. As much as I loved her, I'd loved Father, too, and what kind of daughter would I be if I didn't cry out against the one who had murdered him? Did no one in Pendle Forest have the gumption to rid us of that witch? Ah, but folk were too frightened of Chattox's wrath to speak against her. Still it maddened me that even Gran lacked the courage to take a stand.

"She's an evil soul, Gran. Why should she go unpunished?"

"Our Alizon, I thought you'd more sense in your head than our Jamie, but now I wonder!"

Her words pierced me like arrows and I feared I would burst into tears. How could she speak so, as though Chattox were the wronged one and I the mischief-maker?

"She's an old woman." Gran herself sounded older than the sky as she spoke these words. "She'll die soon enough by God's own hand, then she'll suffer God's judgement, as will we all when our time comes."

"You pity her. But will you spare any pity for her victims?"

Gran softened. "Darling, even if Nowell hanged Anne Whittle tomorrow, it wouldn't bring back your daddy." She stroked my hair as though I were still that little girl bawling over my father's coffin. "You don't want to go round accusing folk, our Alizon. What if Henry Bulcock had run to the Constable and accused you?"

"But I never harmed anybody!"

"And if the Magistrate thought you were lying?"

He wouldn't, I wanted to say. One look into the depths of his eyes proved to me that he was a man of justice, as well he should be. Wasn't he the law in Pendle Forest?

"What if somebody made a complaint about your brother?" Gran asked.

"Jamie? Everybody knows he's a simpleton. No crime in that."

"He's a poacher, love, and for that he could hang."

Her words left me numb. I'd lost my father—that was enough for anybody to bear. I prayed that no one would be cruel enough to hang Jamie. He was touched by God, as blameless a soul as any.

"Promise me, Alizon." Gran was telling me, not asking. "Promise you won't go running to the law. Nowell has his circle and we've ours. He can't begin to understand what we do or what we're about."

"I promise," I said, for she'd left me no other choice, and I knew well enough to keep my word, for it did no good to cross a cunning woman.

"Good lass." She took my arm again as though she were fonder of me than anything on this earth, and I felt ashamed that I'd ever quarrelled with her. Homeward we walked as daylight gate faded into night. In the gloaming bats took to wing, and moths fluttered like tiny stars whilst the swelling moon rode the sky.

That night I knelt beside the pallet I shared with Jennet and prayed long and hard, trying not to mind that Jennet had wrapped our blanket thrice round herself and I would have to go without and shiver the whole night through. I murmured the Latin words Gran had taught me, beautiful and full mysterious, and that rare light of which she'd spoken seemed to enclose me in a golden cloud. What need had I of a blanket when I had this?

*Salve Regina, Mater misericordiae,*
*Vita, dulcedo, et spes nostra, salve.*

I prayed that I might be a vessel of goodness, patient and kind to Jennet. Prayed that I might learn to hold my tongue and mind my words. And then I prayed, tears in my eyes, for my father's soul and that I might find a way of seeking retribution for him without breaking my promise to Gran.

Next morning I rose early, bound for Nancy's. If I sat a spell with her and poured out my troubles, she would find a way to put it right. She always did. Soon enough my Nancy would have me laughing.

Silent and quick, I slipped out before Jennet could awaken and say or do anything to spoil my mood. Soon as I shot out the door, I hitched up my skirts and legged it over hill and stile, the blood inside me singing. Only stopped to catch my breath when I'd reached the gates of Bull Hole Farm. After she had served us all a hearty breakfast, Mistress Holden doled out the chores. That day the little nieces and nephews would card wool and Mistress Holden herself would do the spinning. Nancy and I were to do the laundry.

My friend and I hoisted the baskets of dirtied clothes and linens out to the beck that ran close by the front gate. Catching Nancy's eye, I thought that now would be the time to tell her of my sorrows, yet I found I couldn't bring myself to speak of the Magistrate, Chattox, or witchcraft in this happy place. So instead I started singing a naughty song I'd learned when working at Mouldheels's house in Colne. Nancy joined in, then taught me another song, even bawdier. And so we sang, loud and merry, as we were knelt beside the beck, beating each garment against the rocks. Singing, we spread each wrung-out shirt, kirtle, jerkin, and pair of breeches and hose over the thorn hedge that divided the Holdens' ground from the road.

Merry mischief in her eyes, Nancy leaned close and sang in a low voice the rudest song I'd ever heard, one she'd learned from eavesdropping on the hired men when they'd drunk too much ale. Each verse was more outrageous than the next. When she'd finished, we shook with laughter, our cheeks a-flame. Fair helpless, we hugged each other and laughed till our eyes streamed.

At the sight of a stooped figure staring at us, our mirth turned to terror. There she was stood, that hunched hag. That witch. Come a-begging, so Chattox had, her basket slung over one bony arm. Her glare made my tongue stick to the roof of my mouth. Like a nightmare, it was, seeing Chattox's hateful face, her baleful eyes stabbing us.

"Were you laughing at me?" she demanded.

Neither Nancy nor I could speak, only gawp back at her as though we were a pair of planet-struck mutes. With a grimace, Chattox plucked at the rag that covered her basket, revealing a glimpse of red river clay. Just as quick she hid it again. Nancy made a fearful noise, deep in her throat.

"Nancy Holden! Alizon Device!" She spat out our names like curses. "I asked you: Were you laughing at me?"

Tears in her eyes, Nancy shook her head. She snatched her father's damp shirt off the hedge and held it in front of herself as though it were a shield. But I raised my chin to show Chattox I wasn't cowed. The power was mine. One word to Roger Nowell and she'd swing from the gallows. So great was my need to protect Nancy, I fair forgot my promise to Gran. Slow but steady I strode to the gate and met her stare full on when out of nowhere shot a pitch-black dog, the fur on its scruff raised. That witch had set her familiar on us. But I threw back my shoulders, for my rage was greater than my fear.

"Is that a clay figure you have in your basket?" I bellowed to be heard over the snarling hound. "You'll hang for this, Chattox."

Swayed on her feet did Chattox. She looked at me as though I'd run a knife through her.

"You heartless child. I'm a clemmed old woman without oats or bread. It's clay I eat to fill my belly." She looked fit to weep.

But why should I show a shred of mercy when gazing into the eyes of my father's murderer?

"Get away from here, Chattox. Get away, never to show your face again."

Quivering, the hag looked from me to the dog that now bared its teeth and lunged at her. Her own familiar had turned on her. Well, such was the price the witch would have to pay for doing the Devil's bidding. Away she scuttled, fast as her gimping old legs could carry her.

I smarted in shame, for I almost fancied Gran was stood there, sore disappointed in me. *How could you be so cruel, our Alizon?* I wondered if I should go running after Chattox, offer her some bread. But that was not my place: I was but a guest here.

Turning to Nancy, I saw my own father's face hanging in the air before hers, saw him thrashing in his bed, never to rise again after Chattox had bewitched him. I saw the yellow skull Betty had dumped before our hearth. My heart thumped with enough force to knock me down. Had to wet my lips before I could speak.

"She's well gone, our Nancy." I eased her father's linen shirt free of her fingers and hung it back up to dry. "She'll trouble you no more, I promise."

The horror on my friend's face slit me in half. With a shaking finger, she pointed.

*"Her dog."*

The pitch-black beast was coming right at us. Before I could grab a stone to hurl between its eyes, the creature began to fawn over me, its pink tongue snaking out to slather my arm from wrist to elbow.

A yelp tore out of me. Grabbing Nancy by the arm, I bolted for the house, pulling her along so fast that she near tripped over her skirts. When we reached the Holden kitchen, I slammed the door behind us before sinking to the floor. In the warmth of that summer day, my skin twitched, stone cold where the dog had licked me.

The little nieces and nephews circled round. Nancy's mother rushed over, her face pink from the heat. Since I was struck speechless, Nancy explained what had happened.

"Alizon was well brave and sent her on her way. But Chattox's dog stayed behind to worry us. Mam, I was never so scared in my life."

My friend and her mother raised me to my feet. Nancy took my hands in hers to still my trembling, yet I couldn't bring myself to meet her trusting brown eyes. Our Jamie had foretold what would happen this day. *Alizon will get her powers by and by. She'll meet her black dog.*

My friend had thought that the beast was Chattox's familiar, as had I first off. But no. That creature was mine.

Later, when the men came in for the midday meal, Mistress Holden told her husband about Chattox's visit.

At once Master Holden spoke up. "If ever that witch should dare show her face round here again, bar the gate to her. She'll not have so much as a cup of blue milk off us after this."

I flinched as I went round the table filling the men's mugs with ale. In future they'd drive Chattox away, crying witch, just as Baldwin had done to Gran and Mam and me. Send her away famished.

Master Holden folded his hands in prayer and bade God to ward every soul in this house and every animal in the shippon from witchcraft. During the rest of the meal, no one said a word. The little children could hardly eat, they were so rattled. With each bite of tender stewed lamb, I thought of the clay in Chattox's basket, imagined her gnawing on the stuff to ease her hunger pangs. Had I done wrong? How would God—or Gran—judge my deeds?

After the meal, Nancy and her mother scrubbed the trenchers and pots whilst I alone ventured outside to fetch the dry laundry off the hedge. My heart juddering, I looked round, but saw no trace of any dog.

Walking the dusty road home, I tried my best not to step in the tracks left by Chattox's bare feet. Though I tried to make my mind a blank, Gran's voice was everywhere. *It may happen that an animal crosses your path. Don't fear it, love. Let it come to you. Never dread such things, for there's power to be found there.* The mere thought of that slavering beast with its hot tongue on my skin made me want to dash out my brains on the dry stone wall. Issy Bulcock's words rang out. *Witchblood! You've the witchblood!* The child had vexed me, I'd told her off, then a fever struck her down and only Gran could raise her again. Did that make me a witch, no better than Chattox?

Gran was a cunning woman. She worked for good and her every charm was a prayer of the old religion. Yet her many hardships went to show that there was no way you could win at this game. Once you let folk know you'd the powers to bend and twist, you became a witch in their eyes, even if you sought only to help others. Neighbours would turn to you, all right, call on you if they'd need of you, except you'd never be one of them again, but forever on the outside looking in. A lonely path Gran had chosen. She had us, of course, and I loved her more than anyone, but she'd not a single friend to confide in the way I could confide in Nancy. What kind of life was that? Only a woman as strong as Gran could bear it.

Even my mam, who had renounced the cunning craft, couldn't rid herself of the taint that clung to her like a mantle she could never shake off. Overwhelmed me, it did, to consider what Mam had suffered, throwing herself at Baldwin of all men to purify herself, but the stain remained. If we had been ordinary people and not a family of cunning folk, would Chattox have cursed us with such force? If we had been regular folk, my father might have lived.

With my every step homeward, I prayed to the Mother of God to deliver me from this. May I never again set eyes on that black dog.

When I reached Malkin Tower and unpacked the heavy bundle of bread and honeycake that Mistress Holden had given me, Jennet danced in a circle.

"Cake!" she cried.

But there was no hiding my distress from Mam.

"What's the matter, love? You look ill-done-to."

Up spoke Jamie before I could even open my mouth. "She'd words with Chattox."

Mam bristled to hear that name. From her stool by the hearth, Gran stared with her clouded eyes. She would not let it rest till I'd spilled the story.

"Chattox carried a clay figure in her basket, I'll swear to it." After the long walk in the hot sun, my head was throbbing. When I closed my eyes, I saw blobs of light. I'd tell my family about every last thing—except the dog. That would stay hidden inside me, buried like the skull underneath the manure heap out back. "When I asked her what it was, she said she planned to eat it because she'd nothing else. She was lying, wasn't she, Gran?"

More than anything, I longed for Gran to absolve me of this. Tell me I'd done right to defend Nancy and the Holdens. But when Gran finally spoke, her voice was full of heartbreak.

"May God have mercy upon Anne Whittle."

Next morning I awoke to the racket of hooves and creaking wagon wheels, then somebody pounding on our door. I laced my kirtle and ran, my uncombed hair flying, to find Matthew Holden, his face drawn like death.

"Alizon, will you wake your gran? Our Nancy's taken ill."

Though Gran had barely recovered from the strain of her journey out to the Bulcocks', she rose from her pallet at once and bade me pack her bundle of herbs. Full determined was Gran to do everything she could, for we'd a debt to the Holdens. She'd go if it crippled her. At least this time we didn't have to walk. Matthew, bless him, had lined the wagon bed with straw and blankets to make Gran comfortable. Sat beside Matthew on the driver's plank, I fair wished the horses could gallop all the way, so worried I was for Nancy.

Once we reached Bull Hole Farm, I made Gran take a bowl of porridge and cream to keep up her strength. Blessing the sick was taxing on one as old as her. Whilst she ate, I filled the kettle and brewed the same herbs that had mended Issy Bulcock. Rushing to my friend's bedside, I touched her forehead, clammy from the low fever that left her too weak and dizzy to leave her bed.

"Here." I held the potion to her mouth. "This will make you right again."

"Alizon." She reached for my hand. "Last night I hardly slept for my nightmares. I dreamt you were in danger, darkness and stench everywhere. I tried to help you but I couldn't reach you." Her eyes glistened in fear, not for herself but for me.

"Hush now," I begged her. "Put that woman's evil out of your mind, love."

Mouthful by mouthful, I coaxed my friend to swallow the brew.

When Gran began her blessings, Nancy's parents and brother knelt round and prayed, whilst I stood there, hands folded, not daring to say the old prayers for fear of offending the Holdens who were staunch in their devotion to the new religion.

But Mistress Holden gazed up at me and said, "Please, Alizon, go on and say your Roman prayers if it will take this evil from my child."

So I dropped to my knees and chanted ten Pater Nosters, ten Aves, and the Creed. In the midst of our prayers, Gran took my friend's limp body in her arms, striving to draw the harm out of Nancy and into herself. Looking on, I wept for them both. Gran rocked the girl in her embrace till Nancy's cold sweat turned to warm dew and the colour returned to her cheeks. Then Gran went slack and grey. I caught her before she could hit the floor.

Master Holden bore Gran away to his and his wife's own four-poster and there she lay full spent beneath the embroidered counterpane. Nancy's mother brought Gran ale posset, hot broth, and bread soaked in milk and honey. Afterward, when Gran nodded off, I knew she wouldn't rise for many hours yet. We would have to stay the night.

"My husband shall sleep in Matthew's room," said Mistress Holden. "I shall sleep in the truckle bed in Nancy's chamber. But you, Alizon, shall sleep with your grandmother in the big bed."

Her hand on my arm, she showed me into the master bedroom as though I were a guest of honour. We both smiled to see Gran fast asleep, her head nestled in the plump bolster.

"She must be so proud of you." Mistress Holden rubbed my hair. "You're every inch the blesser, Alizon Device."

How it floored me to hear my dearest friend's mother calling me what I least wanted to be. Too discomfited to speak, I lowered my head. Mistress Holden kissed my brow and wished me good night.

The linens, soft and soothing against my skin, allowed me to forget her words. Such comfort—the likes of which I'd never known. The feather mattress cushioned my hip and shoulder where the bones stuck out. So this was what it was like to lie upon a proper featherbed. The embroidered canopy kept the spiders and beetles living in the thatch from dropping upon our faces in the night. So blessed quiet here, too. Jennet wriggled and squirmed and muttered in her sleep, but Gran slumbered so still that I almost feared she would never awaken. My palm on her flank, I waited to feel the rise and fall of her breath before I allowed myself to drift off.

My dreams were as comforting as the mattress. Before me I saw Nancy, restored to health. We walked along, laughing and sharing secrets. Blushing like mad, she confessed that she was sweet on Miles Nutter, Alice Nutter's eldest son and heir to Roughlee

Hall. I swung Nancy round and teased her that she'd be a grand lady indeed if she married him: mistress of that manor house with its arched windows. She'd wear velvet and silk and lace, and a maidservant would dress her hair each morning. My lips to her ear, I whispered what I knew to be true: *If you marry Miles Nutter, you'll have to accept the old religion. Don't you know they've a priest hidden in their very walls?*

With a start, I awakened to Gran's sobbing.

"Anne," she choked. "My Anne, oh why?"

"Gran, you're only dreaming."

Still she cried out for Anne who could be none other than Chattox. How dare that witch invade my gran's dreams—but wasn't that just what she'd done to Nancy, sending her the night terrors? What bewildered me was that Nancy's nightmare had not revealed her own doom but mine, which proved how vile Chattox was. If it was me she desired to torment, could she not at least be decent enough to leave my friend alone? What game did that woman play with us, and where would any of us be without Gran's charms, the only thing mighty enough to counter Chattox's curses? Yet, in their younger days, Gran and Chattox had been as close as Nancy and I were. There was a time when Chattox had been a girl like any other—a girl no different than I was. That thought made me writhe, the linens twisting round my legs.

"Gran, wake up." I gave her shoulder a shake.

"Tibb," she raved. "The light fair blinds me. The light, how it shines. Tibb, my love, come back."

After that, she quietened down and slept in peace. Then I couldn't rest, for I was too haunted by what I'd heard: her crying out to Tibb with such longing, as though to a husband. In the depth of night I was forced to remember the black dog that had come for me, its eyes locking into mine as though summoning me away to that realm of spirits and visions where the animal would reveal its true shape, appearing, for all I knew, as a man, a lover. Chilled me to the core, that notion did. These were my grandmother's powers and this was what she wished for me.

• • •

In the morning I led Gran into Nancy's chamber. My friend was sat up in bed, eating porridge, just like her old self. Gran looked better, too, her skin bright and flushed as though she had indeed slept in the arms of her invisible husband, but I quickly chased such thoughts out of my mind, fair distracted by the feast of a breakfast that Mistress Holden dished up. Fried eggs, there were, black pudding and griddle cakes, tripe and onion, and the good ale that Mistress Holden saved for special occasions. Sarah Holden sat Gran in their best carved chair and after she'd eaten as much as her fickle appetite allowed, they let her doze for a spell by the fire, which they'd built high and roaring hot even though it was summer. Finally Matthew hitched up his team to take us back to Malkin Tower. Master Holden loaded the wagon with his payment to Gran: a sack of oats, a cask of cider, a side of bacon, and two laying hens.

On the journey back I mulled over my dream of Nancy marrying Miles and living at Roughlee Hall. She'd have servants to do her washing and spinning. Would she be too proud to be my friend then? In truth, there were some mean-spirited folk who said I was too lowly to share her company even now. But I reminded myself that it had been only a dream and nothing more.

As we trundled up and down the hills, the horses straining and flicking flies with their tails, clouds moved in to smudge the perfect blue sky. The sight cheered Matthew, for we'd had a month of drought.

"Looks like the weather's turning, eh, Mother Demdike?" He turned round in the driver's seat to look at Gran where she was nestled in the straw and cushions. "Didn't you predict we'd get rain round the full moon?"

"Weather always changes round about the full moon," Gran said. "Crops will be wanting a spot of rain." But she sounded as though she were a hundred miles away. Was she still spent from blessing Nancy, or was she brooding on Chattox and Tibb?

Clouds kept rolling in from of the west and the air hung heavier and heavier till I fancied I could cut it with a knife and eat it.

When we reached Malkin Tower, Matthew handed Gran down from the wagon.

"Now get yourself home with God's speed," she said, patting his shoulder, "before this storm breaks."

First he let his horses have a rest whilst he hauled in the oats, bacon, and cider. Then he carried the wicker cage, following me as I led the way to the chicken run. Jennet rushed out to watch as we released the hens. Up and down they raced, squawking and indignant. It had been ages since we'd had laying hens.

"Remember to save the slops for them," I told Jennet. So happy I was at the thought of fresh eggs that I dared to ruffle her hair.

"Ugh, don't touch me with your dirty chicken hands!"

Ignoring her pettishness, I ran to fetch water for the horses and wiped the sweat from their necks with a cool, wet rag. A short while later, when Matthew drove away, I was stood at the gate waving.

"Give Nancy our love!" I called out.

Jennet took her place beside me. I tried to be kind, to pretend that I was as tender-hearted as Nancy and that Jennet was one of her little nieces that loved to jump into my lap for a cuddle.

"Matthew Holden's the boy Gran saved and now he's a man with five children of his own," I told her. "Yesterday Gran mended Nancy. Our gran will be needing her rest now, all right." I couldn't keep the pride out of my voice. As much as Gran's powers terrified me, wasn't she the best charmer Pendle Forest had ever known?

Jennet threw me a sly look. "When Gran dies, *you'll* be the witch!"

That made me boil. "Gran was never a witch and you know it."

But Jennet had already scarpered.

# 13

ONE JULY DAWN Jamie and I set off for Bull Hole Farm to help with the hay harvest. Though my mood was as bright as the morning, our Jamie was in a foul humour. The day before he'd quarrelled with Mistress Towneley of Carr Hall.

"She'll rue it," he said as we walked beside Pendle Water. The birds piped and the stream gurgled, but my brother's face was clenched in vehemence.

I strove to soothe him. "Go on, tell us what she said to you, love."

Pained me like a blade in the side to see him suffer like this. Folk were too quick to mock and ill-treat him, for they saw only his affliction and lacked the grace to look beyond it to discover what a good soul he truly was.

"She called me a thief." He kicked at the loose stones in his path, sending them skittering away from his huge feet.

"Oh, Jamie."

At a loss, I was. As Gran had said, he risked enough with his poaching. If one such as Mistress Towneley had evidence of him stealing from her, he was done for. I counted to ten, trying to keep my patience, for I'd never get the truth out of Jamie if I lost my temper.

"Why would she say such a thing to you?" I took his fist in my hands, gently chafing it till his fingers loosened and threaded with mine. "Did you take something of hers without asking?"

"Only some turves of peat."

He couldn't have taken many, I thought, for peat was well heavy. Strong as Jamie was, it was nigh on impossible that he'd made off with more than was his fair reward for the digging he'd done.

"Our Jamie, if you were working for her and took some peat for yourself, all you needed do was ask her. I'll go round and talk to her."

"I was hungry, wasn't I, after digging, so I went into the kitchen. I was fair clemmed."

"Course you were. Anybody would be." But my heart sank at the thought of him seeing something in the Towneley kitchen that struck his fancy. A pewter mug or a brass candlestick.

"She sent me packing." He trembled in his outrage. "She hit me! Gave me a knock between the shoulders."

To my fright, Jamie began to weep at the injustice. Rarely had I seen him cry, but now his tears blinded him. He stumbled and would have fallen had I not held fast to his arm.

"Said folk with thieving hands had no business in her kitchen."

"Jamie!" I wiped his tears on my apron. "She made you dig all day, then never fed you?"

My hands sought the place on his broad back where Mistress Towneley had struck him, and I quaked at the thought of Jamie swinging round and hitting her back. Strong lad like him could kill a woman with one blow.

"She said I was to bide outside and wait for my dinner. Eat outside like a pig. Said I'd no business stepping in her door."

"You'll never go back there. Sarah Holden will treat you a sight better, Jamie, I promise. She'll sit you down at her table with the rest of her family and stuff you till your breeks won't fit anymore."

But Jamie wouldn't leave off brooding on Mistress Towneley. "I'll make her pay. Dandy showed me how."

"Hush," I pleaded. "Our gran wouldn't want you saying such things."

Full sullen, my brother stared off ahead. Presently he pointed.

"She comes," he said in such a voice as to make me leap out of my skin. "Her path crosses yours. There's no running away from her, our Alizon."

I spotted a golden-haired child heading our way from off in the distance. As the sun filled her halo of hair, my nape prickled, for I thought it must be some apparition—a spirit like Gran's Tibb. But when we drew closer, I saw it was only a thin girl, a few years older than our Jennet. Coming up behind her was a haggard woman in a threadbare kirtle that was near to falling off her gaunt frame. Annie Redfearn barely lifted her eyes as she dragged herself past us.

"It was a clay picture what killed our father!" my brother yelled at her.

"No," said Annie. "That's a wicked lie you're telling."

Such a sorry-looking thing she was that I wished I'd some bread to give her, even if she was Chattox's own flesh and blood. But it was all I could do to keep my brother from pummelling her.

"If there's a scalp and teeth buried at Malkin Tower," he fumed, "it's Chattox's doing. Chattox and Betty's, what died from flea bites."

Annie and her daughter fled whilst I seized Jamie round the waist to keep him from charging after them.

In truth, the sight of Annie Redfearn spooked me more than any spirit familiar could have done. I'd never seen anybody so forlorn. She wasn't like her mam, was Annie, no malice or scheming in her eyes, but a woman worn down to the bone, nothing left to her but want and despair. I could picture Annie sending her little Marie off to beg whilst she herself hid in the shadows. With her angel-bright hair, Marie Redfearn was pretty enough to fool folk into forgetting that she was a witch's granddaughter. Poor child was her family's only hope of charity. Gran had told me that Annie, in her younger days, had been a rare beauty, but it seemed a tall tale to look at her now.

Well thankful, I was, when we finally reached the gates of Bull Hole Farm.

"Our Jamie, put a smile on your face. You can smell Mistress Holden's cooking from out here!"

I teased my brother about being such a hard worker that he'd put the Holdens' hired men to shame and wouldn't it be something if Master Holden hired him. Why, then I'd always have an excuse to come round and have a natter with Nancy. Grabbing Jamie's hands, I led him in a wild jig, laughing with him till his bitterness melted away.

Nancy dashed out. "Alizon, look at me! I'm right again."

She beamed and I danced round with her, then Jamie took her hands and whirled her about, but Nancy jumped away from him when her mam came out to gawp at the pair of them. Saddened me, it did, to see Sarah Holden purse her lips at our Jamie.

"Nancy needs to stay quiet and build back her strength," Mistress Holden said.

My friend took my arm and drew me into the kitchen, leaving Jamie and her mother to follow.

"Mam won't let me rake hay!" Nancy lamented. "Instead she'll have me tied to the kitchen, cooking and spinning."

"Keep you out of the hot sun and harm's way," her mam said, fond but firm.

And she'd keep Nancy well away from the road, I thought, for fear of Chattox calling round again out of sheer spite. But it was hard to hold any grudge against Mistress Holden when she sat us down to thick pottage with barley dumplings, and she wasn't the least bit stingy, allowing our Jamie to wolf down five portions till even he could not swallow another spoonful. Looked so contented, my brother did, that I hoped Mistress Towneley was banished from his mind.

After thanking Mistress Holden, Jamie and I stepped out into the gleaming morning where the larks sang and reeled.

"You're a powerful-built man," I told my brother, kneading the muscles in his arms. "Make us proud, lad. Show the Holdens what you can do."

Swell with love, I did, to see him pick the biggest scythe and step into the long, waving grass. With swoop after swoop, he sliced his way through the hayfield whilst Matthew Holden and the hired men struggled to keep pace. Soon my brother's threadbare shirt ran dark with sweat and lay plastered to his chest and back, revealing the might beneath. I prayed that Matthew would see for himself what a fine hired man Jamie would make. If only my brother could find steady work with kind folk, I wouldn't have to fear for him so.

The only girl in a field of men, I didn't shirk my duties. Like the rest of them, I'd a scythe and strong arms to wield it, and I swung in time with Matthew. Out of the corner of my eye, I caught him looking at me, which made my cheeks burn. Was he looking at me in *that* way? *You are growing into a beauty,* Gran had told me not two days ago, her blind eyes fixed upon my face. But Mam had warned me not to get too full of myself, for there was nothing more tiresome than a vain, simpering girl. In truth, I hadn't much of a clue how I looked since we'd no mirror. Besides, I wasn't given to flirting and had vowed never to make the same mistake as Mam had done by throwing away my honour to satisfy the lusts of some wretched man who would just toss me away afterward and call me a whore. Nothing less than true love would turn my heart.

Yet the look Matthew was giving me was enough to make my knees knock. How could this be? He was my best friend's brother and well older than I was: a man of thirty-two with five children. Then again, wasn't Matthew Holden a widower in need of a wife? He was handsome enough in his way, for he shared Nancy's smile and her warm brown eyes. If I married him, my fondest dream would come true. I'd be one of their family, living in their home and spending every day with Nancy till she, too, married and moved away. What's more, if I were a yeoman's wife, folk would call me "Mistress." Mistress Alizon Holden. I'd sleep every night in a fine poster bed. Except I wasn't near ready to marry yet.

In a fit of sadness, I wondered if Matthew would consider me too far beneath him. Man like him could get a girl with a good portion, or a widow with land of her own and a herd of cattle. Perhaps the best I could do was marry a hired man like my own mam had done. Then Gran's voice whispered loud in my breast: *Girl like you could do better than settle for a widower with five children.* Straightening my back, I looked Matthew full in the face. With a fierce sweep of my scythe, I swore that I'd take a man as good as my own father over any yeoman's son.

Sweat poured down my face and the sun scorched my skin. By evening I'd be brown as bread, not that I minded. Folk could call me what they liked, but I wasn't afraid of hard graft. By Our Lady, I'd find a young lad with shapely legs, so I would, who knew how to make me smile. So I laughed and joked with the hired men and thought, *Let them watch me. Let them see my strength and will in each reach of my scythe.*

After the hay was cut, Mistress Holden brought us buttered bread, cheese, and plumcake, whilst Nancy carried out the ale, cool from the cellar, but none too strong as we'd still plenty more work to do. Whilst I gulped from my mug, I thought to myself how clean and neat Nancy looked, not a wrinkle in her apron, her hair tucked smooth beneath her spotless white coif whilst I sprawled on the ground, my skin coated in sweat and grime. But she hung close by, giving me a melancholy look as though she envied me my freedom to work with the men. Catching her eye, I winked, and she grinned. And then, surrounded by the cut hay with its dust clouding the air, she began to sneeze and wheeze and cough till she near doubled over.

I jumped to go to her, but her mam got there first and hustled her back to the house. When I made to follow, Matthew grabbed my arm. I caught my breath to feel the heat of his hand on my wrist, and I thought that there was a bond between him and me no matter what folk said, for once he had been the little boy my Gran had saved from wasting away.

"Peace, our Alizon," said Matthew, smiling into my flustered face. "Nancy will be all right. Just let her mother look after her."

. . .

After we'd raked the hay and forked it into stacks to dry in the sun, we headed to the house for our supper. I yearned to talk to Nancy, but she was sat at the other end of the table, and with the hired men and Matthew's children yammering away, she could scarce hear me above the din. She looked to be in a sad way, and she still coughed now and then. It wasn't till I was helping her clear away the dirty crockery that we'd a short spell alone together. The men had gone out to look at Matthew's yearling colt, and Mistress Holden was putting the little children to bed.

"I'd a dream about you and Miles Nutter," I began, thinking it would cheer her or at least make her laugh, but she only shook her head and rested her pale fingers on my brown arm, which ached from scything and raking.

"Our Alizon, I'd give anything to be as robust as you. I'm tired of being such a frail thing. Mam almost forbade me to carry the ale out to you in the field. When she saw me coughing, she said I wasn't to leave the house for the rest of the day. I'm lucky she didn't send me to bed along with the tots."

"You're mended," I told her. "You're well as you ever were."

"Was I ever well?" Tears fell fast from her eyes, but she swiped them away. "I was never half so healthy as you, our Alizon. You can walk ten miles and be no wearier than if you'd walked from our door to our gate." She took my hand as though to gather strength from me. "Mam has a mind to send me to live with my godmother in Trawden Forest."

This time *I* wept, for I couldn't bear the thought of having her torn from me.

"She has a nephew looking for a wife," Nancy said, her voice flat, her eyes cast down to the floor.

"You're only sixteen!"

"Mam says I *must* go away, out of Chattox's reach. Father says I've the green sickness. My courses won't come. I haven't bled in almost a year and I only grow thinner."

"Green sickness?" My voice caught as I watched her crumple.

Nancy was one year older than I was, but she'd still the body of a scrawny child, no sign of womanliness about her, whilst I, for all my rough living, was shapely and rounded. Her appetite had never been like mine. Though her mother tempted her with the most delectable victuals, Nancy could never get much down. Her once-rosy skin had gone chalky of late. In truth, if I peered at her close, I could detect the palest tinge of green about her face.

She rested her brow upon my shoulder. "It's the virgin's disease, so my father says. The only cure is marriage. The longer I'm a maid, the worse it will get. Then with Chattox casting her evil eye on me—"

"Don't speak of her." Holding my friend's thin body, I wished I'd the powers to spirit her away to a place where she would be safe always. Never had I imagined that her good parents would be capable of strong-arming her into a hasty and unwanted marriage.

At the sound of Mistress Holden's approaching footsteps, Nancy and I pulled apart. I wiped my tears on my sleeve whilst my friend bent over the hearth smooring the ashes, so her mam wouldn't see she'd been crying.

As we trod home, Jamie was in high spirits, rambling on about flying colts and fire-spitting hares and Master Duckworth of Laund who'd promised him an old shirt. I just nodded my head whenever Jamie expected it of me, but I felt too oppressed for Nancy's sake to say much. How soon could her parents force her to the altar? First they'd have to post the banns and, God willing, something might happen in the meantime to strike some sense into their heads.

Next morning Jamie headed to the Duckworths' to do what work they could give him. I'd planned on calling upon Nancy to see how she fared, but Mam told me to go to Carr Hall instead.

"Alizon," she said, "could you not see if you can make sense of what happened between our Jamie and Mistress Towneley?"

I understood her meaning. The Towneleys were an important family and not one we wished to cross. If Mistress Towneley had truly accused Jamie of theft, we'd best make our own amends if that could keep her from reporting him to the Magistrate. So off I went, my guts tied in knots, wondering what manner of welcome I could expect from the woman who had clouted my brother. Carr Hall wasn't that far—less than three miles—but by the time I reached that fine stone house with its windows of diamond-paned glass, I was breathing heavy, girding myself for what was to come.

Place looked deserted, which took me by surprise till I remembered it was market day in Colne. Perhaps I'd have to come back another time, but as long as I was here, I might as well give the door a knock and see if anyone was at home. Well nervous, I was, fair expecting Mistress Towneley to be simmering mad at the sight of me. But when she opened the door, she looked surprised, as if she'd been expecting someone else only to have me turn up.

"Why Alizon Device," she said. "What brings you here?"

"I've come to ask if you'd any work for me," I blurted, having no clue what else to say. I could hardly ask her outright about Jamie without easing into some other subject first.

Seemed to hesitate did Mistress Towneley. Not at all happy to let me in, but still loathe to turn me away and risk folk gossiping that she was a mean-hearted one.

"Well, there's wool to card," she said at last, leading me into her clean-swept kitchen, almost as grand as the one in Roughlee Hall. She'd an oak dresser laden with polished copper and pewter, and a hearth big enough for roasting an ox upon a spit.

A handsome woman, Mistress Towneley was, with curling brown hair and blue eyes. The gentle swell beneath her skirts told me that she was in the early months of pregnancy. One look at her small frame and tiny white hands made me doubt Jamie's tale, for I couldn't begin to picture this woman smacking my brother between the shoulder blades. I'd be shocked if she could reach so high, for my brother would tower over her. Neither was she stingy as he'd made her out to be, for she brought out half a loaf of wheaten bread, some ham, and a jug of cider and told me to help myself before she set me to work with the carding.

She seemed decent enough, but the red rims of her eyes and the over-quick way she trod the slate floor, kicking up the rushes, told me something was eating her, and I could only wonder if it had anything to do with our Jamie. My stomach drew tight as a drum. The bread and ham I gnawed on stuck in my throat and my hunger died.

So I went to the great heap of wool in the corner, sat myself upon a stool, and began to card. Soon my fingers were slick with lanolin. On the other end of the great kitchen, Mistress Towneley could not settle but paced back and forth, glancing out the window. Once or twice she sat down to her embroidery frame, but just as fast she leapt up and gazed out again. A blood red mist seemed to hang in the air, and I began to wonder if Mistress Towneley and I were both bewitched.

A spell later came the clip-clop of hooves and the stable boy's shout. Shuddering with each breath, Mistress Towneley made to open the door, so full of anxious expectation that I could only think she was receiving an adulterous lover. That would explain why she'd been so reluctant to invite me in.

But her guest was none other than Alice Nutter. Seeing her, I called out in greeting, for she had always been kind to my family at Malkin Tower. Now, though, she hardly nodded in my direction. Mistress Towneley whispered something in her ear. With a swish of linen and new wool, both of them retreated to another room. I heard the door behind them close, heard them mounting a stairway on the other side of the plastered wall. They'd some privy matter to discuss, not for my ears, and I knew, dead certain, they wouldn't be speaking of light-hearted things. Some foul business was afoot. What lay at the root of Mistress Towneley's strange humours? If it had anything to do with Jamie, I had to know.

They were in some upper chamber, most likely behind a locked door, so there was no way I could eavesdrop proper. But as I was sat there, I heard ghostly voices coming down the chimney of that great hearth. For Jamie's sake I laid down the carding brush and tiptoed across the rushes to stand beneath the hearth's hood. Then I pricked my ears and listened. The great chimney must have opened up to a smaller hearth in that upper room.

First came Mistress Towneley's voice, higher and more girlish-sounding than Alice Nutter's. "We warned him to be careful, but it was no use."

My knees buckled, for I thought she spoke about Jamie. She'd warned him and then he'd stolen from her, making off with something much dearer than a few turves of peat. I thought of her dresser with the pewter and copper winking and tempting our Jamie, who was too simple to resist. Oh, why hadn't he told me the truth? How could I get us out of this fix?

"Will they come for him?" Alice Nutter asked. "Arrest him?"

Cramming my knuckles between my teeth, I thought I would die right there in Mistress Towneley's kitchen.

"Alice, they already have. He's in Lancaster Gaol."

I held my breath, not believing what I heard.

"When did you find out?" Alice Nutter asked.

"My Henry came back from Parbold with the news yesterday. Today he rode for Lancaster to bring Edward some warm clothes and blankets. God knows, he'll need them there."

"A brave man, your husband," Alice Nutter said. "He puts himself at risk."

"May God rid us of this cursed King." Mistress Towneley began to weep. "He won't be satisfied until he's murdered us all!"

So flummoxed I was. I'd no inkling who this Edward could be or where Parbold was—certainly nowhere near Pendle Forest. I hadn't the faintest notion what they were on about, only that it had nowt to do with Jamie. By all rights I should have crept away then and listened no more, yet I was pinned to that spot in my wonderment and shock, for I'd never heard the gentry speaking so fearful before, as though they were powerless as any common beggar.

"What of the priest?" Alice Nutter asked.

"By God's grace, he escaped. But Edward . . . now they know he harboured a Jesuit."

It fell into place then. The Towneleys, like Alice Nutter's family at Roughlee, clung to the old religion. Everyone knew what happened to priests and those who sheltered them, like this Edward of Parbold must have done. Like Alice Nutter herself did. With a start I remembered the day when, as a five-year-old child, I'd followed her and Gran into that secret recess where her pale young priest dwelt in the gloom. Was the same man still there, or had he moved on and had another Jesuit missionary come to take his place? I'd no business listening to any of this, for it made me a witness to high treason. But I could not draw away.

"My Henry was there at Lawrence Bailey's execution." Mistress Towneley still wept. "Said it was the most ungodly spectacle he'd ever seen. They sliced him right open."

Alice Nutter said something in a voice too low for me to make out.

"But how can you go on like this?" Mistress Towneley asked her. "You know what could happen to you."

Mistress Alice was a widow, the head of her household, and if it wasn't her they executed for hiding the priest, then it would be her eldest son, Miles. Even if they spared her, the sight of her son being drawn and quartered would destroy her.

"Sometimes I fancy there's a noose around my neck," Alice Nutter said. "And it draws tighter each day." Those words of hers raised my flesh as much as any of Gran's talk of spirits ever had.

I left Carr Hall feeling even more wretched than I had upon leaving the Holdens' the day before. In such a maddle, I was, my head fair bursting from the burden of what I'd heard. Such secrets I carried, dangerous enough to get Alice Nutter strung up on the gibbet.

But there was no respite in store for me. When I reached Malkin Tower, what did I see but our Jamie hunched by the west wall. Filling a hole with earth, he was, then stamping it down into place.

"Our Jamie! Are you burying something?"

He shot me such a look over his shoulder, as though I'd caught him up to no good, and then he legged it off and away like a hare.

Such a humming filled my ears—a panic that made me long to run away, too. Instead I made myself dig up the dirt with the spade Jamie'd left behind till I'd uncovered a bit of sacking. I knelt down, pulled the bundle out of the dirt. Upon opening it, I let out such a scream that the birds scattered from the trees. Our Jamie had buried a clay poppet, shaped to a woman's form. What dark business did he meddle in—was this his way of getting even with Mistress Towneley?

I'd no idea what to do. If I tried to destroy this thing, Mistress Towneley, or whoever Jamie had modelled it after, might come to harm. I couldn't burn it or crush it or crumble it. Most I could do was hide it away where Jamie could never find it and ask Gran to do a counterspell. But before I could rise to my feet, I sensed someone stood there watching. Quailing, I looked up to see our Jennet's pinched white face.

"You're a witch. You made Nancy sick."

"Shut it, you witless thing! I didn't make this, our Jamie—" I broke off, not knowing if I could trust that cold Puritan's daughter.

"Jamie means to hurt someone," she said, so full of herself that it was all I could do not to take her over my knee and paddle her till she was blistered. "Terrible wicked, he is. He'll go straight to hell."

"Jamie never harmed a soul. None of us here ever did." But there I was, holding my brother's clay picture in my hand.

"What will you do with it?" Jennet's chilly eyes narrowed to slits.

"Ask Gran to set it right. Keep your mouth shut about this, mind. If you say a word to anybody, I'll birch you and that's a promise." With my free hand, I grasped her wrist and squeezed till she went red in the face and muttered her promise. Only then did I let her go.

"You'll have to fetch Gran," she sniffed, rubbing her smarting wrist. "She's sat on that rock under the thorn tree. I led her out so it's your turn to bring her back." At that, my sister stamped off.

I wrapped the clay doll back in its sacking, and then, looking twice round me, hid it in the hollow of an oak tree, high and out of Jennet's reach, before setting off to get Gran.

From twenty paces away I saw her, her face uplifted. A nimbus of golden light shone about her, bathing her skin. Before me I saw a vision of how she must have looked as a young woman, full beautiful and not blind, for her moist, yearning eyes gazed up at her lover, her Tibb, and though I could not see him, I knew she did. I knew him to be there. Rapt as Gran herself, I stared, unable to look away. Gran spoke to him, her lips moving whilst she listened to his replies. Such awe filled me, and for a spell I fair forgot about Jamie's clay poppet, about Mistress Towneley and Alice Nutter's plight. I'd only eyes for that astounding woman who was my gran.

Such powers! To think that her blood ran in my veins. In the days of the old religion, folk would have called her a saint for her gift of healing. They would have called Tibb her angel. But then I had to admit that wasn't true. Tibb was no angel. Whatever he was saying saddened her, for her eyes clouded and slowly the glow round her faded till I only saw my old gran with her wrinkled skin, alone and weeping.

Hitching up my skirts, I ran to her.

"Our Alizon, an ill wind blows."

"I know it," I said, about to tell her of Jamie's misdeed, and then I found I could not, fearing that such knowledge would break her. Besides, Jamie was only simple and I truly believed he'd no idea of the woe he could wreak.

"Gran," I said instead, "I fear Mistress Towneley is in danger. Can you say a blessing for her? I saw Chattox this day." How I trembled at my lie, wondering if Gran would see right through me. "I saw her with a clay figure in her basket, and this time I was bold and wrested it from her. She wished ill on Mistress Towneley for refusing her alms. If I gave you the clay picture, could you undo the harm?"

I held my breath, waiting, whilst she rubbed the tears from her eyes. If this talk of Chattox distressed her so, how much more despairing would she be if she knew that Jamie was the culprit?

"I've never known Mistress Towneley to refuse alms," she said at last. "Poor Chattox is off her head." She gripped my arm and heaved herself off the boulder.

My arm round her middle, I guided her down the track and back home, getting her settled upon her stool before I sprinted out the door to fetch the clay doll. My hand reached into the tree hollow where I'd left it. But it wasn't there. Jamie must have seen me hiding it, for it was well gone.

Gran murmured her charms and blessing whilst I prayed for Mistress Towneley till my knees ached. As for Jamie, whenever he so much as saw me step toward him, he turned tail and fled. When he had to come in to eat, he closed his ears to me.

"Mistress Towneley means you no ill," I told him, standing over his pallet whilst he lay there pretending to sleep. "She's troubles enough of her own. Our Jamie, please. What about your immortal soul?"

"My soul belongs to Jesus Christ," he said, his eyes squeezed shut. "I gave only part of my soul to Dandy."

"Did Dandy tell you to make that picture?"

"Folk think they can use me however they like. I'll show them."

"Jamie!" I dropped to my knees and stroked his hair as though I were his mam, not his younger sister. As though he were a little boy and not a huge strapping man. "Please, Jamie, if you love the rest of us, have a heart. Stop this mischief or you'll be the ruin of us."

· · ·

An ill wind blew, all right. In the August Assizes, Mistress Towneley's brother, Edward Rigby of Parbold, was hanged, drawn, and quartered, his private parts lobbed off whilst he was still alive, his beating heart yanked from his body, so folk said. Less than a fortnight later, Mistress Towneley miscarried. Though Henry Towneley sent for the best physician he could afford, she died three days on, delirious with fever.

Anne Towneley was buried on a bitter September day with gales blasting down from the moors. When I took my place with the other poor folk come to pay their respects, Jamie jigged up and down to keep warm. A grin spread across his face, as though the sight of Anne Towneley's coffin tickled him. My brother seemed almost smug with what he fancied his clay picture had wrought. His sheer lack of remorse left me so wretched, I hadn't the nerve left to glare at him. Was our Jamie a murderer then? Or had her brother's tragedy broken Mistress Towneley down so that she had miscarried and died of her own despair?

Blessed ignorant of Jamie's mischief, Mam was of a more practical mind concerning Mistress Towneley's demise.

"Her husband was a fool, sending for a doctor when it was a midwife she needed. What do men know about miscarrying?"

Mam made a show of ignoring Chattox, stood only a dozen paces away, but I couldn't keep myself from stealing glances at her. She was even thinner than when I'd seen her at the Holdens' gate. No doubt she'd come for alms, seeing as the Towneleys still followed the old tradition of giving out funeral doles of bread to the poor.

Gran herself, being of frail health, had stayed home with Jennet to mind her, but her stories came alive in my head. She'd told me that when she was young, the Towneleys of Carr Hall used to put on Yuletide revels with feasting and dancing, the humble joining in with the rich, and the Lord of Misrule kissing the girls and showing his bottom to the highborn men. Not a trace remained of those happy times. Master Towneley had lost both his young wife and the unborn child who was to be their first-born. Now he'd have no one but servants to welcome him when he returned to his hall. Maybe he would marry again, by and by, or maybe he would mourn his dead wife forever and die alone, without an heir, and that would be the end of the line for the Towneleys of Carr Hall. The dead woman's voice rang out in my memory. *May God rid us of this cursed King. He won't be satisfied until he's murdered us all!*

Our Jamie laughed aloud, which made everyone in that churchyard stare at us. I ducked my chin right down. Would folk suspect my brother of witchcraft, just to see him with that stupid glee plastered on his face, or would they shrug their shoulders at Idiot Jamie who knew no better than to guffaw at a gentlewoman's funeral? Mam, not one to suffer his nonsense, dragged him off so he could cause us no further embarrassment.

My tears scalded me. Could I have saved Mistress Towneley if I'd told Gran the truth about Jamie's malice instead of lying and laying the blame upon Chattox? Perhaps then Gran's counterspells might have worked.

After the burial rites, after even Master Towneley had withdrawn, Alice Nutter lingered by her friend's grave. The secrets she was keeping must have weighed heavy, as did my own, though mine were well different from hers. Least she didn't have a brother who tried to murder folk by witchcraft.

Shy as the five-year-old child who had once stepped into her hidden sanctuary, I approached her.

"Mistress Alice, I'm dreadful sorry. Terrible, what happened."

The lady's grey eyes held mine as she pressed her bloodless lips together. She looked at me as though she'd powers of her own that made it plain to her I wasn't just saying I was sad that she'd lost her friend. Mistress Alice could tell that I knew things I'd no business knowing.

"You eavesdropped that day, didn't you?" she asked me in a voice quiet as gravedust settling.

For all the high regard she held for my grandmother and the generosity she'd shown to my family over the years, these were trying times, when neighbour turned against neighbour and servant against master. Someone, after all, had betrayed Edward of Parbold, and someone might do the same to Alice Nutter. Had she come to regret the revelations she had entrusted to me when I was a child, my eyes turned in wonder to her statue of Our Lady? Now that I was grown, I could be a danger to her if my tongue was loose, if I proved disloyal. She seemed convinced that her fate rested in my hands.

I stared at the hem of her black gown, smudged by clay unearthed by the gravediggers. What would Mistress Alice think if she knew what lie hidden inside Jamie and me?

"I'm so sorry," I told her again, stammering as though I were no older than Jennet.

My brother had committed the unforgivable and I'd not been able to stop him. Perhaps he and I were both beyond redemption. Still I owed it to Mistress Alice to offer what solace I could, to find the words to tell her that I would never betray her but keep her secrets buried deep as my own. I remembered the words of comfort she had whispered in my ear the day of my father's funeral, nine years ago.

"By Our Lady," I said, gathering my courage to look Alice Nutter in the eye. "I'll pray for her. I'll pray for Mistress Towneley."

Colour flooded her face and she took my hands, for with those few words I'd allied myself with the old religion, as though I'd cast my lot in with hers.

# 14

S OMETIMES FORTUNE GRANTS small favours. To my unending gratitude, Nancy's parents decided not to pack her
off to Trawden Forest straightaway, least not before Christmas,
and that gave us some time together before she was wrenched
from my sight. I visited her every chance I could, doing whatever
work her mam gave me and not minding how hard or dull it was
if it allowed me to sit a spell with my friend.

One rainy afternoon whilst her mam was off visiting a neighbour, the two of us were sat spinning when Nancy arose from her
stool and crooked her finger, beckoning me near. She pressed my
ear to her thin chest.

"Listen," she said. "What do you hear?"

"Your heartbeat, of course. What else would I be hearing? A
herd of mooing cattle?"

"It's no joke, our Alizon."

She sounded so fretful that I could only humour her. Closing
my eyes, I listened with as much care as I'd mustered that day in
Carr Hall, stood in the fireplace and listening to Mistress Towneley's distraught words to Alice Nutter.

Most folk have a heartbeat as steady and even as a patient-
plodding horse, but Nancy's was that of a fresh yearling unsure
of where it wanted to go. It galloped here and there, stopping
in between. I lifted my head and gazed into her eyes, wide and
gleaming. She breathed quick, her kirtle rising and falling.

"Well?" she asked.

"Your heart beats just a little faster than mine."

"You mean to be kind," she said, "but you know there's more to it than that."

"There must be some physick," I said, my mind racing. "I'll ask my gran. All them herbs of hers. She must have some cure."

"It's nowt that even your gran can cure, our Alizon. When Chattox looked at me over the gate that day, she looked into my heart. I haven't been the same since."

"My gran broke the spell!" I cried, stung, for Gran had near killed herself mending Nancy, and yet Nancy still thought she was cursed.

"Do you believe in heaven?" my friend asked me.

"Course I do! You think I'm some heathen?" Then I flushed at the thought of Jamie and his clay picture; of Gran and her Tibb who was no angel; of the black dog that had clung to my side when I'd upbraided Chattox, how the beast had howled and snapped as if to do my bidding.

"I'm not so sure about it myself." She smiled, all crooked. "I don't know for certain I'm part of the Elect. Maybe I'm not bound for heaven."

"Now you're talking rubbish. Stop being such a wet thing. Sure you've more backbone than that."

But Nancy would not be swayed. "When Chattox looked into my heart, she saw me for what I am." An eerie calm took hold of my friend. "Our Alizon, I must be wicked. I don't want to marry this young man they've chosen for me, even though there's nowt wrong with him. He's not even ugly. But I would rather stay ill than be his wife."

"Tell that to your mam," I begged her. "Maybe she'll call it off."

"Alizon, if I live, I'm bound to marry one day. If not that young man, then some old widower. But I fancy I won't live to see the day. I was never that strong or well, even before Chattox over-looked me, and I know my life-thread is short. I've left off fight-ing it. Don't look at me so, Alizon," she said, brushing away my tears. "I'm not asking you to pity me. For all my sinful thoughts and disobedience, I know I'm not bound for heaven, yet I hope I'll escape hell. Is there another place I might go?" She gripped my shoulders. "Don't you Papists believe in purgatory? Alizon, if I go there, you'll pray for me, won't you? Then one day I might reach heaven."

I could only shake my head at her. "Our Nancy, you don't know what you're saying."

But she insisted. "Will you pray for me, Alizon?"

"Course I will." I held her so that her heart beat against mine.

Stumbling home in the rain, I saw only grey. Clouds pressed low and dour, shrouding Pendle Hill. Nancy's talk of heaven and hell nettled me, for it made me ask myself where I was bound. Did I truly believe I would ever reach heaven, and what of Jamie now that he'd worked evil against Mistress Towneley? What of Gran herself, led and beguiled by Tibb? Were we even godly folk, my family at Malkin Tower? In our hearts, we refused to embrace the new church, and yet we weren't proper Catholics like Alice Nutter. I'd never received any of the sacraments of the old faith and had only once clapped eyes on a living, breathing priest, who made quick to show us he'd no high opinion of Gran. Much as I adored Our Lady and took comfort in the forbidden prayers, I couldn't say I fancied laying down my life as a martyr as Mistress Towneley's brother had done, or as Alice Nutter and her son might well do if their luck turned bad. What was I then?

For just a moment I pictured myself a charmer as mighty as Gran. If my soul was damned anyway, why should I not use the cunning craft to unbend what was twisted? What a boon it would be to banish the darkness that hounded Nancy, to bind Jamie to the path of goodness, and to take it on myself without ever burdening Gran—this was too much for her at her age. By rights she should bide her remaining years in peace. One day, far sooner than I wished, she would pass on and then it would be down to me to provide for Mam and my sister, and do my best to keep Jamie out of trouble.

Jennet's voice seemed to call out of the fog. *When Gran dies, you'll be the witch!*

My sight blurred and I slipped in the mud. When I hauled myself up, a dark shape filled my vision, as if in answer to my inmost prayer. The black dog pressed its wet, quivering body against mine.

Too frightened to cry out, I took off running so fast and hard that a stitch sliced my side. But there was no escaping this thing. The creature charged after me, yapping and yowling, following me home to Malkin Tower.

Reaching our gate, I leapt over, praying to leave that thing behind. But the beast found a way to scramble over the drystone wall. I dove for the door, opening it only wide enough to squeeze myself through, then bolted it.

Before I could even wring the rain out of my skirts, Gran limped toward me. Beaming, she was, as though I'd come home covered in gold.

"Our Alizon, did that dog follow you home?"

Outside, the creature scratched upon the door and whimpered, full plaintive. Then what did our Jamie do but unlatch the door and let the thing in. It made straight for me, prancing round me in a circle. Mam let out a fearful moan. For the first time in years I saw her cross herself.

"Alizon got herself a spirit," Jamie said. "Only she doesn't know his name."

"*Her* name," said Gran.

The animal flung itself at my feet and rolled over, belly up, revealing itself to be a bitch.

Gran grasped my elbow. "Has she appeared to you before?"

Too frozen up to say a word, I hid my face in my cupped hands.

"Alizon's time has come," Jamie crowed.

"But she hasn't told you her name?" Gran wouldn't let it rest. "Have you asked her?"

Her eyes big as goose eggs, Jennet gawped at the dog till it jumped up and licked her full in the face. With a scream, my sister pitched herself into Mam's apron, clinging to her.

"It's the Devil," my sister sobbed. "Alizon brought the Devil into the house."

"It's no devil," Gran said, her face glowing with expectation about what I was to become.

Mam gawped at me with frozen, glassy eyes, reminding me of my father in his deathbed, whilst Jennet shook and cried, too petrified to even look my way. I thought I'd gone stark mad. Something inside me snapped, and I hurtled out the door to escape from my family staring at me as though I'd come home a stranger. Weeping like a child who had just lost her father, I staggered up Blacko Hill with the black bitch chasing me. Jamie's voice whispered inside me. *She comes. Her path crosses yours. There's no running away from her, Alizon.*

Flinging myself down, I rocked back and forth, back and forth, as Jamie would do, till my hair and clothes were rain-sodden and I cowered in a pool of mud. When at last I dared to look round, it was gloomy-dark. Tree branches writhed in the wind whilst the damp leaves slithered. But the black dog was nowhere.

When I dragged myself down to Malkin Tower, my brow throbbed in fever. I was chilled through, shivering too hard to speak a word.

The second I crossed the threshold, Mam folded me in her arms and wept over me as though I'd crawled back from the dead. Turning to Gran and Jamie, she spoke up sharp.

"You two stop plaguing my girl. I don't want to hear another word about familiars." First time I'd ever seen her standing up to Gran.

Shooing the others from the room, she stripped off my wet clothes and dried me in front of the fire before helping me into a clean shift. Wrapping a blanket round me, she steered me to her own pallet. Mam, not Gran, brewed feverfew, mint, and valerian. She stayed by my side the whole night through, laying cool cloths upon my forehead till the fever broke.

We were of the same mind, my mother and I, wanting nothing more than that I should awaken the next morning with my health and peace of mind restored. That I would simply be her daughter again, plain Alizon Device. No cunning woman and no witch. No terrified thing chased down by spirits.

Heavy rain had turned the tracks of Pendle Forest into quagmires. Mam wouldn't allow me to walk to Bull Hole Farm, saying I'd catch my death. Instead she brought me and Jennet along to work at Henry Mitton's, his house being only a stone's throw from Malkin Tower. To be dead honest, I'd no liking for the man who had once refused Gran a penny when we were hungry and needy, and his goodwife was just as sour. In their draughty kitchen I was sat spinning with only the poorest of fires and a bowl of watery broth for comfort. But work was work. I spun till my fingers turned to lead whilst Mam carded and Jennet wound the yarn. High time my little sister learned to do something more useful than whine about my devil dog. At least she'd kept her promise not to tell anyone about Jamie's clay picture.

Jamie himself was working for Master Duckworth, in the hope that the man would give him his old linen shirt as a reward for mucking out the cow byre. Gran was left behind at Malkin Tower. Saddened me, it did, to think of her spending her hours so lonely, but I was well nervous round her these days. Though she'd left off even mentioning the dog, I could tell that underneath it all, she was disappointed in me. I'd let her down, so I had, but it was time for Gran to face the fact that I just wasn't made of the same stuff as she was.

On Sunday, with the roads awash in mud, Gran again stayed behind as the rest of us made our cumbersome way to the New Church.

Soon as I stepped through the lych-gate, I sensed something

was not right. From the ash tree with its golden autumn leaves, a murder of crows cawed, raucous as a host of demons. The Holdens were gathered on the church porch with a cluster of folk about them. I spotted Nancy's parents, Matthew, and the little children, every one of them downcast.

Breathless, I raced up, looking for Nancy. Yet I knew even before Mistress Holden clutched me with shaking fingers that my friend had passed in her sleep. Forgetting myself, I wailed as though a hunk of flesh had been hacked from my side. Chattox had robbed me of my father, and now she'd stolen away my dearest friend.

Jagged and raw, I sobbed till Mam wrapped her arms round me and steered me into the church. Held my hand all through the service, she did, and her strength buoyed me. I knew that she understood my pain when Gran did not, so blinded Gran was by whatever loyalty had once bound her to Chattox. My eyes scoured the congregation for that hag's despicable face, but, like Gran, she'd stayed home, being too old and feeble to flounder those miles through the mud. Only Annie Redfearn and her girl had come, their skirts coated in muck.

Surely now the Holdens must lay blame upon Chattox. After church would be the perfect time, with all the parishioners to bear witness. Roger Nowell attended church in Whalley, but Constable Henry Hargreaves was right in our midst. One word to him and he'd ride for West Close, arrest her, and haul her in for questioning. Half of Pendle Forest would be willing to speak against her, so I wagered, and my mam would be first amongst them to denounce Anne Whittle as a murdering witch.

After we'd sung the final hymn and the Curate gave us leave to depart, I turned to Anthony Holden and waited for him to speak out, but he only hastened out of church. I ran after him. *Say it. Just open your mouth and have at it.* I was bold enough to reach for his hand and stare up, beseeching, at his face. My friend's father looked at me with brimming eyes. The man was fair unable to string two words together in the state he was in.

Mistress Holden took my arm. "Would you like to come back with us, Alizon, and see her one last time before we lay her in her coffin?"

My friend rested upon her bed, her hands crossed over her slender breast. Nancy was fresh and lovely as I'd ever seen her. Her mam had bathed and dressed her with such care, I could almost believe she was sleeping and would awaken any minute, smile into my eyes, and laugh at the cruel trick she'd played on us. She was clad in her best gown, trimmed in lace and velvet braid, as though it were her wedding day. A garland of Michaelmas daisies crowned her loosened hair. Stroking her curls, I could not get over how peaceable she looked, happy even, a smile upon her lips. But when I touched her cheek, it was cold as my father's had been the morning I'd rushed to his bedside to find him murdered.

Helpless and undone, I burst into tears. Mistress Holden hugged me close, and I cleaved to her as I'd once done to Nancy. When we drew apart, Mistress Holden took a folded blanket from the foot of Nancy's bed.

"This was hers," she said, offering it to me with both her hands. "Take it, love. She'd want you to have it."

I pressed my face to the wool, so warm and soft, with one of Nancy's long, curling hairs still clinging to the weave.

On my way home I bore the blanket high upon my shoulders to keep it clear of the mud.

That night I kept my promise to Nancy. Whilst the rest of my family slept, I prayed for her immortal soul, chanting my Aves till Jennet burrowed deep in the bedclothes to block out my voice. I prayed till my throat ached and my knees turned to wood, prayed that my friend might step through the gates of paradise into that glorious place where Chattox could never trouble her again.

. . .

The roads had dried out some by the day of Nancy's funeral, making it possible for Gran to make the journey with me guiding her along. When we reached the New Church, we could scarce squeeze our way through the throng gathered from far and wide. Nancy's godmother had travelled from Trawden Forest with her dark-haired nephew who had been Nancy's betrothed. I wondered if he would grieve her a tenth as much as I did.

Nancy's coffin was strewn with asters, ivy, and late-blooming roses, but when the men lowered it into the earth, dirt soon shrouded the lovely blooms. So it had been with my friend's life, snuffed out far too soon thanks to Chattox.

Gran craned her neck, her blind eyes raking the crowd. "She's missing. She didn't come."

"If Chattox isn't here," said Mam, "it's because the Holdens let it be known she wasn't welcome."

Gran's face twisted to one side as though a ghostly hand had slapped her. Even I had to admit I'd never heard of anybody being banned from a funeral. A serious slight, that was. Folk would murmur about it for weeks. This was the closest thing to an open condemnation that could transpire without Anthony Holden taking himself to Roger Nowell and outright declaring Chattox the agent of his daughter's death.

When the burial had ended, Mistress Holden was stood at the lych-gate handing out funeral doles to the poor. She gave us more bread than we could carry. But Chattox and her daughter would go without.

Winter took its toll. That miser Henry Mitton died, and the chill crippled my gran, freezing up her joints. She could no longer mount the tower stairs without one of us guiding her. During those months of cold and darkness, she dwindled and grew ever frailer. Only time she stopped shivering was when she was sat before the fire, though the smoke made her eyes stream. Yet her wits remained sharp as the wind trumpeting down the chimney.

One afternoon when the others were out, I stayed home to look after her, fixing an herbal potion to ease her cough. The herbs were so bitter I worried she'd have a hard time getting the stuff down.

"Next time I go to market, I'll bring you back some honey," I promised.

Gran just screwed up her face and knocked back the physick as though she'd far more important matters on her mind.

"Go up the tower, love, and fetch my pallet. I'll sleep down here from now on."

For all her pride, she'd finally broken down and admitted that the stairs had become too much for her. As long as I could remember, she'd slept in her room at the top of the tower—I couldn't picture that chamber without her inside it.

"I'll bring down your pallet. But come spring, you'll feel more limber. Then you might want to return to your room."

With my whole heart I longed to make time run backward so that she could be her old self—the gran I'd known in earliest childhood, that vigorous charmer who could still see and walk on her own, back in the days before Chattox had laid her curse upon us. In truth, I'd begun to suspect that Chattox's malevolence had cast this dark enchantment on Gran, which made her suffer and pine even as Chattox hungered now that she was cast out by decent folk.

"Bless you, Alizon," said Gran. "But my days of sleeping up the tower are gone for good." She grinned, some of her old spirit shining through. "But you, love, are a hardy young soul. Your blood's still warm enough to withstand the draughts. That room is yours. If you want it."

I turned away, for I knew she was offering me much more than a room. Though Gran had kept her word to Mam not to badger me about familiar spirits, she was now inviting me to take her place at the top of the tower, the place where a cunning woman would sleep.

A hollow buzz filled my head as I stripped her pallet and carried down the bedclothes and the bolster stuffed with straw and mugwort, the herb that gave Gran her visions. On the second trip I heaved the pallet itself up off the creaking oak boards and hefted it down the stairs to the hearthside. Quiet and brisk, I made up the pallet, placing it just so, with its head-end against the chimney breast so that Gran could sit up in bed with the bolster to cushion her back against the warm stone.

"There you are, Gran." I did my best to pretend I wasn't rattled by this.

"Now you'll want to make a pallet of your own since you won't be sleeping with Jennet anymore." Gran's lips curved in a smile. "When I was younger and still had my eyesight, nowt made me happier than lying a-bed and gazing out at the stars."

Lost in thought, she seemed, as though mulling over everything that she had lost to old age. But when I chafed her chilly hands in mine, the caul covering her eyes melted away. A much younger woman I saw, her face bathed in starlight. I blinked and saw the dusky firmament awash with pinpricks of light, the Milky Way sweeping across the heavens. The stars swirled in a diadem, a perfect wheel, spinning round and round Malkin Tower. Then the vision faded. and my heart banged loud enough to deafen me. Gran touched my face as if to draw me back to earth.

Mam helped me stitch the new pallet and bolster, then stuff them with straw, rosemary, catmint, and lovage. Not only did the herbs smell nice, but they also kept the fleas at bay.

My first night in the tower, I thought I'd die of frostbite as the draught whistled through the window slits. Even so, I was well overjoyed to be shot of sharing a pallet with Jennet. Nestled in Nancy's blanket, I lay in blessed contentment with no sister to shove and kick me.

The dark of the moon, it was. In every window the stars blazed pure white fire. As a blast of wind stirred my hair, I imagined I was soaring through the heavens to join Nancy, who took my hand, bearing me aloft, higher and higher till Malkin Tower and then Pendle Hill were lost in the swimming darkness below. Fair thrilled me, that did. Off in the night a hound wailed, rending the stillness. But I shut my ears to the thing and called out to Nancy, letting her draw me above it all.

# 15

I N THE MORNING I set out for Colne Market with my basket of fresh eggs to sell.

Threading my way through the stalls, I pricked my ears to the gossip, fair curious to know if folk would speak ill of Chattox after she'd been shunned from Nancy's funeral, but I heard nowt to do with her. Out of sight, out of mind, she was. Old and infirm, she wasn't likely to show her head outside her door in such weather. Air was so cold it turned my breath to mist.

In hope of soaking up some warmth, I wound my way through the horse market, passing close by those shaggy creatures with their steaming coats. Young lads galloped them over the green to show off their paces whilst the sellers were stood beside their nags, eager to open the animal's mouth to prove how young it was. Our Jamie, who should have been looking for a day's wages, sidled up to a bay mare. The pretty pony, hobbled to keep her from straying, rubbed her head against his chest. Using Jamie as a scratching post, so she was, and fair tolerating his clumsy stroking. Such a look of loneliness burned upon my brother's face as his fingers tangled themselves in her mane.

"Our Jamie!" I called out, sweet and gentle as I could. "Come along with me and watch me bargain!"

My words slid past him. Jerking away from me, he melted away amongst the horses, hucksters, and hawkers, whilst I threw icy stares at the men who muttered unkind things about him. Poor Jamie. When we were still children, I'd at least been able to protect him some, but now he was a man and had strayed beyond my ken.

Heavy-hearted, I shuffled through the warren of stalls in search of honey for Gran's raw throat. After scouring the market-place, I discovered that the only one with honey to sell was Richard Baldwin.

Right torn, I was. On the one hand, honey was honey, no matter how loathsome the vendor, and it would do Gran much good. But did I truly wish to have dealings with this thin-lipped hypocrite who had driven Gran, Mam, and me off his land, calling us whores and witches?

"And what did you come to the market to sell, Alizon Device?" he asked me with a cold gleam in his eye.

For one wicked moment I fancied that I possessed the powers to bowl him over and leave him gasping and full humiliated. Then, shrugging, I made up my mind to turn tail. Before I could walk away, Baldwin did his worst.

"They say your brother's an idiot," he said, making my hands prickle with the urge to slap him. "But that's not the whole story, Alizon, is it now?"

He used his loftiest manner, as if to remind me that he was the Church Warden, a man to be reckoned with. But I saw him for what he was: the fornicator who'd left my mother with his bastard.

"My brother," I said, "is a better man than you'll ever be."

Baldwin's face darkened. "Your brother's an idiot who knows how to curse people."

My boiling rage turned to ice-cold dread. "You're an idiot yourself to believe such twaddle." But the tremor in my voice gave away my fear.

Baldwin smiled, mirthless and cruel. "Plenty of talk going round about you lot at Malkin Tower. Henry Mitton refused your grandmother a penny and now he's dead. Then John Duckworth died after refusing your brother a shirt he'd coveted."

Jamie's clay picture flashed in my mind. Had he fashioned

ones for Mitton and Duckworth? That forlorn look in his eyes when I'd watched him stroking the mare proved that my brother was a lost soul. Seemed he didn't know right from wrong. If this went on, folk would call him an evil wizard and run to the Magistrate with their accusations. Unlike Chattox, Jamie wasn't old or weak or housebound but wandered wherever his wilful fancies took him.

"May God punish you for your slander," I told Baldwin.

Then, to my shame, I broke down into tears. Off strode Baldwin, leaving me to weep and hug my basket of eggs in the middle of Colne Market, and that was how Matthew Holden found me.

"Our Alizon, what happened?"

He looked at me with such concern, but I couldn't bring myself to tell him, not there in the throng with everyone eyeing us. Snow flakes fluttered down and the wind was enough to suck the warmth from a body, so Matthew gave me his arm and I clung to him as though he were my own brother, strong and canny enough to avenge me and Jamie. The good man took me to the Greyhound Inn, sat me upon a settle in the corner nearest the fire, and asked the tavern wife to bring me a mug of mulled ale and a trencher of hot mutton stew.

Took a while before the ale loosened my tongue, but finally I confessed what Baldwin had said about Jamie. Something in Matthew's face changed—I couldn't quite say what. He bided his time till I'd told him everything. Then he leaned close, his elbows on the greasy table, and talked in a low voice so only I would hear.

"Alizon, I know better than anyone that your grandmother's a blesser, not a witch." His voice shook upon that very word. *Witch.* "But you need to keep your brother on a tighter tether."

"What can I do? He's a grown man. Am I to keep him locked up?"

"There's some folk as would do just that with one such as your brother."

"Break his spirit, that would. It would be like killing him."

"You must find a way to rein him in." Never before had I heard Matthew Holden speak like this, grave as any curate. "Before tragedy strikes again."

"What do you mean?"

Did he, of all people, suspect that Jamie was responsible for Mistress Towneley's death? Or, worse yet, did he hold us to blame for what had happened to Nancy? I sickened to remember what little Jennet had said the day she'd caught me unearthing Jamie's clay picture. *You're a witch. You made Nancy sick.* My lost friend's face loomed before me, shivering in terror as she pointed to the black dog wriggling at my feet. Would she still have been my friend had she known it was not Chattox's familiar but mine?

Tears filled my eyes, blinding me to Matthew's face, and he laid a consoling hand over mine. My skin burned to think of everybody in that inn staring at the pair of us. No doubt the story would soon be warped into some lurid tale.

"Best keep yourself out of Baldwin's way," he told me.

"Not so easy avoiding folk of a market day," I said, wiping my eyes. "Everybody's in Colne today. I even saw Roger Nowell—"

"You'd no need to come to market." He smiled at me the way I thought he would have smiled at Nancy when giving her brotherly advice. "If you'd need for anything, you could have asked my mother."

Though I glowed under the light of his kindness, I still had my pride. "Matthew Holden, I'll have you know I'm no beggar to be always banging on your door when I lack something. I've eggs to sell." Then I remembered that our very hens were a gift from Matthew's family.

"So you do. Come, Alizon. Let's get those eggs of yours sold off before market closes. I'll bring some honey round to your gran tomorrow."

I walked through the market with Matthew now at my side, and none dared to slight me. With him haggling on my behalf, I traded my eggs for some smoked bacon and a great loaf of wheaten bread. Then, after searching for Jamie and not finding him, Matthew drove me home in his wagon. Soon he had me laughing, the way his sister used to do. Yet still I worried, for I'd no clue where Jamie had wandered.

Matthew drew his horses to a halt outside our gate.

"If you've need of anything, promise me you'll turn to us, Alizon. We mean to help."

As I gave him my promise, I traced the ghost of Nancy in the curve of his jaw and the depth of his brown eyes.

"Will you make me another promise?" he asked, looking at me so close that I blushed.

"Course I will, Matthew."

"Our Alizon, if you can't put an end to Jamie's mischief, then surely your grandmother can do something. Promise me you'll ask her."

So I gave him my word, for I could hardly deny it after all he'd done for me and mine. But I was red-faced and miserable as I clambered down from the wagon. Now I was bound to tell Gran the truth of what our Jamie had been playing at.

Gran dozed beside the dwindling fire in the darkening room. To her blind eyes night and day, murk and brightness, were the same. Yet when I stepped in the door, her eyes opened and a knowing shone upon her face.

"Our Alizon," she said, her brow creasing. "What's wrong, love? What happened to you?"

"Oh, Gran."

Just the two of us at home. Mam and Jennet had not yet returned from working at the Sellars' and Jamie was off with the fairies for all I knew. Setting down my basket with the bread and bacon, I knelt at Gran's feet and repeated every last despicable word of Baldwin's. Breaking down, I spilled how I'd lied about the clay picture: that it was Jamie's, not Chattox's, handiwork. Said how I'd dug it up and tried to hide it, only Jamie had found it again and I'd never seen it since.

"I don't know how to stop him, Gran." My head rested in her lap. "Do you think he did it? Does he have the powers to kill folk by magic?"

She crumpled. For a spell we cried together, my arms round her.

"Should have seen it coming," she said. "Tibb tried to warn me."

I longed to be in the Holdens' warm kitchen, safe and well-ordered, where nobody spoke of spirits or clay pictures. But then Gran left off weeping and drew herself upright. Before me I saw the cunning woman folk held in awe, my own grandmother whose mere words could send Baldwin wobbling away like a milk-faced coward. My gran whom Baldwin called witch. A steely look flashed in her blind eyes. Her powers seemed to charge the very air I breathed.

"Alizon, before your brother gets home, look about the ground for any loose earth where he might have buried a clay picture."

"Gran, it's well dark. If I go out there now, I'll not see my hand in front of my face."

Defeated, Gran nodded. She looked like an old woman again, knit with worry that the others were out so late.

A while later Mam and Jennet stumbled in.

"Our Alizon," Gran said. "Take your sister up the tower for a spell. I need to speak to your mam."

Jennet was tearing a chunk off the bread I'd brought back from market and cramming it in her mouth when I took her hand.

"Come with me, poppet."

Carrying a rush light in my free hand, I pulled her along up the stairs to the top chamber that was now mine. Setting the rush light down, I hoisted her so she could look out the window slits.

"There's a falling star! Make a wish."

Jennet was having none of it.

"You all *lie* to me," she said with a scowl fit to singe off my eyebrows. "You and Gran and Mam. Just because I'm little doesn't mean I'm an idiot like Jamie."

"Don't you dare say such hateful things about your brother."

"But he *is!* And he's been bad. I know he has."

"You know nothing about it."

She laughed, full scornful, as though she were the big sister and I the seven year old.

"That's what *you* think, our Alizon."

Down below, Mam's anger rose like a tempest, loud enough to stop my heart.

"What, bind Jamie?" she cried. "Oh aye. Some work that would be!"

Had Gran asked Mam's help, even though Mam had renounced her powers? Perhaps this fix was so great that even Gran couldn't mend it on her own. I felt so feeble then, the wind knocked out of me.

Mam started in on Baldwin. That snake, she called him. To think he dared accuse us when he refused to provide so much as a heel of bread to feed his own natural daughter. If it was down to him, our Jennet would starve.

My sister looked at me, tears shining in her eyes. She knew. How could she not? She was cannier than her years, our Jennet, and had probably picked up the gossip. Poor girl trembled from crown to toe as Mam began to curse Baldwin out, wishing every manner of woe upon him. Our mother's rage shook the very walls of the tower.

"Witches, he calls us! I'll show him the measure of his words."

Jennet let out a whimper and launched herself into my arms, hugging me tight as she'd never done before. All that night my sister huddled by my side, not letting go of me, and crying out each time she heard an owl or the wind rustling the thatch.

When I led Jennet downstairs in the morning, she seemed terrified of our mam. Shrank behind me, did Jennet, hiding herself behind my skirts, and I confess that I, too, was a sight skittish round our mother after listening to her fury the night before. But when I saw her fussing over Gran, combing through her hair and coaxing her to eat some bread, I understood that behind Mam's fearsome temper was an even fiercer love. She would stop at nothing to protect us.

After Mam and Jennet had left to work at the Sellars', I searched the ground skirting Malkin Tower for where our Jamie might have buried his clay pictures. When it came to hiding things, my brother was cannier than anyone I knew. I poked my head under every bush and was busy digging at the west side of the tower when a horse trotted up to the gate.

Matthew Holden hailed me. "Our Alizon, what are you digging?"

Must have looked right odd to him, for he'd caught me hacking away at the frost-bitten earth on a steep slope full of thistle and bulrushes. A fair maddle I was in, trying to explain my way out of this.

"These moles!" I laughed as the tale came to my tongue. "Gran asked me to dig them up in winter whilst they're sleeping."

Bemused, Matthew Holden sat back in his saddle. "A lot of labour, that. And they're harmless creatures, you know." He seemed to think it strange that folk common as us would be bothered by moles, and indeed we weren't, but I could hardly tell him the true purpose of my digging.

"I brought the honey for your grandmother," he said, springing off his horse. "My mother sent along a bottle of elderberry wine as well."

"Bless you, Matthew Holden!" Dropping my spade, I ran to open the gate for him. "My gran loves elderberry wine. Come inside and let her thank you herself."

But Matthew swung round with a start. Creeping up behind his horse came Jamie, looking half-starved, his breeches marked with wet clay. Matthew handed me the crock of honey and flask of wine before backing away, a careful hand on his horse's bridle.

My mouth went dry to see him go so pale. Dear Mother of God, Matthew Holden was afraid of our Jamie.

"Come, love," I called as my brother stretched out his long arm to stroke Matthew's horse. The animal snorted and pranced sideways. "No foolishness, Jamie," I spoke up. "Come stand behind me and let Matthew be on his way."

A light inside me died when I saw Matthew leap upon his horse and canter off without a backward glance.

"He's a false one," said my brother. "He'll let you down, our Alizon."

One careful step at a time, I led Jamie behind the tower where we would not be seen or heard from the road. Wanted to talk to him in private before leading him in to Gran. I took his face in my hands.

"Our Jamie, you're my only brother. I'd give my life for you, you know I would. But you must stop whatever wickedness you've been up to behind our backs. Tell me, love, what did you do with that clay doll I saw you bury?"

Jamie set his jaw. "I dried it out in a fire up Stang Top Moor, didn't I. Then I hid it there." Defiant and proud, my brother was. He wanted to get his own back on the folk who had mocked him and made him their fool. "After a spell I went back to crumple it a little each day till it was in pieces, and two days later Mistress Towneley was dead."

My gorge rose to hear my brother confess murder and witchcraft plain as day.

"You know what you did was evil, our Jamie. Don't you want to go to heaven? You can't unless you repent deep in your heart. Beg God's forgiveness and never do such a thing again."

"It was never me. I didn't make the clay picture." He toed the hard ground beneath his foot. "Dandy told me to do it. He made the clay picture. He promised to give me power over folk as do me wrong, if only I gave him my soul. But I wouldn't because my soul belongs to Jesus Christ."

"Jamie." I fought tears, wondering how I could make him face the true weight of what he had done. "You keep this up, you'll hang."

"No one can touch me," he said, aloof now.

"Did Dandy tell you to make clay pictures of Henry Mitton and John Duckworth?"

"Never Henry Mitton!" Jamie seemed scandalised by my very suggestion. "Last night I slept in the Mittons' byre and a thing coloured black, about the bigness of a hare, lay heavy upon me in the night."

"That would be a byre cat, our Jamie. Tell me the truth. Did you or Dandy make a clay picture of John Duckworth? You were right vexed with him, weren't you, when he wouldn't give you that shirt like he promised he would."

"I only touched his arm, our Alizon. Dandy did the rest. There was never a clay picture. Dandy could kill him on account of my touching him."

Leaning against the cold stone wall of Malkin Tower, I slid to the ground. My brother was beyond saving.

Jamie hunched down beside me. "After daybreak this morning I was walking over White Moor when I heard such a foul yowling, like a great number of cats, then voices like children skriking and crying. It was so pitiful, our Alizon."

I seized his hand. "That was your own soul crying out for mercy. You must strive to be a good man and not harm folk anymore, or let Dandy harm them for you."

My brother was silent, his face flushed as though in shame.

"Do you love me, our Jamie? Do you love our gran?" I knew better than to ask him if he loved our mam, since her temper alarmed him, or our Jennet, because she'd never been tender toward him.

"I do," he said, breaking down into long, shuddering sobs.

"Then promise me not to work evil again. *Promise* me, Jamie, or we'll hang for your mischief. Me and Gran will die."

My brother made his promise, and I held him and rubbed his uncombed hair. My heart beat away like mad, for I didn't know anymore whether I could trust him to keep his word. But when I led him inside to face Gran, he fell to his knees and swore how sorry he was.

Jamie was right chastened to see how his misdeeds undid Gran. She seemed to age ten years before our eyes, her breath laboured, her fingers stiffening to claws. Least there was no more talk from Jamie about clay pictures after that.

Our life at Malkin Tower went on, same as always—Mam and Jennet working at the Sellars', Jamie and I finding what work we could, and me leading Gran out to perform a blessing now and again.

To my joy, the Holdens rented the lands near Malkin Tower once more to graze their young stock. Reminded me of the happy bygone days when my father had been Anthony Holden's cowman. Lovely, it was, to watch the heifers and bullocks growing fat and sleek on the rich May grass.

Round about Whitsuntide, Anthony Holden called upon Gran to mend one of his heifers that had taken ill. Jennet led Gran out to the field whilst I looked on from the doorway. Gran held on to our Jennet with one hand and in the other she wielded her birchwood cane. Her limp was getting worse, her bad leg dragging behind her good one. After leading Gran to the tethered heifer, Jennet legged it home. Flew into the kitchen, my sister did, whey-faced and spooked, and helped Mam clear away the stale rushes without being asked. Anything to put Gran's cunning craft out of her mind.

I hoed for a spell in the garden before going to fetch Gran home. Weather was capricious that day, heavy clouds sending down bursts of rain, then moving on to let the sun shine and set the wet grass a-glitter. A double rainbow arched from Pendle Hill to White Moor. All seemed right and good till I found Gran doubled over her cane as though her insides were twisted up. The heifer heaved and limped in a circle whilst Gran's tears washed her cheeks. The look she gave me was so bleak.

"Alizon, I've fair lost my powers."

"No, Gran." I pulled her close.

She gripped my hand. "It's become too much for me. Time a new blesser came to take my place. You're sixteen, love. Not a child anymore."

I shivered in the full sunlight as her cauled eyes rested on mine.

"If I tell you the blessings, will you say them after me?" She was pleading. "Just try, our Alizon."

So what could I do but murmur back the words she chanted? Sinking to my knees in the sodden grass, I prayed over Anthony Holden's heifer with its swollen tongue and rolling eyes. Somewhere at the back of my head was that black dog, but I shut it out, cast it away. No light shone about me. I was empty as a shattered vessel.

When Matthew Holden rode over, he found the heifer dead and Gran weeping over its body as though it were a child that had perished on her watch. Being kind of heart, Matthew paid Gran just the same. But by and by, word travelled round that Old Demdike had failed. Folk muttered that she had grown too old and lost her touch. I wondered if it came down to her broken heart, for we, her family, had let her down. Jamie by his treachery and his ill use of the powers. Mam and I by renouncing the cunning craft. Jennet by her coldness and dearth of love. All this had ground Gran right down.

After the Holdens' heifer died, nobody called out Gran to perform a blessing again. Her cunning craft was the only thing that had raised us up above plain poverty and begging. With her no longer working, we were nowt but poor folk with nothing to show for ourselves. As if that were not enough, Richard Baldwin's lawful daughter died round about the same time as the Holdens' heifer. Baldwin had quarrelled with us, driving us off his land and calling us whores and witches, then a year on, his Ellen lost her life.

• • •

Round Maudlintide, I walked to the Holdens' farm in hope of a day's honest work. Much as it saddened me, I'd left Jamie behind because I knew the Holdens had no liking for him. Yet they'd always been so good to me. Striding up to their gate, I wrapped myself in the best memories I could conjure. How sheltered I'd felt in their home, how my heart used to leap when Nancy came darting out the door, overjoyed to see me. How, even in these dire days, I could count on Mistress Holden to load my trencher with good food and on Matthew to welcome me with kind words.

When I reached the gate, I found it barred. Thinking it must be some mistake, I called out, bright and bold as I always had.

"It's me! Alizon Device!"

I saw no one about. Perhaps the men were off somewhere, down the other side of the shippon, out of sight and earshot. I couldn't even catch a glimpse of any of the children and it was too fine a day for them to be penned up inside. Any other morning balmy as this, Mistress Holden would have them weeding the garden and carrying out the slop buckets to the chickens and geese. I thought I might clamber over the gate and go knock on their door when I saw Mistress Holden come out. With slow, steady steps she made her way toward me, a basket in her hand.

"Mistress Holden!" I waved happily. "Have you any spinning or carding for me?"

My stomach tightened to see her unsmiling face.

"We've no work for you, Alizon," she said, thrusting the basket over the gate at me. "But take this."

Not believing what I'd just heard, I laughed and tried to grasp her hand, but she shrank away out of my reach.

"I'm no beggar, Mistress Holden." My voice stretched thin and high. "It's honest work I'm after. I'd muck out your byre if you asked me."

"I'm sorry, love," she said, speaking too fast for me to cut in. "I know you're a good girl and you mean no harm, but bad luck follows you and yours, and we've had enough bad luck already. If ever you have need, come to us and we'll see to it that you don't go hungry. But we've no work for you anymore."

Turning round, she hurried back to her house, leaving me crying outside her gate, cast out and forsaken as Chattox herself.

In truth, I couldn't say whether I was more wounded or furious. Who were the Holdens to palm me off with a basket of victuals as though I were some leper? The basket Mistress Holden had hurled at me was packed with cheese and curds, oatcake and bread, berrycake and sliced beef tongue, and yet I'd a mind to chuck it down the nearest ditch. But I could scarce let my family clem to save my own pride. Weighed down by my shame and our need, I dragged Mistress Holden's basket home.

After the Holdens shunned me, others followed suit. Though I was healthy and young, strong and canny enough to earn my own living and do for my family besides, I was reduced to proper begging. I learned to gird myself against the rat-faced children who chanted *witch* and *beggar* whilst pelting me with stones. Fair tempted I was to run off to some distant town like Halifax or even Lancaster itself and start over again where no one knew my reputation. But if I took myself off like that, I'd leave my family in the lurch, so for their sake I stuck fast to Malkin Tower and endured the mockery and jibes.

Those days we struggled from day to day. My long-lost uncle Kit gave us what he could, a sack of oats or some turnips when he could spare them, but he'd nine children of his own to feed. If ever we'd meat to roast in our hearth, it was on account of Jamie's poaching. I'll confess he was not above rustling the odd sheep, butchering the unfortunate beast behind Malkin Tower, then burying its bones in our garden between the rows of cabbages and onions.

In times such as these, my family at Malkin Tower came to learn who our true friends were. The Bulcocks hated to see us so ill-done to. When I walked by Moss End Farm, Issy or her brother John came out and invited me into the kitchen where their mam made much of me and gave me a trencher full of whatever she had simmering in her pot. Kate Mouldheels, now a widow, welcomed us like family and was soft as butter with our Jamie, trusting that he was a good soul no matter what folk said of him.

Most generous of our well-wishers was Alice Nutter. Just like Mam, she was getting on in her years, her grey hair dressed high and her collars stiff with lace, but she always welcomed me to sit a spell beside her fire and even gave me some simple chore to do so I could pretend I'd earned the plate of steaming lamb pie and the mug of mulled wine she offered me. If she hadn't been hiding the priest inside her house, I think she would have even taken me on as a servant. As it was, she was already risking so much. If she'd been bold enough to hire me, she'd only draw more suspicion upon herself.

In truth, I couldn't fault her, for she was generous as a soul could be. If a week went by without one of us calling by Roughlee Hall, our Alice Nutter would ride out to Malkin Tower, her saddle bags bursting with provisions. She took special care to bring food and drink that were easy for Gran to get down: soft wheaten bread, sweet elderflower cordial, stewed plums, and egg custard.

So our days passed till the spring of 1612, when I turned seventeen.

# 16

O F A WEDNESDAY MORNING in March, I set out to try
my luck in Trawden Forest, on the other side of Colne, in
hope that some householder there might have work for me. If all
else failed, I could call by Mouldheels's house on the way home
and share a good natter and some pottage with her, for she was
lonely and seemed to cheer right up whenever I came by.

I cut across Slipper Hill, then skirted Colne, crossing Colne
Field, still littered with droppings from the horse fair last market day. Whistling a jig, I was contented enough and up to no
mischief when I saw the pedlar come plodding my way, his great
pack strapped to his back. The man seemed a bit long in the
tooth to be bearing such a load—he wasn't young by any stretch.
Round of belly and red of face, he was, a man who loved his ale,
to be sure. He looked to be heading for the Greyhound Inn.

So what did I do but hail him, for I was in need of pins. My
kirtle was worn down to rags, the seams near to splitting, but I'd
rather buy a few pins to hold my dress together than lower myself to wheedle for someone's cast-off clothes, the way our Jamie
had tried to do with John Duckworth.

Smiled right friendly to that pedlar, I did. Never seen him in
my life and that meant he likely knew nowt of me or my family at Malkin Tower. He'd just see me as an ordinary girl, or so I
hoped, and not as a girl from a family of cunning folk reduced to
begging.

"Good day to you, sir. Would you open your pack for me? I'd
like to buy some pins."

Though I'd used my best manners, the pedlar seemed fair displeased that I was stood between him and his next mug of ale.

"I'm not giving the likes of you any pins." Soon as he opened his mouth, I knew him to be a Yorkshireman and a gruff old gob at that. "I'm a chapman, not a charity."

My eyes smarted at the way he'd taken me to be the lowest sort of person, unworthy of his time. Though I might look to be penniless, I had, in fact, a few silver pennies in my pouch, thanks to our good Alice Nutter. To prove this, I whipped out my coins and passed them beneath his nose.

"I'm not begging. I can pay for your pins all right."

"Wasn't born yesterday," he said, trying to step past me. "I've seen that trick before. Show me some brass and soon as I open my pack, you'll be off with half my gear."

"Now you call me a thief?" I shook, I was so angry. "And me, an honest girl wanting some pins."

"Some honest girl. How did you get them pennies, lass? Did you steal them or did you earn them on your back?"

For a moment I could not speak. Dumbstruck, I was, by the red mist floating in the air between his face and mine. I'd been called witch and beggar, and many other bad names besides, but this was the first time anyone had dared call me a whore to my face. And I'd never so much as kissed a man.

"You'll come to rue your words, you pot-bellied bastard!"

He froze up then, that grown man, the whites of his eyes stark gleaming, and still I could not rein in my fury.

"The Devil take you for your mean heart."

I could scarce recall what other awful words ripped their way out of my throat, but I'd enough of being the butt of everyone's scorn. As my rage wrapped me in its fist, I understood the surge of wrath flying out of Mam when she'd cursed out Baldwin. I understood the throb of anger that had driven our Jamie to avenge himself against those who'd treated him like a witless dunce, as if he'd no feelings at all.

An unearthly humming filled my head, the power thrumming through my veins. Begging for mercy, the pedlar raised his hands as though he feared I'd strike him dead. Staring into his shrinking pupils, I saw the same raw fear I'd witnessed in Nancy the day Chattox had given her the devil.

From behind a hedge the black bitch hurtled toward me, summoned by my wicked ire. The creature danced round the man, snapping and snarling, so that he panicked all the more. Off he bolted toward the safety of Colne, fast as his stubby legs could take him, but his heavy pack dragged him down. The sky seemed to reel in a slow circle, the very birds silenced by the awfulness unfolding.

The fat chapman had run barely two hundred yards when he collapsed. The weight of his pack sent him sprawling, as though God himself had struck him down. Or the Devil. *The Devil take you for your mean heart.* My curse had come true before my eyes. Such a horror gripped me I could no longer feel my own heartbeat.

The black bitch pressed close, nuzzling and whimpering, as if to offer comfort. The powers had been with me all along. Hadn't I both cursed and then helped cure Issy Bulcock? Gran and even Jamie had tried to tell me, only I'd refused to see the truth. Blinder than my grandmother, I'd been. And now it was too late.

This was no blessed event such as when Gran first came into her powers to charm Anthony Holden's sour ale and heal his son. Instead I'd cursed out a stranger, then watched him go down. *No, no, no.* My brother's plaintive claim came back to me: *My soul belongs to Jesus Christ.*

With the black bitch at my heels, I bolted to where the Yorkshireman lay. One side of his face flinched at the sight of me whilst the other side was frozen up as if he'd seen every demon of hell. When I took his hand, he flailed, but one half of his body was so rigid, he couldn't so much as wiggle a finger. Poor man couldn't even speak. If I had allowed her, Gran would have trained me to be a blesser, working for good. But I'd spurned her every attempt, and so I'd become a witch worse than Chattox herself. I'd lamed a man, struck him mute, left him paralyzed in half his body.

"Undo it," I pleaded to the panting black creature who regarded me with fathomless eyes. "I'm sorry," I told the man, my tears falling upon his face, drawn white in shock.

Loud and fervent, I prayed for him till I saw three men passing through the field.

"Help him!" I cried, leaping to my feet and waving with both arms.

I knew these men by sight if not by name: the blacksmith, his son, and another man. With barbed eyes they looked from me to the stricken man and back again.

"Alizon Device, what happened to him?" the blacksmith asked. So he knew my name, though I didn't know his. "Was that dog of yours worrying him?"

"He fell over, didn't he? His pack was too heavy." On my knees upon the cold March earth, I rocked myself back and forth. "Help him, please. We can't leave him here."

So we unstrapped the pack from his shoulders, and the blacksmith and his son bore the pedlar away to the Greyhound Inn whilst the third man carried the pack. Following in their wake, I asked myself what I would tell Gran now that I'd crippled a man and there were three witnesses to my deed. Though I longed to run away into the far hills and never show my face in Pendle Forest again, I was bound to walk to that inn, one foot in front of the other, and stick my head in the door. I was bound to face my deed.

They laid the chapman upon a long wooden settle and spread a blanket over him. The tavern keeper was asking if anyone knew the man's name or his hometown, so that he might send word to his family. One of the men who'd seen him of a market day in Marsden said that the pedlar was John Law of Halifax.

Whilst I shivered in the doorway, the pedlar gazed up at me with his one eye that could still move in its socket.

"I'm sorry. I'm so sorry," I told him.

Then I fled, my feet flying, the cold wind stinging my face.

Part of me wanted to take Nancy's blanket, my only possession of worth, and be off, going to a place where no one knew my disgrace. But where? If I headed off to Yorkshire, I might meet the friends and kin of that pedlar I'd lamed. If I headed west, I'd still be in Lancaster County, still under the reach and power of Roger Nowell, High Sheriff. If I went south, I'd pass through Cheshire where Robert Assheton lay buried, cast down by Chattox herself. And if I travelled north, over the borders, I would find myself in Scotland, that lawless place where folk still raided for cattle and sheep, or so I'd been told. Maybe one as lost as me could find refuge in such a wild and forlorn land.

I wondered if anybody would try to pursue me and how far I could expect to wander, a girl on my own with nowt but a blanket, a threadbare kirtle, and a few pennies. Should I instead run to the nearest fell and leap to my death to spare my family my shame? Flinging myself off the top of Pendle Hill would be a sight easier than telling Gran what I'd done. Maybe it would be better and braver to turn myself in to the Magistrate and confess my crime, in the hope that the rest of my family would be spared. But Gran had made me swear never to go near him.

As my thoughts whirled round, I was frozen as that chapman. Turned to stone, so I was, like an evil witch in an old tale. But at last I crept home, quiet as I could. At this hour of afternoon, only Gran would be in, dozing by the fire. With some luck, I could steal past her and up the stairs, grab my blanket, and be gone, either to try my luck elsewhere or hasten my journey to hell. I still hadn't decided.

When I took my first step over the threshold, Gran's blind eyes caught me. Again I turned to stone.

"Our Alizon."

Her gaze told me that she knew of my misadventure, whether by the far sight or by Tibb whispering in her ear. Tears moved down her face, and she trembled as though Death himself lurked in that room, sickle in hand, preparing to cut us both down. But it was her tenderness that unravelled me and made me hide my face in her lap whilst she stroked my hair. I'd done my worst and she still loved me. I confessed everything, offering up my sin to her as to one of the priests of the old religion.

She wanted to know more of the black dog. "Did she speak to you, love? Did she tell you her name?"

"No! Never. I swear, she only ever took the form of a dog. Afterward I asked her to undo it, but nothing happened. Can *you* undo it, Gran?" My eyes locked with her sightless ones, and for a second I was giddy with the possibility that this burden could be lifted.

Gran seemed to look inside herself, searching for an answer. "This pedlar of yours is a stranger to us, love, from far beyond the bounds of Pendle Forest. I can't go to him unless he sends for me. The innkeeper might bar the door to us. It's down to you, our Alizon. You must pray for him. Pray as you've never done before."

My deed towered over me like some great mountain and I was lost within its shadow. "If you'd seen him, Gran! Lying there as though he were dead on one side of his body. I fear my prayers won't be enough."

Gran lifted my face to hers. "Today you know the true force of your powers. Go back out, our Alizon, and find that dog and pray that the chapman might still be mended."

Up and down the tracks of Pendle Forest I scrambled in search of the black bitch. When I spotted a dark shape dashing up a hill not far from Thorneyholme, I called out till I was hoarse, but it seemed useless enough since I'd never learned her name.

As I was stood there, clutching myself, I heard approaching hoofbeats. It took my last courage to stand my ground instead of scarpering. I would have to live with this now, no matter what, for that was what my loved ones had always done. My Mam hadn't shrivelled up and died after Baldwin ill-treated her and took to calling her a whore. Through it all, she'd held up her head and looked her name-callers in the eye. So I remained on the track and felt again the faint thrumming in my veins, the powers I didn't understand, and wondered if the singing-ringing in my head would be enough to call back that dog.

I braced myself to face that rider, be it friend or foe, even if it was Roger Nowell himself. At that thought, my fortitude deserted me and I was a heap of quivering bones when round the bend our Alice Nutter came trotting upon her chestnut roan mare, the horse's flaxen mane fluttering like a silken banner over its glossy neck.

"Alizon," she said, reining to a halt.

Straightaway I saw in her face that she'd heard the tale of what I'd done to the pedlar in Colne Field. Would she spurn me as the Holdens had done? Yet because I trusted her, I asked her, in a voice half-strangled, if she'd seen hide or hair of a stray black bitch.

The lady's eyebrows lifted all the way to the brim of her tall-crowned hat. But she didn't recoil from me.

"No, Alizon. In truth, I have not."

I dropped in a curtsey. "Thank you all the same, Mistress Nutter."

Instead of riding off then, the way some folk would have done, spattering mud over my kirtle, she reached into her deep saddlebag and pulled out a globe about the size of an apple and the colour of the sun at daylight gate.

"Here, Alizon," she said, stretching out her gloved hand so that I might take the golden-red ball from her hand.

I gazed up at her, full amazed, thinking she must be some conjurer, for I'd never seen anything like this before. Its cool surface was like soft leather, but bright and polished-looking, and when I raised it to my nose, it had the most heavenly smell.

"Take it home and share it with your grandmother. That's an orange. My relations in the south sent us up a box. It's a fruit than can only grow in glass houses in this country, but they grow in abundance in warmer climes. I've been told that the streets of Rome are lined with orange trees."

The picture her words painted made me think of the Garden of Eden. What a marvel to see trees heavy with these fruits.

"You peel off the skin with your fingers," she told me. "Then tear it into segments and eat it. I do hope your grandmother will like it."

As Alice Nutter said her farewell and trotted off gentle and easy, not splashing me once, I clung to her orange as though it were the talisman that could deliver me. So I wasn't despised by everybody in Pendle Forest. Even now there were those who stood by me and mine.

When I reached home that evening, I peeled the scented skin off Alice Nutter's orange and fed half of it to Gran, dividing the other half between Mam, Jamie, Jennet, and me, and I'd never tasted anything more delectable. The taste clung to my tongue for the rest of the evening.

I carried on searching for that dog, scouring every pasture and hillside from Colne Field to Stang Top Moor only to be left with the sinking feeling that I'd never see that black bitch again. The notion lodged itself in our Jamie's head that if we invented some fool ceremony to name my familiar spirit, it would show itself and then I could bid it to lift the curse off the chapman and we'd be out of danger. But Gran said the most we could do was pray—for the pedlar and for ourselves.

Come Sunday I'd no choice but to show myself in the New Church where I burned in my abasement. The Curate glowered at me whilst the Holdens seemed afraid to even look my way. My uncle Kit was stood there like a hag-ridden thing with shadowed, red-rimmed eyes, for I'd brought infamy not just upon myself but all my kin. Even gaunt-faced Annie Redfearn could not keep her eyes off me.

Yet after the service, in front of everyone, Alice Nutter walked up and took my hand, as if to prove to the entire parish that I was neither demon nor leper. I could hear the consternation buzzing round us like a swarm of bees.

"Is your grandmother well?" she asked. "It's a pity the journey has become too much for her. Is there anything she has need of? Just tell me, dear. I'll ride by Malkin Tower tomorrow."

That lady's goodness was enough to make me want to kneel

down and kiss her hand. But before I could reply to her, Constable Hargreaves pushed himself forward and said he needed to have a word with me. My stomach crawled and I feared I would be sick down his leather doublet. I looked past his shoulder to Mam whose lips were pressed thin and worried. Seeing my distress, Jamie stumbled forward, about to say something to the Constable, when Mam hauled my brother off, hissing at him to keep his gob shut. Our Jennet watched everything like some little unblinking toad, as if she believed in her heart that I was wicked and deserved whatever happened to me.

"Alizon Device," said the Constable. "I've three witnesses saying that you bewitched the pedlar, John Law."

My throat swelled tight. "I pray Master Law will soon mend. I never meant any harm, sir. If they let my gran bless him, he'll be right again, I swear."

Constable Hargreaves held up his hand to silence me. "Save your pretty stories for the Magistrate. He's been told."

Chilled to the core, I nodded.

"The people of Pendle have tolerated you lot for many years. That grandmother of yours has half the folk in terror of her. Even Master Baldwin doesn't dare call Demdike to account for shirking the Sabbath. But enough is enough."

So it had finally come down to this. Crying witch and pointing fingers, and not on account of Chattox but me. I'd brought this crashing down upon us.

"My gran's old and lame and blind, sir. Everybody knows that. She can't walk far, and we've no horse or wagon. But she fears God, to be sure, and says her prayers each day."

"Popish prayers and spells," he said. "A letter has been sent to the pedlar's son in Halifax. When it reaches him, he'll likely travel to Colne to see how his father fares."

"And how does Master Law fare, Constable, sir?" My hands folded to my heart.

His answer came curt. "He can speak again."

"Thank the Lord for that." I could scarce keep from crossing myself and calling out the name of the merciful Mother of God.

"The people of Colne have their opinions as to what your punishment should be. But," he said with a sigh, "the law of the land says we can't lift a finger against you unless John Law or Abraham Law, his son, bring their complaint to the Magistrate."

The breath I'd been holding inside my chest came bursting out. I thought I'd fall crashing to the ground like that Yorkshireman. So I wasn't damned, least not yet. I might still be able to atone for my wrong-doing and live a good and decent life.

After the Constable's warning, Mam thought it best to keep me out of folk's eye, so whilst she and Jennet went on their way to work at the Sellars', I stayed home with Gran and tried to be of use, sowing seeds in the garden and digging up weeds. Jamie was off only God knew where, and for once I envied him for being simple since I was never without the hammer of dread, wondering what was to come.

Our only visitor that week was Alice Nutter, her saddlebags bursting with bread and soft cakes and cheese for Gran. She told me she wanted to speak to my grandmother in private, so I showed her into Malkin Tower before going back to the garden and working myself into a cold sweat. I knew the two of them would be talking about me, about what was to be done about me. An age seemed to pass before Alice Nutter came out again and beckoned me. Dropping my hoe, I brushed the soil off my hands and went to her. Rigid with worry, I was. This time she'd no smile on her face.

"Despicable business, this talk of witchcraft," she said.

Head drooping, I nodded, thinking that the moment had come when she would condemn me along with the rest.

"Mark well my words, Alizon," she said, stepping close. "If one person makes an accusation of witchcraft, more could follow. People have whispered base nonsense about your grandmother for years, though, by Our Lady, nobody's dared act on it."

"Gran's a blesser," I said, as I would say to anyone. "She's done nowt but good for folk."

"I know, dear." Alice Nutter took my hand the way she had

after church on Sunday. "But none of us in Pendle Forest can risk another accident like you had with that pedlar."

Her words left me dazed. She believed what had happened in Colne Field to be a mere accident? What had Gran been telling her? Gran would weave any tale if she thought it could save me.

"You must leave off the begging and wandering," Mistress Alice told me.

"I would do just that, ma'am, if I could find steady, honest work."

"I know you're a good girl who would do well at honest work given the chance. This Monday next, if you come to Roughlee Hall, I'll put you to work in my kitchen."

"Mistress Nutter." My eyes filled, not believing my luck or her generosity. Given what secrets she hid in her house, she could hire only servants she trusted with her life and the lives of her children. I thought I would indeed fall to my knees and kiss both her feet, but she carried on talking, practical as my mam would do, saying that if I came early on Monday, she'd see if she could find another kirtle and coif for me and an apron besides and some pattens for my feet, and that I wasn't to be late. I swore to her that I would rise at daybreak and make straight for Roughlee Hall.

Her face broke into a smile. "With God's grace, we may endure this, Alizon. Come hold my horse for me whilst I mount."

So I held steady to the reins and saddle as she mounted up. When her chestnut roan mare nuzzled my neck, I laughed for the first time in a fortnight. Every part of me glowing with gratitude, I waved my farewells to Mistress Alice till she and her horse had passed out of my sight.

Soon as she was gone, I flew into Malkin Tower and threw my arms round Gran.

"What did you tell Alice Nutter to get her to take me as a servant? You charmed her, you did." I rested my brow against hers.

"No, love. She acted from her own heart."

Gran trembled hard as I did, for we both knew how close we'd come to ruin, only Alice Nutter had saved us. I swore to Gran that I would serve my good mistress till her dying day.

Mam was best pleased when I told her the news.

"I've no cause to worry over you anymore," she said, pulling me close. "You'll be sat on a lush meadow serving Alice Nutter. One month at Roughlee Hall, and you'll be too fat to fit through the gate."

Over the moon, I was, to think of my good fortune — working every day in a warm, steamy kitchen and never knowing hunger again or the humiliation of begging or having some pedlar call me a whore when I'd wanted only to buy a few pins.

Jamie asked if he could come along and work for Alice Nutter as well, but I knew that could never be, for he couldn't be trusted to keep the close secrets of her house.

"I'll bring home plenty of cakes and pies for you," I promised. "You'll not clem."

"Maybe you won't be coming home at all," said Mam, fair carried away in her excitement. "Mistress Alice might want you to live up at Roughlee Hall."

My head began to spin at the thought of living in such a fine house, even if it meant sharing the servants' quarters in the attic.

"Once you've served her a good few years and earned her trust," said Mam, always thinking ahead, "you might persuade her to take on our Jennet. Then my work will be done, knowing both my girls have a livelihood and a kind mistress."

"And we'll both look after Jamie," I said, winking at my brother.

Jennet remained sour, as she would do. "Alizon's been bad and she gets rewarded. I've been good and I get nowt."

Gran gave Jennet a glare fearsome enough to turn her bones to ash. "Your sister was never bad. Now shut it."

• • •

"You told Mistress Alice it was an accident," I said to Gran late that night after everyone else had gone to bed. "*Was* it then?" My heart swelled in hope that this stain could be taken from me, that I'd done no evil at all.

"You're coming into your powers," Gran said. "You must learn to control them. Never speak out in anger like that again. Learn to hold your tongue. You'll go to Mistress Alice's hall where you'll be safe and looked after, but of a Sunday you'll come home to me and I'll teach you everything I know."

I held fast to her hand. "The black bitch. What if she's dead?" I could just imagine someone like Baldwin stoning her.

"A spirit is not a thing as can be killed, love." Gran spoke with a conviction that raised gooseflesh on my skin. "But we'll see to that later, after you're at Roughlee Hall and out of harm's way."

Sunday morning I kissed the rose-coloured ribbon Nancy had given me before tying up my fresh-combed hair. "Wish me luck," I whispered, hoping Nancy would hear me in heaven.

No matter what the other Holdens had done, I would always remember her with devotion as she had been my true friend. I vowed to keep her memory alive.

Smoothing my hair into place, I set my coif on my head and danced in a circle. I felt like my old self again, no longer like some hounded boggart. If my kirtle was ravelling apart, then my Mistress Alice would find another one for me come Monday morning. I only had to make it through this day and then my new life could begin.

Bright and eager, I set off for the New Church. Mam and I walked arm in arm, busy talking of my future and how much easier things would be for us. Jennet lagged behind, but we knew that if we ignored her, she'd catch up with us by and by. Jamie lurched about like a moonstruck calf, crashing into hedges and groaning about a mighty pain in his head.

"The skriking," he said, "like a great number of children crying out."

"Peace." I took his hand and tried to gentle him. "It's all right, love. We'll be all right."

In the churchyard Mistress Alice nodded to us whilst Mam and I curtseyed to her for everyone to see. I looked round for Constable Hargreaves and, not seeing him, decided that the bloated man had taken ill. But Baldwin was there, staring slit-eyed at Mam and me as though he were some great hooded crow. I just smiled to him whilst ruffling Jennet's hair, the same mouse brown as his own, then smirked to watch him flush wine-red. Jennet swatted my hand and Mam pinched my arm.

"Don't be too bold," she warned.

So I ducked my head as a modest girl should and filed into church. During the Curate's sermon, I stifled a yawn, for he was even dourer than usual, making every excuse to rant of hell and damnation, as if his preaching weren't endless torment enough. Working himself up was the Curate, till his voice reached a feverish pitch that made our eyes snap wide open.

"There are no accidents in God's design," he proclaimed. "Everything proceeds according to Divine Providence. Those that lead godly lives shall be rewarded in this world and in the next."

Out of the corner of my eye I could see Baldwin smile, smug as anything.

"Whilst those who turn their hearts and souls away from the true God shall be punished and brought low."

Here the Curate hooked his eyes upon Alice Nutter. Feeling faint, I fingered Nancy's ribbon for comfort. With a prickle, I remembered my friend's drained face the day after Chattox had cursed her. I remembered Nancy's fingers gripping mine as she told me of her nightmare. *I dreamt you were in danger, darkness and stench everywhere. I tried to help you but I couldn't reach you.*

"Sometimes God punishes the many," said the Curate, "for the sins of the few. Plagues and famine, storms and flood, and the deaths of those still young are brought upon us by the deeds of wicked souls. And so shall misfortune and calamity continue until we smite the evildoers in our midst."

When the Curate looked straight at me, everyone else did too, their eyes like a thousand bodkins lancing my flesh. Our Jamie began to sway and yammer in the midst of the congregation, forcing Mam to lead him out the door. Then I was left with no family but Jennet, who gazed at me, cool and pitiless, with Baldwin's crow eyes.

Counting the minutes, I was, till I could finally stagger out of that church, and when at last I did, three men awaited me in the churchyard, blocking my way to the lych-gate where Mam and Jamie watched with huge eyes. Jennet glanced from me to them, then burst into tears. I gazed wildly toward Alice Nutter, who looked back at me, her handkerchief clutched to her mouth. But even she was powerless to rescue me now.

Before me loomed Roger Nowell, looking a sight sterner than when I'd seen him last; Constable Hargreaves with his bull's jowls; and between them a strange young man, short and portly, in scuffed black riding boots. With sickening sureness, I knew he must be none other than Abraham Law, the lamed chapman's son.

Gawping at the stranger, I saw his father again, the pain and fear etched on the side of his face that could still move. Like Jamie, I was half-maddened by the voices leaping about inside my head. Alice Nutter's voice, patient and wise, was telling me that what had happened that day in Colne Field was an accident, no more—that was what a just person would believe. But in his sermon, the Curate had decreed there were no accidents.

"Alizon Device," said Roger Nowell. "Abraham Law, cloth dyer of Halifax, Yorkshire, has summoned me and Constable Hargreaves to bring you to his father, John Law, chapman of Halifax, who lies half-crippled at the Greyhound Inn in Colne."

Before I could say a thing, Constable's fat fist closed round my wrist, and I had to rush to keep up with his quick pace as he marched me out the lych-gate to the waiting wagon. I wrenched my head round to take one last glimpse of Mam, weeping whilst Alice Nutter held her shoulders.

The horses strained to drag the wagon along the road, muddy with spring rain. Every so often the Constable and Abraham Law had to leap off and push the wheels free of the mire whilst Roger Nowell stayed aboard to keep his eye on me. So frightened I was, my bones knocking together, that I didn't dare look at him. But when the other men's backs were turned, Nowell cupped my chin and raised my face, giving me a look that was almost fatherly. Odd though it might sound, there was something in his eyes that reminded me of Gran. He looked as though he possessed some of her understanding as to the secrets folk buried in their hearts.

"When we reach the inn and you face the chapman," he whispered, "speak from the heart and tell the truth. With any luck his son will be satisfied and let it lie."

"Thank you, sir," I whispered back, smiling shy at him, but remembering to hang my head when Hargreaves and Abraham Law clambered back into the wagon.

When we reached the Greyhound Inn, Hargreaves made to haul me down from the wagon, but Nowell stayed his hand.

"No need to manhandle the girl," said the Magistrate. "I doubt she'd be foolish enough to make a run for it in front of so many witnesses. Would you, Alizon?"

"No, sir," I promised him.

Obedient as anything, I followed Abraham Law whilst Hargreaves and Nowell followed behind me. We entered the inn, crammed with half the people of Colne, so it seemed, but at Nowell's word, they jumped aside to clear our path. Abraham Law led the way up the stairs, then down a corridor, and finally into his father's room. Even that small chamber was packed: the innkeeper and his sons were there, as well as a scribe sat with his goose quill and parchment. In the midst of it all John Law lay upon a four-poster—the rumour went that Nowell himself had paid to put the man up in the Greyhound's best room. Master Law was no longer fat as I remembered, but wasted-looking, as though he had hardly eaten or touched ale since I saw him last. Though he was still lame and frozen down his left side, both his eyes could move again. He stared at me with such rancour that I wished myself dead.

"John Law," said Roger Nowell, speaking calm and even, with none of Hargreaves's heated huffing. "Here before you stands Alizon Device. Is this the girl you met in Colne Field on Wednesday, eighteenth of March, and who spoke to you before you fell lame?"

"Aye, that's her all right," said the chapman, his every word dripping in venom.

"Would you care to make any accusation regarding this girl?" Nowell asked him.

"She bewitched me, plain as day. I was struck down after trading words with her and you can see for yourself I'm still crippled for it."

Roger Nowell turned to me with his unruffled face as though he were as fair-minded as King Solomon and asked me, "Alizon, what do you say to this?"

I remembered what he'd said to me in the wagon, bidding me to be truthful. When I looked at the chapman's racked body, my eyes filled. Whether what happened that day was an accident or whether it was due to the powers come out of me that I could not control, he had suffered just the same and I was sorry for it. I clasped my hands and fell to my knees.

"Master Law, I am so very sorry. I beg your forgiveness." With the powers inside me I felt his pain as though it were my own.

The pedlar finally spoke up, brusque but not unkind. "Right then, lass. I can see your regret is genuine. I forgive you."

A mighty muttering filled the room. Abraham Law bent to say something in his father's ear, but John Law held up his good hand to call for silence.

"She's only young, Magistrate. Send her home to her mother for God's sake."

Master Nowell seemed as astonished as everyone else. "Alizon Device, you are free to go."

Thanks to God's grace and John Law's forgiveness, I ran home to Malkin Tower. The very air I breathed seemed to spin and crackle with blessing, and then I knew in the depths of my heart that Gran's prayers and charms had warded me this day like a great invisible hand. When I burst in the door, Gran let out a shout and I cried into the crook of her neck. Afterward Mam embraced me and held me firm and safe.

"Tomorrow morning you'll go to Mistress Alice's. The Constable and the Magistrate will dare not trouble you there. She's a rich woman. Her lands rival Nowell's."

I tried to ignore the niggling in my belly, remembering how the Curate had singled out Alice Nutter in his sermon, saying she would be punished for being true to the old faith. If she was wealthy, she was also guilty of high treason, hiding that priest—a far greater crime than witchcraft even. If Nowell chose to turn against her, she too must submit to his judgement. But then I recalled Nowell's fairness to me that very day, and I trusted that he would not persecute so virtuous a woman as Alice Nutter so long as she took pains to remain discreet and not make a display of her popery. If he were to arrest every Catholic in these parts, Nowell would have to take on Henry Towneley, the Shuttleworths of Gawthorpe Hall, even the Southworths of Salmesbury.

Our Jamie twirled round the room with me, so happy he was to see me. "Come Good Friday, I'll conjure up the name of your black dog and call the spirit back to you."

"Hush, Jamie," I begged him. "If you want me to stay out of harm, you must never speak of such things again."

# 17

MONDAY MORNING I rose at first light, got myself up neat and proper as I could, and tied my hair with Nancy's ribbon.

Mam and Jamie wanted to walk with me to Roughlee Hall and watch with their own eyes as I passed into Alice Nutter's protection. So I kissed Gran goodbye and with her blessing set out the door. My brother slowed his long-legged pace to walk beside Mam and me whilst Jennet trailed behind.

"Walk smart, lazy bones," I called out to her. "When we reach Roughlee Hall, our Mistress Alice will give you something wondrous to eat."

We were a mile from Roughlee when a wagon drawn by whipped and foaming horses overtook us, then drew to a halt, blocking our way. Richard Baldwin and Constable Hargreaves jumped out.

"Alizon Device," said the Constable. "You must come to Read Hall. Roger Nowell wishes to examine you regarding the charge of witchcraft brought forward by John Law."

At that moment I took the man for a bigger simpleton than our Jamie.

"Master Law forgave me, sir." I'd a fair struggle not to show him any impudence. "He said so in front of a whole room of witnesses. Master Nowell himself said I could go free."

I made to squeeze past the Constable, but Baldwin thrust out his whip to block my way.

"You also so much as admitted in front of all those witnesses," the Constable said, "that you were guilty of bewitching the man."

"I never did!" My eyes darted to Mam's, wanting to tell her that the Constable was lying, not me.

"You begged his forgiveness," said Constable Hargreaves. "Why would you do such a thing if you hadn't bewitched him in the first place? An innocent soul has no need for forgiveness."

I opened my mouth to protest further, but the Constable cut me off.

"If John Law forgave you, his son will not let the matter rest. Abraham Law has asked us to proceed with the examination."

"But I'm bound for Alice Nutter's," I told him as though her very name were the charm that could release me. "I gave her my word I'd begin in her service this very morning, sir."

Baldwin laughed. "Witches cling to Papists as flies to dung."

The Constable ignored him. "Get in the wagon, Alizon. You are under arrest."

I turned to Mam, whose temper was rising, her wayward eye bulging as though she were set to murder Baldwin and Hargreaves then and there.

"Give my love to Gran," I told her, speaking fast before the men could silence me. "Ask her to pray for me."

"Ask her to work witchcraft on your behalf, you mean. Your grandmother's so-called prayers killed my daughter." Baldwin brandished his whip, but Hargreaves told him to put it away.

"Nowell won't be happy if he sees she's been molested," the Constable said.

Climbing into the wagon, I was thankful that Nowell, at least, was a just man. Perhaps this could still be made right and tomorrow I could begin my service at Alice Nutter's. I lifted my hand to wave goodbye to my family, only Baldwin and Hargreaves were ordering my mother and brother into the wagon.

"The Magistrate wants to question Elizabeth and James Device as well," said Hargreaves.

"Run along home to Gran!" I shouted to Jennet, who was stood there crying. "Run along, poppet! Now!"

My nine-year-old sister took herself off before the men could change their minds and drag her along to Read with the rest of us.

As the wagon trundled past Roughlee Hall, I gazed at the arched mullioned windows and imagined Alice Nutter watching our sad progress. At least they had arrested us on the road and not waited till we had arrived at the Hall. A nasty thing, that would have been, to have Hargreaves and Baldwin bursting into the lady's home in search of us—they might have taken it upon themselves to search for other things as well. With all my soul, I prayed that Mistress Alice could keep her secrets safe.

The driver lashed the stumbling horses as we passed beneath the shadow of the New Church. My eyes caught a leaping shape that I took to be the black bitch. Drawing on the powers Gran thought I had, I sent my inner voice reeling out, begging her to flee far and away from the reach of Baldwin's whip.

When we passed by Bull Hole Farm, where the men were busy sowing this year's barley and oats, I tried not to give Baldwin the satisfaction of seeing me cry, though it seared me to think of Matthew Holden seeing me brought down so low. To humiliate us all the more, Baldwin drove the wagon through Higham, only a stone's throw from West Close. Chattox, I wagered, would be right chuffed they'd come for me instead of her.

We turned on to the shady road leading past the vast Hunt-royde estate, where Nowell's relations, the Starkie family, dwelt, and then on to Read Hall itself.

A grand manse was Read Hall, every diamond-shaped window pane polished to shine. Girding the house was a garden full of shrubs cut to take the shape of birds and beasts, lords and ladies. The lawns were awash in crocus, primroses, and daffodils. Such a splendid sight, this was, I near forgot the reason we were here.

The wagon came to a halt at the back of the house. Baldwin and Hargreaves marched us through a rear door into the kitchen, where a roaring fire blazed in the huge hearth. The smell of baking bread maddled me as I'd eaten nothing that day, but there was no lingering in the warm kitchen, for the men herded us into a chilly little chamber with whitewashed walls, a hard wooden bench to sit on, and nowt else. The bench was worn shiny by the many bodies who'd been sat there before us, awaiting their interrogation. At the far end of that little room was a stout oak door, through which Hargreaves dragged Mam, leaving Jamie and me behind to bide our time till it was our turn to speak to the Magistrate.

Sat on the bench beside Jamie, I took his hand and put my lips to his ear. "Have a care what you tell them. Don't betray us, love."

Baldwin, stood there guarding the door, spoke up, cold and callous. "No whispering, you two, or I'll have you put in separate chambers."

Lifting my head, I strove to see him with clear eyes: Richard Baldwin, Church Warden and the Constable's right hand. I sought to look past my own hate for the man. If the worst were to happen, if Mam, Jamie, and I were never to walk free, what would happen to Gran and Jennet? Would Baldwin take it on himself to look after my sister, his natural daughter? Feeling my eyes on him, Baldwin twitched and pressed his lips down in a brittle line. Mother of God, what had Mam ever seen in the man?

My hand still holding Jamie's, I pricked my ears to make out what was being said on the other side of that oaken door, but I heard only the kitchen maids shouting back and forth. By all rights, their task should have been mine. This very moment I should have been in the kitchen at Roughlee Hall, chopping onions for Mistress Alice's soup or learning how to dress a capon just the way she liked it. I should have been wearing the new kirtle with a clean apron tied over it and pattens on my feet. I should have been there, in her circle of protection, instead of sat upon this bench, half-sick with trepidation.

An hour seemed to crawl by. My brother was so nervous he clutched himself and jigged back and forth till Hargreaves delivered Mam back into our chamber. Then it was Jamie's turn to be questioned. Wild-eyed, Jamie whirled in panic whilst Mam and I threw him pleading glances, praying he'd not say some fool thing that could get us hanged. Before I could blink, Hargreaves had shoved my brother through the door and shut it behind him. Mam sank on the bench beside me and gripped my hand so tight that I could feel each of her bones. Together we bore the looks Baldwin threw us.

His face bleached white, Jamie stumbled back in, looking fit to collapse. When Mam jumped up to guide him to the bench, Hargreaves began to speak, fair bursting with his own importance.

"Elizabeth and James Device, you are free to go. Roger Nowell will now examine Alizon Device."

I gave Mam and Jamie the bravest smile I could muster. Regardless of what might happen to me, they, at least, had their liberty and were not to be punished for my deeds. But my legs wobbled as Hargreaves tugged me down the corridor and into that far chamber.

The grandeur of the room left me dizzy. Oak panelled walls rose to the ceiling, its beams carved with acorns and leaves. Sunlight poured through the great windows to shine upon a tapestry of a woodland scene with leaping stags and hinds. I almost fancied I was stood in that forest. A fire of apple and cherrywood logs crackled fragrant and sweet in the hearth. The mantelpiece was laden with heavy silver candlesticks and painted crockery such as I'd never seen before, and the walls were hung with portraits of gentlemen with ruffs about their necks. Most curious was an oval picture of a girl out of Gran's tales, lovely as the Queen of Elfhame's daughter, her starry eyes wide with wonderment, her face flushed pink, coppery curls escaping her coif. And—what enchantment was this?—the picture moved. I let out a gasp when the girl in the picture blinked as I did.

"That's your own sorry face in the mirror," Hargreaves told me.

Before I could gawp another second at that awe-struck girl who was my own self, he took me by the shoulders and swung me round so that I faced the three men sat at a long elm table. In the middle was Nowell in his velvet doublet with whitest lace at his throat and cuffs. Jewelled rings flashed upon his fingers. At his right, Abraham Law glowered at me as though I were Satan's own daughter. At Nowell's left was his sallow-skinned scribe.

Each man had a goblet of wine at his elbow and, at the centre of that table, lay a great platter of sweetmeats, the sight of which made my stomach groan, for I was ready to faint away from my hunger and I was aching-thirsty besides. No one had so much as offered me a cup of water. But I'd no time to think of food or drink or even of the beautiful things round me. Abraham Law narrowed his eyes whilst Nowell spoke of witchcraft and the scribe scribbled everything down.

"These are very serious charges, Alizon Device," the Magistrate told me as though he were concerned for my welfare rather than scandalised by what I'd done.

At Nowell's bidding, Abraham Law described in his thick-burred Yorkshire drawl how the letter informing him of his father's affliction had reached him in Halifax only four days after my encounter with the pedlar. Abraham Law had then journeyed straightaway to Colne to find his father paralysed down his left side, but he'd recovered his power of speech and was able to describe how I'd bewitched him and struck him lame—I and the black dog.

When Nowell asked me what I had to say, I could only shake my head, for I feared that whatever I said would be twisted by Hargreaves and Abraham Law into proof of my guilt. A grey fog of hunger and fear sent me stumbling to my knees. Though Hargreaves dragged me to my feet, I was too weak to stand and could only weep and not speak at all. Finally Nowell said in his voice that reminded me of my own father that it would be better if he spoke to me in private. He sent Hargreaves to give word to the servants that I was to be brought food and drink.

"There's no sense to be had from a half-starved girl," Nowell told his constable.

After the others had left the room, Nowell himself drew up a chair for me and not just any chair, but one with a broad carved back and a deep-cushioned seat. He sat me by the fire and still I could only weep, for the strain and worry of the last days had left me shattered. Then a maid bustled in with a tray of lamb pie and buttered bread. Nowell poured me a goblet of wine that steadied my nerves.

"All will be well," Nowell promised. "So long as you help me untangle this abominable business of witchcraft. You're just a young girl, I know, and a tender soul, but this legacy stretches far back before you were born."

His words were so fine-spoken that they fair swept me along.

"Will you help me, Alizon?" he asked, his eyes earnest. There was no snobbery in his manner, and I was well flattered that one such as him would appeal to me.

"Yes, sir. I'll help you however I can."

First he bade me to eat and drink my fill, and only then did he carry on with his questions. Just the two of us remained in that beautiful chamber full of dazzling sunlight. Even his scribe had left.

"For the time being, I want you to forget about this Yorkshire chapman," he said, drawing his chair to mine so that he could look into my face. "I'm far more worried about what has troubled people in these parts for years on end. You know something, don't you?" His fine blue eyes plumbed mine. "There's darkest witchcraft going on in Pendle Forest. No one knows that better than you, as your poor father was Chattox's victim. It was murder in cold blood, what she did to him. Will you help me, Alizon? Help me get to the bottom of this evil?"

"That Chattox is a vicious creature," I told him. Yet my tongue was tied, for hadn't I promised Gran that I wouldn't accuse Chattox or ever cry witch? Was I still bound to that vow if Roger Nowell, with all his might and authority, demanded an answer of me? Torn, I was, for Nowell had awoken my grief and bitterness at having lost my father so young and never being able to seek retribution for him. Hadn't I prayed for this chance to avenge him? When I looked at Nowell, I saw Gran's face. Mad as it seemed, Gran and Nowell might have been blood kin, for they shared the same strong chins, the same piercing eyes.

"We have more in common than you think, you and I," Nowell said as if he were gifted with powers as potent as Gran's and could read my thoughts. "My family has also suffered at the hands of one just as menacing as Chattox."

I shook my head in mafflement, for I'd never heard such a thing. Nowell was married to a plump, cheerful lady, and they'd ten children and grandchildren besides who seemed healthy and right, by all accounts, not afflicted by sorcery.

"Have you heard of my nephew, Nicholas Starkie?" Nowell asked me.

"He lives at Huntroyde, does he not?" I asked, proud to show off my knowledge. "We passed it in the wagon on the way here, sir."

"Right you are, my girl. Now he lives at Huntroyde, but seventeen years ago, around the time you were born, Alizon, he lived at Cleworth, many miles away. Back then my nephew's young son and daughter began to suffer fits and convulsions, and, like any father, he was sore concerned. First he hired physicians, one after the other, spending £200, and still the children were not cured."

Near choked on my wine, I did, to hear of such a vast sum. I couldn't imagine having such a fortune in the first place, much less throwing it away on some piss-prophet physician when you could get someone like Gran to do the job for a peck of oats.

"My nephew resorted to a thing that many would consider treasonous." Nowell leaned forward as if he were revealing his deepest secret. "They sought to engage a popish priest to perform an exorcism that would drive out the demons tormenting those unfortunate children. But the priest refused. So finally my nephew found a wiseman named Edmund Hartley to join his household and work to cure his children, and this man employed certain popish charms and herbs. For about a year and a half he seemed to succeed and the children appeared to recover."

I nodded my approval—far more sensible to engage a cunning man.

"But soon enough the wizard showed his true colours. Though my nephew paid him handsomely, Hartley complained that his wages were too paltry, and then an evil influence spread through my nephew's house. Not only did the two children's fits return, furious as ever, but three girls being fostered in his household began to suffer as well, as did a maidservant and a spinster relation.

"A horror, it was." Nowell's eyes went round and wide. "Alizon, picture this: five children and two grown women shrieking, howling, and holding their breath until they went blue, and they delighted in filthy and unsavoury speeches—during church sermons no less—so that they were scarcely fit to enter the House of God for two years. At home, when my nephew read to them from the scriptures, they fell into convulsions and screamed awful depravities.

"My nephew had no doubt that Hartley himself had bewitched these seven souls. But he couldn't condemn Hartley without proof, could he?"

"No, sir." I gripped the carved armrests of my chair, eager to hear how the tale would end. Nowell had made Hartley sound like a slippery character indeed, a world apart from Gran.

"One day, in a woodland, my nephew tricked Hartley into demonstrating his powers in the casting of a magic circle." Nowell looked at me. "Did your grandmother ever speak to you of casting circles, Alizon?"

"Oh, no, sir! Never heard of such a thing in all my life," I told him, plain and honest. "My gran is a righteous woman who prays to God that others will be healed." I folded my hands in my lap. "What happened to Master Hartley then, sir?"

"When my nephew told the judge at the Assizes that he had witnessed Hartley casting a magic circle, the man was declared guilty of witchcraft and sentenced to hang. Still Hartley had the belligerence to protest his innocence. Then, when they hanged him, the rope broke."

"Some luck, that," I said, my tongue loosened by the wine.

"When he fell on the platform, still alive, the wretch at last came to his senses and penitently confessed his crime. Then he was hanged again, this time properly."

I wanted to cross myself to ward off Hartley's sorry fate from befalling any of my kin, but instead I clasped my hands. "What happened afterward to the bewitched children and the maid and spinster, sir?"

Nowell gazed out the window whilst he spoke. "Two godly ministers came to my nephew's house and read from the scriptures whilst the seven possessed souls bellowed, blasphemed, and convulsed, but the ministers never wavered. Eventually each of the afflicted fell into a deep swoon until one after the other awakened, freed of their possession."

That was some tale all right. Left me speechless.

"Let me show you something, Alizon."

Nowell went to a shelf built into a recess in his panelled wall and pulled out a book with golden letters stamped on calfskin. Full reverent, he laid it out upon the table and bade me look at it. How I marvelled. The only book I'd set eyes on before was the Bible in the New Church, but I knew first off that this was no Bible, for it wasn't as massive. A glance at the other books lined up on the shelf told me that Nowell must be a learned man. I tried to imagine what it would be like to read and unlock the secrets hidden inside each and every tome.

"This book," said Nowell, "was written by our King. Did you know our King James was a man of letters?"

"No, sir."

In truth, all I knew of Scotch Jimmy was that he was said to be fat, ill-tempered, and vain, and that he hated Papists even worse than Queen Bess before him had done. Uneasy, I remembered the day I'd eavesdropped on Alice Nutter and Mistress Towneley at Carr Hall and how Mistress Towneley had said, *May God rid us of this cursed King. He won't be satisfied until he's murdered us all!* But if I went pale at the memory, Nowell never noticed, so intent he was on turning the pages of his book.

"It's called *Daemonologie,* the science of demons. The King believes there is a vast conspiracy and veritable army of those such as Edmund Hartley and Chattox and their many cohorts who seek to bring down our Christian nation."

What he said sent my head spinning. Chattox was vile, to be sure, but she was a lonely old woman in her cottage, not part of some devilish army.

"Book learning is all very well," he said with a sigh. "But it's quite another matter to have firsthand knowledge of a thing. In truth, I don't know nearly enough of the ways of witchcraft. I would learn from you, Alizon." He smiled. "Not an hour ago, you promised you would help me. Now that you've heard my story of how black magic nearly destroyed my nephew's family, could you not tell me how Chattox oppressed your family at Malkin Tower?"

He poured more wine into my goblet and pushed the platter of sweetmeats toward me. So warm and comfortable, I was, for I'd never been received in a finer room, and Nowell treated me with such regard that I took it as a sign from God that it was time someone spoke out about Chattox. I was doing it for a higher purpose, after all, not out of spite, and this, I prayed, released me from the promise I'd made to Gran.

So I spilled out the whole story. First, how Chattox's daughter Betty had stolen our oatmeal and our good linen coifs and bands when I was only a small child. Then how my father had tried to make his peace with Chattox by offering her a dole of oats every year, but when he'd stopped the payments in the year of famine when we'd barely enough to feed ourselves, Chattox bewitched him so that he died in agony. Then I told how my dearest friend had died after Chattox accused us of laughing at her.

"It's on account of Chattox that I lost my father and my best friend," I told him, sincere as I'd ever spoken.

Quite something, it was, to have a man as distinguished as Roger Nowell hanging upon my every word, all the while scribbling upon his parchment. Finally I stopped speaking to gaze, full entranced, at the fancy ink shapes he was making that were meant to be my very words.

"Go on, Alizon," he said, lifting his quill. "Have you anything else to say regarding Chattox?"

My speech emboldened by the wine, I told him how Betty Whittle had once begged a dish of milk off the Holdens at Bull Hole Farm only to have Chattox pour it into a can, cross two sticks over it, and begin an incantation till Matthew Holden came charging out and kicked the milk over to break the spell. But the next morning one of his father's cows fell sick, lay for four days, and then died.

Nowell scribbled away with such excitement I thought his inkpot would run dry. After a spell he'd no choice but to rest his hand. He arose then and leafed through the book written by the King.

"Let me read a passage for you."

This seemed a wondrous thing as I'd never heard anybody read from a book just for me.

"'When witches are apprehended and detained by the lawful magistrates,'" he quoted, his finger moving across the page, "'their power is then no greater than before that ever they meddled with these matters.'"

Nowell closed the book.

"Don't you see, Alizon? Your people should have reported this business with Chattox when it first happened. It would have been too late to save your father, but it might have saved your friend Nancy Holden."

Bowing to his reason, I was sat there in silence. He'd given me much to ponder.

"Your own grandmother is even more renowned than Chattox. Some would call her a blesser."

"Oh, yes, sir! A blesser she is, indeed." As the wine went to my head, I bragged quite bold about Gran's many powers. How she mended sick children and cattle, how once I'd left a piggin of blue milk just inside the door of Malkin Tower whilst Gran lay upon her pallet and how I came back a short while later to find a quarter-pound of butter in its place, and Gran had never stirred from her bed! That was stretching the truth, of course, but it was a story I was fond of telling, and everybody knew that Gran was a great cunning woman.

"I'd heard that Anthony Holden of Bull Hole Farm called upon your grandmother to mend one of his cows some months ago," said Nowell.

"Yes, sir, he did. Except it was a heifer."

"The animal died afterward, I take it."

"That was a spot of bad luck, sir. But Gran's a blesser. She's cured many cattle in her day."

"She's blind, is she not? How does she get around, then, to do her blessings?"

"Why, my sister and I lead her about. Sometimes Jennet leads her out and then, after a spell, I lead her back, and sometimes we do it the other way round. Our gran's getting on in her years, bless her, so she never goes very far from Malkin Tower these days."

"But only two years ago," said Nowell, "I understand that she was capable of covering a fair distance. Master Baldwin complained that your grandmother had come to his mill at Wheathead, accompanied by you and your mother, and that she gave him some grief. Soon after his daughter fell ill, languished a year, and died."

"Gran never harmed a soul! She only went to ask Baldwin to pay my mam for the carding she'd done." I trod careful when speaking of Baldwin since he might have been listening on the other side of the door.

"It seems plain that your grandmother has no liking for the man," Nowell insisted. "Was she not angry with him that day?"

"Aye, sir, as most would be if he'd come rushing at them, waving that whip of his, and screeching, *Whores and witches. Get off my ground. I will burn the one of you and hang the other.*" The wine was making me speak freer than I should. I set the goblet down and chewed on my bottom lip.

Nowell's eyes seemed to leap out of his face. "Master Baldwin called your grandmother a witch? How did she respond?"

"The way any decent person would, sir. She offered to pray for him."

Least I managed to keep mum about Baldwin being Jennet's father. Didn't want to push my luck and have Baldwin after me for slander—that stick-legged, arse-faced hypocrite.

I braced myself lest Nowell ask me more of what had passed between Gran, Mam, and Baldwin, but he put the subject to rest.

"Now about the pedlar. I know this is irksome for you, my dear, but as Magistrate it is my duty to address it. Can you tell me, just between us, what truly happened that day?"

I told how I wanted to buy the pins, not beg them off the chapman as he'd claimed.

"Pins," said Nowell. "What need had you of pins?"

"To keep my clothes together, sir," I said, blushing and looking down at my feet, tied up in old rags.

"Understandable," he said. "What happened next?"

"I was angry, sir, that he accused me first of being a beggar and then of being a thief. Said he was afraid that if he opened his pack for me, I'd be gone with half his goods. I've never stolen from anybody in my life, sir! Next he called me something even worse that I'll not repeat, and I fair lost my temper. Then that dog came running out."

Here I stumbled. *Lie,* Mam's voice inside me urged. As much as I trusted Nowell, it would do no good to any of us if I confessed outright that the creature was my familiar.

"It was only a stray, sir, no dog of mine," I said, breaking into a sweat. "The pedlar seemed frightened of it. He ran off, then collapsed and fell lame, and it was a most terrible thing to see. Wouldn't wish it on anyone."

"John Law and his son are convinced that you bewitched him, Alizon, with the help of that dog. Master Law fell lame after you cursed him out."

"I should have never spoken to him in anger like that, sir. I sore regret it. You can believe I'll never do such a thing ever again."

"So it was your anger that lamed the pedlar?" Nowell's voice brimmed with amazement.

"Some might say so, sir. But I never meant to hurt the man."

"What about the dog? Did the animal speak to you as I speak to you now? Did the black beast offer to help you be even of him and lame him for you?"

Such talk set me twisting in the fine chair. If a word of it was true, it made me as damned as Chattox. My stomach seized up. How I longed to be far away from here, out on some windswept moor where I'd never lay eyes on another human being.

"Alizon," he said in the kindest voice. "Pray, turn and face me. Your grandmother is an esteemed cunning woman. Many have turned to her for healing."

Tears in my eyes, I nodded to him.

"You alone of her grandchildren show promise to carry on the family trade. Did she bring you up to be a blesser like herself?"

"Aye, sir, she tried. But I'm nothing like her. I'll never be her match." Least now I took comfort that my every word was the truth.

"Some would beg to differ," said Nowell, "after what passed between you and John Law. Did your grandmother encourage you to befriend this black dog or any other such creature?"

"That was only a stray, sir, what comes and goes." Mam's will

256

seemed to shape my speech. "I've no idea where it came from, sir, but there are plenty of strays running round."

"Have you ever kept an animal as a pet?"

"No, sir," I said, breathing easy again now that we'd left off talking about the dog. "We're only poor folk. We've hens for laying and when they stop laying, we eat them."

He set down his quill. "Well, let's say you had a pet, such as a dove or a squirrel as some gentlewomen have been known to keep. Where would you hold it against you, if you were to show it affection?"

In spite of myself, I laughed. "What would I want with a squirrel, sir?"

Nowell remained grave. "Alizon, stand up, if you please."

My head began to churn from the wine and his many questions, but I did as I was told. Then he stepped close to me, too close, which didn't seem right. Laughing and uncertain, I backed away. Surely he didn't intend to do this, a man such as him. The mirror on the far wall caught my reflection as I tried to smile to show him that I knew he didn't mean it, but the smile died upon my lips and the taste of his claret went bitter in my throat. Backed me into a corner had Nowell, and I hadn't taken him for that sort of man, not in the least. The look he was giving me made me swallow a scream. His eyes were heavy-lidded, his lips parted and wet.

The mirror revealed his back arching over me, my tear-stained face over his shoulder as I struggled to fight him off, only his good wine left me too clumsy and weak. First he brushed off my coif and took my hair in his fists, as if taking pleasure in its softness, but then he yanked it as if its fiery colour proved my guilt. His fingers that had never known a day's hard labour found the lacings of my kirtle. If I cried out, who would come? Baldwin? Hargreaves? What a laugh. Wasn't Nowell the law itself: Magistrate, Justice of the Peace, and High Sheriff? To think that for his sake I'd broken my promise to Gran. Calling upon the Holy Mother, I made one last move to free myself. Only then did he give over, as if banishing sore temptation, and merely pointed to a spot upon my kirtle as though he had discovered a stain.

"There," he said, full triumphant and swaggering as Satan himself. His eyes gleamed wide as though he were about to force a kiss upon my mouth. "Just below your paps, Alizon Device." His thumb kneaded the threadbare wool of my kirtle. "This is where a witch such as you would suckle her imp. Her black dog."

# III

## BY STICK AND STAKE

*Alizon Device*

# 18

**B**ALDWIN SHOVED ME into a low-ceilinged storage chamber where a lantern-jawed midwife and two other matrons awaited. I'd never seen them before, and yet they seemed to know of me and my family's reputation. Later I learned the midwife was a cousin of Baldwin's and believed, as he did, that my gran had bewitched and murdered his only lawful child. In her mind, she'd every reason to treat me with contempt.

The midwife rolled up her sleeves, as did the two others who jumped to the orders she barked, and then the three of them descended upon me. In a flurry they tore off my kirtle, smock, even the rags tied round my feet. The midwife grinned to snatch Nancy's ribbon from my hair and stuff it down the front of her bodice. Before their eyes I was stood there mother-naked. Rough and cold were their hands, prodding and pinching, as they scoured my flesh in search of the witch's teat Nowell had told them to find. A razor in her big red fist, the midwife sheared every last hair off my scalp, humming whilst she worked, as though her grim task delighted her.

To make my debasement complete, the midwife bade her two helpers to hold me down with my legs splayed whilst she shaved every last hair off my private parts, for Nowell had told her that removing a witch's body hair would force her to confess. I pictured him peeping through the keyhole to take his cruel pleasure in this spectacle.

. . .

Afterward they slapped the clothes back on my body and delivered me to Baldwin. His breath blew hot as hell flames upon my shorn and bleeding scalp as he bound my wrists behind my back.

"Nowell told me that we've no choice but to examine your grandmother next," he said, turning me so I could see the elation on his face. "Now that you've denounced her as a bloodthirsty witch."

My tears flew as I shook my head. "I never said such a thing."

I thought of how I'd trusted Nowell, how I'd smiled at him as though he were my father come back from the dead. Lulled by his fine speech and his wine, I'd bragged to him about Gran's powers as a healer whilst he'd scribbled it down.

"What a righteous day it will be," said Baldwin, "when we hang Old Demdike."

My legs turned to putty. Came crashing to the floor, I did. When Baldwin hauled me up, my guts heaved and I spewed Nowell's blood red claret on Baldwin's boots.

"You filthy sow," he railed.

He dragged me out of the house, across a cobbled yard, and down a muddy path. Daylight gate was falling, the cold March air tangy with woodsmoke. The smell of horses filled my nose: their warm flesh and the hay they chewed. A white-faced mare nickered and how I longed to hide my sick-stained face in her mane.

Round the back of the stables, a cellar door was propped open. Baldwin wrested me down a flight of stone stairs, untied my hands, then pushed me so that I toppled into the sour straw. I couldn't bring myself to lift my head off the floor even after I listened to him hurry up the stairs, slam the door, and bolt it behind him. When at last I opened my eyes, I thought I'd gone blind as Gran because that cellar was so dark. Baldwin had abandoned me here without a blanket or rush light. The smell of damp hit me, then the stink of the others who had been kept here before me. The very stones reeked of despair.

My heart would not quieten but kept on banging and banging like a caged thing. I was the most abominable creature on this earth, for I had allowed Roger Nowell to beguile me into condemning my own grandmother.

I could not say how much time had passed in that gloom where fleas sucked at my flesh as though they were a host of demons feeding off the witch that I was.

From fitful sleep I awakened to a thud, to some creature breathing ragged and fast. As I juddered and shook, the dim light trickling from the high, barred window revealed the most awful vision summoned by Satan himself to punish me. It was as if I were gazing into the mirror in Nowell's beautiful room and saw my own reflection warp to reveal how damned I was on the inside. Those empty eyes staring from bruised sockets, that bald and bloodied scalp, that face with its wrinkled flesh hanging loose — the very mask of an aged witch. Chattox peered at me, her mouth curling in scorn, yet I thought that if I tried to touch her, she would vanish, for it was my own forsaken soul I beheld: I, Alizon Device, who had crippled a man in Colne Field.

My mouth went dry to see two other spectres step out from behind her. Annie Redfearn's hollow-cheeked skull floated over a rag-clad skeleton. Then, most painful of all, the vision of Gran hunched in on herself, a stained rag knotted round her head.

Chattox's grip on my shoulder broke the spell. No apparition this, but her flesh and blood looming over my quaking self.

"Is this her then?" she demanded. "The root of our misery."

Before I could speak, Gran fell upon my neck. "Alizon, love, did they hurt you?" Her fingers traced the crisscross of scars on my scalp.

"What hurt will the rest of us suffer before this is done?" Chattox asked. She didn't sound like an addled old woman in the least but like one in full possession of her wits.

Annie Redfearn spoke in a chilled fury that cut even deeper. "I might never see my daughter again, thanks to you. They haven't told me what's to be done with her or who will look after her."

Gran placed herself before me as though to take on the brunt of their wrath.

"Our Alizon made a mistake. But she's suffered as much as any of us."

Cowed though I was, I could not allow my grandmother to fight my battles. So I knelt in the soiled straw before Chattox, the one I'd hated and feared my entire life. My dread of her was nothing compared to my shame.

"I'm sorry," I told her.

If Chattox had done wrong, I'd done worse, sealing my grandmother's doom. Nancy's words came back to me. *When Chattox looked into my heart, she saw me for what I am.* What did Chattox see before her when she looked at my cringing form?

Turned away did Chattox, as did her daughter, who went to help her mother find the least filthy straw on which she could sleep.

"I'm so sorry," I said, reaching for Gran. Sobs racked my body, for I was a useless thing, splintered to pieces. "I broke my promise to you." *Don't go crying witch.*

"You're not alone, love." She stroked my head where the hair used to be. "I broke my promise to myself. A slippery one is Roger Nowell. I played right into his hands and Anne Whittle did no better. He hoodwinked the lot of us."

I shook my head, not understanding.

"Anne and I let him trick us into accusing each other." Gran sounded as aching desolate as I felt. "Something I swore I'd never do. But he knew just how to make me dance to his tune. Said if I spoke against her, he'd let you go. The man's a trickster. Wish I could cut my own tongue out, Alizon."

Gran was crying along with me, and I thought what it must have cost her to go back on her own word, all for my sake and all for nothing. From her shadowy corner Chattox muttered something I couldn't make out.

"Only Annie," said Gran, "was strong enough to keep her silence and not condemn anyone else."

"But why?" I asked. "Why should Nowell even bother with the likes of us?"

"He lusts after the powers of his betters, even the King himself." My gran spoke as if she knew Roger Nowell as well as her own kin. "As gentry go, the Nowells are nowt but upstarts. Can't hold a candle to the Shuttleworths and Towneleys. Your lamed pedlar, Alizon—that was his godsend. You're but his stepping stone. Nowell wants to leave his mark."

"You're talking in riddles, Gran."

"The King believes that witches are everywhere," Gran said, and I thought of Nowell paging feverish through the King's book of demonology. "So Nowell will seek them out and arrest them to gain the King's favour. Make his name as a witchfinder."

My head bursting, I clung to Gran. In that moment her warm, living flesh was the only thing that mattered. Then my fingers found the rag tied to her scalp and the crust of dried blood.

"Christ's wounds, what did they do to you?" With shaking hands I peeled the rag away to discover the gash above her ear.

"On the wagon to Read Hall. Pack of brats throwing stones." Gran sounded just like a broken old woman.

Using my sleeve and spittle, I cleaned her wounds as best I could. Was it too late to learn to become a true cunning woman? If only I could draw the pain out of Gran and into myself. Let me give her ease. Our fingers interlaced. She whispered the incantations of blessing and, though I'd been too wretched to say a single prayer, I whispered each word back to her.

I dreamt of Malkin Tower, of my room with the windows full of stars. I dreamt of Gran crowning me in purest white roses. *Time to lead the procession,* she said, and Alice Nutter appeared by my side to press the rosary beads into my palm. Then all was swept aside in a chorus of birdsong.

When I awakened in the faint trickle of light, the birds still sang. A fine spring morning this must be, though its beauty couldn't reach us down here. Curled beside me, Gran still slept.

Annie Redfearn slumbered beside her mam, who snored like my father used to. Was Chattox truly his murderer then, or had I been wrong about her from the beginning? If she was innocent of killing Father, did that make me innocent of laming the pedlar? My heart began to beat wild as Nancy's had when I pressed my ear to her breast.

The crunch of footsteps upon gravel broke through the birdsong, and then I heard the bolt drawn back. Shaking Gran awake, I helped her to her feet as Baldwin and Hargreaves stumbled down the steps, hesitant and uncertain, as though they didn't know whether to flail before us witches or whether to gloat at how they'd humbled us.

Struggling up from the straw, Chattox wheezed and coughed till I thought the men must show her some pity, but they only gave us water and old bread before binding our hands behind our backs. Wasting not a minute, they herded us out of the cellar and into that glorious morning. Whilst I stared entranced at the red disk of sun breaking through the mist, Hargreaves ordered us into the wagon.

"Where are you taking us?" My voice sounded strange, as if it didn't belong to me anymore.

"Lancaster Gaol," said Hargreaves. "Where else? Did you think Nowell would suffer you on his land another day?"

Bound for Lancaster! Never had I ventured so far from home. The journey of a lifetime, this was, and one that could end with each of us dead. Even if they decided not to hang us, we might die in prison as Chattox's daughter Betty had done.

When the wagon set off, my eyes locked with Gran's clouded ones. Humming under her breath, she was, too low for Hargreaves and Baldwin to hear. The horses made sluggish progress down the muddy road. Again and again, the men had to unload us and heave the wheels free from the mire. A secret smile lit upon Gran's face. It was as though the land itself were rising up against Nowell and his henchmen so that we might stay in Pendle Forest where we belonged.

Chattox's anger hung in the air like an invisible curtain, making me afraid to so much as glance her way, though she was sat, tied and bound, only inches away in the rattling wagon. Sometimes I caught Gran turning to the sound of Chattox's voice as she spoke to Annie.

My grandmother grit her teeth in pain as the wagon jolted along. Needless to say, no one had thought to waste any straw to cushion the splintery boards. Wriggling up beside her, I tried to pillow her body.

"Come, lean your head against my shoulder," I told her. "Rest a spell."

But Gran seemed too troubled to lose herself in the sweet oblivion of sleep.

"What will happen to the rest of them?" she murmured.

I thought of Mam, Jamie, and Jennet, how their lives must go on without us. God willing, Alice Nutter would look after them.

By daylight gate we reached Clitheroe. The weary horses dragged us up steep streets where folk pointed and stared. We passed through the market place with its pillory and then up to the grey castle. Before the castle gates closed upon us, I cast my eyes round at the hills and fells rising in every direction, green slopes dotted with sheep. Above it all, Pendle Hill brooded, bathed golden in the evening light.

Baldwin and Hargreaves took their leave, only too glad to be shot of us. Without a backward glance, they abandoned us to our fate. They'd fare home like brave and conquering heroes—the godly men who had rid Pendle Forest of its witches.

Dour-faced guards whose names we didn't know wrested us down to the dungeon deep beneath the castle. In that cell stinking of shit and vomit, we were locked in for the night. The four of us were given a single bowl of gruel and a bucket of brackish water. High on the wall, a rush light lit up the gloom. Annie Redfearn let out a cry when she spied the first rat, and we'd only the emptied gruel bowl to use as a weapon to beat it off.

"At this rate," said Chattox, "we'll be dead before we reach Lancaster."

She said this with her back to Gran and me, still giving us the cold shoulder. I looked to Gran who touched my face.

"Pray," she begged me.

Though I felt too polluted to mouth the holy words, I sank to my knees in the filth and murmured my Aves. Only then did Chattox deign to look at me.

"Who do you think is going to answer your prayers now?" she asked.

I just prayed on — what else could I do? As the words wrapped themselves round me, the light of mercy welled up from within. The vision came to me of the statue of Our Lady hidden inside Alice Nutter's secret chapel, the Virgin's tender face and outstretched arms. A woman clothed in the sun. How her blinding beauty blazed within my heart as I chanted the prayer charm Gran had taught me as a child.

> Open, heaven's gate, and stick shut, hell's gate.
> Let every christened child creep to its Mother mild.

Opening my eyes, I started to see Annie Redfearn's face before mine. She raised her thin hand with its nails bitten down to the quick. Wrenched from the solace of my devotions, I flinched, thinking Annie would slap me for presuming to pray after landing the four of us in this pit of despair. Annie leaned so close, I could see myself reflected in eyes green as her mother's.

"Can you pray for my daughter? My Marie?"

I bowed to Annie Redfearn, the only one of us who had acted in true honour.

"Course I can," I said, cracking apart to hear how she wept for the girl she'd not see again.

Early the next morning the guards prepared to fetter us for the onward journey. Thinking they would bind our hands with rope as Baldwin and Hargreaves had done, I was stood there with my hands behind my back. But it was cold iron these men laid on us. Manacles were fastened round our wrists and rings round our necks, and to mortify us further, we were chained together like a string of pack horses: me in front, followed by Gran, Annie, and Chattox at the rear.

"Now move your lazy arses," the lead guard told us. "It's onward to Lancaster."

We climbed out of the dungeon and into the forecourt where Baldwin and Hargreaves had handed us over the night before.

"Where's the wagon?" I asked, looking round and not seeing one.

"You'll be walking," the lead guard told us.

"All the way to Lancaster?" I couldn't contain myself. "Sir, my gran's eighty years old. Chattox, too. Sure you can't make them walk so far."

The guards had a good laugh.

"If you witches can fly," said the young guard stood close to me, "then you can walk right enough."

He couldn't have been much older than I was, that lad. Even though I was ugly as could be with my hair shaved off and my kirtle stained with prison dirt, I could sense the lust coming off him. I burned to feel his eyes moving up and down my body just as Nowell's had when he forced me into the corner. Still chuckling to himself, the young guard pinched my cheek. If it weren't for the manacles binding my wrists, I would have belted him. Shackled though I was, I was fair tempted to curse him till his ears bled. Instead I swallowed my anger, for if I lost my temper, I could get the lot of us into more trouble. The lead guard looked like a severe one, just itching for an excuse to wield that club he carried.

Least the chains that bound us were loose enough so that I could take Gran's arm and guide her along, the way I'd always done. If it wasn't for the cold iron biting into my skin, I could almost pretend I'd travelled back in time and was leading her out to bless one of the Holdens' calves.

• • •

First our journey was downhill. We descended the snaking road leading from the castle and out of Clitheroe, then headed alongside pastures full of new lambs, just like the meadows of home. The birds trilled sweet as any I'd ever heard. Wild primrose and dogtooth violets bloomed on the beckside, and every tree was crowned in buds set to burst into new leaves. A lovely and tender time of year, this was, to be marching toward our ruin. Another two Sundays and it would be Easter.

My heart jolted to spy a hare bounding by, seeming to linger near Gran's shadow till it leapt through the hedge, free and away. Gran's face went rapt as though Tibb had appeared to offer her comfort. So sweet her reveries must have been she no longer seemed to hear the clanking iron or cursing guards. Miles away, Gran was, with only my arm on hers to bind her to this earth.

The enchantment faded when we reached Waddington, the next village on our way, where a gaggle of children stormed out, chanting *witch*. Only a matter of time before they started throwing missiles at us, and it looked as if the lead guard had no mind to stop them if they did. Gran's hand in mine went cold and slick, and I saw how the gash on her scalp still wept with pus. Before any of those imps had the chance to hurt her, I drew myself up and yelled for all I was worth.

"Run away, you scabby rotters, or I'll show you what a witch can do."

Head guard told me off, but the young guard who'd been making eyes at me seemed well impressed.

"That's some gob you've got, lass." Though he tried to act stern, he seemed to smile in spite of himself.

"Bless you," Gran whispered, pressing my hand.

Though my ruse had worked and the urchins had legged it, leaving us to pass through Waddington unmolested, I wasn't done worrying about my grandmother. She staggered with each step. Even her spirit seemed to be draining away, her skin gone chalky. We hadn't yet strayed more than ten miles from the boundary of Pendle Forest, and yet she appeared to wilt like a flower cut off from its roots.

Soon as we put Waddington behind us, our way stretched uphill. On the horizon reared a mighty fell, almost high as Pendle Hill itself. The moorland track was treacherous with mud and slippery stone, and the ground on either side was boggy. Up and up we clambered into that desolate heath. Gran foundered, her lungs sounding as though they'd soon burst. Only thing I could do was keep pulling her along, holding her upright so she wouldn't slip. Tried to ease her over every bump, and if there was a ditch or stile, I lifted her over for I didn't trust any of the guards not to bruise her. So spindly-thin Gran had grown I could almost carry her full weight in my arms and, by Our Lady, I'd bear this burden without complaint. Gran had told me how the priests of the old religion used to give folk penances to absolve their sins. Once she knew a man who was sent on a barefoot pilgrimage to St. Mary's of Walsingham. Looking down at my feet, naked and exposed now that the rags that had bound them had worn away, I thought that this was my penance, my ordeal. With each mile I helped Gran along I would prove how sorry I was, how I craved redemption for us all.

Up on the high fell there were no villages, no children to plague us, only wild hares and ewes heavy with lamb. Gran's gasping grew ever noisier the steeper we climbed and Chattox was having no easy time of it either, leaning upon Annie and swallowing her pain with bitter grunts. Then came a stone stile so high it fair overwhelmed me as I struggled to help Gran over. The iron manacles bit into my skin as I pulled on the chains, edging behind her to help push her up the footholds one by one. When at last I got Gran to the top, she nearly tumbled down the other side that plunged six feet to the muddy ground. My arms round her waist, panting in time with her, I racked my brain as to how I could get her down, for on this side the footholds were far apart and well worn away. The two of us were stood atop that stile with Annie and Chattox stuck below, unable to move till we did, and the guards bellowed, baleful and impatient.

Gran said, "Peace. That one has a good heart."

I'd no idea what she meant till I saw the young guard clear the stone wall, nimble as a weasel. But after all, he was better fed than us and he'd no iron chains to weigh him down. Now stood at the bottom of the stile, he reached out his arms to take my gran, but his eyes met mine. The lust I'd seen in them before had turned to something like mercy.

At long last the head guard let us rest a spell. Maybe he feared that if Gran and Chattox both dropped dead, his men would have no choice but to drag their corpses to Lancaster and wouldn't that be a spot of bother. Yet by some miracle we reached the top of Waddington Fell before dusk.

"Best take your last look at Pendle Hill," the young guard told me.

With him stood so close, I'd no choice but to notice his fine hazel eyes. A good-looking lad, he was, who would have made me smile had I not been shackled and shorn. Near brought me to my knees, it did, to think he could be so kind and pay me such attention as if I were still that pretty girl I'd seen in the mirror in Nowell's manor house, my unbowed head crowned in coppery tresses, my body strong and clean, my skin shining with health.

Shame-faced, I ducked away from him, holding fast to Gran's arm, then filled my soul with the vision of that great silent hill that had watched over me since I was a babe. Rising graceful against the eastern sky, Pendle Hill beckoned me like a mother with her vast green skirts. Breathless, I described the view to Gran, painting as true a picture as my poor words would allow. As the tears moved down her face, I told myself that this was my last glimpse of home.

That night there was no dungeon for us but the moon-drenched sky and the cold that forced the four of us to pile together like a litter of puppies. Annie and I huddled on the outside with Gran and Chattox between us so that the old women would be warmest. Gran slept with her spine pressed tight to Chattox's, the woman who had been her dear friend and sworn enemy. Weary to the bone, Gran soon fell into a silent sleep, whilst Chattox snored and Annie, mumbling in her dreams, called out to her lost daughter.

Though I was aching-tired, my eyes stayed open, gazing out at the moon, half full, spilling her silver on the moor. March hares capered in her light. Soon they'd bear their young. Life would go on without us.

My body went rigid to see a dark shape steal toward us. My mouth opened in terror but no sound came out. Then I saw it was the young guard. Noiseless he sat himself down a few feet away. For a spell neither of us spoke.

In that silence I could pretend that I was not his captive nor was he my guard. I could dream that we were two free souls, a girl and the lad who fancied her, and that he could take my hand and off we'd race across this moonlit moorland where his adoring eyes on my face and body would make me beautiful again and so happy that I'd throw my arms around his neck, that I'd start kissing him and never want to stop.

"Are you really a witch?" he whispered.

Was I, indeed? I saw the pedlar falling lame, saw the Yorkshireman's face constrict at the sight of me.

"I can't fly, if that's what you mean," I finally whispered back.

He laughed under his breath and inched closer. Just when I thought he would reach for my hand, his head jerked at the noise of another guard off in the distance.

"What's your name?" I whispered before he could slink away.

"William." Fast as a hare, he was gone.

By morning, mist enclosed us and rain fell, but the air was mild and sweet. I filled my lungs, half drunk on it, for once we reached Lancaster, I knew I'd never breathe such wholesome stuff again. I fair longed to throw myself face-down upon the heath to kiss the heather and bracken, every weed and wort. I'd rather be chained on this fell top, exposed to wind and weather and left here to die, than rot in some prison bristling with rats and fleas. The fog was so dense we lost sight of the way before us. There was nowt but the winding track and the sheep moving in and out of the mist like ghosts. Day bled into day as we trod the remaining thirty-odd miles through the Trough of Bowland. All the while I prayed that we would be lost and stumble round and round in the fog and never reach Lancaster.

Three days after we first set out from Clitheroe, the moors and fells dropped away in long slopes to the sea. Straddling a river in the land far below lay the city with its castle rising mighty and imposing, built to be seen from miles away.

Down off the moors we walked, crossing pastureland where crocus sprang from the damp earth and robins sang in the hedges. How I longed to hold that sunlit morning forever like a perfect stream-washed agate. But the guards drove us along like cattle to market, yanking at our chains if we balked. My feet blistered and raw, I limped past fresh-sown fields, through villages where yet more children came to gawp till I pulled such a fearsome face that they scarpered, howling in their fear of us witches.

The cottages grew ever more plentiful till there were long rows of them. Housewives pattered to and fro with buckets of water and milk. An old man herded goats. Chickens trotted across our path. All these homely things that I would never again lay eyes on.

When the cobbled lane curved past a windswept place where gluttonous crows circled and cawed, I stopped in my tracks.

"What is it?" Gran asked.

She must have felt how my hand on her arm had gone stone cold. Then she gagged, for though she was blind, how could she not smell the rotting flesh, the bodies left to dangle from the gibbet, spinning in the wind?

"Keep walking," William said, marching me along before the head guard could punish us for dawdling.

As I tottered onward, a phantom rope closed round my throat, choking me. So many awful tales I'd heard about hanging. Some folk died quick, their weight causing their neck to snap, whilst others took an age to die. The lighter the body, the longer the suffering. I considered Gran's frame, dwindling ever thinner. How I wished I could charm the manacles off her, transport her through the air back to Malkin Tower and her bed by the fire.

The lane twisted toward Lancaster Castle, towering above us. In its shadow I beheld an apparition of hell. Severed heads stared with frozen eyes from the iron spikes girding the castle grounds.

"Them are Jesuits," William whispered to me.

The sight was enough to make Chattox herself sob aloud. Forgetting myself, I began to pray beneath my breath, mouthing my Aves and Pater Nosters as fast as I could, till William clapped his hand over my mouth and Gran begged my silence.

The gates opened to us, then clanged shut behind us, banishing any thought of freedom. Armed watchmen stalked to and fro with lances and pikelets, and how their eyes raked over us disgraced women, us witches. I turned my head to gaze at the blue spring sky one last time before the guards herded us through a huge door and into the dark tunnels of that castle. They goaded us down passageways, gloomy and cold, where my shackles weighed heavier with each step.

We shuffled by a group of turnkeys, just stood there, idle. "Never fear, lass," one of them called out to me. "I'll save you from the hangman if only you let me get you with child."

I was set to spit in his face, but William, glaring at the turnkey, urged me along till at last we reached a windowless chamber where a heavy-set man awaited us. A black leather doublet he wore over his white Holland shirt. His polished black boots rose above his knees. Upon his little finger he'd a gold and ruby ring that twinkled in the torchlight. A right lordling, he looked, but when he opened his gob, his yellow beard bobbing, he sounded as lowborn as any of us grimy women paraded before him in our chains.

Fat and common, but full himself, this man was. When he cast his piercing eye upon our guards, those hardened men cowered and even William quailed. Seemed the man was accustomed to striking fear into everyone under his command.

"You're late!" he told the guards. "I expected you two days ago."

The head guard grovelled like a beggar. "Not easy to make good progress, Master Covell, sir, with two lame old women in tow."

Covell waved a dismissing hand to silence him. "What a sorry lot you are," he said, looking us prisoners up and down. He'd a good gawp at Gran and Chattox, then threw Annie Redfearn a passing glance before staring at me long and hard. I made myself go cold inside so I wouldn't flinch.

"I am your gaoler," he said. "You whores of Satan took the Devil as your lord, but he has no power here. *I'm* your master now." He thumped his chest. "And it's proper humility you'll learn. It's I who has the final word on how you're kept and what you'll eat, if indeed I grant you leave to eat."

He paced before us, his polished boots echoing on the stone floor, his muscled arms swinging as if to prove how easy he could smite us.

"Our sovereign majesty King James holds witches such as you in deepest contempt and that's how you'll be treated. You're to be closed prisoners. That means no visitors."

Under her breath, Chattox laughed, no doubt in bitter amusement at the thought of anybody being daft enough to seek us out in this place.

Hearing her smothered chortle, Covell's face creased. Flew up to her, he did, with long sweeping strides, and backhanded her across the face. Him, a man in his prime, striking an old woman. Chattox seemed too stunned to even wipe away the blood that ran from her nose. Her daughter wept.

"I'll tolerate no disrespect," Covell told us.

How he loved this, I thought. Bullying the helpless. A mighty wrath took hold of me and I wished horrible things on Master Covell—wished that Gran's Tibb would cause boils to erupt on his pocked, oily cheeks and knot his bowels till he doubled over in torment. I wished that those heads impaled upon the spikes outside would appear in Covell's dreams to deliver the night terrors, that those who had been drawn and quartered, their innards yanked out whilst they were still alive, would stand over him, dripping blood upon him till he drowned in it. I wished him to sup on all the agony he had ever dished out.

Covell addressed our guards. "Take the witches down the Well Tower."

Meek as clipped ducks, the guards rushed us out of his sight.

"You'll not want to cross Master Covell," William whispered as he marched me along. "Edward Kelly was in here and him a gentleman, a friend of Dr. John Dee, the conjurer to the old Queen. Made no difference to Covell. Kelly was in for forgery. Covell had him put in the stocks and slashed his ears off himself. Nasty business, that man. Mind yourself, Alizon. Keep your head down and your mouth shut except when he asks you a question. That's the only way you'll preserve yourself here."

Down spiralling steps they drove us, down and ever down into the bowels of the castle till we, whom Covell called Satan's whores, were delivered into the depths of hell. A tower is meant to be a lofty thing, rising into the sky. Even our lowly Malkin Tower had the wind and starlight pouring through its glassless windows. But this Well Tower sank beneath the earth. Its dank walls seeped and dripped with water. Its only light came from a tiny window at the far end, but the floor sloped down into utter murk. At the very bottom an iron ring was set in the slimy stone floor, and we were chained to the ring and to each other. Then, taking their torches with them, the guards abandoned us in utter darkness.

• • •

We crouched upon sparse straw that was crawling with lice.

"A pity there's no clay down here," Chattox said, her voice ringing out like a ghost's in that murk. "Covell," she began, but even she was too defeated to finish her sentence.

"Clay pictures won't help us," said Gran. I'd never heard her so hopeless.

I chanted my Aves. This time I'd no need to hide my Latin murmurs, for there was no one to hear us at the bottom of the Well Tower. On and on I prayed, pleading for solace, for some vision of salvation. But the chill certainty settled inside my empty stomach. In Covell's mind, we were already tried, sentenced, and damned.

## 19

CHAINED IN THAT INFERNAL GLOOM, I fair forgot the light. A fleeting fancy, it seemed, that we had walked across open moorland and seen nesting lapwings only days ago.

My monthlies began and I'd no rags but could only hitch up my skirts and bleed upon the mildewed straw, hanging my head and not daring to look up when the guards brought in our cold gruel.

Off in the corner was a stinking bucket meant to receive our waste, but it was a struggle to use the thing in the dark. Soon it filled to brimming and we were left to sit chained in our own filth. Though we huddled up together, we were never warm, and we'd huge gaping sores from where our shackles rubbed our wrists and ankles raw. Lice settled into the seams of our kirtles and smocks.

I became a creature of darkness, and feared I'd soon go blind as Gran. More beast than human, I stank worse than any pig. And so we were left to fester till the August Assizes, five months away.

To count the passing days, I made scores by hacking my wrist shackle against the stone. Maundy Thursday came and then Good Friday when Gran asked me to say the old prayers, though they came stiff and wooden off my tongue. In this pit of hell, my faith was slipping away from me as though it were a cord I no longer possessed the strength to grasp. It wasn't that I'd become a doubter like Chattox—it was much worse. Nowell's, Baldwin's, and Covell's words infected me upon this holiest of days. *Whores and witches. Whores of Satan.* Could the three of them all be wrong, the High Sheriff, the Church Warden, and the Head Gaoler of Lancaster Castle? Rotting in this eternal night, I could well believe that I was as debauched and devil-led as they made me out to be.

But for Gran's sake I chanted the prayers till my murmurs settled into an unearthly drone. Then Gran went still as a corpse, which was how she'd whiled away many an hour during our imprisonment. It had taken me some time to realise she wasn't asleep as much as away. She'd the gift to leave her body behind, casting it off as though it were a pile of lousy clothes, whilst her spirit wafted weightless from this dungeon. My chanted Latin became the stream on which she floated into her world of visions. Even Chattox dared not disturb her when she fell into her death-like trance.

*Upon Good Friday, I will fast while I may.* My empty stomach left me with a hollow floating head as I wrestled Nowell's leering devils and sought to picture something holy and pure. The darkness played tricks on my mind, causing me to see things that weren't there, and upon that Good Friday, as I chanted over Gran's unmoving body, I fancied I saw a magpie arise out of her breast and fly upon black-and-white wings through the prison walls. A tug, I felt, as though that bird were transporting me, or a part of me, bearing me along with her.

I thought I must have lost my mind, for I floated insubstantial as a ghost before Malkin Tower on that Good Friday afternoon. Our friends and neighbours had come together: Alice Nutter, pale with worry; the Bulcocks; Mouldheels and some friends of hers; Mam's old friend Jennet Preston, come over from Yorkshire and fussing over our little Jennet, her namesake. There was our Jamie, roasting a stolen sheep upon a spit to feed them all. Even Uncle Kit and Aunt Elsie had come, though from the tight, uneasy look on my aunt's face, I could tell she'd no desire to be there. For as long as I could remember, Elsie had sought to keep Kit and herself well apart from my family at Malkin Tower, as though she feared our ill repute would taint her children.

The others, paying little mind to my cringing aunt, pressed forward to pay their respects to my mother whose grief seemed to devour her from within. Clasping her hands, they told her how terrible it was that Gran and I had been dragged off to Lancaster. Soon everyone gathered round the table to sup upon Jamie's mutton and Alice Nutter's fish. The image before me was so clear I could almost taste the trout upon my tongue. But then a mighty commotion arose as Hargreaves barged through my mother's door and started taking down everyone's name. One after the other, our company fled home, some on foot, others on horseback, vanishing into the low-hanging fog.

The picture faded and another appeared. Hargreaves laid a coaxing hand upon our Jamie's shoulder. He offered my brother a flask of spirits strong enough to make his eyes water. Reeling from the drink, our Jamie pointed to a spot under Gran's old elder tree. As Hargreaves began to dig, little Jennet came to watch, her eyes big as trenchers, till the man unearthed a clay figure and turned it over and over in his trembling hands.

Wrenched from the scene, I fell as though from a great height, plummeting down the Well Tower where my bones smashed to splinters. A band of pain encircled my head like a crown of thorns. In the stillness of that dungeon came a skriking worse than the hounds of hell. Gran writhed full senseless. She raved, her forehead throbbing hot.

*Jennet,* she had screamed. *Jamie. You'll murder us all.* The clay picture—had we shared the same vision?

As I struggled to rouse her, Gran's cries summoned the guards who pretended to be brave though the sight of my blind grandmother shrieking at the invisible seemed to turn their blood to ice. They made like they saw an old witch calling down damnation upon their heads.

"She's mad with fever," I said, looking into each of their torchlit faces.

William was nowhere. Perhaps his master thought he'd been overkind and forbidden him to see me again. In truth, I didn't know whether to be disappointed or grateful that he wasn't there to see me so despoiled. But he, at least, might have done something to help Gran.

"She needs better food than the slop you're giving us," I told the guards, willing myself to speak as bold as Mam would have done. "Can you bring her no broth or blanket? Just feel her skin. She'll burn up and die."

I searched their faces for any trace of compassion, but they drew back, anxious to be gone from this cursed well of despair.

After the men had left, Chattox groped in the darkness, laying one hand on Gran's brow, the other on her heart, and began to sing the charms Gran must have taught her before they became rivals and foes. Lost in bewilderment, I chafed Gran's cold hand and listened as her old enemy strove to heal her. At last Gran's thrashing ceased and she slept on, calm and quiet.

"How long have we been down here?" Gran asked me when she awakened.

"Nineteen days." I moved her hand so she could finger the scores I'd hacked in the stone.

"Only days? Feels like years. Is it May yet?"

"Still April," I told her.

Chattox rubbed her raw hands together. "It will never be May down here."

Three more days passed with Gran floating in and out of fever. When I dared to sleep, my dreams carried me to unwelcome places. I saw our Jennet looking like an abandoned child, her hair dirty and matted, though that couldn't be. Our mam loved her and would never neglect her. But Mam was nowhere. I saw the Constable coming to arrest Uncle Kit and Aunt Elsie, only Elsie went down on her knees, wheedling and pleading. *You can't take us away—we've nine children. In God's name, we've nowt to do with witchcraft. Everyone knows we've lived apart from that lot at Malkin Tower since the first year of our marriage.* Prepared to strike any bargain, Elsie was, if only the Constable left her and Kit in peace.

My false aunt hugged our Jennet to her bosom before scrubbing the child from crown to toe. She dressed the child in her own daughter Martha's best Sunday gown. How Jennet twirled round in her fresh, clean dress, as though she were another girl altogether—a witch's granddaughter no longer. I saw Roger Nowell riding to Uncle Kit's door, saw our Jennet dropping into a pretty curtsey for him. Where had she learned that? Chuckling, Nowell stooped down to smile into her eyes, the way a doting grandfather would do. Then he asked her, speaking kind and patient, if there was anything she wanted to tell him about her family at Malkin Tower. He slipped a bright shilling into her small white hand.

The guards' lantern light revealed my mother's bruised and pummelled face, her shorn head, her wrists and feet shackled to mine and to the ring in the floor.

*No.* I tried to force the vision away, but this was no dream.

Straining against his chains, my brother buried his head in my lap and clung to me, his once-strong body full a-quiver with uncomprehending terror.

Mouldheels swore like a soldier, saying she was no witch, she'd never had any dealings with spells or imps, how could anyone think she was a witch? Her friend Alice Gray squatted on bare stone, as did Meg Pearson. Chattox spat at Meg's feet and called her a hussy, for once Meg had dallied with Chattox's husband, now fifty years dead. Jane and John Bulcock stared round like lost children. On the far side of our circle, her head as bald as the others', was Alice Nutter.

How could this be? How could Nowell throw a gentlewoman in with the rest of us? The Bulcocks, upstanding folk who had never troubled anybody, didn't belong here either. Nor did Mouldheels, Meg Pearson, and Alice Gray, old women who liked to gossip—what had their crime been but to come to Malkin Tower upon Good Friday to ask after Gran and me? Was anyone who had ever shown us fellowship to be suspected of witchcraft? Gran and I had been given a vision of that gathering and now our family and friends had come to join us in the Well Tower. Yet Nowell had spared Uncle Kit and Aunt Elsie. And Jennet.

"What in hell's name are you lot doing down here?" Chattox asked when the guards had gone.

Though weak and fevered, Gran fussed over my mother who sobbed in her arms, the fight knocked out of her, her voice pitched in a wordless moan of loss.

"Liza's bastard," said Mouldheels. "The wench condemned us. Her and her witless brother."

Too shamed to lift his head from my lap, Jamie stiffened as if bracing himself for a blow. Covell and Nowell's cronies must have beaten him, too.

"Your brother told Nowell that your mam murdered Henry Mitton with a clay picture," Mouldheels told me. "He spoke against the lot of us. Said I murdered some woman in Colne. Said Jane Bulcock and her boy used witchcraft to drive some woman mad."

Hargreaves and Nowell had ill-used my simple brother, of that I was convinced. Our Jamie had intended no ill to befall us, his family and friends. But Jennet would have known what she was doing. Spite ruled my cold little sister.

"When we heard of the arrests, we all came to Malkin Tower to offer comfort to poor Liza," Alice Nutter said. "Then Hargreaves stormed in. I've never seen such impudence. He accused us of being a coven of witches gathered for an unholy sabbath on Good Friday." Her voice rang stark in her outrage.

The new prisoners seemed right maffled, for they'd little enough clue what a coven of witches was supposed to be. Apart from my family at Malkin Tower, none of them had dealings with charms or the cunning craft.

"Nowell," said Gran, "has made us his fools."

"They've arrested Jennet Preston as well," Mistress Alice said. "She's been taken to York."

"But what are *you* doing down here?" Chattox asked her. "Couldn't buy your freedom with that brass of yours?"

"It's not as simple as that," Mistress Alice replied, and that was all she would say on the matter.

Her dignity glowed like a candle in the darkness. Still it alarmed me to think that Nowell's powers had waxed to the point where he was emboldened to take on the gentry. Could nothing stop him now? But I wagered he'd met his match in Alice Nutter. A careful and canny one, she was. Even now she clung fast to her secrets, submitting to arrest on the false charge of witchcraft as if in hope that this would turn Nowell's head from her true crime. I knew she'd sacrifice her own life if that could spare her son Miles and the priest she'd sheltered from being drawn and quartered, their heads impaled on the iron spikes outside the castle.

Annie Redfearn broke the silence, asking if anyone knew how her daughter fared.

"Your landlady refused to take her in," Mistress Alice said. "So I asked Miles to find a place for her at Roughlee. She's working in the kitchen."

Annie Redfearn reached across our tangled limbs to squeeze Mistress Alice's hand. "Bless you for your kindness."

"Bless us all," Chattox said, though she sounded well dubious whether any manner of blessing could reach the twelve of us chained together in the dark.

Arresting Gran and me and Chattox and Annie Redfearn was never enough to satisfy Nowell's greed. As Gran had said, he fancied himself a great witch-finder and King Jimmy's fool book of demonology said that witches gathered in covens of thirteen. So what had Nowell done but round up our friends and neighbours till he had thirteen in number, including Jennet Preston, who was held in York.

Not even that was enough to sate Nowell's hunger. In the nearest cell to ours, their cries and dolour sometimes reaching our ears, was another group of wretches: folk from Samlesbury accused of witchcraft on the evidence offered up by a child named Grace Sowerbutts. Roger Nowell would have everybody believe that Lancashire was fair bristling with Satan's army.

Some army! What were we but a lot of half-starved wraiths. Though Alice Nutter did her best to bribe the guards to bring us better rations, Covell would grant us no mercies. After a few days even Mistress Alice was as soiled and sorry-looking as the rest of us, her cheeks sunken and eyes spectral. Soon enough, Gran wasn't the only one ailing with the shakes and shivers. The gaol fever struck our Jamie. A miracle it would be if any of us lived to see our trial in August.

We'd no respite from each other, no escape from the others' moods, or sickness, or stinking flesh. None of us could scratch at our lice without yanking the chains that confined the others. Never any peace, what with Chattox's muttering and Mould-heels's temper. Meg Pearson began to lose her mind, skriking so horrified to make the rest of us leap out of our skins. Jane Bulcock and her son went into a stupor, mute and unmoving, as if wishing themselves dead.

When Alice Nutter prayed, I joined my voice to hers. She took me under her wing and taught me prayers that even Gran had forgotten.

> *Ave, Regina caelorum,*
> *Ave, Domina angelorum,*
> *Salve, radix, salve, porta,*
> *Ex qua mundo lux est orta.*

These devotions of ours were the sole comfort of our lightless days, the one thing that could ease the pain pressing from every side. Our Lady, so Mistress Alice said, was the wide open door to heaven and succour to her people who fell and longed to rise again. Whilst Mistress Alice never seemed to doubt her faith or her innocence, I prayed in atonement for the pedlar falling lame, for bringing on our downfall with my unwitting confession. One question would not stop taunting me: what *was* the power behind the black bitch that had appeared to me? Had it, indeed, been the Devil in disguise as Nowell would claim? If I were only brave enough, I would ask her to reveal her true form so at least I might know, even if the truth tore me apart.

On and on we prayed till our chanting flowed in a tide, carrying me along, transporting me. In my fever that I'd caught from the others, it was a battle keeping my spirit tethered to my aching flesh. Without even desiring it, part of me took to flight. That world of visions that had once belonged to Gran alone opened its gates to me.

Outside the Well Tower it was May—a beautiful May as there ever was. The sun I'd near forgotten shone warm upon my face. Slender white birches bore new leaves and the undergrowth was an endless sweep of bluebells. Three paths stretched before me. I started down the middle one that led deep into a forest.

I heard a singing-ringing. Upon a white mare, a lady came riding and she was so lovely, her red-gold hair floating behind her. Her tinkling music came from bells of gold and silver tied in her horse's mane. The lady smiled with such majesty and tenderness that I sank to my knees, tears in my eyes. Joy swelled up in my breast.

"Hail, Queen of Heaven," I called to her.

The lady shook her head. "No. That name does not belong to me."

Her mantel was not the blue and gold of the Blessed Virgin, but green as the slopes of Pendle Hill. Light streamed forth all about her, dazzling me after my months of darkness. Her overpowering radiance sent me spinning, reeling and turning, till the light vanished and murk enclosed me once more. There I was left, tangled in my chains.

"She fainted whilst we were praying," I heard Alice Nutter tell Gran.

"She'll be right." Gran put her lips to my ear and whispered, "You saw her, too. The Queen of Elfhame."

"There are three paths from which to choose," Gran whispered as I tended her in her fever. "The right-hand path leads to heaven. The left-hand path leads to hell." With her manacled hand, she guided my own hand in a warding gesture. "There's another path, love, betwixt and between. That leads into the heart of the forest where the Queen of Elfhame rides."

She wasn't delirious, was Gran, but uttered each word careful and deliberate.

"She's shown herself to you," said Gran. "Call out to her and she'll come to you again."

I'd no idea what to think about any of this. Seemed too much to wrap my head round. Mistress Alice's faith was straightforward, the rules carved in stone, whilst Gran's was a twisting thing, its shape as ever-shifting as Tibb's.

I'd no chance to reflect over long on such matters, for the very next day Thomas Covell swaggered into our dungeon swinging his cat-o'-nine-tails. The guards' torchlight sent his monstrous shadow leaping over the weeping walls.

"All right, you devil's spawn," said Covell, "I've left you in peace long enough. Tomorrow I will examine you, one by one, in private."

The torchlight turned his white shirt red as he lumbered toward Gran, pointing his cat-o'-nine-tails at her. She lifted her blind eyes to him.

"Nowell says you're the worst of the lot," he told her. "The mother of all this infamy."

One of the knotted tails flicked her wrist, digging into her skin. Gran grimaced but stayed quiet as the stones whilst the rest of us stared at the bloody welt. With Covell glowering over us, not even Mam dared twitch a muscle.

"Prepare your story," Covell told Gran.

My heart sank to the deepest inferno of hell. I didn't need powers like Gran's to guess Covell's plan. After our spell in the dark, he fancied he could drag even wilder confessions out of us.

"Tomorrow," Covell said, taking a torch from one of the guards and shining it in our faces so that we cringed and covered our eyes. Chained for so long in this darkness, we could no longer bear the light.

Late that night I sat up with Gran as she roiled in fever.

"Covell's coming in the morning," she said, labouring to get each word out.

Her lungs were heavy and sore, filled with such a weight of fluid that she said it reminded her of Jamie's tales of great hares pressing down upon his chest.

"If he questions you," she rasped, "blame me. You were innocent, but I led you astray. Maybe he'll go easy on you."

"Easy?" Chattox cut in, for there was no privacy in that place. "Nothing's easy in this hole."

"Gran," I whispered, "I betrayed you once. I'll not do it again."

"Not even if I beg you?" Gran's hand clasped mine with as much strength as she seemed to have left in her. "Save yourself."

Before I could protest, she pressed on, her words coming quick and urgent.

"There's something you must know about Roger Nowell. My mam was a servant at Read Hall when Nowell's father was young. He took a fancy to her, and before long she gave birth to me."

Though I'd always known that Gran was a bastard and though it was nothing unusual for the poor to claim a father from a wealthy house, the revelation that we descended from the Nowells left me legless.

"Roger Nowell's my half-brother. Your great uncle. When next you see him, love, remember that. You're his flesh and blood."

I near spat at the memory of Nowell smiling at me, pretending to be so kind whilst plotting my family's destruction. I sickened to remember his hands groping my flesh.

A fit of coughing kept Gran from saying anything more. Clenching her mouth, she hacked and hacked. When I eased her hands free, they were coated in slime. Using my sleeve, I cleaned her as best I could, murmuring my prayers over her.

"Bless you, Alizon," she said. "It's time you had a rest."

Soon as I lay back and closed my eyes, I drifted off.

I passed through a gate of graceful-twisted iron into a rich man's garden with countless rose beds, with bushes trimmed into the shapes of beasts and lords and ladies. Everything was blossoming and fresh, the lawn a carpet of tiny daisies, for it was May, the most beautiful month. Off beyond the yew hedge I caught a glimpse of Read Hall in its grandeur, the sun gleaming on its many windows, smoke curling from its chimneys. With a curse, I turned my back on Roger Nowell's manse and made my way toward a splashing fountain with a statue of a naked boy. Round that fountain children played, their laughter ringing out. Blameless, they were, Roger Nowell's happy grandchildren, who knew nowt of our lice-covered bodies or the gaoler with his cat-o'-nine-tails. Our little Jennet sported with them, and she was decked out in a new kirtle of yellow stuff with lace at the collar and cuffs. Her mousy hair had been curled with hot iron tongs. How she sang and how she danced, hand in hand with the others. No longer the bastard of Malkin Tower, she shone like Sunday's child, her cheeks glowing rosy and plump from the roast lamb and beef and cakes and pies they'd stuffed her with. Our Jennet's dream come true, this was, pretending to be a daughter of the gentry, lisping along to mimic their soft accents. At last she was shot of her cock-eyed mother and idiot brother; of me, her ill-tempered sister; of her family of witches and misfits. That girl would be only too willing to do and say anything Nowell asked of her. His instrument of God, he called her.

Our Jennet. Baldwin's seed. The cuckoo in our nest. Our little grey-eyed Judas.

I saw the years fly past like the wind blowing through the pages of Nowell's books. Before my eyes, Jennet Device grew into a woman, homely and graceless, as ragged-poor as she'd ever been, discarded by her wealthy protector. Left to beg and scrape, Jennet had a hounded look in her eyes, for the children chased her and pelted her with a rain of horse dung and cried out, *Witch, witch, dirty witch.*

*No, our Jennet,* I called out to her through the chasm that yawned between us. *You'll never be shot of us or our memory.*

I awakened to hear Gran trading hushed words with Chattox.

"Forgive me," Gran was pleading. "I was your false friend."

This shocked me, for I'd always thought that Chattox had first laid her curse upon us. But Gran seemed so intent on speaking her mind that I forced myself to keep quiet and pretend to sleep on.

"Asking my pardon, are you now?" Chattox's voice was dry as snakeskin. "Them fever dreams maddled your brains?"

"Our Anne, I loved you. I'm so sorry."

By going soft and sentimental, Gran only vexed Chattox.

"Show some backbone, Bess. You were never this wet before. Covell will wring you out like a rag and wipe his boots with you."

"I'll go," said Gran, "before I can do any more harm."

"Will you now?" Chattox laughed, hoarse and raw. "Oh, aye, I'd love to see you charm them shackles off. That would be a sight, our Bess."

No longer able to just lie there and listen, I sat up.

"Gran, what are you talking about?"

I reached for her hand only to find it entwined with Chattox's.

"Peace, Alizon," said Gran. "Let us be."

# IV

# ASSUMPTION DAY

---

*Alizon Device*

# 20

IN THE FAR-OFF COUNTRY of my dreams, my friend Nancy still lived. How we laughed together, and I was ever welcome in her mam's kitchen. My second family, the Holdens were. Nancy's mam sat me down to a trencher heaped with spring chicken and tender garden greens, and there were fresh strawberries with cream and more buttermilk than I could drink. Made a game, Nancy's mam did, of seeing how much I could eat, with Nancy looking on and grinning. My friend and I put our heads together, whispering of the men we might one day marry, and I teased her that if she married Miles Nutter of Roughlee, she would have to embrace the old religion. Except Nancy didn't want to marry. She gripped my wrist and gave it a shake. *Chattox saw me for what I was. Do you believe in heaven, our Alizon? Do you believe that any of us are bound for heaven?*

Before I could answer, bony fingers clawed my wrist where Nancy's hand was meant to be. Chattox's green eyes cut through the gloaming to peer into mine. Caught as I was between sleeping and waking, my old dread of her reared up.

Chattox was weeping. "Wake up, lass. Your poor gran's snuffed it."

I crawled to Gran and held her face, then placed my cheek over her mouth and nose so that I might feel her breath, but it never came. Her skin was cold as the floor beneath me.

"Come back," I begged her, refusing to believe that she had deserted us like this without saying goodbye.

Her mouth was frozen wide open as if she had wanted to tell me something. Her eyes were open, too, and I'd no coins to lay upon her lids to keep them shut. An unearthly scream split my ears. Mam was wailing loud enough to topple the Well Tower. She swooped down upon Gran to cradle her rigid body.

Soon enough the guards came scuttling in to see what the skriking was about. When they shone their torches upon Gran, their faces went as corpse-grey as hers. She lay before them, stone dead. But what seemed to terrify the guards most was the shimmer of light rising off her skin to touch us all. There was something holy about her. With her eyes fixed open, she looked as though she had glimpsed paradise from the depths of this hell in which we were mired. The bliss upon her face undid me. Her air of joy and rapture seemed a secret message for us. No matter what Covell and the rest were saying, we weren't damned. We weren't Satan's whores. Gran had wanted to give us hope. Taking her chill hand in mine, I kissed it.

Whilst the guards stood round, frozen as Gran, their torchlight illuminating her, the others stared, full dumbstruck. Annie Redfearn, Mouldheels, Meg Pearson, Alice Gray, and the Bulcocks gazed half in horror, half in awe, whilst Alice Nutter prayed and Mam sobbed and convulsed. Chattox keened over Gran as though they'd been sisters.

Our Jamie was too fevered to take notice of Gran's passing. I laid my hand upon his brow, which burned hot as a brand-iron.

"Bring him a blanket," I told the guards. "Or else you'll soon have another corpse on your hands."

Before they could think of what to say to that, in thundered Covell himself, panting and charging round like a mad dog. Gran, that blind old beldame, had clean escaped him. The most notorious witch of Pendle Forest had up and popped her clogs before he could strong-arm her into another, more damning confession. She'd cheated the hangman. Nowell would be furious to hear that Gran had died under Covell's watch. Her passing might put a damper upon the whole trial.

I ducked my head so Covell wouldn't see me smile at how Gran had bested him, ever the wily cunning woman.

Finally running out of curses, Covell ordered that Jamie be taken away for questioning, never mind that my brother was too weak to stand and had to be carried by two guards.

Chattox's hand found mine. "Let me tell you this before Covell comes for me. Your parents always did think the worst of me, but I swear upon your gran's body that I never cursed your father, Alizon."

Only feet away, Mam muttered in derision, but I knew from the breaking pain in Chattox's voice that she spoke from the heart. I shrank in shame to think how I'd given her the devil at the Holdens' gate, leaving her to limp away hungry and reviled, an old woman with nowt but clay to fill her belly. May God forgive my mean heart.

"The only one I ever wished to harm," she said, "was Robert Assheton and only on account of what he did to my Annie. She was just a girl then, hardly older than yourself."

The rumours I knew—how Chattox and her daughter had cursed their landlord's son after he tried to force himself on Annie. Against my will, I remembered my tussle with Nowell—how he'd shoved me into a corner, his hands voracious as the Devil's. By all accounts, Annie's ordeal had been far worse. How could I fail to understand the hard bargain her mother had struck? Gran would have done no less for me. My grandmother's wisdom and compassion filled me then, like purest well water filling a dry dusty bowl till it overflowed.

"I'm sorry I ever spoke against you," I swore to Chattox. "Can you forgive me?"

"It's gone well beyond that," she said. "We've no time left for grudges or misgivings."

When the guards delivered Jamie back into the dungeon, his jaw bloomed with bruises and his nose was flat and bloodied. As Mam and I bent over him, trying to still his panicked shaking, Covell summoned Chattox to be questioned. My eyes locked with hers before they dragged her off. I offered a silent prayer for her.

Hours later she was returned to us, blue in the lips and sagging so limp it looked as though she might soon go the same way as Gran. So Covell had little choice but to end the interrogations and command his men to bring us decent food, blankets, and fresh straw besides, for he didn't want any more of us escaping justice by dying before the August Assizes.

That very day, after Covell's men had borne away Gran's body, they brought us hot pottage in the place of cold gruel and small beer in place of the unclean water that made our bowels run. They gave us bread, only a day old and still soft to chew. The better rations were Gran's gift to us, and I whispered her name, full reverent, before breaking my piece off the loaf and passing it on as though it were communion bread. Bound together in our circle, we partook of Gran's invisible company. Her spirit quickened inside me, settling into my bones, and I knew that she bided with us, lingering close, ghost and angel, to look after us. When I slept, I fancied that her wraithlike hands stroked my hair and that she whispered in my ear, telling me to hold fast to my courage.

It was courage we needed. Chained to that ring in the floor, we couldn't stand, much less walk. Though we were given better food, paid for, as it turned out, by Alice Nutter, our muscles shrivelled from want of moving. We who lived became ghostly as Gran. Still we struggled along as best we could. Alice Nutter passed her hours in prayer, whilst Mouldheels and Alice Gray sang songs bawdy enough to make the guards blush. Jamie, ailing and weak, clapped his hands over his ears and said that his head would split from the racket. Old Meg Pearson was growing ever madder, raving as Jamie did though she'd no fever.

Chattox could not stop reminiscing about Gran, spinning yarns of the two of them in their younger days. She told me of a private feast she and Gran had once shared at Malkin Tower before I was born. The pair of them had supped upon roasted pheasant and roast beef, the finest cheeses, fresh bread and sweet butter, all washed down with wine and beer. I knew that out of love and yearning she was exaggerating, but I only encouraged her, for her fantastical tale gave me comfort. Her and Gran's familiars had waited upon them like servants, so Chattox said. A great number of dancing imps had lent their magical lights so that Malkin Tower at midnight had been as striking-bright as noontide upon Midsummer's Day, the light far-shining in the darkness.

# 21

A T LONG LAST came the August Assizes. For the first
time in nearly five months, the guards unchained me
from that ring on the floor. Up the long-winding stairs they
heaved me whilst I hobbled as an old woman would do. Though
I was the youngest imprisoned in the Well Tower, those months
in shackles had left me almost as feeble as Chattox. Our Jamie
was so wasted he could neither speak nor stand. Two strapping
guards, it took, to bear my brother along, lugging his limp frame
between them.

When they hauled us into the courtroom and lined us up at
the bar, the sea of staring faces left me stunned. Our trial was
public, open to any soul who could squeeze into that chamber. A
fair wonder that those many bodies crushed together still had air
to breathe, for the room sweltered in the August heat. Pointed
at us and shouted, the onlookers did, as we shrank before them
like underground creatures goaded into the daylight. After being manacled down the cold, dank Well Tower for so long, I toppled and swayed, fighting to keep my eyes open and bear the
light upon my face.

We weren't allowed to speak a word in our own defence,
hadn't even been told what the exact charges against us were. We
were made to stand there like mutes whilst Roger Nowell, our
prosecutor, spoke of our vileness. What a sight he was, calm and
poised, the only one in that courtroom who didn't sweat like a
boar upon a spit. Before the judge and jury he paced, lithe and

supple as a man half his age, and he was clad in spotless linen and silk. Like an angel stepped down from heaven, he appeared, golden rings flashing upon the fingers of the High Sheriff and upholder of the sword of justice.

Except now I'd the power to look right through him, for Gran had revealed his darkest shame. He was our kinsman, blood of our blood. He shared Gran's strong chin, her thick grey hair, her indomitable spirit. If he indeed knew that he was Bess Demdike's own half-brother, it kindled no mercy in his heart but only made him more determined to wipe us out, the hideous growth upon his family tree.

Before that packed courtroom Nowell announced that we witches of Pendle Forest had rejected God and our own baptism to worship Satan as our lord, surrendering ourselves to the Antichrist, body and soul. The Devil's own whores, we suckled demons and so became Satan's instruments, for the Prince of Darkness could only work his depravity through human vessels such as us.

Out into the crowd I gazed, at those countless faces, their mouths hanging open as they beheld the unholy spectacle that was we poor weedy figures gawping back at them. I searched out the throng for anyone who was friend, not foe, anybody at all who wished us well or at least harboured a morsel of sympathy. Perhaps Matthew Holden had come to see how we fared. I saw no trace of him, but my stomach flipped when I glimpsed Uncle Kit. My visions of Elsie's betrayal came back to me, but where did Kit himself, our flesh and blood, stand? Had he simply gone along with Elsie for fear of finding himself chained in the Well Tower along with the rest of his kin? My uncle would not meet my eyes but only stared, looking right queasy, at Jamie, who had fainted in the arms of his guards.

Judge Bromley ordered us to be taken down again. Seemed I had just learned to face the light before they drove us back into the darkness. Our trial would last three days, so Covell had told us.

• • •

Next morning, Chattox, Mam, and Jamie were called to stand trial. Though it wasn't yet my turn, Nowell had ordered me to the courtroom to watch the proceedings. I'd no inkling what his motives were. Perhaps he thought to humble me by forcing me to observe the fates of the others before the assembly.

First up before Judge Bromley was Chattox. A sorry thing, she appeared, her spine drooping, her eyes watering in the unaccustomed light. Lest the jury be moved to feel pity, Nowell was quick to paint an abominable picture of her.

"You see before you a dangerous witch of very long history. I place her in order next to that wicked firebrand, Old Demdike, because from these two sprung the evil deeds of all the rest, who were the children and friends of these infamous witches."

Nowell read out her charge. "This Anne Whittle, alias Chattox, of the Forest of Pendle, feloniously practised, used, and exercised diverse wicked and devilish arts called witchcrafts, enchantments, charms, and sorceries in and upon one Robert Assheton of Greenhead and, by force of the same witchcraft, killed him."

"How do you plead?" the Judge asked Chattox.

Everybody in that courtroom seemed to hold their breath to hear how she would answer. From the looks on their faces, they appeared to suspect she might cry out to Satan to come rescue her.

"Not guilty." Chattox's tears splashed down to wet her kirtle, black with prison dirt.

Nowell turned toward the court clerk, a skinny Londoner with long, greasy hair. City man like him seemed well nervous to be up in our country. Kept glancing round with huge eyes as though we were wild heathens whose like he'd never seen.

"Thomas Potts," Nowell addressed the clerk, "kindly read out Chattox's voluntary confession of witchcraft recorded on the second of April."

In his high nasal voice, Potts read out Chattox's statement of how she had sought to strike down Robert Assheton on account of his trying to force himself on her daughter and drive her family from their home. Next the Londoner read a statement from Gran herself, saying how she'd witnessed Chattox and Annie Redfearn shaping clay pictures of Robert Assheton and his father. Last, Potts read the testimony of a manservant who had worked for the Asshetons at the time of Robert's death. Young Robert had fallen ill, so the manservant had claimed, complaining that Chattox and her daughter had bewitched him.

Looking well pleased with himself, Nowell spoke to the judge and jury. "Since the voluntary confession of the witch herself exceeds all other evidence, I spare to trouble you with the multitude of other examinations and depositions or any other witnesses to come forward and declare her guilt. For I believe no reasonable soul can doubt how dangerous it was for any man to live near such people as Anne Whittle."

A tremor rocked the crowd as though they were unable to shake off the thought of this decrepit old woman toying with clay poppets, torturing her gentleman victim till he dropped dead. Under such fierce attention, Chattox collapsed. Her bones creaked loud enough to be heard over the muttering crowd as she sank to her knees, meeker than I ever knew she could be.

"I'm a wicked creature and pray for God's forgiveness." Beseeching, she gazed toward Judge Bromley and lifted her hands, folded as though in prayer. "My lord, I beg you, be merciful to my daughter, Anne Redfearn. She's innocent. As blameless as I am guilty. The sin was mine, never hers."

In so short a space Chattox's trial was over, though the judge and jury had yet to sentence her. The guards whisked her away, and then it was Mam's turn to take the stand. In a right hurry, Judge Bromley seemed to be. After all, it was steaming hot in that courtroom and he'd a heavy velvet robe to wear and many more cases to hear.

Shoulders drawn back and head held high, Mam took her place at the bar. Resolute, she looked, not giving Nowell the pleasure of seeing her crumble before him as Chattox had done. With my entire will I prayed that she might preserve her dignity. Already the crowd was jeering at her wandering eye as though her deformity proved her guilt.

"O barbarous and inhumane monster," Nowell said to my mother, causing the crowd to rumble even louder, "you are so far from sensible understanding as to bring your own children to the gallows by your wicked example."

How I seethed to hear him speak of the gallows before we'd even been sentenced, as though our trial were a mere spectacle to entertain the slavering throng. I glared at Nowell, who happened to take notice of me, raising his eyebrows and looking at me with a face that so resembled Gran's that my knees knocked.

"This Elizabeth Device," Nowell went on, "was the daughter of Elizabeth Southerns, known as Old Demdike, a malicious and dangerous witch."

Mam lifted her chin even higher, ever proud to hear Gran's name spoken.

"It is very certain that amongst all these witches," said Nowell, "there was none more dangerous and devilish to execute mischief than the woman you see before you, having Old Demdike, her mother, to assist her; and James and Alizon Device, her natural children, provided with spirits and ready to aid her upon any occasion of offence."

Nowell paused then, the way the Curate would, to make sure everybody was paying attention before explaining in detail some choice titbit about hell or fornication or somesuch.

"Such in general was the common opinion in the country where she dwelt, the Forest of Pendle, a place fit for people of such condition, that no man near Elizabeth Device, neither his wife, children, goods, or cattle, should be secure or free from danger."

By and by, Nowell got round to mentioning the actual charges against Mam. He held her to blame for working with Gran and Alice Nutter to bring about the death of Henry Mitton, who'd once refused my gran a penny. Hearing that last bit, I had to bite my lip to keep from laughing. What cause did Mistress Alice have to finish off a nobody like that old miser?

Mam never faltered. Before the packed courtroom, her back unbowed, she declared herself not guilty.

With grim forbearance Nowell asked Master Potts to read out her statement taken on the twenty-seventh of April, when she'd been arrested after the Good Friday meeting at Malkin Tower. Still my mother refused to relent. Stubborn as anything, she denied her previous confession, which Nowell had twisted from her by guile as he'd done with the rest of us.

Judge Bromley then asked the chief witness against Mam to be brought forward. The sight was enough to make my weak shivery legs give out and send me sprawling to the floor. My own sister appeared at the stand. Quite the little lady she looked, her dull hair curled into ringlets and tied up in a velvet band. She'd a rose-coloured gown that made her face seem less pinched and pale. So tiny was our traitor they had to stand her upon a table so the gentlemen of the court could get a gawp at her.

Mam let out such a roar. She wept and screamed and cursed and pleaded all at once. What cold cruelty could move a nine-year-old girl to condemn her own mother? Did our Jennet even understand how Nowell was using her, or did she think it a mere game to pose in her lovely frock and mouth the words he'd told her to say? I could only guess what Jennet made of us with our bone-pale faces and filthy clothes. Maybe that made it easier for her—she could pretend we were strangers.

Nowell could not have contrived a more grievous torture for my mother. The cat-o'-nine-tails would have been kinder. Yet looking at Judge Bromley, the jury, and the onlookers crowding close to stare, I knew they didn't see a woman devastated by her own child's treachery. What they saw was an odious witch and a freak besides, her cock-eye near bursting out of its socket as she railed and sobbed.

Mam's clenched fists were the fists of a weakling with bracelets of oozing sores round her wrists after being chained for months in that dungeon. To see our mother so unravelled, Jennet caved in upon herself and began to cry in shame and confusion, telling the judge she couldn't go on. I wagered that Nowell hadn't warned her it would be quite this harrowing.

Yet instead of removing Jennet from the scene, the guards wrested away my shrieking mother. Soon as she was gone, my sister was made to recite in her thin, shaky voice what Nowell had instructed her to say against Mam. Jennet, our pert little wench—Nowell had made her his creature through and through. His perfect tool. Now I understood why he had called me to court. He wanted me to see how eager my sister was to destroy us. We'd no hope left.

"My mother is a witch," said our Jennet. "This I know to be true. *Sundry* times"—no doubt, she'd learned that word from Nowell—"I saw her spirit come to Malkin Tower in the shape of a brown dog, which my mother called Ball. He'd ask her what she would have him do." My sister gulped for breath, her sweaty hands clutching at her fine skirt and causing it to wrinkle.

"And what *did* your mother bid Ball, her familiar, to do?" Nowell prompted.

"She said she would have him kill Master Mitton," Jennet said, not daring to look in my direction as she spun her lies. "Gran and Alice Nutter wished him dead. Ball said he'd do it and he vanished away. Three weeks later, Master Mitton died."

"Is that all?" Nowell asked my sister. "Do you wish to say anything more?"

Aware that everyone in that room was hanging upon her words, Jennet flushed and simpered as though she'd been crowned the Queen of May.

"My mother taught me two prayers," she said, falling silent as the crowd buzzed in consternation, no doubt assuming that these were no godly devotions but popish prayers that doubled as magic charms. "One to cure the bewitched and one to get drink."

As if that were not enough, Potts then read Jamie's statement of April twenty-seventh so that Mam might be condemned by her son as well as her youngest daughter. Our mother had made a clay picture of Henry Mitton, so Jamie had said, and she had planned the Good Friday gathering at Malkin Tower. His eyes huge, Potts was about to read further when Nowell cut him off as though he wanted to save the juiciest bit for later.

At that, the guards led Mam back to the bar where she was made to listen to how Jennet and Jamie had declared her guilty of murder by witchcraft. Still she denied everything, but that made no difference to Nowell, who then asked Potts to read the most damning part of Jamie's statement.

Potts's hands shook as he held the parchment aloft and read in a half-strangled voice till Nowell silenced him and summed up my brother's confession in the most chilling words.

"Elizabeth Device was the principal agent behind the solemn meeting at Malkin Tower, that great assembly of witches, where they connived a plan to blast asunder this very castle with gunpowder and also to murder Master Thomas Covell, the King's appointed gaoler, who little suspected or deserved any such villainy against him."

Even I forgot to breathe, for this was the most audacious claim yet — far more disturbing than even the clay pictures. Only seven years ago, Guy Fawkes and his band of papist rebels had plotted to blow up Parliament. Now Nowell was accusing us poor simple folk of the same kind of conspiracy — highest treason. Oh, my brother and his foolish talk.

Nowell paused before delivering his final blow. "I shall remind my Lord Judge and the gentlemen of the jury that the evidence against this woman was delivered by *her own children.*"

Riven by those words and by Jennet's hot little face turned away from her, Mam's knees buckled. Finished off, she was, like a horse flogged till it collapsed and lost all will to rise again.

After the guards banished Mam down the Well Tower, Nowell summoned my brother to the bar. Jamie's eyes rolled up with only the whites showing as he slumped in the arms of the two men straining to hold him upright.

"This miserable wretch," said Nowell, "would have us believe that he is too ill to speak or hear or stand. Whether he brought this condition upon himself by his wish for an untimely death to avoid his trial and the just judgement of the law; or whether by his shame to be openly charged with so many devilish practises; or whether his condition was brought on by reason of his long imprisonment, which was done with more favour, commiseration, and relief than he deserved, I cannot say. I can only speak of the charges against him."

Nowell charged Jamie not only for the murders of Anne Towneley of Carr Hall and John Duckworth of the Laund, as I'd expected, but also for the deaths of John and Blaze Hargreaves, kin of our Constable Hargreaves. I couldn't recall that my brother had ever had much to do with those characters. Little difference that made. Seeing that my brother was too senseless to plead either guilty or not guilty, Nowell asked Potts to read out Jamie's previous statements. So the Londoner read out how my brother had wanted to be even with Mistress Towneley who had struck him between the shoulders and accused him of stealing peat, or so he said; and with John Duckworth who had promised him an old shirt and had never given it to him.

When Nowell asked Jamie if these statements of his were true, my brother lolled his head, which Nowell took to be a nod of agreement.

Next Jennet appeared as a witness to Jamie's crimes. Growing used to the attention, she spoke with more mettle than before, smiling to the judge and jury. "My brother fashioned a clay picture of Mistress Towneley to bring about her death. Then my brother called upon Dandy, his spirit, who appeared to him in the shape of a black dog."

I bristled to hear this, thinking she had mistaken the black dog that had followed me home with Jamie's familiar, which he had always spoken of as a foal that flew through the air.

"Within my hearing, Dandy asked what my brother would have him do," Jennet continued. "My brother answered he would have him kill John Hargreaves of Goldshaw and Blaze Hargreaves of Higham. Dandy answered that he would have his best help and so vanished away."

"Do you swear this upon oath, Jennet Device?" Nowell asked her.

"I do, sir," she said, near doubling over in her sweeping curtsey.

In the ground near Malkin Tower, Jennet went on to say, Jamie had buried three human scalps that Chattox had once given Gran. With a lurch I remembered the skull Betty Whittle had left at Malkin Tower, how Jamie had buried it behind the manure pile those many years ago. Loved to tell tall tales, did our Jamie. My brother was a whimsical soul. In his memory, the skulls must have trebled. Now he would hang for his fault of confusing the truth with his unruly imagination.

Before Nowell could usher my sister out of the court, my eyes hooked into hers fearsome as Gran's would have done to burn forever in her memory that I had stood witness to her betrayal. Haunt her all her days, this would. Her deed was worse by far than anything she claimed the rest of us had committed. She, and only she, was the true murderer. After sending us to our deaths, she would never again know a family's love or a moment's peace.

Jennet's sallow face flushed red. Her singed curls flying, she spun away from Jamie and me, her siblings whom she had doomed.

Didn't take long for the jury to reach their verdict. Chattox, Mam, and Jamie were found guilty on all charges.

After the guards delivered us back into the reeking gloom of the Well Tower and chained us once again to the ring in the floor, Mam wept in her thwarted love for Jennet. Pulling against my manacles, I tried to hold her as she used to hold me when I was a little lass crying out for my dead father.

"She's too young to know what she's doing," Mam said, as if scrambling to find any excuse to pardon my sister.

Deep down she must have known, as I did, that Jennet was old enough to know right from wrong. Old enough to know what it meant to hang a person. Our Jennet must have passed by the gibbet same as we had when Nowell brought her down to the castle. Silent, I embraced my mother whilst trying to rid my memory of those bodies rocking at the end of the ropes, left to dangle like hogs on slaughter day.

"My little girl . . . she wants us dead," Mam said, finally admitting it to herself. "Jamie spoke against me, too, but he's only simple. He never meant it to end like this."

My brother shivered on the damp stone. I stroked his face and called his name, but it was like speaking to a straw doll, leaving me to wonder if he would even come back to himself when the hangman fit the noose round his neck. Perhaps he wouldn't survive the journey to the gallows. So far away my brother seemed, as though halfway to purgatory or some other place that he kept secret from us.

"Let him rest, the poor lad." Mam caressed his hair that had grown back crooked and uneven, sticking out every which way. "Listen to me, love." She reached for my hand. "I don't think they'll charge you with murder. That pedlar of yours is only lame. God willing, they might let you go free."

I shook my head, not wanting to be ensnared by some fragile hope that would only be smashed to pieces before my eyes. Even if Mam was right and they released me, how could I return to Pendle Forest and live out the rest of my life if my loved ones had been hanged, thanks to Jennet's lies? I hated to think what I'd do if I ever encountered my sister again.

"Pray," Mam urged me. "Like you used to, love. Pray that you at least will be spared."

Four, five months ago I would have prayed till my knees turned to pins and needles. But I scarce knew how to pray anymore. Five months of darkness and degradation had shaken up everything I thought I knew or believed in. Both the old religion and the new seemed a mockery. I asked myself, as Nancy had done before me, if heaven even existed. What was left to believe in, what anchor for my soul? Only my recollections of Gran gave me succour: her strength and that bliss on her face when she departed this life.

Of the eleven of us, only Alice Nutter's faith endured. When Covell called her Satan's whore, she stared straight into his eyes and shook her head. Bound for the saints and angels, she was. Feet away from us, she prayed even now, the murmur of her words rising and falling with her ragged breath till, of a sudden, Covell and the guards burst in.

"Alice Gray!" shouted our gaoler, shining his torch in the old woman's face. "You are summoned to court."

Alice Gray clamped her lips together as if to keep herself from moaning in fear whilst the guards unlocked her shackles and yanked her to her feet.

"Good luck," Mouldheels called out to her friend. Behind Covell's back, she mouthed the words *you'll need it.*

The afternoon dragged by. Seemed a curious thing that Alice Gray's trial should last so long when Mam, Jamie, and Chattox had been tried and sentenced within the space of an hour and a half.

When the guards finally brought back Alice Gray, we could see straight off that she'd endured a great shock. Her eyes were round as coins, as though she'd beheld a procession of dancing spectres.

Meanwhile, though it was already late, the guards informed Annie Redfearn that it was her turn to stand trial. Chattox's daughter, who had never spoken a word to condemn herself or betray any of us, glanced to her mother before the guards marched her off.

Chattox reached for Alice Nutter's hand. "Pray for Annie, I beg you." Chattox, that old sceptic who'd mocked Mistress Alice's piety as so much nonsense, bowed right down. "May the judge have mercy and let her go home to her daughter."

Before Alice Nutter could reply, Alice Gray let out such a

whoop as to snap my spine. That cry of hers was the first joyful noise I'd heard in an age.

"What is it?" Mouldheels asked her friend.

"Judge says I'm not guilty." Alice Gray was well giddy. "Says there's not enough evidence against me."

We were struck speechless in our amazement.

"I went on trial same time as them from Samlesbury in the next cell over," Alice Gray said. "They're to be freed, too, soon as the Assizes are over. That child Grace Sowerbutts was called up as a witness. Well, the Judge decided she was nowt but a little liar. She'd been misled by a popish priest, so he said."

"So one child's lies count as evidence," said John Bulcock, as bitter as Alice Gray was gleeful. "But not another's?"

Shocked us, John Bulcock did, for we hadn't heard a peep from him in so long. These months in darkness had left him and his mother in deepest melancholy. Yet now that the Assizes were upon us, young John had come back to life with a vengeance as though beside himself with inescapable panic at what was to come.

"If you walk free," he said to Alice Gray, "then so should we all—save for the Chattoxes and the Devices. Hang the real witches and let the rest of us go. We're only here on account of Liza's lying bastard and her idiot son."

His voice lashed through the murk as though he were about to rip out my mother's throat. I gripped Mam's hand, prepared to throw myself between her and young Bulcock if need be. Any other time Mam would have leapt out of herself in fury to hear someone speak ill of her children, but now she only wept in resignation, knowing that John spoke the truth. Jennet and Jamie had destroyed the lives of our friends and neighbours whose only crime had been to visit Malkin Tower of a Good Friday because they were so worried to hear of Gran's arrest.

"Peace, our John." Alice Nutter spoke to him with the gentle authority I imagined she'd once used with Miles. "Such bile will get you nowhere. We must all of us stay calm."

"Calm?" the young man sputtered. "Like yourself, you mean? How can you just kneel there and pray every godforsaken minute? You're damned as the rest of us. If that son of yours cared for you, he'd have found a way to get you out of this hole."

It was impossible to see Mistress Alice's face in the dark, but she went dead quiet as though John Bulcock's words had stabbed her like a dagger in the heart.

The awful silence stretched on till Annie Redfearn returned, trembling so hard that the guards had a fair struggle clapping the irons back on her.

"Well?" her mother asked soon as the men had gone and taken their light with them. The chains clanked and tugged upon us all as Chattox reached out to embrace her daughter.

Annie Redfearn spoke in a voice so hushed and faint as to make each of us hold our breath. "Judge said I'm not guilty of murdering Robert Assheton."

Whilst Chattox cried out in gratitude, Mam's lips found my ear. "You might go free as well," she whispered, my mother who had lost everything, whose one remaining hope was that I might live on and carry the candle of remembrance for her and the others.

# 22

T HE NEXT MORNING Annie Redfearn was called up to trial once more, along with Alice Nutter and Mouldheels. Trying to put aside my lack of faith, I prayed for them till my tongue went dry as a board.

I might have spared myself the effort, for soon enough the three of them were back in the Well Tower, all three sentenced to hang. Though Annie Redfearn had been declared not guilty of killing Robert Assheton, the Judge decided she was to blame for the demise of Christopher Assheton, his father. Mouldheels and Alice Nutter had pleaded not guilty to the charges against them, but my sister stated under oath that Mouldheels had bewitched some woman in Colne and that Alice Nutter had worked with Gran and Mam to bring about the death of old Henry Mitton.

Chattox's grief for her daughter fair deafened us, and the guards told her to shut it. Then they bore me away, together with Meg Pearson, Jane Bulcock, and John, who bellowed out his innocence with every step up those sharp-twisting stairs.

When mad old Meg Pearson limped to the bar, Magistrate Nicholas Bannister, Nowell's friend, charged her with bewitching to death a mare in Padiham. Those months in the Well Tower had indeed robbed our Meg of her wits, for she confessed, blithe as anything, that she and her spirit had climbed into the stable through a loophole and straddled that poor nag till it collapsed. Nowt but a walking skeleton was our Meg, a long string of drool dribbling from her mouth. Perhaps it was all the same to her whether she lived or died.

Next, Jane and John Bulcock took the stand. This time Nowell appeared, assured as ever, and accused them both of using their witchcraft to drive one Jennet Deane of Newfield Edge in Yorkshire insane. As evidence of this, Nowell had the clerk read a garbled statement of Jamie's. The Judge called out my sister, who pointed to John Bulcock and said that during the Good Friday meeting at Malkin Tower, young John had turned the spit to roast Jamie's stolen sheep. Jane and John pleaded not guilty. In the crowd, Henry Bulcock looked on, his face clenched, no doubt praying that the Judge would see reason and let his wife and son go free.

Rushing right along, the jury reached their verdict. As Judge Bromley announced that Jane and John Bulcock would hang, Henry Bulcock blasted out in blistering fury.

"This is no justice!" he yelled. "This is infamy! Infamy!"

Fat good that did. Bromley wasted no time in having the man thrown out of court.

Next, the Judge determined Meg Pearson's fate. Since she had only killed a horse and no human, she was not sentenced to hang, but to stand at the pillory in open market at Lancaster, Clitheroe, Padiham, and Whalley, with a paper tied to her head stating her crime in huge letters. For six hours at each marketplace she would be stood there, her head and hands locked in the stocks, and made to confess her crime whilst every passing drunkard and bully spat and lobbed stones at her. I imagined senile old Meg mumbling our stories in each of the four market towns—with her wandering mind she'd make a job of it, tell tales outlandish enough to outshine Jamie's. Well famous we witches of Pendle Forest would be then. Folk would talk of nowt else.

Then came my turn.

I, Alizon Device, first to be arrested by Roger Nowell on charges of witchcraft, was last to be tried at the Lancaster Assizes.

As to what my chances were, I was right flummoxed. None of the jury's decisions made the least sense to me. Alice Gray, who had been charged with the same offences as our Mouldheels—attending the assembly at Malkin Tower on Good Friday and bewitching some woman in Colne—would go free whilst Mouldheels was doomed to die. Alice Nutter, a gentlewoman who had devoted her life to charity and kindness, would hang alongside Chattox.

Knowing that these might be my last living hours, I looked round with unshuttered eyes, braving the sunlight pouring through the windows. After searching the crowd for Matthew Holden and finding him nowhere, I imagined Nancy watching me from the other side, her face full of sadness. *Alizon.* My friend laid her head upon my breast and listened to my sick-thudding heart. The force of my fear left me faint and yet I remained standing, because I was Old Demdike's granddaughter. Gran would expect me to show some backbone. She would want me to pay attention to every single thing I saw whilst I still had life in me.

Up I gazed toward the huge windows. A few panes had been opened to let air into this scorching room, and upon a high sill perched a magpie. The bird gazed back at me with gleaming-curious eyes. *One for sorrow.* In spite of myself and the bad luck a single magpie promised, I smiled to think that some of God's creatures possessed wings to fly away from their misery.

"On the eighteenth of March," Roger Nowell drawled in his rich man's voice, "the accused, Alizon Device, did bewitch and lame the pedlar John Law of Halifax."

Nowell loomed menacing close, but I'd no awe left for him. He was just a man, after all, only he'd wealth and better clothes than I did. But I girded myself, knowing he would do his worst. No doubt he would call upon our Jennet and encourage her to slander me to my face as she'd done to our mother. As it turned out, Nowell had something even more wrenching in store.

A yelp ripped out of me as a man upon a litter was carried into court and, once again, I found myself staring into the eyes of the Yorkshire chapman. He'd not improved one bit since I'd seen him last. The crowd pointed and shouted, their stares slashing me, for they could see that my victim's head was drawn awry, half his face was deformed, and the entire left side of his body was stark lame. What could this be but the handiwork of a witch?

My doubts and guilt arose anew like hot water threatening to boil over the sides of a pot. Did I do it, or was it an accident as Alice Nutter had suggested? How could such a thing be an accident? It was as though I'd drawn a line down the middle of this man with a magic wand and blasted his left side whilst allowing his right side to remain hale.

"Behold this lamentable spectacle," Nowell said, sweeping his hand toward the pedlar. "What torments this innocent man has suffered at the hands of this damnable witch, Alizon Device, first instructed by Old Demdike, her grandmother, and brought up by her mother, Elizabeth Device, in this detestable course of life."

Mam had begged me to keep my head, admit nothing, and deny my previous statements, as she had tried to do till Nowell broke her by bringing out Jennet. But when I looked into John Law's eyes, I could only sink to my knees and cry.

"Pray, let the court hear me," I said. "Master Law, I beg your forgiveness for your suffering."

"How do you plead?" Judge Bromley asked, showing no pity for my tears. "I bid you to make an open declaration of your offence."

The Judge's words whirled round my head like flies.

"Up on your feet," Nowell commanded. "Tell us. How did you lame this man?"

In those next moments I was at the still centre of a storm—the most important person in the courtroom. All eyes were on me as I stammered out my tale—how angry I'd been at the pedlar, how I'd shouted, how he'd fallen, the black dog leaping out of nowhere. But I'd never meant any of it, never meant to harm the man, much less lame half his body. Yet by telling my story, I convicted myself.

His eyes never leaving mine, my pedlar then told his story under oath. I sensed that he was as sorry for me as I was for him. He alone of those present gazed at me without hate, only yearning.

"So you lamed me, lass," my Yorkshire chapman said. "Can you mend me? Half my body is right. Can you cure the other half?"

With every drop of blood in my body, I longed to do just that. Rise up before all and show them the measure of what a cunning woman could do; what, by rights, Demdike's granddaughter should have been able to do: chant the charms and lift his lameness.

Tears moving down my face, I told him no. "I can't. I'm sorry."

I was no wisewoman. Even if I chanted every blessing Gran had ever taught me, I was nothing like her. She'd shown me the path of power and I'd refused it, run fast as I could in the other direction, the long, bitter road that had led me to this chamber where I cowered, a weak girl covered in prison dirt, so useless that she burst into tears at the sight of a magpie.

Nowell made a great show of calling the other accused witches up from the Well Tower till the eleven of us were stood before the lamed chapman. The sight of Master Law's malady stunned each one of them. Even John Bulcock's mouth hung slack.

"Can any of you lift the bewitchment off this man?" Nowell demanded.

One by one, my fellow prisoners shook their heads. Chattox herself muttered that it was fair hopeless and that she'd never seen anybody as ill-done-to as John Law.

Not waiting for Nowell's leave, I drew myself up to the bar and spoke as loud as I could, to be heard by every last soul in that courtroom. "The only one with the powers to cure him is my grandmother, but now she's dead."

On the high windowsill the magpie fluttered its wings as though it would swoop down and carry me far from this place.

Before Nowell or the Judge could cut me off, I gripped the bar and carried on. "If Gran had lived, she could and would have mended John Law."

# 23

I N THE OLD RELIGION, this would have been round about the time of the Feast of the Assumption. That morning I awakened from a dream of Gran fitting a wreath of roses round my head. *Time for the procession. You'll lead them all on Assumption Day.*

She'd told me how the young girls had gone out to gather wildflowers and herbs, how they crowned each other in garlands and paraded into church, each of them bearing blossoms and fresh-cut greenery to set upon the altar of the Virgin.

Instead of garlands, we'd iron rings round our necks and shackles round our wrists, but our ankles were free as we struggled up the steep cobbled streets. This was the first time we'd been allowed to set foot outside the castle or breathe fresh air or walk beneath the blue sky. The breeze touched my fresh-washed hair, for Alice Nutter had bribed the guards to bring us water and soap. Round my clean body hung a fine kirtle of blue-green wool, for Mistress Alice had procured garments for us at the last moment so that we would not have to march to the gallows in our lousy soiled rags.

The guards had Alice Nutter and me marching side by side at the head of our sorry train with the seven others following behind. Beneath her breath, Mistress Alice murmured of a woman clothed in the sun, crowned in a diadem of stars, who crushed a serpent beneath her heel. How I wished I'd her firm faith, ever unshakeable. But if I lacked Alice Nutter's conviction, at least I could try to bear myself with dignity and grace as she did. Even though the glaring August sun hurt my eyes, I kept them open. This was my last chance to try to make sense of what had happened to us.

Halfway up the hill, our guards took us into the Red Lion Tavern so that we might have one last mug of ale before meeting the hangman. The ceiling was low enough to make the guards stoop, and the rushes on the floor were none too clean. Though it was a sight better than the dungeon, it oppressed me to know that this dingy room was the last I'd ever see. The ale the tavern keeper pulled from the barrel looked like weak and sour stuff. But Alice Nutter took command, a lady once again, for her son had brought her best gown to wear on this, her last living day. Heavenly blue brocade, it was, stitched with silver threads. She told the tavern keeper to put away his ale and bring out his best French claret.

So the tavern keeper poured us each a goblet brimming with blood-dark wine. Sipping the heady stuff, I remembered Chattox's tale of how Gran and her spirits had conjured wine out of nowhere. I pictured Gran and Chattox sat up in Malkin Tower, feasting away in secret, those two most infamous witches of Pendle Forest drinking from the same cup whilst their imps lit up the place like a thousand candles. What a sight that would have been.

Here in the tavern, Chattox gulped down her wine as though it were bitter medicine whilst Annie Redfearn hovered beside her, not touching her own cup, no doubt pining for her Marie, lost to her forever. Mam was giving Jamie her full care, for he was in a bad way, so weak that she had to tip the wine into his mouth for him. What a wretched ending for the lot of us.

Alice Nutter bent close to me as though I were her own daughter.

"Don't give up hope," she said with a knowing in her voice as vast as Gran's. "The one thing they can't take from us is what we carry inside ourselves. By Our Lady, you are bound for a better place."

I wished I could believe her. Though I sought to understand the meaning of our travails, I saw only ruin and approaching death. The Red Lion's finest French claret wasn't near strong enough to blot out my terror of what lay before us. I tried to recall the serenity on Gran's face when she died, yet the memory seemed so fragile.

The guards told us to empty our goblets and move along. Least the wine blurred the edges of things: the ache in my calves, the crowd lined up to heckle us. Out of the corner of my eye, I saw a dark streak and then a black dog crossed my path. A black bitch. To think the creature had followed me all this way to Lancaster and I still didn't know her name. How hard Gran had tried to teach me to welcome my familiar instead of running away. What might I have become if I'd only possessed the courage?

Seeing my face fold up in pain and regret, Mistress Alice reached her manacled hand to mine. "Courage, love. It's not we who must fear death, but those who persecute the innocent. Don't dwell upon dark thoughts. Think of the happiest and most blessed things you know."

I thought about Nancy and how we used to laugh. Of how strong and healthy my body used to be in the old days; how I'd once raced through the fields, swift as the hares; how I had walked ten miles as though it were nothing, instead of staggering along breathless as I did this day whilst the black bitch kept pace with me, walking between me and the mob as if to ward me.

The horde pressing in on both sides gawped at me and I gawped right back. Let them get a good look at the witch about to die before their greedy eyes. I scowled into the faces of the mean-faced brats gathered to point and screech. What a scruffy lot they were, almost as ragged as the prisoners in Lancaster Gaol. Public hangings were the biggest feast days they'd see now that there were no more processions, no more saints' days or holy days like there used to be when Gran was a girl. Pity welled up inside me when I thought of their bleak lives. Seeing a lass about Jennet's age, I offered her a smile, only the poor thing took a fright and covered her eyes.

I'd never have children of my own nor ever know the love of a man, but die a maid like one of the virgin martyrs of the old religion. That notion made me burst out laughing. Glancing backward at Mam, I saw her frown, no doubt wondering how I could find anything amusing at a time like this. How I wished I could clasp her in my arms one last time, but the guards were stood between us, hastening us up the hill.

Too soon the platform was before us, the gibbet with its nine empty nooses. Which would be mine? Swinging my head to search the throng, I saw no sign of Uncle Kit or the Holdens of Bull Hole Farm. But propped upon his litter was my lamed Yorkshire pedlar watching me go with tears in his eyes.

"Pray for me," I begged him as the guards shoved me past.

I choked at the sight of William stepping from the crowd to wave his last farewell. How my heart rattled as I remembered every act of kindness that young guard had shown me on the long march from Clitheroe to Lancaster.

"I won't let you suffer, Alizon!" he shouted before the men could drag me out of earshot. "I'll pull your legs. Make it quick for you."

What he promised was the greatest mercy I could ask for now.

The guards harried us up the steps to the wooden platform where the hangman waited, his face hidden in a black hood. As far as my brother was concerned, hanging seemed like overdoing it. Our Jamie lay in a faint in the arms of his guards. He'd already died in his soul when they first chained him at the bottom of the Well Tower.

We nine condemned witches were lined up; I was between Mam and Alice Nutter. John Bulcock wouldn't shut his gob but proclaimed his innocence to the bystanders who heaved in laughter. Off came our shackles and before I'd a chance to savour the lightness round my wrists, the guard trussed them behind my back, this time with rope. Next we were made to climb upon the long wooden bench. Only thing left to do was say my final prayers.

The Latin words Gran had taught me came rushing from my lips in an unstoppable incantation whilst William and my pedlar stared as though unable to look away. Maybe John Law wondered if my death would break the spell and end his lameness. As I prayed that he would find healing and solace, the black bitch bayed and I felt that hum inside me again, thrumming through my veins and bones, the power rising. If only I'd allowed Gran to teach me before I happened upon John Law, I might have been a cunning woman and not a witch. Through the door of memory I heard her hoarse old voice.

> What hath he in his hand?
> A golden wand.
> What hath he in his other hand?
> Heaven's door keys.
> Stay shut, hell door.
> Let the little child
> Go to its Mother mild.

I gazed straight into the sun, letting it sear my eyes. *Ave, Maria. Ave, Regina Caelorum.* A woman clothed in the sun.

Three paths stretched before me. The right-hand path led to heaven, the left-hand path to hell, but the path betwixt and between led into the heart of the forest. From out of that bluebell wood the Lady cantered upon her moon-white mare with the silver and gold bells twined in her mane. Queen of Heaven—that name did not belong to her. She was a queen of earth, Queen of Elfhame, the one Gran told me about when I was a little lass in her herb garden. *She's shown herself to you. Call out to her and she'll come to you again.* When the Lady raised her hand to bless me, I wept in overpowering awe. In a blink she was gone. In her stead I saw Pendle Hill, its slopes green as the Lady's gown.

The hangman fit the rope round my neck, the hood over my head. Frantic, I prayed as the rope bit deep into my skin. I chanted till he kicked the bench from beneath my feet, leaving me to swing and kick and judder. Queen of Heaven, Queen of Elfhame—I held them both in my heart. A magpie landed in a meadow of lad's love and then that magpie became my grandmother, except she wasn't old or lame or blind. Full beautiful, her chestnut hair crowned in blossoms, she turned to me and called my name.

Inside my bursting skull a rare light blazed. From down the forest path I saw a wreath of roses, a garland of green, a diadem of stars.

# V

## A LIGHT FAR-SHINING

*Bess Southerns*

# 24

Y OU'LL NOT FIND our graves anywhere. God-fearing folk do not bury witches in consecrated ground or even in the unhallowed plot beyond the churchyard walls where the suicides and unchristened go. After I died in gaol, they burned my corpse, then buried my charred bones on the wild heath overlooking Lancaster Castle. Three months on, they did the same to Alizon, Liza, Jamie, and the rest of them hanged upon that dazzling August day. No crosses mark our resting place, just heather and nesting lapwings. Only our names and the lies they told about us lingered on.

Away in Pendle Forest, Roger Nowell ordered his men to bring down Malkin Tower stone by stone till only the foundation remained. Yet he could never banish me and mine from these parts. This is our home. Ours. We will endure, woven into the land itself, its weft and warp, like the very stones and the streams that cut across the moors.

> What is yonder that casts a light so far-shining?
> My own dear children hanging from the gallows tree.
> Hanging sore by twisted neck,
> How they gasp and how they thrash.
>
> Stay shut, hell door.
> Let my children arise and come home to me.
> Neither stick nor stake has the power to keep thee.

Open the gate wide. Step through the gate. Come, my children. Come home.

# Afterword

All the major characters and events portrayed in this novel are drawn from court clerk Thomas Potts's account of the 1612 Lancashire witch trials, *The Wonderfull Discoverie of Witches in the Countie of Lancaster,* published in 1613. In this meticulously documented case, seven women and two men from Pendle Forest were hanged as witches, based largely on "evidence" given by a nine-year-old girl and her older brother, who appeared to suffer from learning difficulties.

Before the reign of James I, witch persecutions had been relatively rare in England. But James I's book *Daemonologie,* a witch-hunter's manual, presented the idea of a vast conspiracy of satanic witches threatening to undermine the nation. Shakespeare wrote his play *Macbeth,* which presents the first depiction of a witches' coven in English literature, in James I's honour.

To curry favour with his monarch, magistrate Roger Nowell arrested and prosecuted no fewer than twelve individuals from the Pendle region and even went to the far-fetched extreme of accusing them of conspiring in their very own Gunpowder Plot to blow up Lancaster Castle. Two decades before Matthew Hopkins began his witch-hunting career in East Anglia, Nowell had set himself up as the witch-finder general of Lancashire.

Thomas Potts paid particular attention to Elizabeth Southerns, alias Old Demdike, the one alleged witch who escaped the hangman by dying in prison before she could come to trial. In England, unlike Scotland and Continental Europe, the law forbade the use of torture. Thus the trial transcripts supposedly reveal her voluntary confession, although Nowell, as magistrate, may well have manipulated or altered her statement. What is interesting—if the trial transcripts can be believed—is that she freely confessed to being a charmer and a healer. Local farmers called on her to cure their children and their cattle. She described in rich detail how she first met her familiar spirit, Tibb.

The belief in familiar spirits appears to have been the cornerstone of British witchcraft and cunning craft. Elizabeth Southerns's charms and spells, recorded in the trial transcripts, reveal no evidence of diabolical beliefs, but use the ecclesiastical language of the Catholic Church, the old religion driven underground by the English Reformation. Her charm to cure a bewitched person, quoted in its entirety on the flyleaf of this book, is a moving and poetic depiction of the passion of Christ as witnessed by the Virgin Mary. The text is very similar to the so-called White Pater Noster, an Elizabethan prayer-charm that Eamon Duffy discusses in his landmark work, *The Stripping of the Altars: Traditional Religion in England, 1400–1580.*

It appears that Elizabeth Southerns was a practitioner of the kind of Catholic folk magic that would have been fairly commonplace only a generation or two earlier. Pre-Reformation Catholicism embraced many practises that seemed magical and mystical. People used holy water and communion bread for healing. They went on pilgrimages, left offerings at holy wells, and prayed to the saints for intercession. Some practises, such as the blessing of wells and fields, may have had pre-Christian origins. Indeed, looking at pre-Reformation folk magic, it is often hard to untangle the strands of Catholicism from the remnants of pagan belief. I am indebted to Dr. Sam Riches at Lancaster University for her course, Late Medieval Belief and Superstition, which made the pre-Reformation Church come alive for me.

Elizabeth Southerns had the misfortune to live in a time and place when Catholicism itself became conflated with witchcraft. Even the act of transubstantiation, in which the communion bread and wine become the body and blood of Christ, was viewed by some Protestants as devilish sorcery. Keith Thomas's social history, *Religion and the Decline of Magic,* is an excellent study on how the Reformation literally took the magic out of Christianity.

Although it is difficult to substantiate that witches and cunning folk in early modern Britain worshipped pagan deities, the enduring belief in fairies and elves is well documented. In his 1677 book, *The Displaying of Supposed Witchcraft,* Lancashire author John Webster mentions a local cunning man who claimed that his familiar spirit was none other than the Queen of Elfhame herself. In 1576, Scottish cunning woman Bessie Dunlop, while being tried for witchcraft and sorcery at the Edinburgh Assizes, stated that her familiar spirit had been sent to her by the Queen of Elfhame. For more background on this subject, I highly recommend Emma Wilby's scholarly study, *Cunning Folk and Familiar Spirits.*

Mother Demdike is dead but not forgotten. In 1627, only fifteen years after the Pendle witch trial, a woman named Dorothy Shaw of Skippool, Lancashire, was accused by her neighbour of being a "witch and a Demdyke," indicating that the name Demdike had already become a byword for witch.

Jennet Device, Demdike's granddaughter and Nowell's "instrument of God," whose testimony sent her mother, sister, and brother to their deaths, was herself accused of witchcraft in 1633, along with eighteen others, including Miles Nutter's wife. Her accuser, ten-year-old Edmund Robinson, later confessed that he had fabricated his tale in order to escape punishment for coming home late when bringing in his mother's cows. Before he revealed his perjury, three of the alleged witches had died in prison.

In the writing of this novel, I have taken some fictional liberties. Robert Assheton in the book is based on Robert Nutter of Greenhead, and Anthony Holden is a composite of John Nutter of Bull Hole Farm, mentioned in the trial transcripts, and his brother Anthony. Anthony Nutter's daughter, allegedly killed by Chattox's witchcraft, was named Anne, not Nancy. I changed both families' names to avoid the confusion of having too many Nutters in the novel. Henry Bulcock is a composite of Henry Bulcock, who believed that Alizon Device had bewitched his daughter but who declined to speak against her in the trials, and Christopher Bulcock, the husband of accused witch Jane Bulcock and the father of John Bulcock.

There is some controversy as to whether Roughlee Hall was indeed Alice Nutter's home. *The Victoria County History of Lancashire: Volume 6,* published by D. S. Brewer, states that she lived at Roughlee Hall, which was built in 1536 by Miles Nutter, her father-in-law. The relevant passage supporting this is accessible online: http://www.british-history.ac.uk/source.aspx?pubid=486. However, Gladys Whittaker, in her pamphlet *Roughlee Hall, Lancashire: Fact and Fiction,* currently out of print, argues that Alice Nutter lived at Crow Trees Farm near Roughlee.

In his speculative local history, *The Lancashire Witch Conspiracy,* John Clayton suggests that Elizabeth Southerns may have come to live in Malkin Tower, a substantial dwelling for someone of her class, because she was the illegitimate offspring of an important family. I have taken this speculation one step further by making her Roger Nowell's illegitimate half sister, although there is no evidence supporting this.

All the magic charms and spells presented in this book are based on documented Lancashire folk magic. Most of the spells were drawn from the witches' own confessions and the information provided by Jennet Device. The spell in which the hen is burned alive was inspired by a nineteenth-century case in which a Lancashire cunning man burned a black cockerel to break a local wizard's curse. This is described in John Harland and T. T. Wilkinson's book *Lancashire Folklore.*

My endless gratitude goes out to Jane Rosenman and Wendy Sherman, who believed in this book from the very beginning. It has been a great blessing to work with editors Adrienne Brodeur and Andrea Schulz, whose brilliant insights and critique proved invaluable in midwifing this book. My copyeditor, David Hough, has been wonderfully supportive and sensitive to the material.

I wish to thank all my readers and well-wishers who helped me along the way. My husband, Jos Van Loo, patiently read draft after draft and helped me explore the tracks of Pendle Forest as we hunted down the sites of my characters' homes. Sandra Gulland, Katharine Weber, and Judith Lindbergh were generous enough to read this novel in manuscript. I would be a lost soul without my fabulous writers group: Cath Staincliffe, Pat Hadler, Trudy Hodge, and Jo Hughes.

Hawthornden Castle International Retreat for Writers, home of the seventeenth-century poet William Drummond, provided the perfect setting for writing the first draft. I am indebted to Dame Dru Heinz for her generosity. Enduring friendship goes out to my fellow writers in residence — Caroline Carver, Helena McEwen, David L. Hayles, Rhona McAdam, and Sian Williams — and to Jacob Larsen, administrator of the gnomes.

Lastly, my heartfelt thanks go out to the people of Lancashire for sharing the stories of their history.